MORE PRAISE FOR BRIAN KEENE!

GHOUL

"Bursting on the scene with an originality and flair, it seemed that Keene was responsible for breathing new life into the zombie story for a vast number of hungry readers in the horror genre. With the publication of his newest novel, *Ghoul*, Brian Keene has finally cemented himself in as a leader of...the horror genre...."

—Horror World

"If Brian Keene's books were music, they would occupy a working class, hard-earned space between Bruce Springsteen, Eminem, and Johnny Cash."

—John Skipp, *New York Times* Bestselling Author

"*Ghoul* reminds me of the early works of Stephen King. I got the same head rush reading *Ghoul* that I did the first time I read *The Stand* or *Cujo* or *'Salem's Lot*...Keene's prose is both disturbing and beautiful...This guy is going to be HUGE. There is no doubt in my mind that I just experienced the future of horror literature and its name is Brian Keene."

—House of Horrors

THE CONQUEROR WORMS

"Keene delivers [a] wild, gruesome page-turner...the enormity of Keene's pulp horror imagination, and his success in bringing the reader over the top with him, is both rare and wonderful."

—*Publishers Weekly*

"Basic and beautiful, simple yet sublime. Keene is a virtuoso writer of...descriptive talents who can also trip out on the minimalism of American Gothic....*The Conqueror Worms* is a...thoroughly enjoyable novel grounded in Keene's fantastic control over his material."

—*Fangoria*

"*The Conqueror Worms* is a classic monster-pulp novel....we've got Brian Keene now. Exactly the voice the horror genre needs."

—*Insidious Reflections*

THE PRAISE FOR KEENE CONTINUES...

CITY OF THE DEAD

"In the carnival funhouse of horror fiction, Brian Keene runs the roller coaster! The novel is a never-ending chase down a long funneling tunnel...stretching the reader's nerves banjo tight and then gleefully plucking each nerve with an off-key razorblade....There aren't stars enough in the rating system to hang over this one-two punch."

—*Cemetery Dance*

"Brian Keene's name should be up there with King, Koontz and Barker. He's without a doubt one of the best horror writers ever."

—The Horror Review

THE RISING

"[Brian Keene's] first novel, *The Rising*, is a postapocalyptic narrative that revels in its blunt and visceral descriptions of the undead."

—*The New York Times Book Review*

"*The Rising* is more terrifying than anything currently on the shelf or screen."

—*Rue Morgue*

"Hoping for a good night's sleep? Stay away from *The Rising*. It'll keep you awake, then fill your dreams with lurching, hungry corpses wanting to eat you."

—Richard Laymon, Author of *The Woods Are Dark*

BRIAN KEENE

GHOST WALK

LEISURE BOOKS NEW YORK CITY

For Joe Branson and Dave Thomas,
until talking pirate cats fight a Yeti...

A LEISURE BOOK®

August 2008

Published by

Dorchester Publishing Co., Inc.
200 Madison Avenue
New York, NY 10016

ISBN 10: 0-8439-5645-3
ISBN 13: 978-0-8439-5645-0

The name "Leisure Books" and the stylized "L" with design are trademarks of Dorchester Publishing Co., Inc.

Printed in the United States of America.

10 9 8 7 6 5 4 3 2 1

Visit us on the web at www.dorchesterpub.com.

ACKNOWLEDGMENTS

This time around, thanks go to:

The Muse and The Familiar—Cassandra and Sam.

The Magic Words—Don D'Auria and everyone else at Dorchester.

The Circle of Protection—Edward Lee, Tom Piccirilli, J.F. Gonzalez, Shane Ryan Staley, Kelly Laymon, Michael Laimo, Bryan Smith, Wrath James White, Maurice Broaddus, Nate Southard, Tim Lebbon, Christopher Golden, James A. Moore, Chet Williamson, Norman Partridge, Douglas E. Winter, F. Paul Wilson, Tom Monteleone, Nick Mamatas, Jack Haringa, Nick Kaufmann, Lee Thomas, Carlton Mellick, Bev Vincent, Joe Hill, Geoff Cooper, Mikey Huyck, and Mike Oliveri.

The Ritual of Banishing—Tod "T. C." Clark, Kelli Dunlap, Mark "Dezm" Sylva, and John Urbancik.

The Ritual of Binding—my readers and the members of the F.U.K.U.

Special thanks to Big Joe Maynard; Bob Ford of Whutta Design Agency; and Lynn Butcher and Gerard Houarner for their technical assistance.

AUTHOR'S NOTE

This book is a follow-up to my novel *Dark Hollow*. Although knowledge of that book's events are not necessary to enjoy this book, you might want to seek it out after you've read this one. Also, although many of the Central Pennsylvanian locations in this novel are real, I have taken certain fictional liberties with them. So if you live there, don't look for your favorite Halloween attraction. You might not survive it....

CHAPTER ONE

Mother Nature held her breath. The woods were quiet. There was no breeze to rustle the few leaves still clinging to the trees, or to toss around the fallen ones littering the forest floor. There were no crickets chirping. No locusts or bees buzzing. No mosquitoes or gnats. No birdsongs. Richard Henry couldn't remember ever being in the woods and not hearing at least one bird. There were no squirrels either. Usually, if he stood still long enough, he'd hear them playing in the branches and chattering at one another—but not now. Back at the forest's edge, near the dirt road where he'd parked, the woods had been alive with activity. He'd seen rabbits, insects, birds, squirrels, and even a mangy stray cat hunting a field mouse. But now there was nothing. Not even a pinecone or dead branch falling to the ground. Everything was still. Even the clouds in the sky, glimpsed between the treetops, remained motionless.

As if the forest was dead.

The silence felt like a solid thing; invisible walls pressed down on him.

Worse, something was out there. Watching him. Rich was sure of it. He felt eyes staring at him through the thick foliage, and the sensation made the hair on his arms bristle. He was nervous. Jumpy. His skin tingled. His mouth was dry and it was hard to swallow. Rich stuffed an unflavored Skoal Bandit in his bottom lip and tried to work up some spit. He cleared his throat. It sounded very loud. The wind briefly whistled through the trees, bringing more sound to the stillness. Shivering, Rich zipped his jacket up to his chin. When his saliva was running again, he spat onto a pile of dry leaves. Normally, Rich smoked, but lighting up a Winston out here would only give him away to the wildlife—if he ever found any, that was. Nothing warned off animals like cigarette smoke. That's why he preferred the unflavored Skoal. Mint or wintergreen flavored would have also warned the animals off. He stuck the round tobacco can into the back pocket of his faded jeans, retrieved his .30-06 from the rock he'd propped it up against, and continued on his way, trying very hard to ignore that watchful sensation.

He felt like an idiot for being nervous.

People in York County told all kinds of stories about the forest, but that didn't make them true. They were just legends. Bullshit folklore. LeHorn's Hollow was supposed to be full of ghosts, demons, witches, Bigfoot, the Goat Man, and hellhounds—but none of those things existed in real life. In real life, there were other things to fear. In real life, Rich had to deal with things like terrorism and cancer scares and health insurance and bills. And his only son, Tyler, getting killed in a war that didn't make any sense—a war that nobody seemed to care about anymore. At least not enough to get off their couches, turn off their televisions, and protest about it in the streets. His parents had protested Vietnam in the sixties. That's how they'd met each other. Rich had a picture of his parents standing at the Mall in Washington D.C., wearing bell-bottoms, carrying placards, and flashing peace signs. His father had been in 'Nam the year before. He'd decided America shouldn't be there and did what he thought was right. Came home after finishing his tour and added his voice to the dissent. Protested. Spoke up about things.

Rich's generation—they'd dropped the ball. Nobody cared anymore. People didn't give a shit about the war. As long as they had Paris Hilton and Britney Spears and George Clooney and Bran-ge-fucking-lina or whatever the hell they called themselves, that was all people cared about. Democrat or Republican—both were part of the problem, rather than a solution.

He'd lost Tyler. And as if that wasn't enough, after his son's death, life poured it on and turned up the heat. It was a mixed metaphor, but Rich didn't give a shit. It was how he felt. Rich had to cope with getting laid off from the feed mill because they said his drinking was out of control. Said to clean himself up if he wanted to keep his job. What the hell did they know? Of course he drank. They would, too, if they had to put up with the shit he put up with. The government—the same government that was responsible for Tyler's death—said he owed back taxes. And now the bank was threatening to foreclose on his home. They wanted their money and didn't care if he was out on the street. The old house sat empty now, except for Rich; the other inhabitants would never return. Tyler was dead. The little bit of him that had made it home was buried in the Golgotha Lutheran Church cemetery; the rest was scattered across the sand. Rich's ex-wife, Carol, was shacked up with another guy. A dentist. They lived in Windsor Hills with the rest of the yuppies. The only things that lived in the old place with Rich were the ghosts of his happiness.

The forest was haunted by the boogeyman? Bullshit. Terrorists and politicians and bankers and bosses and ex-wives and the pain he felt when he looked at Tyler's pictures and remembered when he was so little—those things were the real boogeymen. Real life was scary as hell all by itself. Real life had enough monsters without adding make-believe monsters to it as well. Real life was a horror movie. Pretend monsters were an escape.

Rich had just turned forty-two, but he felt much older.

Middle age had not agreed with him so far. It wasn't the cat-astrophic loss of hair on top of his head or the coarse, gray hairs sprouting in places they had never been before—his ears and nose, shoulders and back. It wasn't that he ran out of breath quicker these days. Or that he was tired all the time. Or that his head ached from the moment he woke up until he went to sleep. Or the extra weight around his waist, or his declining interest in sex and subsequently declining erections, or the way his back and joints hurt after doing simple tasks. He'd expected those things, had watched his own father suffer through them. They were all just part of the aging process. These things didn't depress him, except when he was really drunk.

What got to him, what really brought him down, was how his life had seemed to disintegrate in the last few years. Ever since he'd turned forty, fate had delivered one kick in the balls after another. First there was Tyler's death, then the di-vorce, a mountain of debt, and now the loss of his job and the foreclosure on the house. Everything kept falling apart and there seemed to be no end in sight. His days were one long, endless slide downward. It wasn't fair. This was sup-posed to be the second half of his life, the path leading to the golden years, the twilight years. But sometimes Rich didn't think he wanted to stick around for the second half. Things were supposed to get easier. When would that happen, ex-actly? It felt like things were just getting tougher instead. Could the golden years even be worth living?

He felt betrayed and alone.

Sometimes Rich just wanted to die. He imagined it was a lot like sleep. No cares. No worries. No pain. Just sweet, welcome oblivion, forever and ever—and if there was noth-ing after this, no Heaven or afterlife, he wouldn't care any-way because he'd be dead.

Of course, if that happened, the family name would die with him. He had no siblings, no uncles with sons. Rich was the last male Henry from his father's line. When Tyler had died two years ago in Iraq, a big part of Rich had died with him. The military had never revealed the whole story; just that Tyler had been riding in a convoy across the desert when a roadside bomb—an IED, the government man had called it—shredded his Humvee. One of Tyler's friends, a kid from Mississippi, had died right away. Not Tyler. He'd lingered for almost fifteen minutes. At the memorial service, an American flag was draped over his closed casket. His high school graduation picture sat on top of it in a nice frame from the Hallmark store. In the picture, Tyler was smiling and whole. In the coffin, he wasn't. The preacher talked about God and country and sacrifice. Then Tyler was buried.

The rest of the world moved on.

Rich did not.

Carol left him soon after. She said she'd been planning it for years, and had just wanted to wait until Tyler was grown and out of the house. She'd delayed her plans when he joined the army and went to Iraq. But now . . .

She never finished the last statement. She didn't need to. Sometimes, things unsaid spoke louder than words.

Carol had left him everything—the car, the house, the dirty dishes in the sink, their empty bed, and a mountain of debt. The credit cards were at their maximum, and they still had five years' worth of payments left on the house. Whether she'd done it out of pity or guilt or just an eagerness to be done with him, the end result was the same: she'd fucked him one last time before moving in with her dentist boyfriend. Here he was, one year later, unemployed, almost homeless, poaching deer out of season. All so he wouldn't have to spend his meager unemployment check on groceries, and could instead hold off the bill collectors for another few weeks.

No wonder he fucking drank. "Out of control," his boss said? Not yet. Maybe soon, though, if things didn't get better—and if he had enough bullets . . .

Yeah, he could get *out of control*. Go postal. It would be so fucking easy.

Rich glanced back through the forest. There were no paths or trails. No wide spaces or clearings. This part of the woods had been unscathed by the big forest fire of 2006. Here the trees grew close together, and the rocky soil was covered with dead leaves and twigs. As dense as it was, he was surprised to see thick clusters of late-season undergrowth thrusting up from the ground: fragile ferns, poison ivy, Queen Anne's lace, milkweed, blackberries and raspberries, snake grass, pine and oak seedlings dotted the landscape. All of it would be dead in another week or so. Already, the leaves were turning brown. He couldn't see more than fifteen feet into the foliage, but that sense of being watched remained. It gave him the creeps.

Probably a deer, he thought. *Come on out here and let me put some punkinballs in you, sucker.*

That would be nice. Bag a good-sized buck, field dress it, and haul the carcass back to the truck. Then hide it beneath the tarp and head home. Move it from the truck bed and into the garage without any of the neighbors seeing (Trey Barker, who lived next door, would call the game warden if he knew Rich was poaching). With luck, he could have it strung up, butchered and in the freezer before dark, and he would then have the entire evening to drink a few beers and watch whatever was on the tube. Maybe he wouldn't even cry tonight when he went to bed. That would be an excellent change of pace from his normal routine.

He'd parked on the side of one of the old dirt logging roads. Rich wasn't worried about someone spotting his truck. He was way off the beaten path, hunting along the border of the state game lands. If a game warden or someone else happened to drive by, they'd just as easily assume the truck belonged to a hiker or a fisherman or somebody digging up ginseng roots as they would a poacher. They might even think it was broken down or abandoned. As long as he was careful when he dragged the deer's carcass out, he'd be fine.

Of course, first he had to shoot one. Hell, shoot anything, something.

But there was nothing.

It was late October—almost Halloween. Small-game season had just ended and deer season was still a month away. The only thing he could legally shoot right now were coyotes and crows, but eating a coyote was like eating a dog and crows didn't have enough meat on them—and what little meat they did have tasted like shit.

But even the crows were absent today.

Rich wondered if he'd have had better luck coming in from the Shrewsbury side of the woods. Maybe so. He hadn't come in that way because the volunteers from the fire department and other civic groups were busy working on their Ghost Walk—a haunted attraction that would open Halloween eve and run until the first weekend in November. Even though it was the first one, the organizers had said they expected thousands of people over the next month, ferried back and forth on hay wagons, walking the trail through the forest while people in masks jumped out and scared them. It only took up a small section of the woods, but there were a lot of people working there currently, and he couldn't risk anyone spotting him poaching.

He spat tobacco juice again and listened to the silence. Then he walked on. As he wound his way through the trees, he reconsidered his skepticism. He could understand why people told ghost stories about this area. This far in, the woods had atmosphere. The stillness was unsettling. He wondered what it meant. Did the wildlife know there was a predator in their midst? He'd been quiet, had walked lightly, dipped instead of smoked, made sure not to wear any deodorant. He'd even worn dirty clothes rather than clean ones that would smell like detergent. But nothing was out there.

Well, almost. Something was out there. He just didn't know what it was.

He felt those invisible eyes boring into him again, right between his shoulder blades. When Rich wheeled around, there was nothing there but trees and foliage.

"Come on," he whispered. "Give me a rabbit. A pheasant or squirrel—anything, goddamn it."

He was smack-dab in the middle of over thirty square miles of protected Pennsylvanian woodland, zoned to prevent farmers and realtors from cutting it all down and planting crops or building housing developments and strip malls. The pulpwood company and paper mill in nearby Spring Grove had logged a great swath of the forest in years past, but lawmakers, the raging forest fire, and the rising availability of cheaper paper from China had put a stop to that. The old logging roads still existed, however. They were rutted and washed out in some places, but even so, they still provided access to the deeper parts of the forest. The adjoining land on the outskirts of the woods that hadn't been ravaged by the fire was zoned agricultural and filled with corn, strawberry, and soybean fields. Other outlying areas housed hunting cabins. Beyond the farms and hunting cabins were the small towns of Shrewsbury, Seven Valleys, Jefferson, New Freedom, Spring Grove, Glen Rock, and New Salem. York County's heartland.

Rich had grown up in Seven Valleys, and other than a four-year stint in the Marines during the early eighties, and a vacation trip to New York City when Tyler was ten, he'd spent his whole life there. Rich had been in these woods thousands of times, but he'd never gone farther than he had today. With the game nonexistent, he forgot about the unseen presence spying on him and pressed on, ignoring that creepy feeling and venturing into areas he'd never seen before. He wasn't worried about getting lost. He had his compass and he'd be able to find the road and his truck again. His only concern was not finding some meat in time to get home and watch some TV. He wished now that he'd shot something when he had the chance, closer to the road where he'd parked. At the time, he hadn't wanted to risk somebody hearing him. But it appeared that all the wildlife had gone deeper into the forest, so Rich did, too.

This close to the center, the woods seemed lifeless.

And that damned sensation of being watched didn't go away.

The distant drone of a chainsaw broke the silence, and Rich jumped at the sudden sound. The buzz ceased, and was followed by pounding hammers. Rich shrugged. Probably the volunteers from the fire department, building something for the Ghost Walk. It occurred to him that maybe that was why the game was so scarce. Maybe all the noise had scared the wildlife away. He hadn't realized that he was so close to the haunted attraction's location. Grumbling to himself, Rich pushed through the foliage and moved on.

A few minutes later, he came across the first of the dead trees. Soon, the tangled undergrowth cleared, replaced with a vast swath of desolate, barren ground. He was nearing what had once been the true heart of the forest: a burned and blackened area known as LeHorn's Hollow, named after the farmer who'd once owned it. The big forest fire in the spring of 2006 had destroyed over five hundred acres of woodlands and totally eradicated the entire hollow. Several people died in the inferno. Investigators suspected arson or perhaps an accidental blaze, but they were never able to determine the exact cause. In the end, it was speculated that a careless cigarette or an untended campfire had sparked the conflagration. The event made national headlines. CNN and FOX News even sent reporters out to cover it. For five minutes, York County, Pennsylvania, was in the news for something other than the Intelligent Design versus Evolution court case.

A lot of Rich's friends and coworkers had been relieved to see LeHorn's Hollow burn down. It had been the main source of most of the ghost stories and legends associated with the forest, including a violent murder in the eighties, a series of cult-related killings in 2006 (right before the fire), and whispers of everything from witchcraft and devil worship to crop circles and flying saucers. Then there was the more recent legend of a Bigfoot-like creature called the Goat Man who was said to haunt the area. All of it was bullshit, of course, but standing here among the burned-out tree skeletons, with no breeze blowing and no sound or movement, and that persistent feeling of being watched—Rich could understand how folks would believe the old tales.

His stomach grumbled. His tobacco tasted sour, so he spat it out and then put a new dip in. Rich checked his watch and sighed. Then he pressed forward. Burned tree limbs disintegrated beneath his feet. A splintered log crumbled into charred bits as he clambered over it. With each step, ashes and dust shot up into the air, swirling around him and clinging to his jeans and boots. It was like walking through black baby powder. He wondered why the vegetation hadn't started to come back yet. There should have been green shoots and fragile saplings thrusting upward from the soil. He shrugged. Probably because it was so late in the year. Next spring might bring it back to life. Maybe the lack of new growth to forage on explained why the hollow was empty of wild game. The surface was devoid of any tracks or footprints, except for his.

He was just about to give up and start back to the truck when he came across the stone. It was gray and stood out sharply against the dark landscape. It reminded Rich of a tombstone: knee-high, curved, rounded edges, and covered with carvings. It had definitely been shaped and smoothed by human hands. Despite the fire that had obviously raged around it, the stone appeared untouched. There was no soot on its unmarred surface. No burn marks or heat-induced damage.

Curious, Rich approached the rock and knelt down beside it. The carvings looked weathered, which meant that the stone was probably old. Had it been here before the fire, or had someone brought it here after? And if it had been here before, then how had it escaped undamaged? He studied it closer. There was no moss or lichen clinging to its sides, and no cracks or crevices in its surface. The rock was totally featureless except for the weird carvings. They weren't like anything he'd ever seen before. They looked like runes of some kind, or maybe Native American symbols, like the ones they showed on the History Channel documentaries. He remembered the cult that was supposed to have been based here before the fire. Could they have carved these? It didn't seem likely. Rich couldn't explain it, but the strange symbols felt much older than that.

Maybe it was worth some money. A stone like this, covered with what might possibly be Native American glyphs? That was a pretty big archeological find. Maybe he could sell it to the Indian Steps Museum near Wrightsville. They had all kinds of artifacts there—spears and arrowheads, stone clubs, bowls, and other things. If he remembered correctly, they had some rocks with markings on them, too: displayed in a showcase were several pieces of slate that somebody had pulled from the bottom of the Susquehanna River, each segment containing several ancient carvings. He'd seen it on the local news.

Rich nodded his head and spat again. Yeah, the more he thought about it, the more certain he was. This had to be worth some money; if not to the museum, then maybe to somebody at York College, or maybe even down at the Smithsonian in Washington. How much? He didn't know. Surely enough to get him out of debt—allow him to pay off the house and credit cards, and stop all the phone calls and letters from the bill collectors once and for all.

He'd be free. Suddenly, Rich had options again. A way out that didn't involve eating a bullet or drinking himself to death. There was a light at the end of the tunnel and it wasn't an oncoming train. He could keep the house, or at least pay it off and then sell it to someone else. Get a fresh start. Be free of his family's ghosts.

Faint hammering sounds drifted to him again. He wondered if any of the people working on the Ghost Walk had discovered this yet. Probably not. If so, he'd have seen their footprints in the ashes.

He sat his rifle down and pulled out his compass, trying to figure out where he was. He blinked, staring at it. The needle was slowly spinning around, not fixing on a location. Almost as if there were no true north.

"That's weird. Cheap piece of shit."

Rich glanced around and spotted three more stones jutting up from the ground. Each of them looked just like the other. They were spaced out about ten feet apart forming a half circle of sorts. Could there be others, hidden beneath the ash? An entire circle, perhaps? An American version of Stonehenge? If so, then his fortunes had just gotten even better. One of these markers had to be worth money, but a dozen of them? He'd be set for life.

"Payday!"

Grinning, Rich placed his hands on the stone. It was cool to the touch, and for a brief moment he thought he felt it vibrating beneath his fingertips. He paused, wondering if the ground was shaking. An earthquake? Although rare in this part of the country, they'd happened before. But it wasn't. The soot and ash remained still, as did the burned hulks of timber. They didn't shake. Only the stone moved—and only this one. He could definitely feel it. Its brethren, the ones he wasn't touching, remained still, at least to the naked eye. The flat surface warmed slightly as he ran his palms across it. Then the vibrating sensation faded and the rock turned cool again. He noticed that the woods were quiet again, too. The hammering sounds had faded.

"Spooky shit."

Even though he spoke softly, his voice boomed across the blasted landscape, sounding too loud in the silence. It occurred to Rich that he hadn't felt watched—hadn't felt those unseen eyes on him—since discovering the stones.

Thoughts of money helped him brush his fears aside. He pushed the stone, wiggling it back and forth, disturbing the scorched soil. Flakes of ash fluttered into his face, sticking to his sweaty forehead and cheeks. Brown tobacco juice dribbled down his chin as he pushed harder, grunting with the effort, trying to determine how much of the stone was buried beneath the ground. The rock was heavier than it appeared. His fingers found purchase in the carvings. Again he felt a warm sensation in his palms and fingertips. The hard surface throbbed. He was sure of it this time.

Bewildered, Rich gave it a final shove. The rock tore free of the dirt and tumbled over onto its side, sending more ash into the air. Rich coughed, his eyes tearing up as the cloud obscured his vision. He tasted soot in the back of his throat. He wiped his nose with the back of his hand. It came away grimy and black. His skin itched.

When the dust settled, Rich peered down at a small, round hole where the stone had been. He couldn't see the bottom, just a deep shadow. He leaned closer, peering down into the crevice. The air seemed colder at ground level. Rich's eyes widened in surprise as the darkness inside the hole moved, swirling around just like the cloud of ash had done.

The darkness was a solid, shapeless thing.

Still on his knees, Rich shuffled backward, gasping as the darkness floated out of the hole and into the air, forming into a small funnel like a miniature tornado. It moved in silence and of its own volition, slowly spinning round and round. There were no breezes to twirl it. The black cone glided backward, away from Rich and the stones. Rich saw more rocks sticking up now. They did indeed form a circle. He was standing outside of it. The cloud hovered in the center of the circle. Its speed increased.

"Oh shit . . ."

Still coughing from the ash in his throat, Rich jumped to his feet. His knees popped and his head pounded. The darkness continued turning. His stomach lurched as he watched it. His feet and hands felt like lead. The darkness spun faster. His mouth was suddenly parched; the plug of tobacco felt like a dry sponge between his gums and lip. Forgetting about his discarded rifle, he stepped away from the hole, watching the funnel cloud with wide, fearful eyes.

"I believe," Rich whispered. "Okay? I believe now. Everything they say about this place is true. You win. You proved your point. I believe. I believe in God and the Devil and the motherfucking boogeyman. I believe in it all. So just let me go. I won't come back."

The darkness spoke. It sounded far away.

Dad . . .

Rich sobbed. He knew that voice.

Dad . . . it's me. The voice grew louder.

"T . . . Tyler?"

The darkness coalesced, its form shifting again, changing into something else.

Changing into his dead son.

"Tyler . . . is it . . . what is this?"

This couldn't be happening, but it was. His dead son's ghost stood before him, still dressed in his desert khakis, as if he'd just returned home. Just like that, Rich became a believer. He couldn't deny his own eyes. This wasn't a vision or hallucination. This was Tyler, solid yet ethereal, his feet hovering inches from the forest floor. His death had been horrific, but now Tyler appeared unharmed and complete, looking as perfect and proud and strong as he had the day he left for boot camp.

Dad. Tyler held out his arms and smiled. *It's good to see you. How's Mom?*

Rich tried to respond, but he couldn't. His words died in his throat, strangled by his sobs. His eyes blurred with tears.

"Oh, Tyler . . . I miss you. I miss you so fucking bad."

I miss you, too, Dad. You and Mom both.

Rich took a hesitant step into the circle. As he did, Tyler seemed to grow clearer.

It's so cold here, Dad. Not like the desert. It's really cold.

Wiping his tears away with the back of his hand, Rich stepped fully into the circle and reached for his son. Tyler drifted toward him, drawing closer. Weeping, Rich touched him. As he did, Tyler changed shape. The darkness returned. Rich's fingers sank into the substance. It felt like frigid cotton candy. Black, smokelike tentacles erupted from its center and snaked across his hand and up his arm. Whimpering, Rich tried to pull away, but the darkness held fast. It slithered up his shoulders, wrapped around his neck and raced toward his mouth.

Rich screamed, frozen in place.

More of the darkness flowed over him. It poured through his mouth and ears and the corners of his eyes, slipped beneath his clothes and snaked into his anus and urethra. Anywhere there was an opening, the darkness found it. The black cloud grew smaller and smaller as more of it pulsed into his body. Rich screamed throughout it all.

When the cloud disappeared, Rich's screams turned to laughter, echoing through the dead trees. The voice wasn't his. Nor were the thoughts inside his head. There were no more worries about his financial situation or unemployment. Gone was his depression and anger. Gone were his memories of Carol and Tyler and everything else. Those memories, just like their owner, didn't exist anymore. They were just ghosts.

Richard Henry was no more. He'd been replaced by something else.

He would not be missed because there was no one to miss him.

As night fell on the hollow, the laughter ceased. The moon shone down through the burned trees, but the light did not penetrate the desolate spot. The figure that had once been Rich retrieved the .30-06 rifle and went hunting. There was much to do and only a short time to do it. Halloween was coming and the barriers between worlds grew thin.

CHAPTER TWO

Maria Nasr held her breath and counted to ten.

I will not snap. I will not snap. I will not snap.

She repeated the mantra over and over in her head. It didn't help. Her anger swelled. This was ridiculous. Her hands curled into fists and her long fingernails dug into her palms, the French manicure from the day before all but forgotten. Her legs twitched in annoyance, rocking the tablet, pen, and digital voice recorder precariously balanced in her lap. The clock on the wall refused to move, the hands seemingly frozen in time. Maria's temples throbbed.

At the front of the room, the fat man, Orvil Hale, one of the town commissioners, droned on and on about his kid's private Christian academy and how marvelous it was and how all of the other board members should consider enrolling their children at the school, too. His bald head shined under the fluorescent lighting. Hale's pudgy, red-splotched cheeks jiggled as he talked. Long hairs dangled from his nose, swaying with each breath. Maria could see them even from where she sat. And he wheezed between words, as if the very act of talking left him breathless. So why didn't he just shut up? Weren't they on taxpayers' time? Yes, of course they were. But rather than getting down to business, Hale kept talking.

It pissed her off. She had better things to do on a Wednesday night than sit here and listen to an elected official proselytize on township time. Okay, maybe laundry, cleaning her apartment, and grocery shopping weren't exciting, and sure, these meetings were about as thrilling as watching flies have sex, but enough already! Get to the matter at hand, address the taxpayers' concerns: the new sewage system and who was going to pay for it. That's what she was here to cover for the newspaper, not this personal fucking nonsense. They could save that for after the meeting.

Occasionally, Maria would skim through *Writer's Digest* and other magazines and websites directed toward writers. They always made freelancing sound glamorous and fun.

This was neither.

Maria exhaled, took another deep breath, and forced herself to relax. She stretched her fingers and toes and twisted her head from side to side, cracking the cartilage in her neck. The guy in front of her, a writer for the *York Daily Record*, turned around and smiled. Maria smiled back.

Don't get the wrong idea, buddy, she thought. *You're like twice my age and still working as a freelancer. No career drive or higher financial aspirations there, obviously. And besides that, you pick your nose and wipe it on your pants.*

It was true. She'd seen him do it at dozens of these township meetings, as well as other municipal government meetings, car wrecks, ribbon cuttings, Jaycee bean suppers, Lions Club pancake breakfasts, and everything else they covered.

The reporter—Mark was his name, she remembered now—turned back around and focused on the front of the room. His index finger crept toward his nose again. The township supervisors were discussing last week's episode of *American Idol*. Maria glanced at the clock and sighed. The hands had barely moved.

Somebody kill me now . . .

She hated this. Hated her job as a freelancer and everything it entailed. This wasn't how she'd pictured things would be after graduating from college three years ago. She'd imagined moving to New York City or Los Angeles and getting a job for a major newspaper, or maybe writing for *Time* or *Newsweek* or *Vanity Fair*. Instead, she was stuck freelancing here in York County, Pennsylvania, scrambling to sell articles for anyone who would send her a check, and barely making a living at it.

Maria had grown up in Paramus, New Jersey. Her father was a Jordanian Muslim and her mother was a Brazilian nonpracticing Catholic. Both had immigrated to the United States to go to college, and both had ended up living here afterward. They'd gotten married, after her mother converted to Islam. Maria's father was an engineer. Her mother was a doctor. Both had wanted the best for their daughter, especially since she was an only child. But they also insisted that she earn things on her own. Her father was especially adamant about this. They could have sent Maria to the finest journalism schools in the country and paid her tuition in full, but instead, they'd declined to help her financially. "You must do it on your own," her father had said. "If you do not work hard now, you will never appreciate the opportunities you are given. You may hate us for it now, but you will thank us one day."

Maria had ended up picking York College. It was highly accredited, yet still affordable on her college loan. Moving from Paramus to the small Pennsylvania town was a bit of an adjustment, but she managed. She got a job working part-time at a video store, shared an apartment off campus with five other girls, and stayed focused. No boyfriends during her four years in school—there was no time. Becoming a journalist was what mattered. Serious relationships could come later, after she'd graduated and went to work for the *New York Times*.

Except that it never happened. Maria received her degree, but the job offers weren't forthcoming. She applied in Baltimore, Philadelphia, Pittsburgh, New York, Washington, D.C., and all the other nearby cities. When she had no luck there, she tried the smaller cities like Allentown, Scranton, Trenton, and Richmond, but they weren't hiring either. Some of them offered her other positions or freelance work, but nothing that was financially feasible. She needed full-time employment—a staff gig. Maria had her student loan to pay off, as well as the cost of living, and moving expenses to wherever she took the job. She couldn't move back home. Her father remained adamant that she do things on her own, so living with her parents again wasn't an option. She could have asked them for a loan, but that would have been admitting defeat—and besides, she was already far enough in debt.

In the end, Maria opted just to stay in York. She got a small apartment in York City, bought a Hyundai Accent, and added even more to her debt. Then, still working at the video store—full-time now, rather than part-time—Maria started supplementing her income with freelance assignments. After all, what good was her degree if she didn't put it to use? So in the evenings, after she got off work, Maria began writing for various markets. It was slow going at first. She had to build up a list of editors and markets that she could submit regularly for. Webzines, travel guides, magazines, newspapers—all of them were looking for freelancers, even the papers who had refused to hire her as a full-time employee. After a year and a half, she had an impressive amount of clippings and could afford to quit her job at the video store—even though she was really only earning the same amount she'd made working there. She continued working hard and stayed prolific, and so far, she wasn't behind on her bills and could buy groceries and hadn't crawled back to Paramus to tell her parents she was a failure. The key to being a successful freelancer was the ability to write quickly for a variety of clients.

Like now. Maria focused again on Orvil Hale. She hadn't missed anything. The officials were just now calling the meeting to order.

Finally, she thought. *It's about fucking time. Maybe we'll be out of here before Halloween.*

Maria crossed her legs. She needed to pee.

Tonight, Maria was freelancing for the *York Dispatch*. Unlike their rival, the *York Daily Record*, they used freelancers to cover most local government meetings. Maria earned sixty dollars per story, and while it didn't seem like a lot of money, every check counted—that was the freelancer's mantra. On any given week, she could get paid for several magazine articles, half a dozen reviews online, and two or three freelance stories for the newspaper. It all added up. And besides, the local government stories only took her a few hours to write. They weren't exactly hard work. The only drawback was sitting through the tedious meetings themselves. Maria had yet to discover a way to make sewer lines, street repair, or refuse collection interesting and exciting. No matter how you dressed it up, it was still the most boring shit in the world. Still, she wasn't getting paid to make it thrilling. She was simply supposed to report the facts, no matter how uninspiring they might be.

The other downside was the fact that she had very few personal relationships and little time for socializing, other than with business contacts and peers she met on the Internet. Maria posted regularly on a few message boards for freelance writers, and had several friends she exchanged e-mails with, but she didn't go out much. She couldn't. There was no time. She spent her days and evenings working on the next assignment or trying to line up more. As a result, her social life outside of the Internet was almost nonexistent. Three years after college, she still had no serious boyfriends. Maria could count the number of dates she'd been on with one hand. And other than a drunken one-night stand with a guy she'd met on assignment six months ago, she'd slept alone.

Yep, she thought, *the thrilling, glamorous life of a freelance writer.*

Nuts . . .

Two long hours later, the township officials finished their business and Hale adjourned the meeting. Maria turned off her digital voice recorder, put it in her purse along with her notebook and pen, and stood up. Her notebook was filled with doodles—cat and dog faces, a hexagon, and labyrinthine, concentric circles. She hadn't taken any notes, confident that the important stuff was on the recorder. She'd play it back when she got home, transcribe it, and make sense of things. Boil two hours' worth of discussion into a four-hundred-word news brief that would end up buried on the last page of the local section, right after the farm report and church worship schedules for the week. She'd e-mail it to her editor before her one A.M. deadline, and then get some sleep.

Maria filed out with the rest of the attendees. Mark from the *Daily Record* smiled at her again. His pants legs were covered with dried boogers. She smiled back, and then looked away, pretending to be interested in some Halloween decorations hanging on the wall.

Yeah, her life was really working out the way she'd planned.

Maybe tomorrow she'd look into moving again. Try getting out of York. Search Craigslist for an apartment in New York or Philadelphia. And maybe she'd win the lottery, too. That was the only way she could afford to move, after all.

Like it or not, she was stuck here. Alone.

On her way out the door, she glanced back at Mark. His finger was in his nostril up to the first knuckle.

So she wasn't the only thing that was stuck.

Maria finished her assignment half an hour before the deadline and e-mailed the attachment to her editor. Her little television flickered in the corner. Conan O'Brien was interviewing Canadian stand-up comedian Pete Zedlacher. The two were laughing at something, but Maria couldn't tell what because she had the sound muted.

Her apartment was small but comfortable—bathroom,

living room, kitchenette, and two bedrooms, one of which served as her office. The place was furnished with a curious mixture of leftover dorm furniture from her college days and more recent purchases from Ikea and Target. A new couch. A used futon. The eggshell-colored walls were sparse—a framed Monet print, a montage of photos from high school and college, and a collectible spoon rack. There was only one picture of her parents in the whole apartment, subconsciously hung above the entertainment center where she didn't have to look at them every day. Maria spent little time in the living room—when she was home, her evenings were spent sleeping or working. Her office wasn't much. Two desks had been lined up in an L-shape in the corner. One held her laptop and the other her older desktop. A two-drawer filing cabinet contained her various clippings and bylines, as well as contracts, receipts, and financial records. Two bookshelves leaned against the wall. One overflowed with paperbacks and compact discs. A green vase sat precariously at the top. The other bookshelf held her television and more books.

Conan gave way to an annoying commercial for a headache medicine. She was just about to turn the television off and go to bed when her laptop beeped, signaling a new e-mail. She clicked on Outlook Express and saw it was from Miles, her editor at the paper.

It read:

> *Got the piece. Thanks. Will run in the local section to-morrow. Meanwhile, how would you like a bigger assignment? Looking for a special feature on a new local Ghost Walk. At least one full page, plus pictures. Maybe more, if material warrants. One of the staff photographers has already made arrangements for pics. Just need someone to do the story. Normally, Hilary would cover this, but she's still on maternity leave and the Ghost Walk's owner, Ken Ripple, is adamant about coverage. The attraction opens the night before Halloween,*

*so we've got to get hopping. Not a lot of time. It's a rush
job. You interested? —Miles*

She was surprised to see that Miles was still awake this time
of night. But then again, judging by how often he complained
about his wife and kids, maybe he was happier at work.

Maria hit REPLY. Was she interested? A full-page feature?
That paid a lot more than a sidebar item about local government. Hell, yes, she was interested, and she told him so. A few
minutes later, Miles responded with Ripple's contact information and a suggestion that Maria come in and go through the
newspaper's archives tomorrow. There was a lot of history associated with the haunted attraction's location, and since she
wasn't a local, she'd have to brush up on it.

Assuring him that she would, and promising to stop by the
office in the morning, Maria logged off and went to bed. It
was a long time before she fell asleep.

When she finally did, she had a nightmare about her parents. They were displeased with the path she'd taken in life
and had decided to talk to her about it—with knives.

They were very angry, and the knives were very sharp.

CHAPTER THREE

Ken Ripple wiped the sweat out of his eyes. Then, hands on hips, he stretched his aching back. He let out a satisfied sigh as it cracked.

"Getting too old for this shit?" Terry Klein asked.

"No," Ken said. "I was banging your wife last night and threw my back out."

"Well, at least one of us is getting some from her." Terry pulled off his leather work gloves and flexed his fingers. "Damn, blisters."

Ken grinned. "Too much jerking off."

"Like I said, at least one of us is getting some from her."

Both men laughed, and then turned back to the business at hand: rigging a pulley system to an outhouse door. When triggered, the series of cable and pulleys would open the door, allowing a dummy to lurch out at unsuspecting passersby. All they had to do was step on the hidden switch. The dummy wasn't much—straw and plywood covered with some of Terry's old clothes, and a rubber monster mask for a face—but in the dark, it would suffice.

The Ghost Walk had been Ken's idea. He'd always enjoyed haunted attractions. Central Pennsylvania was loaded with them—Field of Screams, Jason's Woods, The Spook House, The Haunted Mill, Scream in the Park. But it wasn't until last year, when Ken had attended a trade convention in Baltimore for haunted attraction operators, that he'd gone from an enthusiast to designer. He'd gone to the convention out of curiosity, hoping for a glimpse behind the curtain, some trade secrets, how the magicians pulled their rabbits out of the proverbial hat. Instead, he'd come away with a deep desire to build an attraction himself.

And dedicate it to Deena's memory.

Two years ago, Ken's wife, Deena, while suffering from a slight cold, had missed her period. A home pregnancy test showed a positive result. This was a joyous event. They'd been trying to have a child, without success, for the last three years. But the subsequent follow-up visit with the doctor brought grim news—her slight cold was anything but, and Deena wasn't pregnant. Instead of a baby growing inside her, she had a tumor. The cancer had already spread. Four months later, she was gone, and Ken was alone again. He missed her more and more each day. His friends and family told him that it would get easier with time, but it didn't. Yes, the emotional wounds healed, but the scars still ached.

To honor his wife, Ken decided to build a haunted attraction, and donate the proceeds to women's cancer research. The area around LeHorn's Hollow seemed like the perfect location. It was steeped in local folklore—ghosts and witches and all kinds of creepy phenomena. Murders, both solved and unsolved. The place was perfect. Sadly, he couldn't construct his Ghost Walk on the LeHorn property, since the land's ownership was tied up in a lengthy battle between the state and surviving family members. But the woods around LeHorn's Hollow were vast, and a lot of it was untouched by the fires, which had consumed so much two years before. And the area that had been burned wasn't suitable; it was ash and rubble—a wasteland.

Ken decided to situate his attraction as close to LeHorn's Hollow as was legally—and environmentally—possible.

First, he approached the board of directors at the Glad-

stone Pulpwood Company, which owned some of the neighboring forest (the state and local governments, and several
farmers and companies owned the rest). After several meetings and a lot of pleading, he secured the company's support
and the usage of their land. More importantly, he benefited
from their insurance coverage.

Then he took his idea to the township and got the proper
permits and permissions. That had been a little trickier. There
was a lot of red tape to cut through. Zoning wasn't an issue,
since the Ghost Walk was situated on Gladstone property and
privately owned land donated by neighboring farmers. But he
needed to apply for building permits, provide a site plan and
all sorts of documentation, and fill out a seemingly never-
ending pile of applications. Eventually, however, he got it
approved.

Finally, he put out a call for volunteers. Men and women
from various local organizations and churches answered the
call—students, youth groups, retirees, volunteer firemen and
medical responders, and members of the Lions Club, VFW,
American Legion, Rotary, Masonic Lodge, and Knights of
Columbus. All donated their time and labor while Ken funded
the undertaking and oversaw construction. He obtained some
corporate sponsors. The local hardware store donated supplies, as did the lumberyard. Ken studied back issues of
Haunted Attraction magazine and contacted some professionals via a message board for haunt enthusiasts, all of whom
were very helpful. He'd been stunned and grateful beyond
words at the kindness and enthusiasm the community had
shown.

Construction had started in August. Ken and a few volunteers had scouted the forest, marking trees to indicate in
which direction the trail should go. Then they cut through
the brambles and brush, clearing the undergrowth so that
they could commence with the design.

And here he was, just a few days from the grand opening—
and there was still a ton of things to do. He'd taken his two

weeks of paid vacation from his day job, and was using it to get everything completed in time.

His only regret was that, because of the time the whole process had taken, he wouldn't open until Halloween Eve. Most haunted attractions were open for the entire month; the Ghost Walk would only run from the night before Halloween to the first weekend in November. Still, if it was a success, maybe they'd be open sooner next year.

Finished with the pulley system, the men tested it out. Ken stepped on the hidden pressure switch, which was hidden beneath dirt and leaves. On cue, the outhouse door banged open and the dummy lunged out. Then it leaned back inside and the door slammed shut again.

"Perfect," Ken said.

"What's next?" Terry asked.

Ken sighed. "Too much. The guys from the VFW are almost done with the maze house, but we need to rig some strobe lights inside it. The trail needs to be raked again. We have to make sure we remove all rocks, roots, and anything else somebody could trip over. Last thing we want is someone taking a tumble and suing us. Someone with a pickup truck needs to make a run to Nelson Leiphart's place. He's got a field of dead cornstalks that we can use for camouflage along the trail."

"Camouflage?"

"Sure. In addition to the buildings and scenarios, we're gonna have volunteers in masks or makeup hiding along the trail. When people walk by, they'll jump out and hopefully scare the shit out of them. So we need to camouflage their hiding places."

Terry frowned. "Shouldn't we use tree branches and leaves? Would look more natural. Or plywood sheeting, maybe?"

"Sure, but part of the fun is knowing there's something up ahead. People see the cornstalks and they'll be dreading taking another step. But at the same time, they'll have no choice.

Helps to ramp up their fears. Plus, cornstalks are suited to Halloween. It's all about the ambience."

Smiling, Terry shook his head.

"What?" Ken asked. "What are you laughing at?"

"You, man. It's amazing. I've known you since high school, but I've never seen you as fired up about something as you are this. I mean, just listen to you talking about this—I'm impressed. By day, you hang drywall. But after work, you become an expert at this shit. I've got to hand it to you, Ken. When you first came up with this idea, I figured you'd lose your shirt. But you've really pulled it together."

"Well, I could still lose my shirt. It's all for nothing if nobody shows up on opening night."

"They'll come." Terry put his hand on Ken's shoulder and gave him a squeeze. "Deena would be proud of you."

"Thanks."

Ken's voice was thick with emotion. They stood in awkward silence for a few seconds. Then Terry cleared his throat and removed his hand.

"Okay," he said. "Where do you want me next?"

"Can you give Sylva and Clark a hand unloading those bags of lime? We need it to outline the trail."

"Sure. What are you gonna do?"

"Walk the trail. Check up on everybody. See if I can spot any last-minute things we might have missed. And later, I'm supposed to meet with some reporter. Trying to get a write-up in the paper. They'll probably do a hatchet job."

"Better you than me."

"Yeah."

Terry gathered his tools and then strolled back up the trail, vanishing around the bend. Ken turned around and walked the other way, following the trail deeper into the forest. He inspected various locations along the way, making sure they were functional. The guillotine, whose dummy had a removable head. The spider's grove, an area of the trail overrun with gauze "webs." A pit in the earth, made up to look like a flying saucer crash site, complete with bits of twisted metal and several "alien" bodies. Scattered hiding places, small sheds that housed generators and first-aid stations.

The sound of hammering greeted him as he approached the maze house. It was a ramshackle construct. Low-hanging branches scraped against the corrugated tin roof. Various grades of plywood and weathered planks made up the outer walls. It looked exactly as Ken had wanted it to—like something out of a backwoods horror movie. *House of 1,000 Corpses* or *Texas Chainsaw Massacre* or *Cabin Fever*. He pushed past a sheet of plastic nailed over the doorway and stepped inside. The interior was far different. Black plastic covered the walls, floor, and ceiling, blocking out all light. Three different passageways led off into the darkness. The center hall glowed dimly. Ken followed it to the source of illumination: a string of work lights hanging from the ceiling. Four retired VFW members were putting another dead end into place, driving nails into the thick plywood.

"Hey, guys."

The men stopped hammering and turned to him.

"Howdy, Mr. Ripple." The speaker, Cecil Smeltzer, pulled a red bandanna from his back pocket and wiped his brow. "It's coming along good. Darned if we don't get lost trying to find our way back out."

Ken laughed. "Let's hope not. Wouldn't want to send a search party in here after you."

"No, we wouldn't."

"It looks good, guys. I really appreciate your help. You've done a great job."

"No need to thank us," Cecil said. "It's for a good cause."

The others murmured their agreement.

"And besides," Cecil continued, "it ain't like we've got much to do during the day anyway."

Ken allowed them to show him all they'd done, and nodded with satisfaction. Then he exited the maze and continued down the trail. The work sounds faded, and silence enveloped him. The forest was still, the quiet noticeable. Ken supposed that all the activity had scared off the wildlife, but the absence of even the birds and insects was a little unsettling.

He reached the end of the trail, which opened up into a barren field. Stubs of harvested cornstalks jutted from the rocky soil. When the Ghost Walk was up and running, hay wagons and tractors would be positioned in the field to transport the customers back to their cars. There were supposed to be two teenaged volunteers working here. They'd been tasked with roping off the trail's end and clearly marking the exit. Since they were seniors, the high school allowed them to leave school in the afternoon and help out with the Ghost Walk; all part of the workplace credit program. The idea was that they'd learn valuable skills that could be applied in the job market after they'd graduated. But reality was something different. Instead of working for him, they'd apparently played hooky.

Ken swore under his breath. The rope lay on the ground, along with the exit signs. There was no sign of the teens.

"Hey," he hollered, trying to remember their names. He searched his memory, to no avail. "Hey, you kids!"

His voice echoed through the forest. He paused, listening. Then he remembered their names.

"Sam! Rhonda!"

They were good kids, for the most part. Except for now, when he needed something done. He called out again but there was no answer.

"Goddamn it. Want something done right, you've got to do it yourself."

Sighing, he gathered the rope and began stringing it up between the trees. The echoes faded and the unnerving silence returned.

Won't be quiet for long, Ken thought. *Hopefully, on Halloween, there'll be lots of screams.*

"What was that?"

Rhonda Garrett squeezed Sam Freeman's hand. She halted,

glancing back through the forest. Sam cocked his head and listened.

"Sounds like Mr. Ripple," Sam said.

"He's probably looking for us. Maybe we should go back."

"Screw that," Sam argued. "When we go back, if he says anything, we'll tell him we had to go piss."

"In the woods?"

"Why not?"

"Poison ivy, for one thing."

"It's October. There's no poison ivy now."

Sam tugged her hand, leading her forward. Rhonda halted again, reluctant.

"I don't know, Sam. We could get in trouble. I don't need anymore drama from my mom. She's still tripping about catching us in the hot tub."

"She's just mad because you're getting some and she's not."

Rhonda gasped. "That's terrible!"

"It's true. Your mom would be a lot nicer if she'd just get laid. When was the last time she went out on a date?"

"I don't remember. Probably years."

"Well, there you go."

"It wasn't just the hot tub," Rhonda whispered. "I think she suspects."

"No way. She can't. We were careful."

"I know, but I still think—"

Sam interrupted her. "I thought we weren't going to talk about that. We need to move on. It's a nice day. No need to bring ourselves down."

Rhonda's bottom lip quivered. Her eyes grew watery. Feeling guilty, Sam tried to change the subject.

"Maybe we should fix her up with somebody," he suggested.

"How about Mr. Porter?"

Sam grimaced. "The shop teacher? He's like seventy and shit."

"He's nice."

"He's old. And he scratches his ass."

"Oh, he does not."

"Straight up. He sticks his hand down the back of his pants when he thinks nobody is looking. Then he scratches his ass and sniffs his finger."

"That's disgusting!"

"That's Mr. Porter."

Rhonda laughed. "Well, then who would you suggest?"

"How about a little mother–daughter action."

Rhonda slapped his shoulder. "You're disgusting."

"I can't help it. Your mom's a MILF."

Rhonda pulled away. "I'm going back. You can stay here."

Sam grabbed her arm. "I was just playing. I'm sorry."

"It's not funny. That's my mother you're talking about."

Sam pulled Rhonda closer and kissed the top of her head. Her hair smelled like strawberry-scented shampoo. His lips grazed her forehead, then dipped to her ear. He nuzzled her neck. Rhonda sighed.

"I'm sorry," he repeated. "Let me make it up to you?"

"Not here. Let's go a little further. This close to the trail, I won't be able to relax."

"Okay. We'll go where they can't find us."

He led her deeper into the forest. The trees were close together and the air grew colder. They could see their breath like smoke. They walked hand in hand, not talking, comfortable in their shared silence. Sam wondered what Rhonda was thinking about and decided it was probably how much trouble they'd be in if they were gone too long. She always worried about getting into trouble. Rhonda wondered what Sam was thinking about and decided it was probably sex. He was usually preoccupied with it.

Though neither of them knew it, they were actually thinking about the same thing.

Their baby.

Sam and Rhonda had known each other since the sixth

grade. They'd been dating since the ninth. Their relationship was surprisingly free of all the usual teen angst. But seven months ago they'd faced their first big hurdle when Rhonda missed her period. They'd been careful. Sam always wore a rubber. But despite that, Rhonda got pregnant. After coping with the initial shock and dread, the two agreed to keep it a secret from their families.

Rhonda was terrified of what her mother would say. Her mother, twice divorced, had gotten pregnant with Rhonda at seventeen and never missed an opportunity to remind her daughter what a mistake that had been. Also, Rhonda wanted to go to college. How could she juggle that with the demands of being a parent?

Sam was frightened of the responsibility it would bring. Sure, he loved Rhonda. He always had. But he wasn't ready to get married yet. Although he hadn't told her, after graduation, he wanted to join the Marines and go to Iraq or Afghanistan. She'd have enough problems with that without adding a baby to the situation.

The abortion was a mutual decision, if not an easy one. Pennsylvania law stated that women under the age of eighteen needed permission from a parent before having an abortion. No way would Rhonda's mother ever agree to such a thing, and the only contact she had with her father was the monthly child support checks. Her stepfather had moved to North Carolina after her mother divorced him. Parental consent was out. And Pennsylvania required women to go through a "state-mandated information session"—basically, they tried to talk you out of getting an abortion. She didn't need that drama.

After Rhonda confided in her best friend April, they came up with a solution. Washington, D.C., had no parental notification or consent laws, and it was only a three and a half hour drive from York County. Sam went online and bought fake IDs for them both, stating that they resided in the District of Columbia. Then, on a rainy Tuesday, they called in sick to school and made the drive.

They'd been haunted by it ever since.

Both were thinking about it when a man stepped out from behind a tree and pointed a rifle at them.

"Don't scream," he rasped. "Don't make a sound. Move and I'll blow your fucking brains out the backs of your heads."

Rhonda's grip tightened. She squeezed Sam's hand, grinding his fingers together.

"What do you want?" Sam asked, trying to hide his panic.

The man grinned. "*You.*"

The entity inside Richard Henry had many names, yet none of them were its true name. To speak that aloud was to invite certain death and destruction. It, along with its twelve brothers, was one of the oldest things in the universe. Indeed, it had been old before this universe was even created. It was not a demon, though many throughout history had mistakenly thought it as such. Nor was it a god, though it had occasionally been worshipped as one over the centuries.

Since well before the dawn of humanity, it had taken different forms, used different faces—a satyr, a pillar of fire, a small child, a storm cloud, a black goat, a giant serpent, and others. Anything that mankind feared, anything that haunted them, this being could replicate. Each guise had a different name attributed to it. Verminus. Nuada. Lud. Shub-Niggurath. Pahad, who hungers. Lilitu, the cold one. The Mesopotamians knew it as Lamashtu. Cain's tribe called it Nud. Another clan, forgotten by history, called it Othel. To some civilizations, it was the Father of Pan. To others, the Living Darkness. One obscure sect had believed it to be the sire of Kali. The Celts figured out its real name, mistakenly thought it a benevolent deity, and had paid the price for that tragic error. The Romans had also known its real name, but refused to speak it out loud, instead referencing it only in their texts. Humanity had since mistakenly believed that the Romans didn't know its real name either. The Greeks had believed that merely acknowledging its existence could lead to madness. To avoid the risk of speaking its name, many cultures struck all references to it from their histories and grimoires. Others simply called it He Who Shall Not Be Named.

Its real form was a shapeless, shifting darkness—the absence of light made solid.

Its real name was Nodens.

Nodens' temples could be found everywhere across the universe. On distant planets unknown by mankind, like the twin moons of distant Yhe and the fungal gardens of Yaksh. In the deserted tunnels beneath Mars and in the center of Jupiter's Great Red Spot. On frozen, barren Io and several hurtling asteroids. And on Earth, in the ruins of Mesopotamia, Babylon, Rome, and Persia, and more recent diggings in Oregon, Hawaii, Peru, Kenya, the Yian-Ho province in China, and the Welsh counties of Gloucestershire and Monmouthshire.

Nodens existed in none of these temples. Instead, it resided in the center of a place—a Labyrinth—that spanned space and time, dimensions and realities. From there, it sent out tendrils to different worlds, searching for the slightest opening. When conditions were favorable, these exploratory feelers breached the barriers between dimensions, allowing it to infect entire worlds with its darkness. All it needed was an open door.

Nodens had corrupted other Earths before. Alternate Earths. Ones whose dominion wasn't given to Ob or Leviathan or Behemoth or Kandara or any of the others among the Thirteen.

Now it was this Earth's turn.

It studied the male and the female through Richard Henry's eyes, sensed their fear, and tasted their terror.

The darkness quivered with excitement.

No matter how many times Nodens had done this over the eons, it never tired of the destruction and violation—the utter desolation that followed in its wake.

The time was near. The barriers were weakening. But first, before Nodens could totally engulf this world, it had to finish the breach. The seven sigils carved into the rocks encircling the doorway prevented that. It couldn't touch the sigils or move the rocks.

But these creatures—and others like them—could.

"Keep walking. Bear to the right."

"Look . . ." Sam turned around.

The man thrust the rifle at him. "I said keep walking. You stop again, or turn around, and I'll blow your fucking head off. You'd better just do as I tell you."

Despite the threatening words, the man's voice was flat. He looked bad—spoiled. Smelled like it, too. Judging by the condition of his clothes and his unkempt appearance, he'd been out here in the woods for a few days. His skin was pale and sallow. His fingernails were caked with dirt. Leaves and twigs clung to his greasy hair, and his bald spot and other exposed areas were covered with scabs and bug bites. But it was his eyes that disturbed Sam the most. They were black—two impenetrable obsidian holes floating above the guy's nose. No iris. No sclera. No cornea. No color. Just darkness.

Normal people didn't have eyes like that.

The man stroked the rifle's trigger. Sam trudged forward, ducking the low-hanging branches. Rhonda reached for his hand. Her palm was sweaty. Sam felt her pulse hammering beneath the skin. Its rate matched his own.

"Look, mister," he tried again, careful not to turn around or stop walking. "Let my girlfriend go. Whatever the problem is, she doesn't have to—"

"I need you both," he said with that same inflectionless tone. "Straight ahead. Don't stop until I tell you."

Guy's a freak, Sam thought. *Maybe he's sick. Infected with something that made his eyes like that. Or maybe he's just fucked up. Wants to watch us get it on or something. Or maybe he's gonna kill me and do something to Rhonda.*

He shuddered. But if that was true, then why hadn't the man shot him already? Probably because they were still in earshot of Mr. Ripple and the other volunteers. He was forcing them to march farther into the forest, away from the Ghost Walk. That couldn't be a good sign. Sam considered shouting for help, but his fear wouldn't let him. If he called out, the man might shoot him on the spot.

The ground sloped downward. They came to a thin, trickling creek.

"Go across."

Sam and Rhonda did as ordered. Rhonda slipped on the far bank and her foot splashed into the water, soaking her shoe.

"Keep going. Straight. Not much farther now."

Thorny vines tugged at their legs as they continued on. Occasionally, the man would give them a direction—left, right, or straight ahead. Otherwise, he said nothing. The forest was silent. Sam winced as a branch whipped his face. A red welt formed on his cheek. He rubbed it gingerly, then wiped tears from his eyes. Rhonda stumbled over a rock, but Sam kept hold of her hand and held her upright. Eventually, the dense undergrowth thinned out. They passed by some dead trees, and soon entered a burned-out hollow.

"Almost there."

Rhonda sobbed. "Please don't hurt us. We'll do anything you want."

"Yes, you will."

The ground was covered with a thick layer of ash. It swirled around their feet as they plodded forward. Some of it flew into Sam's mouth and nose, and he coughed. Unable to help himself, he halted. Rhonda did, too. When he could breathe again, Sam glanced back at the man, ready to beg forgiveness for defying his orders to keep moving. The plea died in his throat. The man had stopped, too. He held the rifle in the crook of his arm, pointed away from them.

"I'm sorry," Sam said. "The ash . . ."

"Doesn't matter. We're here."

"W-what are you going to do to us?" Rhonda stammered. "We did everything you asked."

"Yeah," Sam said. "We won't tell anybody. We promise."

"Just let us go. Please?"

"You can both leave here once you've moved those rocks."

Sam blinked. "Rocks?"

The man nodded his head at something behind them. Slowly, Sam and Rhonda both turned. Their eyes widened. A circle of round, gray stones jutted up from the ash. Judging by the marks on the ground, some of them had only recently been uncovered. The stones had strange carvings on them. One of them lay on its side, revealing a hole in the earth.

Sam turned back to the man. "You want us to do what?"

"I can't touch the stones. But you can. I want each of you to move one."

Rhonda frowned. "What for?"

"Because if you don't, I'll kill you."

He pointed the rifle at them again and stepped forward, forcing the teens toward the circle. Sam and Rhonda walked backward, their eyes not leaving the gun.

"Besides," the man said, his tone still emotionless, "there's somebody waiting for you inside the circle."

Sam balled his fists up at his sides. "Who?"

The man didn't respond.

"His eyes," Rhonda whispered. "What's wrong with his eyes?"

Sam hushed her with a warning glance. Rhonda fell silent.

They reached the stones. The man kept the rifle aimed at them, holding it at waist level. He nodded at Sam.

"You first."

Grimacing, Sam slowly turned his back to them and knelt down. He tensed, expecting to feel his head split apart at any second, but their captor made no move. Sam put his hands on the stone in front of him. It felt cool, but quickly warmed to his touch. He could have sworn that it was vibrating slightly. The fillings in his teeth began to ache. Sam winced. He needed to piss. His bladder felt like it was going to burst.

"Don't pull it out yet," the man warned. "Your turn, girl."

Rhonda knelt next to Sam. They both waited. As they did, something occurred to Sam. Obviously, they were in the part of the forest that had burned down two years ago. The area was barren and desolate—but shouldn't it have been alive again? It *had* been two years. Surely, new growth would have started by now—saplings pushing their way through the ashes, small plants seeking new footholds in the wide open space. Instead, there was nothing.

"Okay," the man said, interrupting Sam's thoughts. "Pull those rocks out and toss them aside."

Ignoring his bladder's insistent urgings, Sam tugged and pushed until the heavy stone came free. Rhonda did too, but couldn't get the stone to move. Grunting, she pushed as hard as she could. Veins stood out in her neck and forehead. She sat back, exasperated.

"It won't move."

"Do it."

"Sam can do it. He's stronger than me."

"He's already touched one. It's your turn."

"I can't!"

"Do it or your boyfriend dies."

With an angry shout, Rhonda freed the rock from the soil. It rolled aside, revealing more of the strange carvings.

"What now?" Sam asked, not looking back.

There was no response.

With the sigils removed, Nodens sent two more tendrils surging through the doorway and into the world.

Sam and Rhonda heard it at the same time.

A baby. Crying.

"Oh, God," Sam gasped. "Oh, my fucking God."

The baby's cries grew louder.

"I'm sorry," Rhonda sobbed. Tears streamed down her anguished face. "I'm so sorry. I want to take it back."

In the center of the broken circle, darkness swirled, coalescing into a cloud. They watched, terrified but unable to turn away, as it formed their greatest regret. Their greatest loss. Their greatest fear.

It opened its eyes and curled its little hands into fists.

The ghost of Sam and Rhonda's dead baby screamed for its parents.

They screamed, too.

And then the darkness took them.

CHAPTER FOUR

The newspaper's archives were located in the basement of the building. It was a bright, well-lit area with a state-of-the-art climate control system. Dozens of rows of alphabetized filing cabinets dominated the center of the room. Each one held copies of every article the newspaper had printed in the last thirty years. Microfiche units lined one of the walls, allowing reporters access to articles older than thirty years. During their last quarterly meeting, the newspaper's owner had promised the staff that he would digitize the entire library, making them available via computer, but had balked at the idea a month later. Something to do with profits.

Maria hated him for it.

If the archives were stored electronically, if she were able to view the files using some sort of search database, this would go a lot faster.

It was one in the afternoon. She'd been here since eight thirty that morning. She'd intended to be there for an hour or two, tops. Check in with her editor, Miles. Then do some research, familiarize herself with background for the story, interview Ken Ripple, write it up and turn the article in. After that, all she'd have to do is wait for the direct deposit to hit her checking account. Sadly, what was supposed to be a quick fact-finding session had turned into much more.

Maria closed her eyes and rubbed her temples. She had a headache, and it didn't look like the pain would subside any-time soon. She sipped cold coffee from a Styrofoam cup and sighed. The area the Ghost Walk was located in had a lot of history—far more than she'd ever imagined. Every article she uncovered led to three more. So instead of jotting down a few notes, Maria found herself unraveling a dense, spiral-ing series of events, folklore, and local history.

Maria started by researching LeHorn's Hollow, but quickly determined that the stories associated with it actually included far more land than the hollow itself. The woodlands surround-ing the hollow contributed to the folklore. The forest was over twenty miles wide and encompassed five different townships. Most of it was untouched by the explosive development that had marred other parts of the state. The land was owned by many different people—farmers, the Gladstone Pulpwood Company, various local governments, a paper mill, and the State of Pennsylvania. LeHorn's Hollow had sat almost in the center of the woods, surrounded by cornfields, until a massive fire destroyed the hollow and some of the surrounding coun-tryside in 2006. She remembered the fire. It had made national headlines at the time, even warranting coverage on the cable news channels. Eventually, accidental arson had been deter-mined as the cause. The perpetrator was never caught.

All sorts of supernatural phenomena were associated with the forest—crop circles, ley lines, strange balls of light, un-identified flying objects, mysterious sounds, trees that seemed to move on their own, and a roster of creatures that would make any cryptozoologist salivate with delight, including numerous sightings of a large black dog with red eyes. The locals called it a hellhound. In the early nineties, a group of researchers from Penn State decided to investigate some of the paranormal activity. They discovered strange pockets of magnetically-charged ground scattered throughout the forest.

There were stories about the hollow long before it had

even *been* LeHorn's Hollow—anecdotes from before the time of William Penn and his fellow white men. Before the endless waves of German, Irish, Dutch, Quaker, and Amish settlers. The Susquehanna Indian tribes had considered the land to be "bad ground," and avoided it altogether, refusing to hunt or dwell there. They thought it was cursed; believed that the hollow was infested with demons and that a portal to another world lurked beyond the trees. Their only documented usage of the hollow was as a place for their criminals and insane. According to legend, none of those who'd been banished to the hollow were ever seen again.

Apparently, that continued to the present day. Maria found numerous accounts of missing persons from over the years— hunters, hikers, teenagers, and a logger for the pulpwood company. All of them had one thing in common: they'd last been seen in the vicinity of the hollow.

There were deaths, too. A group of deer hunters perished when their cabin burned down in 2000. A state surveyor was found dead atop a tree in 1990; the official cause of death was listed as a heart attack. A little girl had been murdered by a child molester inside the surrounding forest. The killer, Craig Chalmers, abducted the girl three days after making parole on a similar charge. He was captured alive, babbling about demons. He told State Police investigators that the forest was full of monsters trying to kill him.

And then, of course, there was the most famous murder and disappearance of all.

Nelson LeHorn himself.

Depending on the source, Nelson LeHorn was either a simple farmer teetering on the edge of bankruptcy and divorce while the modern world encroached on his home, or a powerful witch devoted to dark folk magic, or both. Public opinion seemed split. Whatever he was, in 1985 LeHorn killed his wife, Patricia, by pushing her out of their attic window. He'd supposedly believed that she'd had sexual relations with the devil. After the murder, he promptly disappeared before police could capture him. He'd been missing for over twenty years, despite a sizeable reward for information leading to his arrest. His three children were adults now, and had forsaken their heritage. They were scattered across the country—a son in a Northern Pennsylvanian prison, a daughter in Idaho, and another in New York. Maria found notes from other reporters detailing their attempts to interview the children, none of whom had ever consented. They refused to talk about their father or their mother's slaying.

Maria took another sip of coffee and grimaced. There were grains floating in her cup. She drained it, crushed the cup in her fist, and tossed it into the trash. Then she continued poring over the clippings.

LeHorn had supposedly practiced powwow—a rustic mix of magical disciplines, folklore, and Judeo-Christian teachings and mythology. The same superstitious beliefs were known as hoodoo in the Southern states, but here in Central Pennsylvania, it was called powwow. Its history was as mixed as its structure. The Susquehanna Indians had a form of shamanism called pawwaw. When the first German settlers arrived in Pennsylvania, they brought with them a magical discipline called Braucherei. Over time, the two beliefs mixed, and became known as powwow.

Powwow practitioners relied on a book by John George Hohman called *The Long Lost Friend*. First printed in 1819, this was the primary powwow sourcebook. Its material was derived from many different sources, including the Hebrew cabala, African tribal beliefs, German mysticism, Gypsy lore, Druid ceremonies, and ancient Egyptian teachings. The book offered an eclectic range of cures, spells, and magical protections. There were remedies for everything from pink eye to cholera to parasites in livestock. Maria guessed that none of the recommendations were approved by the American Medical Association. There were also numerous spells, chants and incantations, complete with symbols and lists of ingredients. Two other tomes that were usually included in a powwow library were a three-volume set by Albertus Magnus entitled *Egyptian Secrets*, and *The Sixth and Seventh Books of Moses*, which was supposedly based on magic and cures that Moses learned while he lived in the house of the Pharaoh.

Powwow doctors, who cured their patients using magic and methods from *The Long Lost Friend,* were mentioned in several articles. They had been quite prevalent in the area up until the late sixties. Many of the county's older residents visited powwow doctors before consulting a physician. Nelson LeHorn had been just one of several well-known powwow practitioners in the area. Others had included Nelson Rehmeyer (murdered in the 1930s for his copy of *The Long Lost Friend*); a woman who lived along the Susquehanna River named Mary Knowles, considered a witch by her neighbors, who'd passed away in 1941; and an Amish resident of neighboring Lancaster County named Amos Stoltzfus, who'd died in 1980.

What Maria found most surprising was that in a county with a population of over 373,000 people, powwow was still practiced in some of the more rural parts. She shook her head. How could anybody still believe in this superstitious nonsense? Especially today, with all of the advances in modern science and medicine? Growing up in Paramus, there had been no magic, no witch doctors. Instead, there were shopping malls and boutiques, espresso bars and cafes, cell phones and community activism. Here she was, a three-hour drive away from home, and it felt like she'd gone back in time. Yes, York, Pennsylvania, had all of the luxuries that Paramus, New Jersey, had offered, but beneath that veneer, there was a weird, backwoods mentality. It was depressing, and yet, she wanted to know more. Maria was fascinated with LeHorn. The entire tragic story would make great fodder for a true-crime book. But what she discovered next was even more bizarre.

Alive or dead, Nelson LeHorn had remained an enduring,

if somewhat infamous, figure. For years following his disappearance, there were purported sightings of him in the hollow and surrounding woods, but subsequent searches turned up nothing. Others reported that they'd seen his ghost walking among the trees. But otherwise, things quieted down again. There was the occasional UFO sighting or encounter with a hellhound. Usually these reports involved couples who'd gone to the hollow after dark, looking for a secluded spot to party or get amorous.

Then, in the spring of 2006, things heated up again. A witches' coven took up residence in the hollow, practicing black magic rituals and worshipping LeHorn as a deity. They were involved in several murders and disappearances, including several people connected to a local author named Adam Senft.

Adam Senft had lived in the area all his life. By 2006, he'd had some national success as a midlist novelist. He'd written three mystery novels: *When the Rain Comes, Cold as Ice*, and *Heart of the Matter*. Senft was inextricably tied to LeHorn's Hollow, and not just by acquaintances whom the coven had murdered. On the night the forest fire destroyed the hollow and some of the surrounding acreage, another murder victim had been found in Senft's home. A homicide detective named Ramirez cleared Senft of any wrongdoing, but Maria was unable to find a conclusive follow-up on who *had* committed the crime. Ramirez retired soon after, and moved to south Florida. She made a note to track down his contact information, if possible. He might have more background information not available in the archives.

Six months after the fire and the murders, Adam Senft killed his pregnant wife, Tara, in the exact same manner that LeHorn had murdered his wife twenty years earlier—by pushing her out of the attic window. At his trial, Senft claimed that the baby was half human and half goat—the malignant offspring of a satyr. He'd killed his wife to prevent its birth. He also claimed that the creature had been summoned by

none other than Nelson LeHorn. Despite the best efforts of the
district attorney, Senft's defense lawyer was able to secure an
insanity plea—something that was normally very difficult to
do in the Pennsylvania court system. He was remanded into
the custody of officials as a "forensic"—basically criminally
insane—patient and currently resided in the White Rose Mental Health Facility in East York.

Nelson LeHorn had murdered his wife because he believed
she'd slept with the devil. Adam Senft had done the same because he believed his wife had slept with a satyr. The psy-
choses were remarkably similar. Could both be linked to the
hollow's Goat Man mythos?

Maria was intrigued. There was far more she could do with
this story than just a fluff piece in the local paper. The possibility of a true-crime book, or even a series of them, was tan-
talizing. The more she uncovered, the greater the possibilities
became.

Her headache forgotten, Maria glanced at her watch. She
still needed to meet with the Ghost Walk's owner, Ken Ripple,
later that evening. It took her another hour to make copies of
all the articles. By the time she was done, she'd decided on
her next course of action. She'd finish the write-up on the
Ghost Walk and get it turned in on time, but then, she'd start
collating her information and put together a book proposal.

She also decided to track down Ramirez, the detective who
had originally cleared Senft in the first murder, and then try to
secure an interview with Adam Senft himself. She anticipated
a lot of red tape with the security hospital, but was sure she
could cut through it. Maria had been lucky enough to nurture
some professional relationships and contacts among several
individuals employed within the county's medical system.

Maria packed up her copies and hurried out of the newspaper's offices without saying good-bye to Miles. She whistled on her way through the parking garage. Her headache
had vanished. For the first time in a long while, she felt excited by an assignment. She couldn't wait to dig deeper. Her

gut told her that there was more to this story—a hidden narrative woven between the newspaper articles and records. The public details were dark, no doubt, but she suspected that beneath the surface, it was even darker.

CHAPTER FIVE

There was no danger of Richard Henry being missed, but Sam Freeman and Rhonda Garrett had families and friends who would note their absence. Like some of the others among the Thirteen, such as Ob of the Siqqusim, Nodens had the ability to pick through its victim's memories and experiences before it devoured them. It had done so with Sam and Rhonda, scanning their lives and the moments leading up to their arrival at the doorway. The teenagers had arrived at the hollow that morning in Sam's car, a Mustang GT. The vehicle was parked at the edge of the forest, along with those belonging to the other volunteers. Nodens had Rhonda retrieve the car keys from Sam. Then, to prevent discovery, Nodens sent Rhonda to move the automobile while Richard and Sam stood guard around the circle. There were too many humans in the woods now. Sending its pawns out to collect more of them was too risky. If they abducted another, it might arouse suspicion. They could be overpowered.

Instead, it would wait. Nodens knew patience well.

Nodens was hungry. The desire to totally consume these three, to drain their physical forms of energy, to snuff them out like candles, was strong. It was hungry. But not yet. The other sigils needed to be removed first. The doorway must be opened. Then it would feed.

The sun began its descent. In a few hours, darkness would reclaim the forest.

And in a few more days, when the walls between the worlds were at their thinnest, Nodens would do the same, and then spread out into the world, bringing eternal darkness in its wake.

Ken nodded at Rhonda as she walked past him. Sweat ran into his eyes. He hoisted a dummy into the air. A noose was around the dummy's neck. Ken had tossed the other end of the rope over a sturdy oak tree branch jutting out over the trail. Customers would have to walk directly beneath the hanging "victim" as they made their way along the path.

"How you doing, Rhonda? You and Sam finished up for the day?"

Without stopping, Rhonda nodded. She kept her gaze averted, staring straight ahead. Ken noticed that her shoes and jeans were smudged with dirt and ashes. More filth covered her hands and the back of her neck. Twigs and leaves dangled from her hair.

"I was looking for you guys earlier," Ken said. "Thought maybe you'd left already."

Rhonda didn't respond.

Ken tied off the rope and flexed his aching fingers. "You okay?"

"I'm fine, Mr. Ripple." She kept walking, not turning to face him. "Sorry. We didn't hear you calling for us before."

"Well, that's okay. I just want you kids to know how much I appreciate your help. Couldn't do this without you."

"It's no problem. Really. I have to get going now. I'm late."

Rhonda rounded a curve in the trail and disappeared from sight. Sam heard leaves and twigs crunching beneath her feet.

"Don't mention it," he muttered. "Wouldn't want to inconvenience you."

Ken noticed that she hadn't looked at him. Hadn't let him see her eyes. The girl's reaction was uncharacteristic. Usually, Rhonda was friendly and outgoing. Terry called her a chatterbox. This wasn't like her at all. She seemed sullen. Maybe she'd gotten into a fight with her boyfriend. That might explain why they hadn't completed their tasks earlier.

"Oh well. Kids . . ."

Shaking his head, Ken studied his handiwork. The dummy swung slowly back and forth like a pendulum. The rope creaked against the rough tree bark. Ken grinned at the sound—it would add to the ambience. The dummy's clothing had been splattered with red paint. He debated hiding a spotlight in the undergrowth beside the trail and positioning it to shine on the dummy, but decided against it. The sight would be more effective in darkness.

"Perfect."

He glanced up at the sky. The sun was a red ball. The clouds glowed, tinted with orange and yellow hues. It was a beautiful sight. Ken enjoyed it for a moment, wishing Deena was there to see it with him. How many evening walks had they taken together through the woods behind their house? How many sunsets had they watched together, not knowing that those moments weren't infinite?

He remembered one in particular. His favorite. Early in the morning, on their fifth wedding anniversary, Ken packed a picnic lunch—crackers, cheese, fruit and vegetables, bottled water, whipped cream. He put it all in a wicker basket, grabbed a beach blanket from the hall closet, and then left the house. When Deena woke up, she found a note from him in the kitchen, telling her to get dressed and walk down to the edge of their property. She'd find further instructions along the banks of the stream that served as their lot's boundary line. Deena found a second note nailed to a tree along the creek. That one told her to follow the trail along the brook. She kept following the notes Ken had left behind like a trail of bread crumbs until she found him. The blanket was spread out along the stream bank. They'd sat there all day, eating their lunch, swimming, making love, and then swimming again. The land was owned by the Sportsman's Club, of which Ken was a member, so they didn't have to worry about anyone stumbling across them. They stayed all day and when sunset came, they'd watched it curled up together on the blanket.

Now his sunsets were solitary affairs.

Ken sighed. The loneliness made his stomach ache. Tired and sore, he trudged back toward the exit. It would be night soon, and he'd watch another sunset by himself. It occurred to him that the reporter was probably on her way. Ken decided to get ready for the interview to take his mind off of things.

All around him, the shadows lengthened.

Rhonda unlocked Sam's car and slipped behind the wheel. Before starting the vehicle, she rummaged through the glove compartment and found a pair of sunglasses. She put them on, hiding her obsidian eyes. Then she turned the headlights on and drove away, navigating winding, treacherous back roads. She passed cornfields and pastures and farmhouses. The homes were shuttered for the night. Lights glowed softly behind their curtains.

Soon, there would be no lights at all. They'd be snuffed out, consumed by the living darkness.

The back roads gave way to main roads. She did the speed limit and obeyed all traffic laws. She drove in silence, staring straight ahead. She did not turn on the radio or Sam's iPod. When her cell phone rang, she ignored it. She had no family or friends now. She was part of something bigger and greater.

Eventually, she reached Route 30. She drove east, crossing the Susquehanna River and into Lancaster County. She took the first exit off the highway and cruised through the bucolic riverside town of Columbia, passing antique shops, beauty salons, small cafes, and used bookstores. The streets were relatively empty.

At the other side of town, she pulled into the parking lot of a Safeway grocery store and parked the car at the far end, away from the overhead lights. Most of the spaces were full—cars, trucks, and a few Amish buggies. Rhonda turned off the car and headlights, exited the vehicle, locked the doors, and walked away. She stared straight ahead. Her stride had purpose. She passed by a mother pushing both a shopping cart and a baby stroller. The baby began to cry. The mother hushed her child. Rhonda felt their fear. It was made stronger by the fact that neither human knew why they were afraid.

The last hint of the sun disappeared below the horizon and darkness engulfed the town. Rhonda slipped into the shadows. Consumed with their own lives and agendas, nobody else in the parking lot even noticed her.

Except for one person.

Levi Stoltzfus was putting his grocery bags in the back of his buggy when he saw the girl. She was young and pretty, dressed immodestly and wearing dark sunglasses at night. But that wasn't why he noticed her.

Her aura was what attracted his attention. It was black.

All human beings have auras. Levi had been able to see them since birth, and his father and grandfather had taught him how to read them. Their colors varied, encompassing the entire spectrum. A trained eye could tell if a person was healthy or sick, happy or sad, just by noting the color of their aura. Different colors meant different things. But auras were never black. At least, not human auras.

Black meant something else.

His horse, Dee, whinnied nervously as the girl passed near them. Pointedly turning his attention away from the young woman, Levi patted the animal's neck and stroked its mane, whispering soothing words of assurance that only the horse could hear.

"Easy now, Dee. I feel it, too. Calm down. This too shall pass."

Her footsteps echoed on the blacktop. His free hand drifted to his coat, patting the bulge over his left breast. A battered copy of *The Long Lost Friend* lay snuggled in his inner pocket. It had been his father's, and his father's before him. The front page of the book held the following inscription: *Whoever carries this book with him is safe from all his enemies, visible or invisible; and whoever has this book with him cannot die without the holy corpse of Jesus Christ, nor be drowned in any water, nor burn up in any fire, nor can any unjust sentence be passed upon him.*

Levi had never had reason to doubt it, except for maybe the last part—the bit about unjust sentences. His excommunication from his church and professed faith still chafed at his pride, even after all these years. It had cost him everything—his love, his friends, his community. He didn't like being an outsider, didn't like being alone. Who would? But still, it was God's will, and a small cross to bear, all things considered.

As his father, Amos, used to say when he thought no one else was listening, "Thou shalt not suffer a witch or a charismatic evangelical Christian to live."

Dee stomped her hooves and whinnied again. The air grew colder as the girl passed by. Across the parking lot, a baby shrieked. Dogs barked somewhere in the night. Levi mouthed a silent prayer:

"The cross of Christ be with me. The cross of Christ overcomes all water and every fire. The cross of Christ overcomes all weapons. The cross of Christ is a perfect sign and blessing to my soul. Now I pray that the holy corpse of Christ bless me against all evil things, words, and works."

The young woman stopped a few yards away from him. Levi stole a quick glance at her. The girl turned her head toward him. Levi saw his reflection in her sunglasses. Dispensing with pretense, he continued out loud, his voice barely a whisper, issuing a challenge of sorts.

"Enoch and Elias, the two prophets, were never imprisoned, nor bound, nor beaten, and came out of their power.

Thus, no one of my enemies must be able to injure or attack me in my body or my life, in the name of God the Father, the Son, and the Holy Ghost. *Ut nemo in sense tentat, descendere nemo. At precedenti spectatur mantica tergo.*"

Ignoring him, the girl walked on. Dee calmed down after she was past them. Levi kept petting the horse, watching her go. Darkness swirled around her, blacker than the surrounding night. Levi shivered. He suddenly felt very cold. His stomach clenched and his breath caught in his throat.

Something was very wrong with the girl. She wasn't human. Well, she had been at one time—recently, judging by her appearance. But no more. Now, she was something else. Not *evil*. Levi had faced evil many times, had seen it reflected in both human and inhuman beings. The girl wasn't satanic. He was sure of it. If she had been, she would have responded to his challenge. This was something else, something beyond the Judeo-Christian pantheon or any of the world's other major religions. Whatever the girl was—possessed, otherworldly projection, or pan-dimensional manifestation—she wasn't evil. Her presence went beyond evil. He sensed it. Saw it in the girl's aura. In the way she'd ignored his prayer.

Levi had some experience in such matters.

The Lord had put him here, that much was certain. God had sent him to the Safeway for groceries tonight so that their paths would cross. So that he would recognize the threat. This was his calling. His birthright. His curse.

He sighed. It was still a long ride home, and there was much to do once he got there. Levi rented a small, one-story house in Marietta. His neighbors pretty much left him alone, whispering quietly to each other about "the nice Amish man next door." Levi found that mildly irritating. He'd tried explaining to them over and over that he was no longer Amish, but they still insisted on referring to him as such. Maybe it was because he still preferred the long beard of his former people, or perhaps because he still adhered to their plain dress code: black pants and shoes, a white, button-down shirt, suspenders, and a black dress coat, topped off with a wide-brimmed straw hat. Or because he drove a horse and buggy rather than a gas-guzzling SUV.

The rental property had a two-car garage out back. One half had been converted into a stable for Dee; Levi had turned the other section into a woodshop. During the week, he made various goods—coat and spoon racks, plaques, lawn ornaments, and other knickknacks—and sold them every Saturday at the local antiques market. It was an honest, decent living. The Lord provided. But Levi also had another, more secret occupation.

He worked powwow, as his father had, and his father before him. Patients, mostly the elderly who remembered the old ways, or the poor who couldn't afford the more modern methods, came to him seeking treatments for various ailments and maladies. He dealt with everything from the common cold to arthritis. Occasionally, he'd be called upon for more serious matters: stopping bleeding or mending a broken bone. He usually saw two or three patients a month—not nearly as many as his father had tended to when he was alive—but, modern age, modern sensibilities. People didn't need his help anymore. They didn't even need doctors. Modern man had the Internet—a font of medical knowledge. The first thing Levi had done when he left the congregation was purchase a computer and dial-up Internet service. He hoped the Lord would grant him enough money to get a cable modem, but so far, none had been forthcoming. Levi loved the Internet. It symbolized all that was right and wrong with mankind. He found it fascinating. And useful to his trade. Many times, he'd exchanged notes and information with others around the world—faith healers, witch doctors, warlocks, shamans, hougans. Their differences in beliefs didn't matter. They all answered to a higher purpose, and they all had something in common. They were outsiders, Levi and the others.

Despite his knowledge, Levi's abilities had limits. There

were no herbs or ingredients to combat cancer, for example. Only prayer could cure that, and the Lord didn't seem inclined to oblige. Levi had experienced failures. They haunted him. But so far, his successes had far outweighed his failures. Yet there were times when he was charged with doing more than helping the sick or curing livestock.

This was one of those times.

"Thy will be done, Lord. Thy will be done. Although I wish you'd have let me get my ice cream and milk home before you called on me. They'll go bad sitting out here. And I've still got to feed Crowley. Wouldn't do to let him starve, unless you plan on sending him some manna."

Dee neighed in agreement. Or maybe displeasure. Levi couldn't be sure.

He needed to face this—whatever it was. Defeat it. But to do that, he needed its name. He needed to know what he was fighting. All power stemmed from naming. And the only way to discover the girl's identity was to follow her. She was on foot and hadn't gone far. He still sensed her, although distant. She was heading west, toward the river. He couldn't follow her with the buggy. There was no telling how far she would travel, and Dee was already tired. Also, if she crossed the river, he'd have to use the bridge. Such an undertaking was dangerous. Tractor trailers barreled across the two-lane bridge at seventy miles an hour. If he was in front of them, they'd never be able to stop in time. He couldn't do the Lord's work if he was dead.

Even as he considered his options, he felt the girl's presence getting farther away. If he followed on foot, he might lose her. Already, her aura was fading. No, there was only one way to follow her.

And he didn't like it. He loathed it, in fact. It had been a long time since he'd done it, but now, it was a necessary evil. There was no other way.

Levi was afraid of flying. Afraid of heights. He had a fear of gravity.

"Thy will be done . . ."

He ran back into the grocery store and asked the manager if somebody could keep an eye on his horse and buggy. Levi explained that he had an important errand to run. The manager eyed the clock on the wall and pointed out that they closed in two hours. Unblinking, Levi stared him in the eye, made a slight motion with his finger and asked if the night shift would be willing to watch it for him. It was very important. Sighing, the manager agreed. Levi thanked him and left the store.

On his way back to the buggy, Levi rummaged through his pockets and pulled out his cell phone. He dialed his closest neighbor, Sterling Myers. The older man answered on the third ring. He sounded drunk. Southern rock music played in the background.

"Hello?"

"Hello, Sterling. This is Levi Stoltzfus. I hope I'm not disturbing you?"

"Hey, Levi. What's up? I was just sitting here watching some stupid reality show. People singing. Don't know why the wife likes this stuff."

Levi silently agreed. When he'd finally gotten his first opportunity to watch television, he'd been underwhelmed. It wasn't a tool of the devil. It was a tool of stupidity.

"Kids out trick-or-treating," Sterling continued. "Don't know why the township doesn't wait and have that on Halloween night, but what the hell. At least the house is quiet. Anyway, enough about that. How's it going?"

"Well," Levi said. "Not too good, Sterling. I need a big favor."

"Sure. What's that?"

"I'm going to be late getting home tonight. Something's come up. I was wondering if you could feed my dog, Crowley? He's tied out back."

"Yeah, I can do that. You know, those are weird names for your animals. Crowley and Dee. What's the deal with that?"

"Old friends of the family. A long time ago."

"I had a dog named Shithead, once."

"Sterling, I have to get going."

"No problem, Levi. I'll take care of the dog. You got a key to the house hidden somewhere?"

Levi's heart hammered in his chest. Sterling couldn't enter the house without Levi being there. That would invite disaster.

"No," he said, speaking carefully. "His food is in the garage. It's unlocked. There's no need to go inside the house at all. And Crowley has the doghouse to go into if it rains, so he'll be fine."

"Okay. No problem."

There was a burst of static and then Sterling came back again.

"You on your cell phone?" he asked.

"Yes," Levi said. "I'm sorry about that. The network coverage is spotty in this area."

"Let me ask you something, Levi."

Levi rolled his eyes, anticipating what was coming next. He didn't have time for this. Not tonight.

"What's that, Sterling?"

"If you're Amish, then how come you can use a cell phone?"

Levi sighed. "I've told you before, Sterling. I'm not Amish anymore. I use a cell phone for the same reason everybody else uses a cell phone: because it's a lot more practical than a carrier pigeon."

"Yeah," Sterling cackled. "You got that right! Still, I hate the things. Wife has one, but I don't. I think they're just evil."

"Perhaps," Levi agreed. "But they are a necessary evil. Sometimes a little evil is necessary to achieve a greater good."

Levi cut Sterling off in midreply and thanked him again, then hung up. He slipped the cell phone back into his pocket.

He did not smile.

There was nothing funny about what he had to do next. But it was necessary.

Thick clouds glided over the moon, engulfing it. The night grew darker.

CHAPTER SIX

Maria drove from York City to the site of the Ghost Walk. Urban row homes, ethnic restaurants, liquor stores, and pawnshops gave way to deserted industrial parks and factories, followed by the excesses of suburban sprawl, and then wide-open expanses of countryside. Along the way, she got lost on the back roads and had to turn around twice. Before leaving, she'd gone online and printed out directions; unfortunately, those directions landed her in the middle of nowhere. She'd never had to travel to the rural parts of York County before. It was a little scary after dark—just trees and shadows and darkened houses. Several of the porches held garishly carved jack-o'-lanterns. Their eyes and mouths flickered with an orange glow as candles burned inside them. Other than the pumpkins, the houses seemed deserted. No lamps or television lights. She passed only a handful of other cars. It was like she'd driven back through time. This part of the county seemed divorced from the rest of civilization. She felt like an astronaut exploring a different planet. In locales like this, it was easy to understand why primitive man had been so afraid of the dark.

The radio was on. Warm 103, the local easy listening station, played softly in the background. Whoever programmed the station relied heavily on songs from the sixties, seventies, and eighties—almost as if elevator music had died after 1989. Maria hated the selection, but for some reason the only other channel she could pick up in this remote area featured a preacher screaming at his audience. She tried again, scanning the dial, but found more of the same.

"Luke tells us, in chapter twenty-three, verses forty-four and forty-five, that there was a darkness over all the earth and the sun was darkened and the veil of the temple was torn in the midst. DARKNESS, brothers and sisters! It engulfs the world."

"That's wonderful news." Her tone dripped with sarcasm.

"And in that darkness," the sermon continued, *"only the light of the Lord can shine. All other lights will be snuffed like a candle flame. Only the Lord's light shall prevail. Can I get an amen?"*

There was a chorus of amens, and then the preacher continued.

"Great," Maria said. "My choices are hellfire and brimstone or Whitney Houston and The Righteous Brothers."

Sighing, Maria turned off the radio and drove in silence. She found it preferable to the preaching. Although she considered herself a spiritual person, Maria had little patience for organized religion or its spokespeople. At her father's insistence, she'd been raised in the Islamic faith, albeit a watered-down Western version. She didn't know what she was anymore. She disliked the agnostic label and she didn't consider herself an atheist, but she didn't believe in the Muslim, Christian, or Jewish versions of God, either. She'd always felt that God, if He or She existed, was probably more of a personal, singular deity—a God that was specific to the believer's current needs rather than beholden to the dictates of an entire world. A personal Jesus, just like in the Depeche Mode song, or an instant karma, like John Lennon had sung about. She'd never told her parents this. If she did, she'd never hear the end of it. While neither of them were particularly religious behind closed doors, they were all about keeping up appearances—doing what was expected of them by the community and their peers. They expected the same of Maria. It wouldn't do for the Nasrs' only child to be labeled a nonbeliever, especially in times like this, when Islam was so misunderstood by so many others. She was supposed to embrace her Jordanian father's Muslim heritage, not turn away from it—even if she didn't truly believe.

Her attention was drawn to something black and red lying in the road. Her headlights flashed off it. Her nose wrinkled at the sharp, pungent smell of a skunk. She swerved around the dead animal and sped up.

Eventually, Maria found some roadside signs for the Ghost Walk. Simple and crude—block letters and crooked arrows spray-painted onto cheap plywood: GHOST WALK—3 MILES. Following them, she turned onto another winding road, then off the road and into a massive field. The terrain was bumpy. She bounced up and down in the seat. Her teeth clacked together.

"Jesus . . ."

Fragile wisps of fog swirled in her headlight beams. A paunchy man with a flashlight appeared, waving her in and directing her to the parking area. Maria smiled and nodded, indicating that she understood. Then she realized that he probably couldn't see her in the dark, so she waved her hand instead.

There were about a dozen other cars parked in the field. Maria turned off her headlights and got out of the car. The man with the flashlight approached, smiling. As he drew closer, she was able to make out more details. He was in his late thirties or early forties. A few days' worth of whiskers covered his pale face. His red flannel shirt fit tightly over a middle-aged gut. He also wore a hunting jacket, dirty jeans, and a Mack Truck ball cap. Thin, brown hair jutted out from beneath the hat's brim.

"Howdy," he said, pointing the flashlight at the ground. "You the lady from the paper?"

Nodding, Maria stuck out her hand. "I sure am. Hi. Maria Nasr."

"Pleased to meet you." He shook her hand.

"You must be Ken Ripple?"

"Sorry, no. I'm his friend, Terry Klein. I'm sort of a second-in-command here, I guess."

"Oh. Where's Mr. Ripple?"

"He'll be along in a minute. Rudy Snyder, the Winterstown fire chief, wanted to inspect some things real quick. He showed up late. Said this was the only time he could do it, and we can't open up without his blessing."

"I see."

"So Ken's with him. He sent me up here to make sure you knew. Shouldn't be too long."

"Okay." Maria quickly recovered from her initial surprise. She reached into her purse and pulled out a small notebook and pen. "Well, while we're waiting, since you're involved with the construction here, would you mind if I asked you a few questions about the Ghost Walk?"

"I think you'd better wait for Ken. No offense."

"None taken. They were just general questions, really. What you think of Ken's idea and things like that. What people can expect. You know, a chance to talk it up?"

"Sure, but no thanks. Like I said, you'd better wait for Ken. He'll do the talking."

Maria decided to try changing the conversation. "Do you happen to know if the staff photographer from the newspaper showed up? He was supposed to take some pictures to accompany the feature article."

"Yeah, he was here earlier. Took some shots of Ken and a few of the volunteers. Then he walked the trail and took a bunch more. You ask me, he took too many. No way they'll use all those photographs. Seems like a waste of film—and money."

"I guess you don't care much for the media?"

"Not really." His whiskered cheeks turned red. "I'm sorry. Does it show?"

Maria grinned. "Just a little."

"Sorry about that." Terry shrugged. "It just seems to me like they're doing our country a disservice. You know? CNN or FOX News, it's all the same bullshit. None of them really report on anything that matters anymore. There's no news on the news. They just give screen time to a bunch of talking heads who only further whatever agenda is important to them. They let these clowns in Washington dictate the news, rather than going out and finding it."

"Actually, I agree with you. Cable news services are businesses, and these days advertising dollars and ratings come first. But what about the newspapers?"

Terry laughed. "Shit. Who has time to read the paper these days? I'm lucky if I get a chance to read *American Rifleman* from cover to cover every month. I don't bother with the newspapers anymore. Nobody does."

Maria was speechless. Part of her wanted to laugh and another part wanted to scream in frustration.

"And besides," Terry continued, "you guys are a business, too. You've got advertisers, just like the networks. Instead of ratings, you have to worry about circulation."

"Perhaps. But I'd like to think we try to do better."

Still chuckling, Terry said, "I'll go and fetch Ken for you. I'd call his cell, but the coverage is shit down there in the woods. You okay waiting here by yourself?"

"Sure. It's not Halloween yet. I'll be fine." She grinned.

Terry turned and walked away. Maria leaned against the hood of her car and watched him leave. Despite his jovial, engaging tone, he looked exhausted. His shoulders slumped and his head hung low. She wondered how many hours a day the organizers were putting in on the Ghost Walk.

After he was gone, she looked around, studying her surroundings. The field was large and could probably hold hundreds of cars on opening night. Two large trailers sat in one corner of the field. She guessed that was where they stored their tools and supplies at night. The woods were a long distance away—she couldn't tell how far for sure in the dark. Maybe the length of a football field. Possibly farther. The tree line was nothing more than a wall of thick, gnarled shadows—skeletal black fingers reaching for the night sky. Their tops swayed slightly in the breeze. She heard dry leaves rustling, even from this distance. Then an owl screeched. It sounded like a screaming woman—just like it had on a special about owls she'd seen on Animal Planet. The cry chilled her. It sounded far more terrible in real life. She idly wondered if owls ever attacked humans. She didn't think so, but wouldn't it just be her luck if this one did?

Maria waited, cold, restless and bored. She flipped the hood of her blue sweatshirt over her head and fought to keep from shivering. It was getting chillier with each passing minute. She tried to be patient, tried to fight back her annoyance, but it was hard to do. She wanted to get this article wrapped up and turned in, so she could focus on the book, instead. It was all she'd thought about that afternoon. A true-crime publisher would flip over it. The story was something different, something unlike the usual serial killers and crimes of passion they normally focused on.

A few volunteers walked by her, nodding with polite indifference, but none of them stopped to talk. Instead, they got into their cars and drove away. Maria noticed that all of them had the same weary gait as Klein. The field emptied of vehicles, leaving only four, including hers. She assumed the others belonged to Terry, the fire marshal, and Ken Ripple.

The owl shrieked again, and Maria jumped, banging her leg on the car.

"Go on," she hollered. "Scat! Get out of here."

She was glad, at moments like this, that her parents didn't ask her much about her career as a freelancer. Although they had never said it out loud, Maria knew that they were

disappointed with her. They'd expected far more for their
daughter than the hardscrabble life of a freelance writer. They
wanted her to marry someone successful—a good American
Muslim—and move back to Paramus and have an important
career as a journalist and give them lots of grandchildren. If
they could see her now, standing in a field in the backwoods
of Pennsylvania, jumping at owls, what would they say?

The night grew quiet.

"Hello," Maria called. "Anyone there? Mr. Klein? Mr.
Ripple? Mr. Owl?"

Silence. Then the wind moaned through the trees.

"Goddamn it. I don't need this shit."

Maria unlocked her car, reached inside the glove compartment, and pulled out a flashlight. It was long and black—a
Mag light just like the cops used. The heavy steel cylinder felt
good in her hands, gave her confidence. She plucked her digital voice recorder from her purse, tested it, dropped the notebook and pen back inside, and then hid the purse beneath the
driver's seat. Then she locked the car again and flicked on the
flashlight. The darkness seemed to press against the brightness.
The spotlight beam showed a clear path to the forest. She'd
been right. The woods were farther away than they'd looked. It
would be a long walk.

"This is bullshit. These shoes aren't made for traipsing
around in the woods."

Cursing, her hood pulled low, Maria trudged toward the
hollow. The mud sucked at her feet, as if the ground were
trying to prevent her from going forward.

Levi climbed into the back of the buggy. His weight made
it shift, rocking the suspension. The wheels groaned. At the
front, Dee shuffled her legs, hooves clattering against the
pavement.

"I know what I'm doing," he told the horse. "Trust me."

Dee chomped her teeth together. They sounded like a
mousetrap snapping shut.

"There's just no pleasing you, is there?"

A car drove through the parking lot, hip-hop music blasting from the speakers. The bass rattled the windows. The driver's face was painted to look like a skull—white and leering. Obviously, they were getting a head start on the holiday. Levi waited for the car to pass. If the driver parked next to him, he'd be unable to proceed until they left.

When the coast was clear again, Levi pulled a canvas tarp off a long wooden box and laid it aside, stirring up dust. He sneezed. The box was padlocked, and covered with charms to protect its contents from thieves, witchcraft, and the elements. The sigils were painted onto the wood, and in some cases, carved deep into the surface. There were holy symbols and complex hex signs, as well as words of power. Levi ran his fingers over the two most dominant etchings.

I.
N. I. R.
I.
SANCTUS SPIRITUS
I.
N. I. R.
I.

SATOR
AREPO
TENET
OPERA
ROTAS

He'd carved them himself, just as his father had taught him, carefully inscribing the words from *The Long Lost Friend* and other books. Levi smiled. All of the books had been passed down to him from his father. He wondered what his father thought of him now, as he looked down on Levi from the other side. Was he proud of his son? Did he approve? Did he understand that sometimes you had to use the enemy's methods and learn the enemy's ways if you were to defeat them? Or, like the rest of Levi's people, did his father disapprove, even in death?

There was no way of knowing—not until the day when Levi saw him again. The day the Lord called him home. He prayed for that moment. Yearned for it.

And feared it, too.

Dee whinnied softly and pawed at the pavement again with her hooves.

"Okay," Levi said. "I'm hurrying."

He pulled a key ring from his pocket and removed the padlock. Then he opened the box. The interior smelled of kerosene and sawdust and dirt. They were comforting smells. They spoke of hard work and effort and honesty. Many people had boxes like this, on the backs of their buggies or in the beds of their pickup trucks. Usually, they held tools. Chainsaws, shovels, hammers, spare engine parts.

Levi's box held different tools; the ones of *his* trade.

He sorted through the contents, pushing aside a bundle wrapped in duct tape. The package contained a dried mixture of wormwood, gith, five-finger weed, asafoedita, and salt—a charm against livestock theft, to protect Dee when Levi left the buggy unattended. As long as it remained in the box, no harm could befall the horse. Too bad that didn't go for the rest of the buggy, which was why he'd asked the store manager to keep an eye on it for him. He'd tried perfecting a charm for the buggy, but so far his efforts had been unsuccessful. The last time he'd tried it, Levi parked the buggy in downtown Lancaster. A street gang had tagged it with spray paint ten minutes later. He'd been ready to forgive them until they turned their attention on Dee. Then the charm had kicked in and Levi had shown them the error of their ways.

The memory made him smile. The looks on their faces . . .

But as long as Dee and the box were safe, that was all that mattered.

He moved a few books and trinkets around, and found what he was looking for.

A stick.

Levi's stomach fluttered. His lips felt numb. He started to sweat.

He didn't want to do this, but he had no choice. The girl was getting farther away. If he didn't follow her now, he'd lose her for sure, and thus lose any chance he might have of learning the entity's true name. Then, whatever befell this community would be on him. He was charged with the task.

Swallowing, Levi reached into the box and pulled out the stick. It looked like a walking staff—four feet long, an inch thick, and round. It had been cut from a tree and the gnarled wood was smooth and hardened with age. It was a Rod of Transvection and Levi was terrified of it.

Since the time of King Solomon, Levi knew, scholars had believed that witches could fly with the aid of a broomstick or similar implement. Lambert Daneau, in *Les Sorciers*, and witch-finder Henry Boguet in numerous writings, both believed that the stick was covered with some type of magic flying ointment and that was how the witches traveled. Other scholars had believed it to be nothing more than delusion. Prierias argued in 1504 that it did not matter if a witch actually flew or not. Simply believing that they flew indicated a clear devotion to pagan goddess Diana, rather than God, and thus branded them a witch. Sir George Mackenzie, Scotland's King's Advocate, also explored the psychological side, writing in 1678 that the witches he'd interviewed only dreamed they were flying.

None of them were correct. Like many men, they presumed to know not only the mind of God, but of His enemies as well. In reality, flying was a combination of both theories. Transvection involved a displacement of the inner self—what some people called an "out of body experience." Levi's staff had been cut and cured according to the rules, and then lathered with a special home-brewed oil that seeped into the wood. Holding the stick in a certain way, Levi could indeed leave his body and "fly."

He just didn't like to.

Levi sat the rod beside him and locked the box again. Then he picked up the stick, climbed down from the buggy, and gave Dee a kiss on the nose, stroking the horse's thick mane.

"I'm ready. Stay here and mind the groceries. I'll be back as soon as I can."

The horse stared at him with sad, brown eyes.

"Now don't you start with that, Dee. I'm about to undertake the Lord's work. It's not like I have a choice. If I don't do it, who will?"

Dee snorted, then lowered her head and closed her eyes.

"I'm sorry, girl."

Levi glanced around the empty parking lot. He needed seclusion, some place where he wouldn't be discovered or disturbed. The back of the buggy was out, as were the street and sidewalk. He considered using the grocery store's restroom, but decided against that as well. What if somebody came in while he was out, and they removed the stick from his hands?

That would be bad. Without the physical tether, his astral form would have no means of staying anchored to his body. Unable to return, he'd simply float away.

He tied Dee's bridle to a light pole so the horse wouldn't wander away. Then he chocked the buggy's wheels. Finished, Levi quickly walked across the parking lot and crept around the side of the building. Behind the grocery store sat three large, green garbage Dumpsters. Beyond them was a vacant lot, choked with dead weeds and debris. The sight made him sad. Why didn't the town do something with the lot? Perhaps turn it into a park for children. Make it green again. Fill it with life and good things.

He squeezed between the Dumpsters, breathing through his mouth. The small space reeked of curdled milk, spoiled food, and urine. Frowning, Levi studied the pavement, looking for a spot that was free of broken glass, cigarette butts and other trash. Pickings were slim. He swept some of the debris out of the way with his shoe and then crouched down, satisfied. He lay back, stretched out, and positioned the stick between his legs. He lowered it, the tip touching his nose while the other end remained clenched tightly between his thighs. The phallic symbolism was not lost on him, but he ignored it. This was how it was done.

Grasping the staff with his fists, he closed his eyes and exhaled. He forced himself to relax, tuned out the sounds of traffic and the public address system inside the store, over which the manager was calling for a cleanup in aisle seven. A late-season gnat flitted around his face, but he ignored it. Levi shut out the world and focused on his breathing. He couldn't feel the hard pavement beneath him. Couldn't feel the pebbles digging into his back or the breeze on his skin. All he felt was the wood. All he heard was his heartbeat. His ears hummed. His pulse slowed. Within minutes, he'd entered a trance. His arms and legs began to tingle, as if asleep.

And then he was gone.

Up, up and away . . .

Levi tried not to scream.

Maria stepped into the tree line and followed the path. The Ghost Walk's trail was clearly marked. Both sides were outlined with something that glowed white in the darkness. It was almost phosphorescent. Curious, she bent over and touched it. It felt cool and dry. Powdery. She sniffed her fingertips. Lime.

"Pretty smart."

Even without her flashlight, she'd have been able to see where she was going because of the lime, but she kept it turned on just the same. The beam held the darkness at bay and made her feel more secure. She wasn't afraid of ghosts

or any of the other folklore connected to the area. But there
were animals out here. Raccoons, possums, deer, coyotes,
maybe even black bear. The light would keep them at a distance.

She hoped.

Maria shivered, pulling her hood tighter. It was colder here
in the woods than it had been out in the open field. This struck
her as odd. The trees should have acted as a windbreak of
sorts, making the forest's interior warmer than the field. She
stuck her free hand in her pocket. The other gripped the flashlight. She sniffed the air and caught a faint hint of burning
leaves, even though there was no fire, as far as she could tell.

"Hello?" She stopped walking. "Mr. Ripple? It's Maria
Nasr, from the paper. We had an appointment?"

Something rustled overhead. Off to her right, a twig
snapped in the darkness.

"Who's there?"

The noise ceased.

Maria took a deep breath and continued on. She swept the
flashlight beam back and forth, illuminating both sides of the
trail. As she rounded a curve in the trail, Maria gasped, startled. A figure loomed overhead, slowly swaying back and
forth. She heard a creaking sound. Maria swung the light upward, illuminating a hanged dummy.

"Jesus Christ . . ."

She passed by more attractions. There was a guillotine,
its phony blade covered with tinfoil and red paint. A dummy
sat propped against it. Next came a section of trail that had
been lined with tied-together cornstalks. Plaster skulls, rubber bats, and other trinkets hung from mosquito netting overhead. This was followed by a giant bird's nest, complete with
an animatronic pterodactyl, turned off for the night. The path
went right through the center of the nest, which was littered
with fake body parts and a generous amount of red paint for
blood. Maria had to admit, it was sort of neat. Not her type of
thing, but she could see where others would enjoy this. It was

certainly more creative than just dressing in a sheet, jumping out at someone, and shouting, "Boo!"

She pulled out her cell phone to check the time, and realized that Terry Klein had been right when he said service was spotty in the forest. She had no signal beneath the trees. That meant she couldn't call Ripple and find out where he was.

"Mr. Ripple?" she yelled. "Anybody here?"

Her voice seemed muted. It didn't echo like it should have.

That's weird, she thought. *Maybe there's something to all that folklore after all. Some kind of sound-dampening phenomena? I didn't see anything about it in the research, though.*

She continued down the path, deciding that she'd go a few more minutes before turning around and heading home. If she hadn't found Ripple by then, she'd explain to her editor that he hadn't shown up for the interview. Miles would be pissed, but he'd see it wasn't her fault. Maybe she could call Ripple tomorrow and do a quick phone interview. Otherwise, the feature article would become a sidebar. At this point, Maria didn't care. It had been a long day. All she wanted now was to go home, eat dinner, check her e-mail, and then relax in the bathtub. Maybe she'd read a little bit tonight before bed, or paint her toenails—not that anyone ever saw them.

Maybe she'd even give her mother a call.

Yeah, right. Staying out here in the woods all night was better than that.

She went down a gradual hill, passing by several more attractions. In the distance, just off the trail, she noticed a small shack. It was painted white and stood out in the darkness. Maria pointed the flashlight at it and stepped forward. As she did, the shack's door flew open, banging against the side, and a figure lunged at her.

Maria screamed, dropping the flashlight.

The woods turned pitch black.

"So what's the verdict, Rudy? You gonna let me open on time or what?"

The fire chief shrugged. "It's hard to check everything in the dark, Ken. I can't see shit out here."

Frowning, Terry glanced at Ken, then back to the chief. Behind them, windblown tree branches skittered across the roof of the maze house. It sounded like nails on a chalkboard.

Ken sighed. "Are you serious?"

"Well, yeah," Rudy said. "I can't inspect if I can't see."

"Goddamn it. Then why the hell did you want to do this tonight? Why not wait until morning?"

"It's the only free time I had," Rudy explained, holding up his hands. "I'm a busy man. You think I just sit around in the firehouse, jerking off to midget porn and waiting for a call?"

"Yeah, as a matter of fact, I do."

"Well, fuck you."

Both men stared at each other for a moment. Then they both laughed. After a second, Terry joined in. Rudy reached out and squeezed Ken's shoulder.

"Had you going for a minute there, didn't I?"

"Hell, no," Ken said. "But seriously, are we cool?"

Rudy nodded, smiling. "You're fine, Ken. I hereby give the Ghost Walk my official seal of approval. I'll sign off first thing in the morning—let the township office know so they can file the paperwork."

"That won't hold us up, will it?"

"No. The paperwork is just a formality. Like I said earlier, just make sure you have fire extinguishers stationed every hundred yards, and that all of your volunteers know where they are and how to operate them. Other than that, I don't see any major problems."

"Terry will pick them up tomorrow."

"Sure will," Terry said. "That's on my list for tomorrow, along with making sure the portable toilets get delivered. Anything else you can think of, Rudy?"

"Just what I said earlier. You guys can't have a Carve Your Own Pumpkin tent for the kids. I think it's a sweet idea, but we can't have a bunch of elementary school kids running around with knives."

Ken nodded. "But the apple bobbing tent is okay?"

"Sure," Rudy said. "Just make sure it's supervised."

"Anything else?" Terry asked.

"No. I think that's it. You guys have done a good job here. Seriously. You should be proud, Ken."

"Thanks, Rudy." Ken's voice grew soft. "That means a lot to us. In truth, I couldn't have put this together without Terry's help."

"It was your idea," Terry said. "You're the brains. I'm just the brawn."

"I just wish Deena could see it, you know?"

Rudy put his hand on Ken's shoulder. "Maybe she does, man. Maybe she does."

"Yeah."

They lapsed into an uncomfortable silence. Terry broke it by clearing his throat.

"That reporter is still waiting," he reminded Ken. "Maria something-or-other."

"Nasr," Ken said.

Terry shrugged. "We ought to get back up there. She's probably pissed."

"I'll make it up to her." Ken stifled a yawn.

"You okay?" Terry asked.

Ken nodded. "Just tired. Seems like the last few weeks I've frigging lived in these woods."

"It will be worth it," Terry said.

"Damn straight," Rudy agreed. "I can't wait to see this place filled with people. You guys think you're tired now, you better get a good night's sleep while you can. In a few days, you'll be busier than ever."

"You're a ray of fucking sunshine, Rudy. You know that?"

"That's why you love me."

"Any other words of wisdom you want to lay on us, Captain Obvious?"

"Your face is about as ugly as Terry's ass."

Ken blinked. "Nothing's that ugly."

Chuckling, the three men began hiking back up the trail. They were almost to the outhouse attraction when they heard a woman's scream. It pierced the night, echoing through the trees. Startled, Ken dropped his flashlight. They halted, glancing around in confusion while Ken fumbled for the light.

"What the hell was that?" Rudy gasped.

"That reporter," Terry said. "It's got to be her. Maybe she's hurt."

"Come on!"

Ken dashed up the trail, his footsteps pounding in the darkness. Terry and the fire chief ran after him. Another scream rang out.

"Hello," Ken shouted. "We're coming!"

"Miss Nasr?" Terry cried. "Is that you? Sound off!"

Wincing, Rudy stayed silent and concentrated on breathing. He reminded himself for the hundredth time since turning forty that he needed to get in shape.

As the three men charged forward, the screams abruptly stopped.

"Who's there?" A woman's voice.

"It's Ken Ripple. I've got Terry Klein and Rudy Snyder with me. Is that you, Miss Nasr?"

"Yes."

"Are you okay?"

"There's someone hiding in this fucking outhouse! He ducked back inside."

Ken and Terry glanced at each other. Terry snickered.

"It works," Ken whispered. Then he called out to Maria, "It's okay, Miss Nasr. Just stay where you are. It's a dummy. You triggered it when you walked by."

"What?"

"Oh, shit," Terry muttered. "She sounds pissed off. Hope she's not the suing type. Last thing we need is a bullshit lawsuit."

"It's a Ghost Walk," Ken said. "What the hell does she expect?"

Rudy nodded in agreement. "It *is* supposed to be scary."

They reached Maria a moment later. She stood just off the path, amidst heavy undergrowth. She stepped out onto the trail as they approached.

"You okay?" Ken asked.

Maria turned away from his flashlight beam, shielding her eyes. "You mind not shining that thing in my face?"

"Sorry." Ken switched his flashlight off. "I'm Ken Ripple. This is Rudy Snyder, Winterstown's fire chief. And you've already met Terry."

Maria nodded at Rudy and Terry and shook hands with Ken.

"Nice to meet you—finally. What the hell just happened?"

"Well, you see Miss Nasr—"

"Maria. Please."

"Okay, Maria. There's a pressure switch buried just under the path. When people step on it, the switch sends a signal to the outhouse. The door flies open and a dummy jumps out. Then it resets again."

"You were our first victim," Terry joked. "Scared you good, huh?"

Maria glared at him. Then her expression softened.

"If you want me to be honest, I think I may have peed my pants a little. And I broke my flashlight. Dropped it when the dummy popped out."

Ken grinned. "Can I use that as an endorsement?"

"That depends. Are you still going to let me interview you tonight?"

"After making you wait and then scaring you? Sure. I haven't eaten since lunch. You hungry?"

Maria arched an eyebrow. "I could eat. I spent most of the day doing research."

"How about we conduct the interview at the Round the Clock Diner? My treat."

"Mr. Ripple, you've got a deal."

"Call me Ken. Please."

Maria smiled.

The four walked out of the woods together. The darkness closed behind them.

CHAPTER SEVEN

Levi's body remained on the ground, lying hidden between the Dumpsters behind the grocery store. The stick was still clutched in his hands, touching his nose and groin. The rest of him, his astral self, soared above the parking lot, rocketing higher with each passing second.

When he was eight years old, Levi had ignored his father's warnings and climbed to the top of the family grain silo. He'd done it to show his brother, Matthew, and their friend, Elias, that he wasn't afraid. But he had been. Levi had stopped halfway up the ladder, unable to proceed and too terrified to climb back down. He'd remained there, whimpering, clinging to the iron rungs, his eyes squeezed shut, until his father climbed up and rescued him.

He looked down now and remembered that day. All of his old fears came rushing up to meet him.

Levi screamed soundlessly.

The ground got farther away.

Get control . . .

He focused, forcing himself to halt, rather than fly. His speedy ascent stopped. Gently, slowly, he glided downward until he was hovering just over Columbia's roofs and treetops. He looked in all directions, seeking the girl and trying not to focus on the ground. He noticed signs of her passing—dogs barking, children crying in their beds, birds fallen from tree limbs—but not the girl herself. Willing himself forward, Levi followed the carnage left in her wake. Distracted, he floated higher again. If he didn't focus on staying anchored when he flew, he'd continue to rise. To stay tethered to his body, he needed to concentrate.

The cross of Christ be with me; the cross of Christ overcomes all water and every fire and all heights.

He risked another glance below, and immediately regretted it. His butt puckered and his stomach fluttered.

So far up . . .

Levi was always amazed at the sensations during flight. He was nothing more than an astral projection. He didn't have a stomach right now, but he felt it just the same. Felt the fear making it clench. He didn't have eyes or a nose or ears. They remained behind with the rest of his body. And yet, the senses remained; sight, smell, and hearing still functioned in this psychic form, sharper than they were in his physical body. Levi didn't know how or why. The only person who could have explained it to him satisfactorily was his father, and Amos had passed away long before Levi attempted his first flight. He was sure there were other folks who had theories. New-Agers. But nothing annoyed Levi more than New Age mystics, except for maybe Evangelicals. Both were hypocrites and cons—wolves dressed in sheep's clothing. Part of the problem disguised as the solution. So Levi had never sought out help from the crystal-worshipping, herbal supplement crowd. Not that they would have welcomed him anyway. Even among the fringe, Levi was alone.

Still on the girl's trail, Levi picked up speed. He tried to ignore his fear of heights and focused instead on tracking his quarry. He swooped over more homes and apartments and quickly reached the waterfront. The area was dominated by a large, desolate-looking furniture factory. Like the rest of the town, the building had seen better days. Once the center of industry, it now appeared tired and run-down. Bucolic, just like the rest of Columbia's citizens.

Beyond the factory lay the Susquehanna River, broad and swift and glittering in the moonlight. Its waters ran cold and deep, a little over half a mile wide. Twin bridges crossed the span. On the far shore were the ruins of a Civil War–era ferry crossing.

Levi's attention was drawn to the center of the waterway. A patch of darkness spread out across the river's surface, halfway between the Lancaster County shoreline and York County on the other side. In its center was the girl, like a rotten spot inside a cancerous tumor. The darkness was blacker than the night around it, engulfing everything in its path. It flowed from the girl like mist. The tendrils formed a cloud around her, extending from her body almost five feet in each direction. Her aura was brighter, now that he viewed it from his astral form. The darkness pulsed like a living thing as she swam across the river with jerky, spasmodic strokes. Levi watched her movements, convinced that this was further evidence of something supernatural. Even athletes tired when crossing the expanse. Many had drowned in this section over the years. And yet, the girl showed no signs of tiring.

Where are you going? And more importantly, who are you? What's your name?

Levi drifted over the water, gradually slowing down again so that he could keep a safe distance and avoid detection. At the same time, he flew higher, lifting himself out of easy range in case the entity became aware of his presence and launched an attack.

Lord, he prayed, *I am your servant and your sword. Guide my hand tonight as if it were your own. Though my methods might not all be yours, let their purpose be to thy glory.*

He glanced down again, rather than ahead. The river seemed so far below. From this height, the water's surface shined like glass. Moonlight flickered off the waves. The girl was a dark smudge.

And, he continued, *if you're so inclined, Lord, please don't let me fall . . .*

Maria took another sip of coffee.

"So you don't believe in any of it at all? You don't think Nelson LeHorn's ghost still haunts the hollow?"

Her digital voice recorder lay between them on the tabletop, recording the conversation. Ken had seemed nervous of it at first, speaking in halting, self-aware sentences. But gradually, he'd relaxed, forgetting about the device altogether. The leftover remnants of their late dinner covered the rest of the table. Ken had ordered a hamburger and fries. Maria had ordered a grilled chicken salad. The waitress had done a good job of keeping their coffee cups filled.

Ken was apologetic at first, determined to make up for delaying their interview, and for the bad scare Maria had suffered. In return, Maria had remained clinical and distant, seeking only the facts. But as the evening went on, they both warmed to each other. Maria found Ken to be genuine and friendly. He liked her determined attitude and her playful sense of sarcasm. She'd been interviewing him for the last half hour, learning about the Ghost Walk, his deceased wife, and more.

Despite the late hour, the diner was crowded. Long-haul truckers sat at the front counter, reading newspapers and magazines or talking to each other. A group of boisterous college students occupied a large booth, playing an apparently high-stakes game of *Magic: The Gathering*. Even though it wasn't yet Halloween, several of them were in costume. An elderly couple sat at a corner table, ignoring the others around them, sharing the comfortable silence that only longtime partners seemed to enjoy. A younger couple sat nearby, engaged in the type of small talk and forced conversation that indicated a first date. The sleepy-eyed waitress moved among them all, lost in her own thoughts, only coming out of her reverie long enough to ask if anyone would like dessert.

"No," Ken answered Maria's question. "Not really. I mean, some weird things have happened there over the years. There's no denying that. Folks have died. But that was from accidents or stupidity, mostly. Not because of ghosts or demons or shit like that. Oh, sorry. Didn't mean to curse."

"That's okay," Maria said. "I can edit that out. So you don't believe any of it?"

"Nope."

"What about Patricia LeHorn's murder? What do you think contributed to that?"

"Simple. Nelson LeHorn was a nut job. Just because he believed he was a witch, that doesn't necessarily make him one. He murdered his wife because he was crazy, not because she'd actually slept with the devil."

"How do you know for sure?"

Ken smiled. "Don't tell me you believe this stuff?"

Maria shrugged. "Not really. But it's my job to keep an open mind, right? Reporters are supposed to be analytical. Explore all options and find the truth."

"If you say so. I don't know. I never met a reporter before. I thought you were just writing up a little article on the Ghost Walk."

"I am. But everyone in York County knows about LeHorn's Hollow. And people love a good ghost story. It wouldn't be much of an article if we didn't mention this. I mean, that's the whole reason you based your operation in those woods, right? To be near the hollow?"

"True." Ken glanced down at the recorder and cleared his throat. "Well, you asked how I know LeHorn was crazy. It wasn't a big secret or anything. My dad used to know him."

"Really?"

"Yeah, back in the seventies and eighties. Before he . . . you know."

Maria nodded in encouragement.

"My dad was a beekeeper," Ken said. "Well, actually, he worked at the paper mill, like everybody else did back in the day. But in his spare time, he kept honeybees."

"I grew up in New Jersey," Maria interrupted. "Was the paper mill the county's main employer?"

"Didn't think you were from around here," Ken said. "Your accent gives you away."

"I have an accent?"

"Sure. Not a bad thing. I figured you for New York or New Jersey. Like a girl from a Springsteen song, you know?"

He paused, smiling. After a moment, Maria smiled back. She felt her cheeks flush.

What the hell's wrong with me, she thought. *He's, like, twice my age.*

She stared into Ken's soft, brown eyes. Even when he smiled, a great sadness seemed to cling to him.

Poor guy. Maria looked away. *I'm just feeling sorry for him. That's all. Need to keep my mind on work.*

"Dude," one of the college students shouted at his friend. "You can't un-tap that card this turn!"

His friend turned a few cards and then slammed another one down on the table. "Take that, bitch. Twenty points of damage and you can't fucking block it! That's game."

Everyone in the restaurant glanced at them in annoyance. The waitress walked over and asked the students to keep it down.

"In the seventies," Ken said, turning back to Maria, "pretty much everybody in York County worked at one of five places. We had the Caterpillar and Harley Davidson plants in York. There was Borg-Warner over in West York, who made stuff for the military—tanks and half-tracks and bomb shelters. All kinds of shit. And then there was the paper mill in Spring Grove and the foundry out in Hanover. That was it, unless you were a farmer or an auto mechanic. But by the mid-eighties, right around the time I graduated from high school, Caterpillar and Borg-Warner had closed down, the paper mill was in the middle of a yearlong strike, and Harley and the foundry had both downsized. But yeah, my dad worked in the paper mill, and in his spare time he tended to his beehives. During the strike, when he wasn't on the picket line with his union buddies, he was fooling around with his bees. He had hives all over the place. In orchards and on neighbor's farms. Anywhere somebody would let him. I think he had over forty of them during his busiest year. Every autumn, he'd harvest the honeycomb, extract the honey, and then sell it to the local grocery stores and farmer's markets. Had his own label on the jars and everything. 'Ripple's Apiaries.' He made a nice little secondary income. I bet if he was still doing it today, he'd make a lot more, what with everybody into all that organic shit."

"I'm sure. But what does this have to do with Nelson LeHorn?"

"LeHorn had bees, too. More than my dad ever did. Occasionally, my father would go over to LeHorn's farm and buy beehive materials from him. Frames. Parts for his extracting drum. Smokers. Protective clothing. Stuff like that. It was easier and cheaper to get them from LeHorn than through mail order."

Maria signaled the waitress, indicating another refill. "So did he ever see LeHorn do any powwow?"

"No. My old man didn't believe in that stuff. But he did say several times that LeHorn was crazy. I remember this one time, these little microscopic mites got into Dad's beehives. Killed several of his queens—just destroyed whole hives, you know? My dad asked LeHorn what he should do and LeHorn drew some kind of weird symbol and told Dad to paint it on each hive. It was supposed to keep the mites out."

They stopped talking while the waitress refilled their mugs.

"Did your father do it?" Maria asked after they were alone again.

Ken chuckled. "No. He bought some pesticide. And that did the trick. When I asked him why he didn't use the powwow doctor's method, Dad said, 'I'd be a damn fool to go drawing that nonsense on my beehives. The boys down at the American Legion would have never let me live it down. Old LeHorn is nuttier than your grandma's fruitcake.' And he was right. Another one of my dad's friends was cutting down a Christmas tree near the hollow. Back on the pulpwood company's land. He damn near cut his finger off. LeHorn came across him as he was walking out. The old guy told him not to go to the hospital—said he could stop the bleeding by 'laying on of the hands' or something like that."

"Faith healing," Maria said. "Did your father's friend take him up on the offer?"

"Shit, no. He ran to his car and got the hell out of there."

Maria snickered, then laughed. Smiling, Ken dumped a container of cream into his fresh cup of coffee. Maria composed herself and asked the next question.

"So, will your attraction feature anything based off the LeHorn legend?"

"Not directly, no. At least, nothing about the murders or anything like that. LeHorn's kids are still alive. That just wouldn't be right, capitalizing off their mother's death or their father's mental illness. There are enough weird stories connected to the hollow without getting into the LeHorn stuff. Bigfoot. Demons. The Goat Man. Native American spirits. We can do stuff featuring them."

"What about the more recent murders; the witch cult and the mystery writer?"

"Adam Senft?" Ken shook his head. "No. Again, it wouldn't be right to capitalize off something like that. Like I told you earlier, this whole thing is to honor Deena's memory. What she stood for. Her strength. She wouldn't want me using other people's misfortunes like that."

Maria reached out and turned off the recorder.

"You really miss your wife, don't you?"

Ken nodded, glancing down at the table. When he spoke again, his voice was barely a whisper.

"Yeah, I do. I thought it would get easier with time, but it doesn't. It just gets worse. I feel haunted."

Maria arched an eyebrow. "Her . . . ghost?"

"No, nothing like that. I told you, I don't believe in ghosts. I just mean her memory, you know? I'm haunted by her memory."

"Perhaps that's what ghosts are," Maria said. "Maybe they're just memories."

"Could be," Ken agreed.

"I'm sorry. Hope I didn't offend you?"

"No, not at all. It's something to think about, I guess. I'll tell you, though. Sometimes, I wish there were ghosts. I wish I could believe in them."

"Why?"

"Because then maybe I could see Deena again."

Ken reached out and picked up the check. Then, before they could continue the conversation, he excused himself and slid out of the booth. Maria watched him walk to the register. She collected her recorder and purse and smiled politely at the waitress. On her way to the ladies' room, Maria mulled over the last part of the conversation, wondering what ghosts haunted her.

The girl didn't stop until well after midnight. Levi followed her, his dread increasing with every mile. Even before she'd reached her final destination, Levi had guessed where she was heading.

LeHorn's Hollow.

He knew it well. Nelson LeHorn and Amos Stoltzfus had been peers and associates, if not friends. Occasionally, their individual endeavors had given them cause to consult with each other. LeHorn had called upon the Stoltzfus farm several times when Levi was growing up, and his father had traveled to York County once or twice to visit LeHorn. His father had passed away five years before the events at LeHorn's farm.

Levi knew what most of society thought—that Nelson

LeHorn had gone insane, believed his wife was consorting with the devil, and then pushed her out of the attic window, killing her. Then the old man had disappeared, and no one had heard from him since. Twenty years passed. And then, in a bizarre twist of fate, a local author named Adam Senft became obsessed with the story and committed a copycat murder, slaying his own wife. Now he was a guest at the White Rose Mental Health Facility—a fancy, politically correct title for what amounted to an insane asylum.

Those were the facts, as far as the public was concerned. But the public was wrong. Levi knew the truth. It had taken him several years of painstaking investigation, and had taxed him both physically and psychically. He'd used everything at his disposal—divination, fortune-telling, his grandfather's seer stone, the bending of wills, and exploring the woods themselves, walking around, poking his nose into things and finding out what was what—and eventually discovered several doorways and standing stones. He was certain that not all of them had been crafted by LeHorn, but he wasn't sure who had built them. Some looked Native American in origin. Others were even older. But all of them were closed and barred, guarded by circles of protection and other means. There was nothing of concern. Nothing that posed a danger. The hollow was a dead zone, and in the end, his diligence had paid off. He'd finally learned what really transpired.

In a misguided attempt to bring good fortune to his failing farmstead during a statewide drought, Nelson LeHorn had attempted to summon a minion of Nodens. Nodens belonged to a pantheon called the Thirteen, a race of entities that had existed before this universe came into existence. LeHorn was misled by a black magician from Hanover named Saul O'Connor—a foul, degenerate little man who'd foolishly worshipped the Thirteen and eventually paid the price. O'Connor told LeHorn that Nodens' minions could bless his crops and ensure a bountiful harvest. But he was wrong.

LeHorn conducted a summoning ritual, opening a door

between this world and another. He called forth a satyr named Hylinus, who was indeed a minion of Nodens. However, instead of blessing the farmer's crop, Hylinus managed to break through LeHorn's carefully crafted circle of protection and impregnate Patricia LeHorn. A distraught LeHorn bound the creature and imprisoned it, transmuting the satyr into stone. He'd murdered his pregnant wife, so that she wouldn't give birth to the satyr's spawn. Then, in his final act on this world, he'd opened a doorway into the Labyrinth and disappeared to somewhere else. Levi wasn't sure where. Another plane or another world. Nelson LeHorn was never seen again. He closed the door behind him. Somewhere, in the State Police barracks in Harrisburg, or maybe hanging in the corner of a rural post office somewhere, was a wanted poster with Nelson LeHorn's picture on it, a picture from twenty years ago. But he would never be captured. Never be found.

Years after LeHorn's departure, Adam Senft somehow came into possession of the farmer's books. Nelson LeHorn had an impressive collection of esoteric tomes—things like *The Sixth and Seventh Books of Moses*, Jean Bodin's *De la Demonomanie des Sorciers,* Johann Weyer's *De Praestigiis,* and a partial transcript of the dangerous and deadly *Daemonolateria.* Most of these had been destroyed in the forest fire, but from what Levi had determined, Senft had made off with LeHorn's journal, pages from the *Daemonolateria,* and a complete English translation of *The Long Lost Friend.* Around this same time, Hylinus had been freed from bondage. Levi was never able to determine how, exactly, but his educated guess was that Senft was somehow responsible. Whatever the cause, Adam Senft became involved in a struggle against the satyr—a confrontation that ultimately resulted in the deaths of several of Senft's friends and finally, months later, Senft's wife, Tara, who ultimately suffered the exact same fate as Patricia LeHorn. The courts deemed Senft insane and he was now in a mental health facility.

But neither Nelson LeHorn nor Adam Senft had been insane.

They were just fools.

They'd believed written history. Trusted the words of men. Assumed that Nodens was some Roman or Celtic god of harvest and fertility. And they'd paid the price.

Unlike the others, Levi was no fool. Since the forest fire and the last round of deaths, he'd kept a cautious eye on the region. But the hollow and the surrounding forest had remained quiet. Levi became convinced that whatever evil had lurked there was now purged.

Maybe I was a fool after all . . .

Levi floated far above the treetops, hovering as the girl disappeared into the forest. He resisted the urge to flee, even though he wanted to. Dread overwhelmed him. A darkness was brewing down there beneath the trees—a pulsing black cloud, more obsidian than the gloom that surrounded it. A twisting, coiling mass that permeated the foliage, the ground, the very air itself.

Levi knew what it was, but he dared not speak the name out loud.

The thing in the forest—and in the girl—was Nodens, greatest among the Thirteen, brother of Ob and Ab. Of Leviathan and Behemoth. Of all the others. He watched the writhing shadows. This was its true form. It was a living darkness, a force that traveled from world to world, consuming everything it touched, sucking the life and energy out of every single thing until there was nothing left. Then it moved on, leaving a barren, lifeless wasteland in its wake.

And now it was here.

Apparently, LeHorn's summoning spell had worked after all. The effect had just been delayed.

Levi wished his astral form had tears so that he could cry.

Not me, Lord. Please, find somebody else. I can't fight this. I'm not strong enough. Nobody is.

If God was listening, He did not answer. Levi hadn't expected Him to, even though, just this once, it would have been nice. Especially now.

Steeling his resolve, Levi drifted closer. The darkness remained finite. Although it moved, it did not grow. Did not expand. That meant it wasn't completely in this world yet. Most of it was still in another dimension, slowly bleeding through into this world. Obviously, someone—or something—had disturbed one of the portals, accidentally broken one of the circles. Levi cursed his own arrogance. He should have checked back here more often. He'd known those places of power still existed in the forest's perimeter, but he'd thought them closed and useless.

This is my fault. I should have guarded them better. But still, what idiot left the door open? If you leave the barn door open, you know the cow is going to get out. More importantly, what am I going to do about it?

Nodens wasn't completely through the doorway yet. Its corporeal form in this world was weakened and bound by limitations. It wouldn't be at full strength until it had completely breached the barriers. That bought Levi some time. Levi considered all that he knew regarding the situation— the events transpiring below, the hollow's past history, the time of year and position of the stars.

Even though his astral self didn't need to breathe, Levi felt his breath catch in his throat.

Halloween was only a few days away. It was one of the rare times of the year when the walls between worlds grew thin. If he didn't figure out a way to stop Nodens before then . . .

Terrified, Levi recited a benediction against evil. Even though he knew the words were useless against such a foe, doing so still brought him some brief comfort.

Ut nemo in sense tentat, descendere nemo. At precedenti spectaur mantica tergo. Hecate. Hecate. Hecate.

If the thing below heard his prayer, it gave no sign. Levi

listened. He heard no birds, no insects, and no wildlife of any kind. The forest was silent. Even the wind had stopped. But despite the stillness, he was sure that the entity was laughing.

Horrified, Levi willed himself back to his body. He rushed backward, away from the hollow, soaring like a rocket past the river and the towns. He zoomed down to his body and felt it jump.

Levi opened his eyes. Blinked once. Twice. Smacked his lips together. His throat was dry and his mouth tasted like Dee had used it for a toilet. Slowly, painfully, his fingers uncurled from around the stick. His knuckles popped. Levi's upper lip was warm and wet. He touched it gently and looked at his fingers. The tips were red. His nose was bleeding.

Stumbling to his feet, Levi leaned against one of the Dumpsters until he had regained enough strength to walk. After a few minutes, he felt better, but still dizzy and weak. He weaved across the deserted parking lot, using the flying staff for a cane. Dee whinnied in excitement when she saw him. Despite his fears, Levi smiled at her greeting. He pressed his face into her mane and sobbed. Tears flowed, mingling with the blood. He trembled against her until the storm had passed. When he pulled away, Dee nuzzled him. This made Levi cry again.

"Why me, Lord? What did I do to deserve this? Why not one of Your other warriors? Why is it that You always demand the most from those who love You the most? Should we not be rewarded, given an occasional rest, instead of just running from crisis to crisis, cleaning up Your messes?"

His stomach cramped. Levi bent over and threw up all over the pavement. The bile burned his throat. He brushed the tears from his eyes and then wiped his mouth with the back of his hand. His nose was still bleeding. Straightening up again, he scratched Dee between the eyes. The horse's tail swished back and forth.

"Come on, girl. Let's go home."

Levi climbed up into the buggy and stowed the flying

staff. Then he grabbed the reins. His hands wouldn't stop shaking. He found a crumpled handkerchief lying beneath the seat and stuffed the ends of it into his bleeding nostrils.

He couldn't fight Nodens alone. There were things he needed. Items he had no access to. He needed help. Help from one of the people indirectly responsible for this mess.

It was time to prepare.

Tonight, he would begin fasting, so that he might be cleansed for the task ahead.

Tomorrow, he would pay a visit to Adam Senft.

CHAPTER EIGHT

The wind promised blood.

The coyote's stomach growled in anticipation when she smelled it.

The coyote wanted nothing more than to return to her den before the sun came up, but she had a long way to travel before she could sleep.

The blood called to her. She intended to answer.

It had been a long, weary, and demoralizing night. At dusk, she'd risen from her den to hunt and forage. First she encountered a small dog that had strayed far from home. The coyote gave chase, but the dog was faster. It escaped. She decided not to pursue it. Panting, she drank cold water from a creek and looked for the darting, silver forms of fish. The stream was empty. She flipped a rock over with her paw and found a tiny crayfish. She snapped at it, dancing around to avoid the angrily waving pincers. The coyote devoured the crayfish in one bite, but the small morsel simply fueled her hunger.

Her wanderings had then brought her to the edge of the forest. The coyote sneaked through the backyard of a nearby farmhouse. She was careful. Cautious. The sounds of humans came from inside the home. The coyote stayed alert, listening for any sign that they were aware of her presence. After deciding it was safe, she crept undetected to the front porch. A fat, yellow cat lay on a lawn chair, licking its paws. The coyote's muscles coiled. She tensed, preparing to charge, but the feline spotted her and leapt from the porch. The coyote dashed after her fleeing prey, across the yard and down a one-lane dirt road. Trees lined both sides of the driveway, but the terrified cat ran straight. The chase ended when the cat ran out into the main road and was crushed beneath the wheels of a tractor-trailer. The truck didn't stop. The coyote watched from the bushes along the side. Twitching, the cat let out a pitiful, gurgling mewl. Then it stiffened and lay still. Steam rose from the body. The coyote stepped forward, drooling at the sight and scent of the fresh innards splattered all over the pavement—the rich liver, the tender intestines, an eyeball, warm blood. Before she could feast, another car came along. Then another. Their wheels thumped over the carcass, further spreading the gore. The coyote darted out into the road and snagged a shred of intestine, but oncoming headlights chased her back into the bushes again. Not wishing to suffer the same fate as her prey, the coyote left the area.

She came across a deserted campground and knocked over the garbage cans, snorting through their spilled contents with her snout. She found a few scraps—French fries, a pizza crust, and half of a hot dog—but not nearly food enough to sate her hunger.

The coyote felt sad—a lingering shame that couldn't be cured with sleep or food or water. She was a hunter. Her kind were predators, unmatched by any other animal in these woods except for the black bear. And yet here she was now, nothing more than a scavenger. No better than a raccoon or a possum, stealing from trash cans, eating humanity's refuse just to survive. Every year, the humans came farther into the woods, chasing away the other wildlife, and reducing her kind to this.

She missed her mate. She'd met him during her second winter, when the moon was full and yellow and new-fallen snow covered the ground. The scent of her heat had called him to her. He was strong and lean and large, standing over the other males that answered her call. She remembered his pelage colors: gray washed with streaks of black, with beautiful tan and reddish markings running down his legs. His ears had been erect and his tail full.

They'd rutted on the frozen ground, their body heat melting the snow around them. The coyote howled her passion to the full moon when her mate's teeth nipped the back of her neck, holding her in place. Four months later, safe in their den beneath an overturned tree, she gave birth to a litter of seven pups. Her mate had gone hunting while she nursed and cleaned their young. He'd paused along the stream bank, looking back at them once over his shoulder. He had seemed so proud.

Then, while she waited for him, the human thunder that was different from sky thunder echoed across the forest. She knew what that thunder brought with it.

Her mate never returned. She waited four days, but he never came back.

She'd raised the pups on her own, as best she could, teaching them how to hunt and track, where to shelter and when to sleep, what was good to eat and what would make them sick. Most important, she taught them about man.

So, when men arrived a few months later, and shot her with something that made her sleepy, the mother coyote's last thought before losing consciousness was that her cubs would escape. They'd know to run. To flee from man, just as she'd taught them.

When she awoke, there was a small metal clamp in her ear, and her young were gone. She sniffed around the forest floor. Their scent was mixed with the stench of humans. She cried out for them but there was no answer. The coyote waited but her cubs didn't return. They had vanished. Just like her mate.

She missed their yips, barks, and howls. Missed their warmth. The way they crawled all over her when they were playing. How they tugged at her ears with their sharp little teeth or snuggled against her when it rained. Their individual scents.

Scent . . .

The coyote's memories faded as she caught the scent of blood again. It was stronger this time. Perhaps an injured deer or a wounded dog. It was too heavy, too thick, to be from anything smaller. Whatever the source, it was near.

But so was something else. Something without a scent. Something . . . dangerous.

She just didn't know what.

Parting the field grass, she peered into the woods. The coyote's nocturnal prowling had brought her here, to the edge of a bad place. She had never been here before, had never strayed so far from her usual area. But after the failed cat hunt, she'd smelled the blood and followed it. Now she felt alarmed. This place was wrong. Menacing. She knew it instinctively, as did the rest of the animals in the area. The trees were different. The air was different. It was dangerous to proceed.

And yet, the blood-smell called to her, promising a feast if only she would enter.

Whimpering, the coyote stepped out of the field and into the shadow of the trees. She sniffed the air, cautious. Now she caught a new scent in addition to the blood: burning leaves. She paused, but sensed no signs of fire. Her ears twitched, alert for the slightest sign of activity. The forest was quiet. No birdsongs or insect conversations. The ground vibrated slightly beneath her paws, as if something deep inside the earth was turning. It felt unnatural. Not of man, but not of nature either. This was something else, something that was neither. The coyote wanted to run. Instinct and common sense told her to flee, but her stomach rumbled. She took another tentative step forward, and raised her snout. The woods smelled like humans. There had been many of them here recently. Signs of their presence were everywhere: downed trees, gasoline and sweat, urine, footprints, threads from clothing snagged on branches. She considered this new information. The humans had been here, and nothing bad had befallen them. Perhaps the danger was overstated.

She smelled the blood again. It was fresh. The coyote drooled. Hunger overrode her caution. She darted forward, following the scent toward the center of the forest.

While Rhonda got rid of the car, Richard went hunting. He traveled far to find a deer, since they were afraid to enter the proximity of the hollow. He'd left the forest, crossed through the harvested remnants of soybean and corn fields, and found another patch of woods where the game was plentiful. He climbed a tree and perched among the branches, patiently waiting. When a doe finally appeared, he shot her through the neck. The crack of the rifle echoed over the hills. The doe thrashed and snorted as her lifeblood jetted from her body. Then he hauled the dead animal back to the hollow. He gutted the carcass and spread the entrails and internal organs all over one of the sigils, careful not to touch the stone directly. Using the barrel of his rifle, he wedged the animal's heart between the ground and the stone. He grunted in frustration. How much easier would this be if Nodens had the strength to move the stones itself? If Nodens could just use the rifle to pry them free? But the sigils sapped Nodens of its strength, and thus, it had to rely on these methods.

Rhonda arrived shortly after, dripping with the stink of the river. Finished with his task, Richard disposed of the deer's body. He dragged it far away and buried it, digging the grave with his hands. After he'd returned, his fingers torn and bleeding, Richard withdrew into hiding, along with Rhonda and Sam.

They watched from the darkness, waiting for something to take the bait.

The coyote's uneasiness grew with every step, but so did the gnawing in her stomach. Her nose twitched again. Her tail hung limp and low, tucked firmly between her legs. Her senses warned her to flee, but she couldn't. She was compelled now. Driven. No matter how strong her fear, she couldn't ignore the promise of the meal, borne on the night breeze. It was waiting for her just ahead.

She padded across a vast wasteland of ash and charred wood. The ground sloped steadily downward into the burned-out remnants of a hollow. She stepped over a dry creek bed filled with ashes. It was dark here—darker than the rest of the woods. In this place, the night seemed to gather, as if drawing together. It reminded the coyote of her den beneath the overturned tree. The place she'd shared with her litter and her mate. The hollow was like that—a den for darkness.

The coyote felt far from home.

She turned to flee, to find safer ground, but then she saw it. A pile of fresh deer innards lay splattered on and around a nearby rock. Liver, kidneys, intestines—all covered in a thick, rich coating of blood. The guts were no longer steaming, but the flies had yet to discover the remains and the blood was still fluid, rather than congealed.

Dispensing with caution, the coyote approached the rock in four quick strides. It didn't occur to her to wonder where the rest of the corpse was. Her pink-white tongue shot out, lapping experimentally at some drops of blood on the nearby ground. She licked her lips, and then dug in, chewing and swallowing as fast as she could. Famished, she ravaged the organs without thought or care to anything other than filling her belly. When she'd consumed the solids, she licked the rock clean. It wiggled back and forth at her ministrations, and made her tongue tingle. She barely noticed. Her attention was focused on another morsel sticking out partially from beneath the stone.

The deer's heart.

She pawed at the ashen ground, digging a hole around the heart. Then she pushed at the rock, straining hard until it toppled out of the way, revealing a small depression. She gobbled down the heart in four quick bites and was swallowing the last shred when the darkness rose out of the hole and she heard her mate and cubs.

They called for her inside the swirling blackness. Mesmerized by this unexpected reunion, she stepped closer, yipping with excitement. Too late, the coyote realized that although they looked like her brood, their smell was different. She froze.

This was the something else—the bad thing she'd sensed before.

The darkness surged toward her and the coyote howled.

And then the sun greeted a new day, filling the land with light.

But the light did not penetrate the hollow.

There were only three stones left and less than forty-eight hours until the walls between worlds collapsed.

CHAPTER NINE

"This is fucking bullshit."

Maria sat in her car, in the parking lot outside the White Rose Mental Health Facility, talking on her cell phone to her editor, Miles. Despite the fact that it was late October, it was a warm day. The sun beat down through the windshield, and Maria had rolled down her window. She was tired and the fresh air kept her awake.

"What can I tell you?" Miles said. "Come on. Did you really think you could just walk into a security hospital and speak with the guy?"

"No." Maria pouted. "Not right away, at least. But I didn't know I'd have to go through all of this crap."

Miles laughed. "Listen, kiddo—"

"I hate it when you call me that. It's demeaning."

"You're right. I'm sorry."

"Me, too. And I'm not pissed at you. I'm just disappointed. I even called in a few favors with some contacts in the medical system."

"And?"

"No dice."

"Maria, it's very tough for a reporter—any reporter—to legitimately get an interview with a patient in one of these facilities, let alone a freelancer for a local rag like ours. The last thing any psychiatric hospital wants is publicity. They don't want a reporter sniffing around. They're like a methadone clinic or a group home; they want to stay nestled in communities without people even knowing they exist. They like things kept quiet."

"But I'm not writing about them. I'm writing about Adam Senft."

"No therapist, and certainly no administrator, wants their patient exploited for a news story. I mean, can you imagine that headline? 'Satyr Killer Still Believes Wife Was Pregnant with Anti-Christ.' There's no way they'd give a reporter free rein with something like that. And you're not even there as a reporter. This isn't on behalf of us. This is for a true-crime book you want to write."

"I know," Maria said. "I'm sorry."

After her late-night dinner with Ken Ripple, Maria had returned home and found herself too wired to sleep. Instead of just lying in bed, tossing and turning, she got up and made herself a fresh pot of coffee. While it brewed, she set her iPod for random play. Then, armed with a cup of coffee and a can of Red Bull, she banged out the first draft of the feature article on the Ghost Walk while Usher sang in the background. The article clocked in at just over three thousand words—perfect for what Miles wanted. Finished with that and still wide-awake, she'd gone online and tried to track down Ramirez, the former police detective who'd been involved with Adam Senft and the last spate of murders in LeHorn's Hollow. She was disappointed to learn that he'd apparently dropped completely off the grid. His last known address was in Florida, where he'd been working as a security guard for a private firm. Two early morning phone calls confirmed that he was no longer employed with the company, and that he'd moved out of his apartment six months ago and had left no forwarding address. There was a possibility that she could still find him—access driver's records, employer databases, things like that. But doing so would take time, and the star of her story—Adam Senft—was right here in town. Plus, even if she did track Ramirez down, there was no guarantee he'd consent to be interviewed, or that he even had any pertinent information. She decided to find Ramirez later, and focus on Senft instead. She put out a few feelers to several of her contacts in law enforcement and private investigation, letting them know she was interested in information regarding Ramirez's whereabouts. Then, still unable to sleep, she'd revised the Ghost Walk piece and e-mailed it to Miles. Finally, she'd showered, ate breakfast, chugged another Red Bull, and drove to the White Rose Mental Health Facility.

Where she'd hit a brick wall—rebuffed by the receptionist and ignored by the officials. When she raised a stink, she was escorted out by a smiling, uniformed guard.

"Can't you pull some strings for me, Miles? Isn't there somebody we can talk to?"

"No, there isn't. And even if there was, it would still take time. First, we would have to get in direct contact with Senft and find out if he wants to be interviewed."

"I know. They just told me that. They said I'd have to put in a request to get on his visitor's list and that could take up to two weeks."

"And they're right," Miles said. "But it would probably take even longer than that. Trust me. I know these things."

"How?"

"I'm an editor. I know everything."

Maria smiled, but refused to let him hear her laugh.

"Patients at mental hospitals," Miles continued, "even murderers like Adam Senft, retain most of their rights. They can have visitors, but the tricky part is that all visitors, even their family members, have to be approved by the medical staff. This guy is criminally insane. His life hangs on the thread of a committee of professionals who decide when he can get off the ward, for how long, when he can go outside the facility, see a movie, visit the park. Whatever. So let's say you contact

Senft. You send him a letter, ask to be added to his visitor's list, and arrange to interview him. And let's say he agrees—"

"He will."

"Say he does. Senft then has to take the request to his treatment team. We're talking a psychologist, social worker, behavioral analyst, unit director, head of security, and a doctor or nurse. All of these people have to determine whether or not the visit would be detrimental to his current treatment plan. You know how long that would take?"

Maria sighed. "A lot longer than two weeks."

"Exactly. And that's just if Senft agrees to the interview. He might not, you know. If he wants to get discharged eventually, he wouldn't want to make waves."

"But I could get him to consent to an interview. I know I could."

"And maybe you could. God knows you've convinced me to do stuff for you in the past. Things I took a lot of heat for. But even if you did convince him, there's still no guarantee. Even if you get past the treatment committee, you then have to face the judge who was originally involved in the case. And he's the one who is ultimately responsible for letting these people back into the community, so you can bet your byline that he's going to have something to say about it. Senft's lawyer would be involved, too—if he even has the money to afford a lawyer. State lawyers never get involved with things like this."

"He was a novelist," Maria pointed out. "He's got money."

"He was a midlist paperback genre writer. They get paid even less than you do. And whatever assets he *did* have are probably frozen. Either that, or they got sold to pay for his defense the first time around. His publisher isn't going to help him out. But let's say some well-meaning fan pays for his lawyer, and the lawyer convinces the judge to consider your request. Then you've got the hospital and their lawyers stepping in to ask the judge, 'Why do you want a raving lunatic with paranoid delusions about half human, half goat monsters running around York County impregnating housewives to speak to a reporter?' End of interview, Maria."

"Goddamn it . . ."

"On top of that, there's HIPPA regulations—those forms the doctors make you sign guaranteeing confidentiality? Those get taken very seriously. Technically, the staff can't even confirm they have any particular patient in the facility without that patient's signed consent."

"I know," Maria said. "They gave me that song and dance earlier, until the receptionist let it slip that Senft was there."

"Well, there you go. What I don't understand is this. Why is it such a big deal to just wait the two weeks—or however long it takes? After all, this is for a book, not an article. A book that you haven't even pitched yet, let alone sold. Why the rush?"

"I just want to get started on it. I'm excited about the idea. I want to dive in while it's still fresh."

"You want some free advice? Sit on it and wait. What are you going to do if you sell this thing on proposal and then lose your sense of excitement halfway through? Then you've still got a book to finish. One that you no longer want to write."

Yawning, Maria glanced around the parking lot, blinking at the bright glare coming through her windshield. It was deserted. Lots of cars and even an Amish horse and buggy parked at the rear, but no people. She assumed most of the vehicles belonged to the staff.

"Come on, Miles," she pleaded one more time. "Isn't there something you can do? Anything? Help me out here. Throw me a bone, for Christ's sake."

He laughed. "There's no way I'm getting involved with this."

"Thanks for nothing."

"Look, Maria, for what it's worth, I think you've got a solid idea. I think LeHorn and Senft and the whole weird story would be perfect for a true-crime book. It's got sex, murder, and black magic. I think you'd sell a ton of copies.

But my duties are to the newspaper. If you start rattling cages or getting into trouble, and it reflects badly on us, I'd have no choice but to cut you loose as a freelancer. And then, with you gone, they'd hold me responsible. Shit rolls downhill, right? You know what the owner is like. I like my job here. They pay me for it, and in turn I get to keep things like my house and my car and that goddamn inground pool my wife made me buy last summer—the one we never use. Those things cost money and I'm a big fan of money. Therefore, I'm a big proponent of keeping my job. I can't help you with this."

"Not even unofficially? Just whisper the name of someone that might be able to help? You owe me, Miles."

"Nonsense."

"Who covered that antiabortion rally for you when all your staffers called in sick?"

"You did. And if I remember correctly, we had to publish an official apology because you called that evangelical minister a fuck-head while you were interviewing him."

"Well, he *was* a fuck-head. But never mind that."

"Never mind? I *still* get my ass chewed out for that!"

"Who got the county commissioner to admit on tape that the County Parks Department's public domain seizure of the Larue Farms property was wrong? Who got you that quote when no one else could?"

Miles sighed. "You did."

"So hook me up."

There was silence on the other end of the cell phone. Maria thought that maybe her call got dropped, and was ready to curse her service provider, when she heard Miles sigh again.

"Damn it, girl. Okay, look. This is off the record and completely unofficial."

Maria smiled.

"Are you recording this?"

"You know I wouldn't do that to you, Miles."

"There's a couple of things you could try. Let's call them 'backdoors.' If Senft wants to meet with you, he could lie to his handlers about who you are. Remember, he's got rights. In Pennsylvania, the staff aren't permitted to read his mail or monitor his phone calls. So instead of telling his treatment team that you're a reporter, he could say you're an old friend or a fan of his books or something like that. They can't eavesdrop on your conversation when you visit, so you could ask him questions then. But if you got caught doing that, no reputable newspaper, webzine or magazine in the country would ever let you freelance for them again. It would totally discredit you, and you'd be stuck doing blogs."

"Not necessarily. Reporters do that kind of thing all the time. It's just part of getting the story."

"Not anymore. Not with the corporations in charge. This is the New Media. Welcome to the age of accountability to the shareholders."

"Well, then is there anything else? Something that doesn't involve me dropping a nuke on my career?"

"Sure. Here's something else to consider—these facilities have fences, and people can talk through fences."

"What do you mean?"

"Senft has to have fresh air, right? He has to have exercise. Are you still sitting in the parking lot?"

"Yeah."

"See the double security fence going around the place? You could try sneaking up to that and talking to him through the mesh."

"But that's even riskier than the other method."

"Correct. So why not just let this go? Move on?"

"Because that receptionist pissed me off. And because I'm stubborn."

"Yes, you are, Maria. You're like a goddamned pit bull when it comes to a story. That's why you're my favorite freelancer. And that's why I wish you'd just walk away from this."

"I can't. But thanks, Miles. I really do appreciate your help."

"Don't mention it. And listen . . . I'll ask around. See if I can't find you someone more sympathetic. But it's got to be totally on the down low, okay?"

"No worries. I promise."

"I'll call you if I hear anything. And again, good job on the Ghost Walk story. It'll run in this afternoon's edition. Hawkins got some great photos to go with it."

"Awesome. Talk to you later, Miles."

"Stay out of trouble."

"There won't be any trouble, as long as I can talk to Adam Senft."

"Maria!"

"I'm kidding. Bye."

Grinning, Maria disconnected the call and bent over, putting the cell phone back into its charger, which was plugged in to the car's cigarette lighter. She yawned again, rubbing her tired eyes. She decided to go home and get some sleep. When she sat back up, a shadow fell over her. A dark-haired, bearded man stood next to the open window. Startled, Maria gasped. She reached for her purse, intent on grabbing her can of pepper spray.

"I'm sorry," the man apologized, taking a step backward and holding up his hands. "I didn't mean to startle you. Are you okay?"

Maria's hand slipped inside her purse. She closed her fingers around the can of pepper spray and paused, studying him. To her surprise, the stranger was either Mennonite or Amish. She couldn't be sure which. His clothing and hat were a dead giveaway, though, as was his long, bushy beard. When Maria was younger, her mother had liked a rock group called ZZ Top. The band members all had flowing beards. This guy reminded her of them. His age was hard to determine. She guessed that he might be in his early thirties. She remembered the Amish buggy she'd noticed earlier while talking to Miles. If it belonged to him—and she assumed it did—that made him Amish. People from the Mennonite faith drove cars and trucks. Only the Amish still insisted on horse-drawn buggies.

"I'm really sorry," the man said again.

Her shock dissipated. Whoever he was, she doubted very much that he was a rapist or carjacker. His expression was apologetic, his tone concerned.

"It's okay," Maria said, taking a deep breath. "You just surprised me, is all. Can I help you?"

The man lowered his hands and smiled. "Possibly, Miss . . . ?"

"Maria Nasr. And you are?"

"You can call me Levi Stoltzfus."

Maria thought that was odd. Not *my name is* but *you can call me*. She chalked it up to an archaic speech mannerism. She'd heard the Amish sometimes favored those.

"What can I do for you, Mr. Stoltzfus?"

"Well, I'm sorry about this, but as I was passing by, I couldn't help but overhear your conversation. You seemed very . . . irate."

"My boss," she explained. "It's a long story."

"Would that story have anything to do with Adam Senft?"

Maria paused, keeping her poker face. She studied him closely, trying to figure out his intentions. Had he recognized her name? Remembered her byline from a previous story? Amish people read the newspapers, just like everyone else. Indeed, since they couldn't watch television, listen to the radio, or go online, newspapers were their only source for news. Or maybe, like millions of other Americans, maybe he was just fascinated with morbid stories and had recognized Senft's name.

"How would you know that, Mr. Stoltzfus?"

"I heard you mention him, I'm afraid." He glanced at the hospital. "Adam Senft is a patient here, isn't he?"

"And may I ask what your interest in this is?"

"If you tell me what your own interest in him is, then I might be able to help you."

Maria laughed. "I really doubt that, Mr. Stoltzfus, but I appreciate your—"

"You want to speak to him, right?"

She nodded.

"So do I. And if you tell me what your involvement is with him, I can make it happen for you. May I sit in your car while we talk?"

Ken stifled a yawn and cracked his aching back.

"Long night?" Terry asked, grinning.

"Yeah." Ken rotated his arms and stretched his shoulders. "Didn't get to bed until well after midnight, and couldn't fall asleep until past two."

Terry's grin widened. "Had a little company, did you?"

"Fuck you. You talking about Maria?"

"Hey—first-name basis now, huh? Come on, Ken. You banged her, didn't you? Tell the truth."

"No," Ken protested. "Not that it's any of your business, but we had dinner. That's all. It was a business meeting, Terry. She interviewed me. We ate. And then I came home."

Ken felt defensive. It seemed disrespectful to Deena's memory to be having this conversation. But before he could explain that to his best friend, Terry continued.

"You should have banged her, man. That's some ass on her. I bet you went home and thought about it."

"Dipshit."

"What? She's cute."

"She is. And she's also too young. Look, I just couldn't sleep. That's all. Had stuff on my mind. In case you forgot, we open tomorrow night."

"I know," Terry said. "That's why I got a good night's sleep."

"Wish I could say the same. I ended up doing a few shots of Woodford Reserve just so I'd nod off."

They walked the trail, checking off things that were completed and making a last-minute list of what still needed to be done. Terry had taken some vacation time so that he could give Ken a hand. Both men felt overwhelmed. Most of the volunteers wouldn't arrive until the evening. There were only a few on hand, and two who hadn't shown up at all.

"Have you seen . . ." Ken snapped his fingers, trying to remember their names. "Rhonda and Sam? The kids from the school?"

Terry shook his head. "Not this morning. Maybe they had something going on at the school?"

"Maybe. I know that I shouldn't bitch about it. I mean, they're volunteers. It's not like they're getting paid. But we've got a lot to do yet. We could really use some extra hands."

"We'll get 'er done," Terry said, doing his best impression of stand-up comedian Larry the Cable Guy. "Don't worry, man. You've just got the jitters. Just like back in high school, right before a game."

"Maybe," Ken agreed. "I just want everything to go smooth, you know? I want this to really be a good thing."

"It will be."

They finished their tour and walked back to the beginning of the trail.

"Listen," Ken said, fishing his car keys out of his pocket. "I've got to run to the costume store and pick up our masks. Think you can handle things while I'm gone?"

"Damn straight. What do you want us to focus on?"

Ken handed him the list. "Everything on here. You've got Cecil, Tom, Russ and Tina to help you this morning. I sent Jorge to pick up more lime. He should be back in an hour or so. Have him outline the trail some more. Make sure we get a good coating of lime down so people know where the trail is and don't go wandering off into the woods tomorrow night."

"Will do."

"Everybody else will be here this afternoon, after they get off work and stuff. We'll do a final walk-through and then have a staff meeting out here in the field, so that everybody knows what they're doing tomorrow night."

"No worries." Terry took the list and looked it over.

They said good-bye and Ken climbed into his truck and

shut the door. He started it up. Johnny Cash's rendition of
Soundgarden's "Rusty Cage" filled the cab's interior.

"No," Ken muttered as he drove away. "No worries at all.
Nothing's gonna go wrong."

CHAPTER TEN

"So what do you want him for?"

"No fair," Levi said. "I asked you first."

They were still in the parking lot, sitting in Maria's car. She'd hesitated at first when he had suggested it, but finally relented. He was definitely Amish—no way that beard was a disguise. She decided he didn't pose a threat. Even so, she made a point of keeping the canister of pepper spray within reach, and letting him know that she had it.

"Okay," Maria said, "but I'm warning you. If this is some kind of trick . . ."

"I assure you that it's not, Miss Nasr. My interest in Adam Senft most likely parallels your own. In any case, it's really important."

"You can call me Maria if you like. Nobody's called me 'Miss Nasr' since I got out of college."

"Very well. It is nice to make your acquaintance, Maria."

"Yours, too." She paused. "Um, not to be rude, but what do I call you, anyway? Brother Stoltzfus or something?"

He appeared confused. "No, I'm not a clergyman. You can just call me Levi if you like."

"Okay." Maria relaxed. "I wasn't sure. I've never actually talked to an Amish person before. I took one of those tours in Lancaster when I first moved here, but that's all. I didn't know if you guys referred to each other as Brother and Sister or not."

"Oh, I'm not Amish. At least, not anymore."

"I see." She frowned. "I'm sorry. I just assumed, what with your clothing and the buggy and all. Are you Mennonite, then?"

"No. It's a long story. I was once a part of the Amish faith, but sadly, I left the community many years ago. Now, I'm just . . . well, I don't really *know* what I am. Certainly not Amish or Mennonite. Or even Protestant or Catholic. I guess I'm just trying to live my life right and do God's work, the way that feels right to me. What would you call that?"

"Noble?"

"I like that." He smiled. "I would call it nondenominational."

"That would work, too."

Levi's stomach rumbled loudly. He smiled, embarrassed. "Sorry. I haven't eaten today. I'm fasting."

Maria nodded. Although she didn't ask, she wondered what the reason for the fast was. Was it religious or medical?

"So, I've got to ask. If you're not Amish anymore, then why the clothes and the beard? What's up with the hat?"

"I'm single. I thought that women might be attracted to the beard. And as for the hat, it's to keep the sun out of my eyes."

Maria tried to suppress her laughter, but failed. She snorted once, twice, and then laughed out loud, jumping up and down in the seat. Tears streamed from her eyes.

"What?" Levi asked, seemingly puzzled. "What's so funny? You don't like my beard?"

"I . . ." Gasping for breath, Maria wiped the tears from her eyes. "I think it's great. It's unique, you know? A lot of guys these days just go with a goatee. You've got a very retro vibe going on. It works for you."

"Excellent." He sounded pleased.

She stifled another burst of laughter and smiled. When she

felt she had control again, Maria explained her assignment—the feature article on the Ghost Walk and how it had inspired the book idea. She told him about her research into LeHorn's Hollow, powwow magic, and, ultimately, Adam Senft's involvement. Levi stayed silent throughout. He absentmindedly stroked his beard and listened. His face was expressionless.

"I guess it must all sound pretty bizarre to you," she finished. "But there are people who still believe in this stuff, even today."

"Oh, there's no doubt. I'm one of them."

Maria was stunned. "W-what?"

"My father worked powwow, as did my grandfather. It's sort of a family tradition."

"Wait a second," Maria said. "Stoltzfus. Your father was Amos Stoltzfus?"

Levi cocked his head. "You've heard of him?"

"He was mentioned in some of the articles I read when I was researching. Sort of a famous guy, right?"

Levi shrugged. "He helped a lot of people."

"So then you already knew all about Nelson LeHorn and the murders and all the legends about that area?"

Levi nodded. "I did."

"Then why didn't you interrupt me?"

"I needed to see what you knew. My reasons for speaking with Senft are related to your research into LeHorn's Hollow. In fact, I was just there last night."

"When? I was there, too. Are you helping with the Ghost Walk?"

He frowned. "No. But tell me more about this Ghost Walk. Your article sounds interesting."

"Well," Maria said, "it's a Halloween trail that Ken Ripple is building for charity. It's located in the same forest as LeHorn's Hollow—or, at least where LeHorn's Hollow used to be, before it burned down. My article about it runs this afternoon."

"I see."

"You must have noticed them working on it when you were there."

"No," Levi said. "I was preoccupied with something else. What is it, exactly?"

Maria shrugged. "People dress up in scary costumes and hide in the woods. Then other people pay money to walk through the woods and be scared."

"Hmmm." Levi's frown deepened. "A lot of people probably attend an event like that."

"Sure," Maria agreed. "At least, that's what the organizers are hoping. The proceeds go to help fight women's cancer."

"When does it open?"

"Tomorrow night. The trail opens at seven and stays open until midnight, followed by a party with live bands and stuff. You know, to celebrate the start of Halloween, since the holiday begins at midnight. I know a lot of people don't really celebrate until the next night, but technically, the holiday starts at midnight."

Levi's face grew pale. He looked startled—or maybe sick. He sank into the seat, shoulders slumped, head hung low. He closed his eyes and sighed.

Maria leaned forward, concerned. "Are you okay? You look like you're going to throw up."

Levi didn't answer her right away, and when he did, his voice was panicked. He covered his mouth with one trembling hand.

"Tomorrow night. Of course . . . The walls will be at their thinnest then, just after midnight. If it breaches with all those people in the area . . . My Lord! There's no time . . ."

"What are you talking about?" Alarmed by his reaction, Maria inched her hand toward the pepper spray.

Levi bolted upright, reached out, and snatched her wrist. He squeezed—gently, but firm. Alarmed, Maria tried to pull away.

"Hey!" she shouted. "Let go of me or I'll fucking scream."

She hated that. Hated the threat of screaming, like that was the only thing a woman was capable of. *If you don't stop, the widdle girly will scweam.* It sounded pathetic. There were other ways to defend herself. Her fear dissipated, replaced with anger. She was furious that he'd made her feel this way.

"I'm not going to hurt you," Levi said. "Please calm down."

"Don't tell me to calm down." She tried to get free again. "Let go of me, you son of a bitch."

Maria raised her free hand and slapped at him. To her dismay, she missed. Levi blinked as the blow whizzed by. Her hand glanced off the seat. It seemed impossible to her. This close, there was no way she could have missed.

"I'm not going to hurt you," he repeated, his voice patient. "Please. I just need you to listen to me and I don't want to be hit. Okay?"

Breathing hard, Maria nodded.

"Okay." He released her wrist and folded his hands in his lap. "I'm sorry if I upset you. That wasn't my intention. I'm just scared, is all."

"What you are," Maria said, "is lucky. Lucky I didn't knock your head off."

He smiled slightly. "Even if you'd wanted to, you couldn't have."

"Oh, believe me—I wanted to. You gonna tell me you're an expert at Amish karate or something?"

"No, not at all. It's just that I carry something on my person that prevents attacks like that. Your aim was true. It just wasn't effective."

Maria started to protest, but Levi held up his hand.

"Please, let me continue. I'm sorry for upsetting you. I shouldn't have touched you and I know it was wrong. But we have a very serious situation here and not a lot of time to deal with it. I can't do this alone. I need help, starting with Adam Senft."

"Is this some kind of powwow thing?"

"No. The powers that I'll be calling on and the methods I'll be using have nothing to do with powwow. They are a much older and much more dangerous form of magic."

"I think I've heard enough," Maria said. She reached for the pepper spray again. "I'd like you to leave. Now."

"Listen to me," Levi pleaded. "You don't understand what's going on. If I could just—"

"I want you to get out of my car *right now*."

"Please . . ."

"Let's see if powwow has a cure for pepper spray to the fucking face!"

She raised the canister and pointed the nozzle at him. Her thumb was on the button.

"When you were eight years old," Levi said quickly, "you had a pet turtle named Lucky. You called him that because your father found him in the middle of the Garden State Parkway, crossing several lanes of traffic. He was lucky to be alive."

"What—" She lowered the pepper spray and stared at him, gaping.

"One day," Levi continued, "you came home from school and took Lucky out into the backyard. You had a small, plastic wading pool with green and pink fish painted on the sides. You used to let Lucky splash around in it. On that day, Pete Nincetti, the bully from next door, came into the yard and stole Lucky from you. Your parents weren't home yet, and you were scared of Pete because he was older than you were. You tried to get Lucky back but Pete shoved you down. You started crying. Then he tossed Lucky into the air and hit him with his baseball bat. He did this four more times, cracking the shell and finally knocking Lucky down into a sewer drain."

Tears streamed down Maria's shocked face. "Stop it. How do you—"

"You told your parents when they came home. Your father hollered at Mr. Nincetti, but nothing ever happened. The police did nothing. His parents did nothing. Pete wasn't punished."

"I . . . I never told anyone."

"Wrong. You told Clarissa Thomas, your roommate during your freshman year in college. But what you never told anyone was that three months later, it was you who wrapped the rat poison up in a piece of bologna and fed it to Pete's dog."

"Shut up," Maria sobbed. "Just stop it."

"The dog vomited blood and died. Pete cried. So did you."

"Are you some kind of stalker or something? Have you been following me?"

"No."

"Then how do you know this? Tell me!"

"I just know."

She buried her face in her hands. "You son of a bitch."

"I'm sorry that I had to do this," Levi said, "but I needed to get your attention. I had to show you proof that this isn't just the ramblings of a crazy man. I need you to listen to me, Maria. More importantly, I need you to believe what I'm saying."

"But you just—"

"If it's any consolation, you might like to know that, years later, Pete was shot in the head by two men named Tony Genova and Vincent Napoli, after he ran afoul of the mob. Despite the severity of the wound, it took him a long time to die. He suffered. His body is buried in an unmarked grave near Manalapan."

Maria opened the console between them and pulled out a tissue. She wiped her eyes and blew her nose, then tossed the crumpled tissue on the floor.

"How the hell do you know all this?"

"The methods don't matter," Levi said. "What matters is that you've seen incontrovertible proof that I can do things like that. Things that you don't believe in. Except that now you've got no choice but to believe in them. This was no parlor trick. It's real. Do you believe?"

She hesitated. "Yes."

"Good. Because I've got a lot more to tell you, and if you're going to help me, then you can't have any doubts."

"Help you? I'm not involved in anything, Levi. I'm just researching a book."

"No," he said. "You're involved. Whether you realize it or not. It feels . . . right, to me. You're a part of this. Not by your own hand, but because that's what God wants of you."

"I may believe you're some kind of mind reader, but I definitely don't believe in God. I was raised to believe in Allah, but I'm not even sure about that anymore."

"It doesn't matter. God. Allah. Yahweh. These are all just different names for the same being."

"Whatever. I've heard that before, too. Still doesn't mean I believe in any of them."

"Well, that's unfortunate."

Maria smirked. "Is this the part where you tell me that's okay because God believes in me? If so, save the clichés for somebody else. I've heard that one before."

"No." Levi shook his head. "I'm not going to tell you that. Because by tomorrow night, if we don't stop what's about to occur, you'll have your disbelief resolved whether you like it or not."

"How?"

"All souls, whether they believe in Him or not, stand before God after they die. And unless we act soon, there are going to be a lot of people dying—us included."

"What are you talking about?"

"The end of the world."

"Okay," Maria agreed. "You've got my attention, at least. Let's hear what you have to say. Should we go somewhere more secluded or are you comfortable here?"

Levi glanced out the window and checked the parking lot. While his attention was diverted, Maria reached down and quickly turned on her digital voice recorder, which was sitting in the console's cup-holder. She sat back up and smiled as Levi turned back to her.

"We should be okay here," he said. "I'm sure it will put you more at ease."

"Whatever you prefer."

He took a deep breath and exhaled. "Much of what the human race thinks it knows is actually wrong. The history of our planet—of our past—is full of inaccuracies. This is especially true of our religions. The primary texts of Judaism, Christianity, Islam, Buddhism, Jainism, Hinduism, Shinto, Satanism, Wicca, and all of the others are fundamentally flawed. They've been tampered with and rewritten by man so much over the years that much of them are now filled with falsehoods. It takes many years of study and searching to learn the real truths."

"And that's what it means to be Amish?"

He snorted. "No. We're just another Christian denomination—and we're just as flawed. Perhaps more so. I no longer believe what they believe, because I've seen the bigger picture. I believe in God, the Father Almighty, maker of Heaven and Earth, and in Jesus Christ, one of his sons."

"I remember that from the times I went to church with my Christian friends. I thought the mantra was, 'His only son'?"

"So do a billion other people, Maria. And they are wrong. All of them. That's my point. The Bible isn't the inspired word of God. Nor is the Koran or the Torah or any of the other holy books. They are the words of man. Of many men. Edited and changed to reflect their will, not His. To truly know God and to seek His will, you've got to look beyond the Bible. Read between the lines. The book we know today as the Bible is not the complete text. It's not the inspired word of God. It is made up of a number of scrolls and tablets that men decided should be in it. Men, not God. But there are other texts, and they are just as valid. Texts from the same time that give us *true* understanding. The Bible we know speaks of Heaven and

Hell, but it never mentions places like the Labyrinth or the Great Deep or the Void. The Bible tells how God created our universe, but there's nothing in it about the universe that existed before this one. Or the enemy that came from that other universe."

"You're talking about the devil?"

Levi shook his head. "Which devil? There are more than one. Do you mean Lucifer, the Morningstar? Or maybe Satan? The old serpent? The dragon? The Beast? All of these appear in the Bible, and we're told to believe that they are the same entity—but they aren't. In any case, I'm not speaking about any of them. I'm talking about the Thirteen. They are far worse than any devil."

A car alarm blared across the parking lot. Maria jumped. After a minute, it faded.

"To create this universe," Levi continued, "God destroyed a universe that existed before ours. Think about it—the act of Creation must have required an unimaginable amount of energy. Where did He get it?"

Maria shrugged.

"He tore down the old universe and used its material as building blocks for our own. The old universe ceased to exist down to its last atom—except for the Thirteen. Somehow, they escaped the destruction. And they've been the enemies of God and all of His creations ever since."

"Demons?" Maria asked. She tried not to sound skeptical. Levi obviously believed what he was saying, and it seemed important to him.

"Not demons." Levi shuddered. "Although mankind has often mistaken them for demons. And gods. Entire—incorrect—mythologies have been created around them by foolish people who didn't know the true nature of what they were worshipping. No, the Thirteen are much worse than demons. They have nothing to do with Hell's legions. And each one of them is more terrifying than the next. Kandara, Lord of the Djinn. Ob, the Obot, who commands the Siqqusim. His brothers, Ab and Api. Leviathan, Lord of the Great Deep. Behemoth. And others—all terrible. But the greatest among the Thirteen is one who can't be named. Simply speaking its real name out loud causes unimaginable destruction. It is the reason mankind has such an unreasonable fear of the dark, for this thing is darkness incarnate. It sits in the heart of the Labyrinth and infects world after world."

"Hold up," Maria interrupted. "The Labyrinth? As in the minotaur and King Minos?"

"No," Levi said, "although I guess it could be the source of that old myth. The Labyrinth is sort of a dimensional shortcut between different worlds and realities. It weaves through time and space—nowhere and yet everywhere all at once. It connects to everything via a series of dimensional 'doors.' This is how the Thirteen travel between worlds. How they traverse the dimensions. And how some humans have traveled, as well. Normally, the only time we see the Labyrinth is when our spirit has departed our body. But there are ways to pass through it while still alive. You just have to know how to open one of the doorways. That's what Nelson LeHorn did."

"He traveled to another dimension?"

Levi shrugged. "Possibly. Another dimension. Another Earth."

"An alternate reality?"

"Exactly. There are many different Earths—mirror versions of our own world with alternate versions of ourselves. On one of them, you might be just like you are now. On another, maybe you're the first female president of the United States."

"Freaky. You're talking about string theory, right?"

"String theory?"

"Yeah, you know. Different dimensions stacked up against each other like membranes?"

"Is that what the scientists call it?"

Maria nodded.

Levi smirked. "They have no idea. And even if they did

figure it out, they wouldn't know how to stop what's happening. The Thirteen seek to destroy all of these Earths—and all of the other alternate worlds, as well. They've sworn to destroy anything created by God. After all, he destroyed their universe. They figure turnabout is fair play. So, on one of these worlds, perhaps Ob is the threat. On another, it might be Leviathan. Sometimes the Thirteen work together. Sometimes they work alone. Think about the end of the world. It can happen in so many different ways. Global warming. Nuclear war. Disease. Maybe it starts raining and doesn't stop. Perhaps the sun explodes or a comet collides with us. Or maybe zombies—"

"Zombies?" Maria interrupted.

"Sorry," Levi apologized. "But when you know the things I know, it doesn't seem so far-fetched. Anyway, yes, the end of the world happens every time the Thirteen are loosed upon one of these other realities. And there have been many ends of the worlds."

"And Nelson LeHorn escaped to another one of these Earths."

"Another Earth or another planet. Who knows? He could have miscalculated and ended up on Mars or anywhere else in the universe. Just as there are multiple Earths, there are alternate versions of the other planets as well. Imagine a Mars where life still exists, or a Jupiter that was formed out of rock and dust, rather than gases. All I know for sure is that after he murdered his wife, Nelson LeHorn opened a doorway in the hollow and fled through it. He closed the doorway behind him, but it still exists. LeHorn took precautions. He knew what waited out there. Knew that if he wasn't careful, something else could come through the portal. So he placed a circle of protection around the door, ensuring that nothing else could use it. But something went wrong. I don't know what. Maybe the sigils were removed or the circle was broken. Whatever the cause, this entity—this living darkness—is now seeping through into our world. It hasn't made it all the way through. Not yet. But tomorrow night is when the barriers between all worlds are at their thinnest. When that happens, it will surge into our plane of existence, and there's not a thing we can do about it."

Maria studied him closely. He seemed so earnest, so self-aware. Whether or not he was crazy—and he had to be to spin a story like this—Levi honestly believed every word of it.

But how had he known about Lucky? And Pete's dog? She'd never told *anyone* about that. Indeed, she'd been ashamed of it all her life. No matter how much time passed, she still felt the guilt.

Levi had known.

"Okay," she said, still keeping her tone neutral. "What happens then? Once it's loose. Everything goes dark?"

"Yes. Eternal night. Like a total, planet-wide eclipse. It would start at the doorway and then quickly sweep across the land. But that's just the beginning. Every living thing that this creature touches gets consumed. It sucks up all their energy, leaving an empty husk behind. Within days, our planet would be a lifeless shell. Once the Earth's energies had been depleted, the creature would move on to the next world."

Maria decided to change tactics.

"You seem to know a lot about this . . . thing that can't be named. But how? I mean, if all of our history books and religious texts are wrong, then how can you be sure you've got the right information?"

"Because of my source. Yes, over the centuries, a lot of people have got it wrong. The Celts, for example, believed this creature was a deity from their pantheon. That's because the entity tricked them into thinking so. It can shift shapes, appearing as anything it wants. Quite often, it takes the form of things we fear, long for, or regret. As I said, it feeds off our energy. Quite often, it is our fears that generate the biggest amount of energy."

"But you said it feeds off all living things. So what does it appear as to a tree or a flower? They don't know fear."

"Sure they do. A tree fears the roar of a chainsaw or the crackle of flame. A flower fears the hum of a lawn mower or the voice of a young man intent on picking it for his girl-friend."

Maria stared at him, speechless.

"It doesn't always use that attack, however. It can appear as a benevolent being—a friend or parent or lost love. It appeared to the Celts as a human male with a silver arm replacing its original arm, which had supposedly been lost in battle. It appeared to others as an old man carrying a great wooden staff in one hand, and riding in a seashell chariot drawn by flaming beasts. Again, this was a falsehood. Historians have misidentified it. Archeologists, too—attributing ruins and sites to its name, even though the things worshipped there were far different. Fiction writers like Arthur Machen and H. P. Lovecraft have added to the confusion over the years. One of them even labeled the entity as the Lord of the Great Deep, which is actually Leviathan's post. In reality, there's only one, true source of information on this thing—and the rest of the Thirteen. It's the only source I trust."

"Let me guess," Maria said. "You hear the voice of God?"

"Please don't tease me. This is a very serious matter. My source is something called the *Daemonolateria*."

"You know Latin?"

"It's not Latin. I know it sounds like it, but the word is from a language not spoken on this planet. The *Daemonolateria* is sort of a book, although it's unlike any other book you've ever heard of. There are different versions; each copy is unique. Some of it exists on this plane of reality. Other parts exist . . . elsewhere. Its contents can change, depending on the owner and translation, but much of it deals with all of this forgotten history. It contains methods of stopping or banishing the Thir-teen, including the thing we face."

"Sounds awfully confusing."

"It is. It's definitely not for amateurs. There's as much misinformation about the *Daemonolateria* as there is about the Thirteen. In short, if he wants to be sure, a magus has to build his own version of the book. That's what I'm in the process of doing. It can be dangerous. Nelson LeHorn's copy was fairly complete and very accurate. But it also made him paranoid. A lot of people like us coveted it."

" 'Like us'?"

"Magicians. Powwow doctors. Priests. Warlocks. Witches. There are more of us than you think. There are different disciplines and social orders, of course. Some of us are loners. Others have their own little groups and clubs. Black Lodge. The Kwan. Things like the O.T.O. and the Starry Wisdom Sect. Teenagers playing at satanism. Senior citizens giving their money to charismatic leaders."

"I thought Black Lodge was a division of the CIA?"

"That's what they would like you to believe."

"All I know is they're a conspiracy theorist's wet dream."

"It doesn't matter," Levi said. "My point is, there are a lot of us—most of whom can't be trusted. LeHorn became convinced that others might try to kill him for his copy of the book, so he hid several of the most important pages, rendering the rest of the book incomplete and, hopefully, worthless. My father told me of the hiding places that he knew of. One of those pages—the one we need to stop this—was hidden in LeHorn's copy of *The Long Lost Friend*. He thought it would be extra safe there. And he was right about that."

"So you need to find his book?"

Levi nodded. "And that's why I need to speak with Adam Senft. He was the last person to have LeHorn's book. I need to know where it is now. It might be in his possession, though I doubt it. Senft was certainly dabbling in magic before his wife's murder, but I don't think he'd progressed far enough to secrete something like a page from the *Daemonolateria* on himself while in a psychiatric hospital. Not without it being detected. It's more likely that the book—and the page—are hidden somewhere on the outside."

"What if he doesn't know where it is, or he doesn't remember? What then?"

"There are other ways to find it. Divining would work, but that takes weeks and we don't have time. So we'll just have to *make* him remember."

"You said 'we' again. I'm not a part of this. Like I told you before, I'm only interested in Senft for my book. That's why I'm here. God didn't bring us together. It was just a coincidence."

Levi sighed. "You don't believe what I just told you?"

Maria chose her words carefully. "I believe that you believe it. But, look—I don't believe in God in the first place. I don't believe that He created the Earth, so why would I believe that He destroyed another universe to do it and that it's been covered up ever since? And even if I did believe any of that, it's not God. It's Allah."

"I told you before. Allah and God are the same being. Names have power. Those are just two names for the same divinity."

"So you say. And so have others. But how do I know that?"

"You take it on faith! Just like any other belief."

She shook her head and sat in silence.

"Maria," Levi begged, "I can't do this alone. I . . . I don't have anyone else."

"I'm sorry, Levi. I really am. You seem very nice. But I'm not some occult avenger. I wouldn't mind interviewing you some more, specifically about powwow and your father and LeHorn. But that's all."

"Interviewing me?"

"If you don't mind, that is?"

"Would it matter if I did?" Smiling, Levi nodded toward

her digital voice recorder. "After all, you've been secretly taping our conversation since we started."

"I . . ." Maria felt her face flush. "I'm sorry. It made me feel better, just in case . . ."

"Just in case I turned out to be crazy after all?"

"Yeah, if you want the truth."

"Go ahead and play it back."

"Why?"

"Humor me."

Slowly, Maria picked up the recorder, pressed the stop button and then played back their conversation. Except that instead of Levi's voice, somebody else spoke to her. A different voice boomed from the device. She couldn't distinguish its sex or age. There was no accent or distinguishing characteristics. It had a hypnotic, musical quality, and flowed like water.

"MARIA. PLEASE HELP."

Maria's jaw went slack. Her fingers tightened around the recorder until her knuckles turned white. The voice was replaced with a feint, electronic hiss—white noise. Maria advanced the recording, but there was just more silence.

"How . . ." She turned off the recorder and looked at Levi, her eyes wide. "How did you . . . your voice?"

Levi's smile grew broader.

"Let me guess," he teased, mimicking her earlier taunt. "You heard the voice of God?"

Maria started to respond, but couldn't. Her mouth felt dry, her tongue swollen. She tried licking her lips. They seemed puffy. Heavy. Her ears rang. She struggled to sit up straight, but the car's interior began to spin. Her fingers grasped the seat, but she couldn't feel the upholstery.

"Maria?" Levi reached for her, concerned. "Are you okay?"

Levi's voice sounded far away, as if he were speaking from the other side of a long tunnel. Maria tried to answer him but had trouble forming the words. She felt weak and her senses seemed deadened. She bowed her head, grasping for something to hold on to. Her hand felt heavy—made of lead. It suddenly seemed very hot and stifling inside the car, yet she was shivering.

"N-no . . . I . . ."

Then her eyes rolled in their sockets and she fainted.

CHAPTER ELEVEN

Ken went through the masks and costumes, making sure everything he'd ordered was there. He ticked them off in his head. Werewolf. Gorilla. Boar with tusks. Witch. Evil clown. Phantom of the Opera. Both Boris Karloff's and Robert DeNiro's versions of the Frankenstein monster. A leering jack-o'-lantern. A gargoyle. Gollum from *The Lord of the Rings*. The Creature from the Black Lagoon. Jason Voorhees. Freddy Krueger. Pinhead. A few zombies, including Bub from George Romero's *Day of the Dead*. Several different mutants and aliens. Leatherface. The Fly. A man with one latex eyeball hanging down his cheek. Another man with a hard foam axe jutting from his latex head. And Ken's personal favorites, masks of veteran horror actors Bruce Campbell and Michael Berryman, cast from molds of their faces. Two of his volunteers were going to dress like the actors' characters in *Army of Darkness* and the original version of *The Hills Have Eyes*. For the former, they'd even built an attraction that looked like the inside of the windmill from the movie. Hopefully, the attendees would recognize it. In any case, these masks would cap the ensembles off perfectly. Satisfied with the results, Ken then double-checked the costumes and found they were all in order, as well.

"All set?" asked the clerk, a college-aged kid who still hadn't outgrown the curse of teenage acne.

"Yeah," Ken said. "I think we're good to go."

"Sweet. I'm glad you picked these up early. We'll be busy tonight."

"Because of Halloween?"

"You got that right. We make nine months of rent during the month of October."

At the counter, Ken grabbed a few compact discs of Halloween music and added them to the pile. He already had dozens of sound effect and ambience recordings, but a few more wouldn't hurt.

"Want to add a fog machine, Mr. Ripple? I can give you a discount since you bought so much."

"That's okay. To be honest, the ones you guys have here are too small for my needs. The Ghost Walk has a creek that flows through one part of it. We're gonna use dry ice. Drop it in the creek and place buckets of it at intervals along the trail. According to some haunt enthusiasts I've talked to online, once it starts evaporating, the dry ice should have the same effect."

As he handed the salesclerk his credit card, Ken's cell phone rang, playing the main orchestral theme from *Young Guns II*. While the clerk rang up his charges, Ken glanced at the phone and saw it was Terry calling.

"Hey," he answered. "What's up?"

"The police were here."

"W-what? Why? What's wrong?"

"It's Rhonda and Sam. The kids from the high school? Turns out they never went home last night. Their parents called it in. Last time anybody saw them was here, at the Ghost Walk."

"Yeah," Ken agreed. "I saw Rhonda yesterday evening, before Maria and Rudy showed up."

"I told the cops that. They want to talk to you about it when you get a chance."

Ken twitched. "Why? They . . . they don't think I had something to do with it, do they?"

The clerk looked up from the register. Ken turned his back on him.

"No," Terry said. "At least, I don't think so. They found Sam's car in Lancaster this morning, parked at a supermarket in Columbia. That's all they'd tell me. Don't know if they ran off together, or had a fight, or what. I wouldn't worry about the cops thinking we're involved. You know how kids are. Remember the shit we used to get up to?"

"Yeah."

"The cop left a business card for you and wrote his cell phone number down on the back. I told him you'd be out running around most of the day but would get back to him as soon as you could. I also gave him two free passes. Hope that's okay? He seemed really into the Ghost Walk."

"Sure," Ken said. "That's fine. I'm finishing up at the costume shop right now. I'll be back as soon as I can."

"Sounds good," Terry said. "I just figured you'd want to know right away."

"You did the right thing. Are the others saying anything?"

"The cop talked to Cecil, Tom, Russ and Tina. Jorge ain't back yet with the lime. I walked out here to the field so I could call. You know how bad cell coverage is in the woods."

"Okay. Hold down the fort. I'll be there soon. And Terry?"

"Yeah?"

"Let Cecil and the others know that I'd appreciate it if they didn't go blabbing about this. We don't need that kind of publicity, and it's not going to help the cops find them."

"Agreed."

Finished, Ken disconnected the call and stuffed the cell phone back in his pocket. Then he turned back to the clerk, who was holding out the store copy of his receipt and a pen for him to sign it with.

"Everything okay?" the clerk asked.

Ken nodded. "Fine. Just one of those days, you know?"

"Tell me about it. Seems like I'm having one of those lives."

Ken signed the receipt. "Ever get the feeling something bad is coming? You don't know what, but you can feel it—looming like a thunderstorm?"

The clerk stared at him. "No, can't say that I ever have."

"Oh." Ken shrugged. "Must be me, then."

"I'll give you a hand loading up," the clerk offered. "And then you can be on your way. Bet you're excited! Tomorrow's the big day."

"Thanks," Ken said. Then he muttered under his breath, "It's just getting more exciting all the time."

"Time to piss," Cecil Smeltzer announced.

"Thanks for sharing," Tom McNally said. "Want me to hold it for you?"

"No need. This ain't no union job and we don't work for the state road crew. Doesn't take two men to hold my pecker. It still stands up every time. Unlike you younger guys with your Viagra."

"You get a hard-on when you piss? Maybe you'd better see a doctor about that."

"No, sir." Cecil frowned. "I don't guess I will. You get to be my age, any visit to the doctor involves him putting his finger in your ass."

The sound of their laughter filled the forest.

"I'm gonna go back to the field," Tom said. "Check in with Terry. See how he made out with that cop. You want anything from the cooler?"

Cecil shook his head. "No, I'm good. I drink anything else, I'll just have to piss again."

As Tom strode away, he called over his shoulder, "Careful you don't cut your dick off with that machete while you're pissing!"

"Young people," Cecil muttered. "No respect for age or beauty."

After Tom was gone, Cecil drove the blade of his machete deep into a rotting tree stump. Splinters of dry wood fell to the ground around the stump's base. When he let go of the handle, the machete was still vibrating from the force he'd put behind the blow. He grinned, flashing his dentures and feeling happy. At his age, he was lucky if he could lift the machete most days, let alone swing it hard.

Volunteering for this Ghost Walk had been good for him, more than he'd even at first suspected. Initially, Cecil had gotten involved because he liked Ken Ripple and appreciated what the younger man was doing to honor his wife's memory. Ken and Deena had gone to Cecil's church for a while. Good people. Deena had one of those smiles that made people feel better, no matter what kind of day they were having. Ken had stopped coming to services after Deena's death. Cecil couldn't blame him much. Cecil's wife, Gladys, had been gone two years now, struck down in the night by a blood clot. But if she hadn't been such a bitch to him for the last thirty years of their lives together, then maybe Cecil would be pissed at God, too. Instead, he was secretly grateful.

Maybe it was the fresh air or just the fact that he'd been more active these past two months than he'd been for the last five years, but Cecil felt better. Healthier. He felt strong again, like he had in his forties and fifties. The exercise was definitely helping. He'd swung that machete all morning long, stopping only to drink coffee and talk to the police officer, but his back and shoulder muscles barely ached.

"Yes, sir," he whispered. "Maybe I'll head on down to the Lutheran Home's Senior Center tonight and see if I can't meet a lady. Play a few hands of strip cribbage."

He left the trail, pushing through the undergrowth. Although Tom and Terry were up in the field, Russ and Tina Farnsworth were around somewhere, putting up cornstalk walls along parts of the trail. Wouldn't do for Tina to come strolling down the path and find Cecil with his penis hanging out of his pants. She might get one glimpse of it and leave Russ for him.

He stopped after he'd gone about fifty yards. He glanced behind him. The brush was dense enough that he couldn't see the trail, which meant that nobody could see him either. Satisfied, Cecil unzipped his pants and freed his penis. Rather than the usual pathetic trickle, his stream was strong.

A twig snapped somewhere behind him.

Cecil turned his head, but couldn't see anything. He focused his attention on the business at hand again, amazed by his renewed vigor.

"Yep," he breathed. "Hard work does a body good."

Then he thought of his brother, Clark—a reminder that honest labor didn't always have the same positive results.

Cecil tried not to dwell on Clark. For years, he'd refused to speak or think about him at all. He'd put all of his brother's pictures in a shoe box and hid them in the attic, beneath Gladys's cross-stitch collection and a pile of old record albums. He'd tried to contact his nephew, Barry, a few times over the years, but the boy had turned out just like his father, and Cecil had given up. Talking to Barry just made him think of Clark. Thinking of Clark caused pain, so the easiest way to deal with it was to pretend his brother had never existed.

But, Cecil was learning, these days it wasn't so easy to ignore the past. Maybe it was because he was lonely, or that he had so much free time on his hands since he'd retired, but lately, he thought of Clark more and more. The pain was just as strong now as it had been back then, like an old scar that had been reopened and was bleeding out fresh again.

Cecil felt haunted.

While Cecil had taken a good job at the paper mill, Clark Smeltzer had gotten work as the cemetery caretaker for the Golgotha Lutheran Church in Spring Grove. At first, Cecil had been a little jealous of his younger brother. Sure, Cecil had union benefits and a fine hourly wage, but Clark's position entitled him to a home along with his weekly paycheck. He and his family lived across the street from the cemetery in a house owned by the church. They stayed there rent free, paying only for their utilities. It was a good job.

Until Clark fucked it all up.

Somewhere along the line, Clark went crazy. Cecil blamed himself for not seeing it sooner. Perhaps he'd just been bad all along—keeping his insanity brewing beneath the surface, hidden from everyone but himself. Maybe it was the booze or the gambling, or the whores he'd slept with on the side. Clark beat his son, beat his wife, and drank himself nearly to death. Then he'd started robbing graves—stealing from the people he was supposed to be burying. Worse, when the hookers apparently weren't doing it for him anymore, he'd kidnapped two women and held them in a tunnel he'd dug beneath the cemetery, raping them repeatedly. He'd died in that same tunnel, killed while trying to murder his own son and the boy's friend, both of whom had discovered what he was up to. And even in death, he'd continued to poison those around him. Cecil's nephew Barry was living proof of that. Despite everything he'd gone through, the boy had turned out just like his old man.

As Cecil's stream slowed to its more normal trickle, another twig snapped behind him, closer this time. Leaves rustled.

"Hello?"

Snap . . . snap . . . snap . . .

"That you, Tom? Don't you be messing around now or you're liable to get a surprise."

Something growled, low and deep.

"Clark?"

Cecil immediately felt stupid. Clark had been dead since 1984. Why would he call out his name now?

Because I'm getting senile in my old age?

Cecil stuffed his shriveling penis back in his pants and

quickly pulled up the zipper. The noises continued, coming from three different directions now. When he turned around, something brown and red darted between the trees.

Coyote, he thought, *or maybe a fox.* He'd never heard of either attacking a full-grown man before, but he didn't intend on waiting around to find out.

"Go on!" He tried to holler, but it came out more of a whisper. His mouth was suddenly very dry. "Scat! You get out of here now."

He hurried back toward the trail. To his left, the predator—whatever it was—growled again.

"Let me get my machete and you won't be growling like that, I goddamn guarantee you."

Sam, that kid the cop was looking for, stepped out from behind a tree, holding the machete in his right hand. Cecil noticed that the boy's hand had what appeared to be dried blood on it. The teen looked sick. His clothes were dirty. Patches of his hair were missing. Cecil remembered seeing pictures of the prisoners in the Nazis' death camps during World War II—living skeletons, flesh stretched parchment thin over sharply angled bones. That was what Sam resembled, which made no sense, since two days ago, when he'd helped Cecil and the others with construction on the maze house, he'd looked fine.

"Kid," Cecil gasped. "What the hell happened to you?"

Ignoring the question, Sam raised the machete over his head. "Looking for this?"

"Put that down before you hurt yourself. Listen, there's a coyote or something back there. Let's get back to the trail. You don't look so good. You got the AIDS or something?"

Smiling, the teen shook his head.

"You know the cops are looking for you?"

Still smiling, the teen shuffled closer, holding the machete as if to strike. As he closed the distance between them, Cecil got a good look at his eyes.

They were black.

"I . . ." Cecil tried to talk, but found that he couldn't breathe.

Another man stepped out of hiding. Cecil didn't recognize him. He wasn't one of the volunteers. The stranger pointed a hunting rifle at him.

Cecil desperately tried to call for help, but could only wheeze. The forest seemed to spin and his heartbeat was very loud in his ears. Sam grabbed his wrist, hard. The boy's fingers felt like burning ice.

"Want to see your brother again, Cecil?" Sam asked him. "Come along. We'll show him to you. But first, you'll have to do something for us."

"I feel better," Maria said. "Seriously, you can let go now. I'm fine."

Levi released her hand. He'd been pinching the skin between the thumb and index finger on her right hand.

"Are you still light-headed?"

"No. Honestly, I'm okay. Just sweaty and thirsty. My senses are coming back again. Whatever you did, it worked. What was that anyway? Acupressure?"

He nodded. "Something like that. It wasn't magic, though, if that's what you're thinking. A lot of what I do—a lot of powwow in general—has no basis in magical theory and discipline. It's just herbs and prayer."

"But you're not just practicing powwow. You admitted as much yourself."

"No," Levi admitted. "I'm not. Some of the places the Lord has led me over the years—well, let's just say that powwow wouldn't have been effective. I've had to use other methods."

"But doesn't that fly in the face of God?"

"Not if I'm using those methods to further His will."

They were sitting in Levi's buggy, which was still positioned at the rear of the parking lot. He'd led Maria there after she regained consciousness, so that she could lay down. Her car didn't have enough space for that, and despite the time of year, it had been hot and stifling inside the vehicle. The buggy sat beneath several trees, and it was better for her to be in the shade rather than the sun. Maria laid down on the long, wide bench at the front of the buggy. Once he'd gotten her situated, Levi crossed the street to the local gas station, bought her a bottle of water, and then hurried back. While Maria sipped the water, he'd applied slight pressure to her hand until her dizziness and nausea passed.

"Do you . . ." he hesitated. "Do you want to talk about what happened?"

"I don't know," Maria admitted. "I mean, it's not every day that you hear . . . whatever that was."

"Oh, God—or Allah, as you think of Him—speaks to us every day. We just don't listen."

"But not like this."

"No," Levi agreed. "Not like this. Not in a long time. These days, there are no burning bushes or voices from the mountaintop."

Maria breathed a heavy sigh. "Part of me still thinks it was a trick. Maybe you got to my recorder earlier or something— except I know that's not true."

"I promise you that I did nothing of the sort."

"And part of me believes it really happened. That G . . ." She paused. "That *whoever* . . . somebody left a message."

"I can't sway your belief one way or the other, Maria. All I ask is that you believe what I've told you. For anything other than that, you'll have to look to your own heart."

"Listen, I'm sorry about my behavior earlier. I don't think you're some psycho killer or Amish rapist or anything like that. At least, not anymore. And yes, some things have happened that I can't explain. But I just don't know what to think yet. I'm overwhelmed and exhausted. I got no sleep last night. I was already in a bad mood and then all this . . . this *weirdness* started up. I just need to chill for a bit. I need to take a step back and think about things. I can't just totally, one hundred percent accept on blind faith that Allah spoke to me through my voice recorder. I want to. I really do. But I need to think about it more. Call it my journalistic side."

"Fair enough."

"But I do want to help you. I just don't know what you need from me."

"Simply having you involved is enough. Certain numbers have power. Six and seven. Nine. Twelve and thirteen. Twenty-two. Six hundred and sixty-seven, the number of the Beast."

"I thought it was six-six-six?"

"No, that was another thing scholars got wrong."

"Lost in translation, huh?"

"Something like that. But there *is* power in numbers. Twelve disciples, for example. Jesus picked twelve for a reason. Or consider the universal belief in the unluckiness associated with the number thirteen, regardless of the culture. Three is considered a very lucky number. Not as powerful as seven, but still very good."

"How is three a lucky number? There weren't three disciples."

"No, but there were three Stooges. No cosmic evil could stand against Moe, Larry and the original Curly."

It took Maria a moment to realize that he was joking. They both chuckled.

"You, me, and Adam Senft make three," Levi said. "Those are good odds."

"If you say so."

"I do." He took her hand and squeezed it gently. "Thank you for helping me, Maria."

She returned the gesture and then he released her hand.

"But let's be honest," Maria said. "Helping you is helping myself. We both want to talk to Adam Senft and neither of us has time to go through the official channels. So my reason for helping you make that happen isn't exactly charitable."

"Nevertheless, it is still appreciated."

At the front of the buggy, Dee whinnied.

Levi smiled. "And Dee appreciates it, too."

"She's a beautiful horse. Have you had her long?"

"Since she was a foal. She comes from an old line. Her family has aided my family for a very long time. She's my best friend. I don't know what I'd do without her."

Dee snorted and then looked away. Her tail flicked back and forth in agitation.

"And she never lets me forget it," Levi said.

"I always wanted a horse when I was a little girl."

"Your parents wouldn't buy you one?"

"We lived in the Jersey suburbs. There was nowhere to keep one."

"I can't imagine growing up like that, with no livestock or wide-open fields to play in."

"Yeah. It's definitely two different worlds. Do you have any other animals?"

He nodded. "An old hound dog named Crowley."

"Crowley and Dee—odd names. How did you come up with them?"

He hesitated before answering. "I named them after Aleister Crowley and John Dee."

"Oh." Maria nodded in affirmation, but privately, she wondered who they were. She vaguely recognized the names, but that was all. She didn't want to appear stupid, so she tried to change the subject. She held out her water bottle. "You want a sip?"

"No thank you," he declined, waving his hand. "As I said, I'm fasting. I can drink water, but only at specific times. So I'll have to wait."

"Must be tough."

"It is."

They sat in silence for a moment. While Maria finished her water, Levi bowed his head, folded his hands in his lap, and closed his eyes. His breathing grew shallow. She wasn't sure if he was praying or just resting, but decided not to disturb him in either case. Instead, to occupy herself, she looked around the buggy's floor. It was messy. Levi had road maps, emergency flares, a flashlight, assorted wrenches and screwdrivers, a pack of tissues, and even an empty soda cup from a fast-food restaurant. The buggy contained everything a regular vehicle would have. She considered this. Levi had said he was no longer Amish, so it shouldn't be that surprising, and yet, Maria couldn't help but be amazed. She was surrounded by hints of normalcy from someone who was anything but normal. She was no longer wary of him. She'd been honest with him about that. He wasn't crazy, at least, not in a violent, harmful way. She liked to think she had a pretty good sense for such things. Eccentric, certainly, but not crazy. The buggy's interior seemed to reinforce that.

A car pulled into the parking lot and drove slowly past them. The driver glanced their way. His gaze lingered on them for a moment. Then he drove on, finding an empty space several rows away. She saw brake lights flash. A moment later, the driver got out of the car and pointed his key ring at it. The car's alarm system chirped. The man looked at the buggy one more time and then walked toward the building.

For a few seconds, Maria felt paranoid. The driver had seemed awfully interested in them. Technically, she was trespassing. The parking lot was private property, and she'd been asked to leave by the staff. How would she explain her presence here, if discovered? But after she'd thought about it, she decided her fears were unjustified. The guy was probably just looking at Dee. Or maybe he'd recently moved to Central Pennsylvania from Maryland, as had thousands of other residents seeking a break from higher taxes. He might be unaccustomed to seeing an Amish buggy. After all, they were far less common in York than they were in Lancaster.

Before she could consider it more, Levi opened his eyes and sat up straight. Maria drained the last drop of water from her bottle.

"All set?" he asked.

She nodded. "I feel much better, thanks. Where should I put this bottle?"

"Just throw it in the back. I'll get rid of it later."

She tossed it over her shoulder and turned back to him. "So, what do we do now?"

"Well, first of all, we should probably get out of here before we attract attention."

He grabbed the reins and flicked them. Dee trotted forward on command. The buggy started to roll.

"Where are we going?" Maria asked.

"I've got to get a few things. If you want to catch a nap or get something to eat, now would be a good time. We've got several hours to kill."

He pulled alongside her car. "You should probably move your car, as well."

"What's the plan?"

Levi shrugged. "Like I said, you've got some free time. I've got to go home and retrieve a few things we'll need. We'll meet back here after dark. See that line of trees behind the hospital?"

Maria nodded.

"We'll meet there," Levi said. "Let's say ten o'clock. It should be dark enough by then."

"It'll be dark by six or seven."

"But the facility will have quieted down by ten, as well. The night shift will be on hand."

"Okay. And then what?"

"Then, we meet with Adam Senft."

"But how?"

"Simple," he said. "We just open the door and let him walk through it."

CHAPTER TWELVE

Russ and Tina Farnsworth finished lashing together a stack of dried cornstalks and then stood back to admire their handiwork. The air was cool in the shade between the trees, but their clothes were soaked with sweat. They'd worked hard all morning on last-minute preparations. The visit from the police, and the subsequent delay while they were questioned, had set their schedule back an hour, and now they rushed to complete everything.

"I wish some of the others would get here," Russ complained. "Seems like we're doing all the work."

"Wait until tonight," Tina said, wiping her hands on her jeans. "We'll take a break while everyone else busts their ass. We've earned it."

"Yeah." Russ fished a crumpled pack of cigarettes out of his shirt pocket and lit up. "Still, it seems quiet today. Hard to believe tomorrow is opening night."

"I know."

"Wonder what happened with those kids?"

"Rhonda and Sam? They probably just skipped town. Ran away together."

"Maybe," Russ said. "Or maybe something else happened to them."

"What?"

He shrugged. "I don't know. You see stuff on the news all the time. Boyfriend kills the girlfriend, buries her in the woods, and then tries to run. Like that Scott Peterson guy."

"You think Sam killed Rhonda? I don't know, Russ. Isn't that a little far-fetched? I mean, sure, he had some anger issues. We saw that here, while he was working. He could be hotheaded and arrogant, and sometimes he was belligerent to Ken and Terry, but that doesn't make him a killer. I never heard that he beat her or anything like that."

"Yeah, but who really knows these days? Look at all those people that got murdered right here in these woods a few years ago."

"They were a witch cult, Russ."

"Well, still. You wait and see. I bet you she's buried right out here in these woods."

"Terry said that Ken saw her leave last night, you dork. They found Sam's car in a grocery store parking lot across the river."

"You never know, Tina." He took a deep drag off his cigarette and smiled. "You just never know."

"I know one thing," Tina said. "You promised me you'd quit those things."

"Don't start that again. I'm going to. On New Year's day."

"That's three months from now."

"Well, I can't just quit cold turkey. Got to wean myself off them."

Grinning, she playfully smacked him. He reached around and tapped her ass.

"Love you," Russ said.

"I love you, too."

Russ and Tina had been married for twenty-eight years. Graduating the same year but from rival high schools, they'd met in Ocean City, Maryland, during Senior Weekend and had been together ever since. They'd had two wonderful children together, owned a nice home nestled deep in a secluded valley in Red Lion, and had no major debt. They stayed involved with their community. Decorated their house for Christmas and Halloween. Kept their lawn mowed. Were kind to their neighbors. Bought Girl Scout cookies every year. Life was perfect. They were happy and still in love. They shared everything.

Still, they had their ghosts, unknown to each other.

When her mother was in the final stages of Alzheimer's disease, Tina had faced a tough decision. The assisted care home her mother was in was expensive, and her mother's money had run out. Russ and Tina didn't have the funds to keep her there, not even with a second mortgage. Although her mother's mind was gone, her body was still in fine shape. The doctors said she might live for several more years. Tina cried as she pressed the pillow over her mother's face and held it there. She did it with love. When her mother was gone, she leaned over and gently kissed her cheek one last time.

Russ had a gambling addiction, bordering on obsession. There were weekend trips to Atlantic City, long hours spent at the off track betting parlor on Route 30, and many late nights spent online at various gambling sites. The problem—and his debts—both grew to enormous proportions. He'd eventually broken free, put it behind him after months of secretive counseling without Tina or his family's knowledge. But he had to hit bottom before he got the help—bottom being burglarizing his own home and pawning Tina's jewelry, including her great-grandmother's diamond ring, just to satisfy his debts. He'd called the police and reported it as a break-in. Russ had watched enough cop shows to know how to make it look like a real robbery. The regional cops never suspected otherwise. But when Russ saw the pain that he'd caused his wife, and the fears he'd stoked in his family—fears that their home was no longer safe—he'd shed the habit once and for all. Sadly, shedding the guilt was much more difficult.

Hand in hand, they double-checked the cornstalks one more time.

"Perfect," Russ said. "No way will people see behind them as they walk down through here."

"Whose hiding place is this?"

"Doug's. He's going to be dressed as a werewolf. He'll hide here and let folks walk by, unchallenged. Then, Shane's going to be hiding a little way up the trail. Doug will creep out behind the last person in the group and follow them. Then, when Shane jumps out, Doug will scare them from the rear. It's gonna be—"

Tina held up her hand, abruptly silencing him. Frowning, she tilted her head and listened.

"What's wrong?" Russ asked.

"I heard something."

"Russ? Tina? Somebody help me!"

Tina gasped. "That sounds like Rhonda!"

"Come on," Russ urged. Still clasping her hand, he led Tina forward, off the trail and into the woods. Their quick pace turned into a run as Rhonda called out for them again. Low-hanging branches tugged at their clothes, and Russ almost tripped over a root jutting from the soil. They followed Rhonda's shouts until they found her.

"Jesus," Russ breathed. "She doesn't look very good."

Rhonda leaned against a tree. Her clothes were tattered and dirty. Her face and hands were caked with mud. Dried blood covered one cheek, directly beneath a shallow, untreated cut. The most shocking aspect of her appearance, however, was the tremendous amount of weight that she'd apparently lost in the last twelve hours. Her arms and legs were rail-thin. The flesh hung off them like sallow curtains. Her face was sunken. Much of her hair was missing, revealing raw, glistening red patches on her scalp.

Then she raised her head and they glimpsed her eyes: two black holes full of swirling darkness.

"Rhonda!" Tina ran to the sickened girl. "Are you okay, honey? What's wrong?"

"I need help."

"It will be okay," Tina soothed, stepping closer. "Just calm down."

"I'm glad you both found me. Is there anyone else with you?"

"No," Russ said. "It's just us. Everyone else is up in the field. What's wrong with you, Rhonda? You look like you've been exposed to radiation or something."

"Russ," Tina snapped, glaring at him.

"I need help," Rhonda repeated.

"We'll get you some help," Russ promised. "Can you tell us where Sam is? Do you know?"

Rhonda smiled. "Sure. I can tell you where he is. He's right behind you."

"What?"

Russ turned in time to see Sam and a man he didn't recognize step out from behind a tree. Both men were obviously suffering from whatever malady Rhonda had. The stranger was especially gaunt, almost skeletal. Their eyes were like Rhonda's. Russ held up his hands as the man pointed a deer rifle at him. Sam clutched a machete. Russ recognized the weapon. It belonged to Cecil Smeltzer, one of the volunteers for the Ghost Walk. The old man had been using it to cut undergrowth earlier this morning, between nursing cups of coffee. Russ suddenly realized that he hadn't seen the old veteran since shortly after the cop had left.

"Hello, Russ," Sam said.

Russ struggled to keep the alarm out of his voice. "What the hell's going on here?"

Behind him, Tina whimpered. Russ whipped around again. Tina cowered against a tree trunk, flanked by Rhonda and Cecil. But that wasn't what had her terrified. It was the coyote that stood in front of her, legs spread, haunches rigid, teeth bared. A low growl emanated from its chest. It turned briefly and glanced at Russ. The beast's eyes were black, just like those of the humans. Although it wasn't emaciated like the others, some of its fur was missing.

"Russ," Tina sobbed. "Do something."

"Jesus fucking Christ," Russ whispered.

"No," Cecil said. "Not even close."

The old man's eyes were black, but physically, he was in much better shape than the others.

"Cecil," Russ pleaded, "that's a coyote."

"Once. Now it is us. Soon, you will be, too."

"Come with us," Rhonda commanded. "If you scream or try to run, Rich will shoot you."

The coyote backed away, allowing Tina to step forward. She stumbled away from the tree, swooning. Russ hurried to catch her. They sank to their knees on the forest floor.

"What's this all about?" Russ demanded. "This is crazy!"

"We need your help," Rhonda explained, her voice calm.

"Help? What kind of help?"

Sam ran his thumb along the machete's edge, drawing a thin bead of blood. He smiled as the blade parted flesh.

"We need you to move some rocks," he said. "That's all."

Blood dribbled down the blade. Russ was mesmerized by it.

"Now get up." The stranger, Rich, motioned with the rifle. "Follow us. We don't have far to go."

Russ got up and pulled Tina to her feet.

"Or what?" he challenged.

"Or we'll kill you right here. The roots of this forest have drank much blood over the years. Yours will just be the latest to feed them."

Ken pulled alongside one of the storage trailers that were parked at the edge of the field. He left the truck on while he got out to open the trailer door. The engine idled choppily. Waylon Jennings and Willie Nelson rumbled from the truck's speakers, singing about a good-hearted woman in love with a good-timing man. Ken had been a metal-head when he was in school, but as he got older, he found himself gravitating more toward the country music of the seventies. Listening to it reminded him of when he'd been a kid. His father had always liked Willie and Waylon, along with the other outlaws, Johnny Cash and Kris Kristofferson.

The song drifted across the field and into the forest. If anyone heard it, there was no indication. There were other cars parked near the entrance to the Ghost Walk: Russ and Tina's SUV, Tom's Dodge Charger, Cecil's old pickup truck, and Terry's Jeep. Jorge's truck was absent. Ken swore, wondering if Jorge had made it back with the bags of lime he'd sent him for that morning. But despite the vehicles, there were no signs of activity. The forest was silent.

Ken checked his watch. He had two more hours before the other volunteers arrived for the walk-through and staff meeting—and a shitload of things to do before then.

Grumbling to himself, he began unloading the costumes and masks, putting them inside the trailer. The interior was full of items for the Ghost Walk: gas generators, extension cords, lights, tools, spools of rope and wire, plastic sheeting, landscape fencing, dry erase boards and markers, propane bottles, and numerous other odds and ends. He cleared a space for the costume boxes and sat them down. Finished, he exited the trailer and locked the door behind him. Waylon was now asking, "Are you sure Hank done it this way?"

Ken started to hum along, but his song turned to a shout when a hand fell on his shoulder. He spun around, fists raised, and almost punched Terry in the face.

"Jesus Christ," Terry laughed, scampering backward. "Didn't you hear me calling for you?"

"I didn't hear shit," Ken said.

"That's because you play this honky-tonk bullshit too loud, man. Hell, Ken, you're worse than my kid."

"Your kid likes country music?"

"No. But he drives around with that rap music playing loud enough to shake the goddamn windows."

Ken turned his truck off and shut the door. "Better?"

"Much. My eardrums thank you."

"So where is everybody? Jorge make it back with that lime?"

"Yeah. We got it spread. Then him and Tom took off to get something to eat before the staff meeting. They took Jorge's truck."

"Where's Tina and Russ and Cecil?"

Terry shrugged. "Don't know. Tom was working with Cecil for a bit. And Russ and Tina were way back in the woods, near the spot where the trail loops around and starts heading back up here. I haven't seen them for a while. Probably still down there."

"I wish cell phone coverage worked down here," Ken complained, not for the first time. "It would be a lot easier if we could communicate with walkie-talkies or something."

Terry grinned. "Ken, do me a favor?"

"What's that?"

"Take a deep breath and calm the fuck down. You're worrying about everything, and you don't need to. It's fine. This is gonna go off without a hitch. Russ and Tina and even old Cecil are good people and hard workers. If they're not here, then that means they're busting their ass somewhere along the trail."

"I know," Ken agreed. "You're right. It's just . . . I've got this feeling. Like something is going to go wrong."

"That's just the jitters. Only thing that's going to happen is we're going to make a lot of money for charity starting tomorrow night."

"Let's hope so. Speaking of which . . ." Ken climbed back into his truck and grabbed a stack of newspapers. He exited the vehicle, smiling proudly. "Check it out."

"That the article?" Terry took a copy from Ken and flipped it open.

"Front page of the local section, and then it continues on page four. And they've got a photo on the front page of the main section, too."

Terry whistled. "Nice! And look there—she mentioned my name, too."

"Yeah," Ken replied, his tone dry. "Seeing your name in there will really sell tickets."

"Fuck off."

Laughing, they walked toward the entrance to the trail.

"I think we'll have everybody gather right here," Ken said. "That way, everybody can hear me. Then we'll do the walk-through." He glanced up at the sky, and then added, "Might have to do it by flashlight. It's getting darker already. Weird."

"Not really," Terry said. "It's late October. It gets dark early. The days are growing shorter."

Nodding, Ken zipped up his jacket and shivered.

Not only are they getting darker and shorter, he thought. *They're getting colder, too.*

CHAPTER THIRTEEN

Evening rush-hour traffic was in full swing, moving at a crawl along Route 30, through the heart of York County. Construction signs substituted as mile markers. One of Maria's first impressions upon moving from New Jersey was that orange traffic cones seemed to be Pennsylvania's state plant and road workers were the state animal. They were everywhere. Drumming her fingers on the steering wheel, she crept by fast-food restaurants, run-down shopping malls, abandoned industrial complexes, shuttered factories, and dilapidated warehouses. Like the traffic cones, all were part of the natural landscape of this stretch of highway.

She watched, shaking her head in dismay as other drivers talked on their cell phones, applied lipstick and mascara, and in one particularly disturbing case, read a comic book—all while driving. Cursing, Maria gave the finger to no less than five different drivers, for offenses ranging from tailgating to cutting in front of her.

Despite the annoyance, she was actually glad that traffic was moving so slowly. Her head felt foggy from the lack of sleep, and her eyes were red and gummy. It wouldn't do to fall asleep behind the wheel at sixty-five miles per hour. If it happened at the current pace, she could just gently bump into the car ahead of her.

Exhausted as she was, Maria was worried that if she went to bed, she might sleep through her alarm clock's annoyingly shrill wail and miss everything. She still had her doubts that Levi could actually get them face-to-face with Adam Senft, despite everything she'd seen. But if there was a chance, then she wanted to be there. So when she arrived back at her apartment, instead of going to sleep, she made a fresh pot of coffee. While it was brewing, she stripped out of her clothes and took another shower. The combination of caffeine, hot water, and scented body wash stimulated her senses, waking her up. Wrapping herself in two oversized, fluffy towels—one for her body and another for her hair—she decided to log online and check her e-mail.

When she'd left that morning, Maria was certain that she'd hit a dead end as far as tracking down Ramirez, the police detective who'd been involved with the first Adam Senft–connected homicide, as well as the murders of several of Senft's next door neighbors, one of whom had been found inside Senft's home. To her surprise, a new lead on his whereabouts was waiting in her e-mail inbox. Maria subscribed to several different online services that were frequented by journalists and private investigators. For a nominal fee, they would track people when other avenues failed. While she'd been at the psychiatric hospital, they'd found something for her—a new landline phone number supposedly connected to Ramirez, with a Fort Myers, Florida, area code.

Maria checked the clock in the lower right-hand corner of her computer monitor. It was just after six. If Ramirez worked a day job, he should be home by now—if, indeed, this was his home number. Crossing her fingers, Maria snatched her cell phone off the coffee table and dialed. A man picked up on the third ring.

"Hello?"

"Hi. My name is Maria Nasr. I'm calling from—"

"I'm not interested. Take my name and number off your list."

"Wait! Don't hang up."

"I said, I'm not interested."

"I'm not a telemarketer," Maria explained.

"You're a bill collector, then. And I'll tell you what I've told all the others. No, I can't send you any money because I'm fucking broke. I can't pay what I don't have."

Maria took a deep breath, trying to keep her tone patient and friendly.

"Sir, I'm not a telemarketer or a debt collector. If you'll just let me speak?"

"Well, then who the hell are you? The only people that ever call me are bill collectors and salesmen. Or wrong numbers."

"My name is Maria Nasr. I'm calling from York, Pennsylvania. I'm looking for Detective Hector Ramirez."

There was silence on the other end of the line.

"Are you Detective Ramirez?"

"Not anymore. Nobody's called me 'Detective' in a long time. What do you want, Miss Nasr?"

"Well, I'm writing a book about powwow magic and the murders associated with LeHorn's Hollow. I was wondering if I could ask you some questions regarding Adam Senft, the mystery writer."

"Don't you ever call here again."

Maria was so stunned by his vehement reaction that it took her a moment to realize Ramirez was no longer on the line. She glanced at the phone, trying to figure out if the call had been dropped or if he'd disconnected. She guessed the latter.

"Goddamn it."

Maria redialed. This time, Ramirez picked up on the first ring.

"Hello?"

"Mr. Ramirez, I think we might have gotten disconnected. I just—"

"Hell, yes, we got disconnected. That's because I disconnected the call! I mean it, lady. Don't call here again."

"Wait!" Maria shouted before he could hang up again. "Listen, I just want to interview you, sir. I respect your privacy. I'm not out to disparage you over how the case was handled or anything. I'm just curious as to what you believe really happened."

"You want to know what I believe?" Ramirez laughed. "Okay, I'll tell you what I believe. I believe that there are things in this world that don't make a lick of fucking sense. Things that should not be—that we're not supposed to know about. I saw it once during that bank robbery in Hanover, and—"

"Bank robbery?"

"Shut up! It's got nothing to do with your book or the hollow. But it's got everything to do with what I'm saying. I saw it then and I put it behind me. But it fucked with my beliefs—in God and in mankind and in what was real and what wasn't. And then Shannon and Paul Legerski went missing and I canvassed the neighborhood, interviewing potential witnesses and I met Adam Senft. If it hadn't been for that . . ."

Maria stayed quiet, jotting notes while the man rambled. She hoped he'd begin making sense. His cadence was short and clipped. Forceful. It was obvious that this had been festering inside him for quite some time. She got the sense that he wasn't even talking to her anymore.

"That night—the night of the fire. I'll never fucking forget it. How could I? When Senft and his buddies came marching across the field, armed to the teeth with shotguns and spell books, like some blue-collar Van Helsing. Even his dog was in on it. And I helped them. What was I supposed to do? People were dead. Their wives were missing. So I went out there into the woods. Me and Uylik. We went with them. And I was responsible . . . for that officer's death. The trees . . ."

His words turned into unintelligible sobs.

Maria stammered, unsure of how to proceed.

"Um . . . Mr. Ramirez? Hector? I'm afraid that I don't understand."

"The trees were alive! Don't you understand? They fucking moved around. They killed Uylik. And Senft's friend—Swanson. A lot of people died that night. All because of Senft and his goddamned Goat Man."

"But, sir, your own investigation concluded that Adam Senft wasn't involved. The State Police and the district attorney agreed with your determination. Those murders were committed by the LeHorn's Hollow witch cult, of which Paul and Shannon Legerski were members."

"There was no cult. It was a fucking monster! Half man, half goat. And I'm not talking about those murders, anyway. I'm talking about *belief*. What was I supposed to do after I saw all of that? Magic spells and devils and men ripped apart like soft marshmallows. I damn sure wasn't raised to believe in that. So how was I supposed to react? How could I do my fucking job when I knew what was really out there? You asked me about my beliefs? I had them confirmed and then shattered that night. At the same time. Senft, too. Isn't any wonder he killed his wife. He saw her there, around the fire in the woods, rutting in the dirt with that . . . thing."

Confused and frustrated, Maria threw her pen down on the notepad and sighed. Ramirez started crying again.

"I'm afraid I don't understand," she said softly, trying to sound sympathetic.

"You want to understand? You want to believe? Tell you what. Go on down there to the hollow and have a look around. Even now, with it all burned up. You don't even have to go to the heart of it. Just walk around the woods for a bit. You'll believe. And then you'll have that belief sucked away, along with everything you've ever felt. Love. Hate. All your thoughts and emotions and feelings. It will suck them all away and leave you with just darkness inside."

"Mr. Ramirez, what about—"

"Just darkness."

He hung up again. This time, Maria did not call him back.

Depressed, she had the sudden urge to call her mother, but she resisted. Instead, she poured herself another cup of coffee and got ready for the night.

"And over there," Ken said, pointing to a part of the field where a makeshift stage had been constructed, "is where the bands will play. We'll have a local rock band and a hip-hop group from Baltimore here tomorrow night for the afterparty. Subsequent nights will feature country, pop music, and the Red Lion High School marching band. We'll also use the stage to make announcements and such to the crowds while they're waiting to enter the trail."

He paused, surveying the assembled crowd of volunteer staff members. There were over fifty of them, along with private contractors, concession stand operators, a representative for the emergency medical specialists who would be on duty at the site, the farmers handling the hay rides, and dozens of others. He'd never spoken to a crowd this big before and he found it daunting. He'd never been much of a public speaker.

There was still no sign of Cecil, Russ, or Tina. No Sam or Rhonda, either. He searched the crowd, trying to distinguish their faces. Instead, he saw Terry, who smiled at him from the front row, nodding in encouragement to go on.

"Here's how it will work," Ken continued. "When they come in from the road, we'll park them in the designated sections of the field. That's where you folks parked tonight. We can hold up to five hundred vehicles at one time. Hopefully, we won't run out of room—although that would be sort of nice, from a financial perspective."

The crowd laughed, filling Ken with more confidence.

"Those of you on flag duty will collect your orange safety vests and flashlights tomorrow night. Then you'll take your positions. You guys are lucky. You're the only volunteers that get walkie-talkies, because radio and cell phone signals don't work in the forest. So use them to stay in contact with each other. Figure out who has empty spaces and who's full.

"Over here," he pointed, "is where we'll have our concession stands and merchants. I see that some of you are set up already, which is good. The rest of you will want to get here early tomorrow, and take care of your preparations. We're happy to have Bricker's French Fries, Porky's Barbeque, and other local vendors. I'm sure you've seen them at the state fair and local carnivals, so you know how good their food is. All you have to do is look at my waistline to know."

More polite laughter.

"The Golgotha Lutheran Church Ladies' Auxiliary will have a bake sale booth, and the VFW, American Legion, Knights of Columbus, and Lions Club will also be on hand. All of these groups have been kind enough to donate their profits to our cause, so please be sure to thank them. We'll also have some games for the kids, along with a petting zoo and a dunk tank."

"Who gets in the dunk tank?" Tom shouted.

"You do, Tom." Raucous laughter greeted this. Ken grinned, amused. Shielding his eyes against the glare of multiple spotlights, he went on. "No, in all seriousness, we've got a fine slate of volunteers. The principals from Kennard-Dale, Red Lion, and Spring Grove High Schools have all volunteered, along with the chief of police for Windsor Township, the mayor of Wrightsville, and a few other elected officials. Again, all proceeds will go to the charity."

"That's good," a man called, "because I'll spend a hundred bucks to drown the mayor!"

Ken chuckled along with everyone else. When the commotion had subsided, he continued, the last of his nervousness fading.

"People can mill about in the concession area for as long as they like. We'll have a row of portable toilets at the rear of the area. But to actually enter the Ghost Walk, they'll have to line up at the ticket booth. We'll have stanchions and ropes to keep the line orderly and to prevent folks from cutting in. Hopefully, we won't have too much of that sort of thing. Our big concern is people sneaking in through the woods, and to counteract that, we'll have spotters positioned at strategic points along the trail. Their job is twofold. As I said, they'll watch for people who try to get in without paying. But they're also there to protect you. They'll be very easy to recognize—each of them will be wearing a baseball cap that says 'Ghost Walk Staff' in glow-in-the dark letters."

"Yeah," a fat woman yelled, "but then the people sneaking in without paying can see them, too."

"Maybe," Ken conceded, "but we're more concerned with the safety of our staff and volunteers. So if any of you get into trouble—be it an unruly attendee or a bunch of kids messing things up or a medical emergency—find the nearest security spotter and let them know. They'll get a message back up here to operations and we'll help you out. As I said, communications are spotty in the woods, but we've got runners who will do that very thing—run messages back and forth all night long. They'll also bring you coffee, hot chocolate, water, or spot you while you go on a bathroom break."

"What about beer?"

Ken couldn't see the speaker. They were hidden in the glare of the spotlights.

"No alcohol," he said. "We're not going to let people in if they're intoxicated, and we ask the same of our volunteers. You can drink all you want at the afterparty tomorrow night, though. Just make sure you've got a designated driver."

Ken paused, running over his mental checklist to find his place again.

"Once they've bought their ticket and are cued up in line, the hay wagons will bring them down in groups of twelve, with five-minute breaks between groups. That will give all of you on the trail a chance to catch your breath, adjust your costumes, and things like that. It will also help cut down on congestion. As you'll see when we do the walk-through here in a moment, the trail loops around. The exit is about fifty yards from the entrance. We'll have wagons waiting there as well, ready to bring folks back. To walk the entire trail from beginning to end, including a stop at each attraction, will take the average person about forty-five minutes. So although we're going to try to give you breaks in between groups, stay on your toes. I'm sure there will be stragglers."

His cell phone rang, but Ken ignored it.

"A few thoughts on scaring people. Obviously, people who attend a haunted attraction like this enjoy being scared. But we want it to be fun for them, and we want to keep safety in mind. So absolutely under no circumstances should you touch an attendee. Scaring them is fine. Physical contact is not. And be mindful of who you're scaring. If it's a little kid, and they are obviously terrified—not in a good way, you know what I mean—then consider making them feel better. Maybe be funny instead, or act like you're scared of them. Where's Christopher Jones at?"

"Here!"

"Chris, you're playing Leatherface, right?"

"Hell, yeah!"

"Make sure you take the chain off of your chainsaw. The last thing we need is you cutting somebody or tripping over a tree root and hurting yourself. Some of us here remember how you almost cut your finger off field-dressing that spike buck two years ago."

"You just *had* to bring that up, didn't you, Ken?"

"Well, we made fun of Tom earlier. Gotta spread the love, brother."

The throng laughed again, but Ken could tell by watching the first few rows that they were getting restless. He decided to wrap things up and get on with the walk-through, before he lost them.

"Okay!" He raised his voice a little, commanding their

attention once more. "That's about all I have. Any questions before we begin the walk?"

A dozen hands shot up.

Ken sighed. It was going to be a long night.

CHAPTER FOURTEEN

Maria parked at a twenty-four-hour convenience store about a block and a half away from the White Rose Mental Health Facility. This section of town was still relatively unscathed by crime and drugs, so she felt safe walking the distance. The sidewalks were clean and in good shape, free of cracks or holes. The streets were lined with sprawling elm trees and bright streetlights, and the old houses were neat and tidy, populated mostly by retirees or converted into professional offices for doctors and lawyers. Many of them were decorated for Halloween. Paper cutouts of witches and ghosts hung in the windows. Pumpkins sat on porches and stoops, carved in a wide array of designs—everything from smiley faces to demons to something that resembled Pac-Man. Some of the homes had dried cornstalks or varieties of squash and melons arranged in tasteful displays. One home even had strings of orange Christmas lights strung all over the exterior.

She looked for Levi's buggy as she stepped onto the sidewalk, but didn't see it. Was he here yet? Although she didn't know much about his personal life, he struck her as the type of person who'd be punctual. Still, there was no sign of the buggy—or of Dee. Levi couldn't have been stupid enough to park it at the psychiatric hospital, could he? That would surely attract unwelcome attention.

She still had no idea what he intended to do. "Open the door"? Did that mean they were breaking in? Did he know a back entrance, perhaps unguarded and unlocked? No, that was impossible. She was sure that whatever Levi's plan was, it involved some form of magic. That's why he'd been so secretive and vague. He was probably worried it would sound far-fetched to her, despite everything else that had happened today.

Maria shook her head in disbelief. What a day it had been. This morning, the world had looked very much the same as it always had; now, things were different. She still didn't totally believe in powwow or magic or sorcery or whatever Levi wanted to call it, but neither could she remain skeptical any longer.

She yawned, wishing she'd brought along another cup of coffee. The earlier rejuvenating effects of the hot shower and caffeine were starting to wear off. Worse, she doubted there would be time for sleep anytime soon. If Levi actually got them a sit-down with Senft, she'd have to transcribe her rough notes while they were still fresh in her head. It would probably be another long night.

Maria approached the hospital from the rear, cutting behind a dentist's office and then across a vacant field. She moved safely under the cover of darkness. There was a thick cloud cover sliding over the moon, and although the psychiatric hospital's parking lot had sodium lights, their radiance didn't reach beyond the lot itself. She crept through the underbrush, alert, pulse throbbing in her throat.

It was so murky that she didn't even see Levi until he spoke.

"You made it."

Maria yelped, barely biting back a scream.

Levi shushed her. He was hiding in a thicket of vines and

small trees, concealed in shadow. The only thing she could see clearly was his hat, silhouetted against a brief ray of moonlight.

"Jesus fucking Christ," Maria gasped, crouching down beside him and trying to catch her breath. "You scared the hell out of me, Levi."

"Language. I may not be Amish anymore, but that doesn't mean I approve of or enjoy hearing you take the Lord's name in vain."

"Well, I'm sorry, but you shouldn't have surprised me like that."

"I apologize. But if I, as you said, scared the Hell out of you, then that's a good thing. The purer we are, the better our chances of defeating this."

Maria bristled. "Are you saying I'm not pure?"

He didn't respond. Maria peered closer and realized that he was grinning.

"You're just messing with me again, aren't you, Levi?"

"Yes. Just playing off your words. Sorry about that. But in truth, purity does add strength to our fight. And by purity, I don't mean being a goody two-shoes. I'm just talking about a healthy body, mind, and spirit. Righteousness. A sense of self-assuredness and confidence. Making the universe revolve around you—understanding that you are the focal point of all that occurs."

"That doesn't sound like purity."

"But it is, in a sense. Being pure in thoughts and deeds means never second-guessing or doubting them. Knowing that what you're doing is right and having the determination to see it through. That's the kind of purity I'm talking about."

Maria nodded in fake understanding and decided to change the subject. "So where's Dee?"

"I left her stabled at home. I thought the buggy might attract too much attention at this time of night."

The clouds parted again, revealing the moon. Light spilled

into the thicket. In front of the building, out on the street, a car drove by, bass-heavy music reverberating from the speakers.

"So how did you get here, then?" Maria asked.

Levi smiled. "By other means. Did you get any sleep?"

"No. How about you?"

"I meditated for a bit, but you can't really call that sleep. Mostly, I just read. Studied. Prepared."

"Like cramming for an exam?"

Levi shrugged. "I guess. I don't know for sure. I never had to do that."

"Amish have schools, too. You never had to stay up late studying for tests?"

"There was no time. We had chores to do. If we got a chance to sleep, then we took it."

They fell silent for a moment, watching the building. Although a few lights burned, most of the windows were dark. There was no signs of activity or movement.

"Seriously," Maria whispered. "How did you get here?"

"I told you—by other means of transportation."

"Magic?"

"No. A taxi cab. I had the driver drop me off several blocks from here and then I walked. I forgot my deodorant, so you might not want to get too close. How about you?"

"I parked a few blocks away, too. But I remembered to put on my deodorant."

"Now *you're* messing with *me*."

"Hey, turnabout is fair play. And besides, we're a team. Remember?"

"That we are. Are you ready?"

Maria shrugged. "I guess."

Levi took a deep breath, held it, and then exhaled.

"Before we go any farther," he said, "I have to say something. Regardless of whether you believe or not, you must do as I say from this point on. If you question or falter, it could be very dangerous for us both. Okay?"

"We're not going to kill a chicken or anything like that, are we?"

"Not for this ritual, no."

"Okay, then we're agreed."

"Good. That's a relief. We're going to open a doorway tonight. Remember when I told you that there were ways to enter the Labyrinth and cross space and time, like Nelson LeHorn did?"

"Yeah."

"Well, this is something different. We don't want to travel to another world or dimension. We want to transport someone from one point to another right here. On our Earth. To do that, we're going to create a shortcut—a temporary hole in the Labyrinth's fabric. That's not really what it is, but it's the easiest way to explain it. In any case, we must be quick and sure and cautious. And very, *very* careful."

"Why?"

"Because we don't want anything else using the doorway. And because we don't want it getting wider or becoming permanent. That would be very bad."

Levi's demeanor had changed. He seemed more solemn. Finished speaking, he reached behind a thorny bush and pulled out a wicker basket.

"Are we having a picnic?" Maria whispered.

Levi lifted a finger to his lips, silencing her. His eyes conveyed seriousness. He reached into his pocket and pulled out a compass. After consulting it, he nodded. Then he glanced upward.

"Good," he said. "We're facing north and there are no tree limbs hanging directly over our heads. We can begin."

Maria watched as Levi opened the wicker basket and pulled out a container of salt. She recognized the brand; the same kind was in her kitchen cupboard. Levi poured the salt all around them in a circle, emptying the container. Then he sat down cross-legged in the center of the circle and indicated that she should do the same. Her joints popped as she followed.

"Whatever happens," he told her, "do not go beyond this circle. This is important. Don't reach beyond it. Don't stretch beyond it, not even the tip of your toe. Don't even spit beyond it. Nothing must break the circle. Do you understand?"

"Yes."

Nodding, he reached into the wicker basket again and pulled out a red cloth. He spread the fabric out on the ground in front of them, smoothing the wrinkles with his palms. Then he pulled more items out of the basket: a small copper bowl, four red candles, a chrome cigarette lighter, a broken, collectible silver spoon with a sharp, jagged edge, and a small bottle of shampoo—the kind usually offered as an amenity at hotels. Maria started to make a joke, but then thought better of it. Levi lined up each of the items on the cloth, placing the candles at four different positions— north, south, east and west. He sat the copper bowl directly in front of him and then picked up the tiny shampoo bottle. When he unscrewed the lid, Maria smelled a pleasant, aromatic scent—some type of oil, rather than shampoo. She tried to place it, but couldn't. It smelled a bit like sandalwood, but heavier, more musty. Levi poured the oil into the bowl, careful not to spill any. The bouquet grew stronger, filling the air around them. He screwed the cap back on the bottle and placed it inside the basket. He retrieved one final item from the basket: a piece of white paper with strange symbols and a series of letters drawn on it. Maria tried to read the words, but they were nonsensical—strings of vowels with no consonants, and vice versa. He laid the paper directly above the bowl of oil. Then he lit each candle and bowed his head. Maria did the same. When he spoke again, in a strong, authoritative tone, she wasn't sure he was talking to her.

"I have fasted according to the Nomos, which is the Law,

and have eaten none which is unclean and have drank only water. I have avoided spilling my seed and have abstained from worshipping at the temples of Ishtar or Lilith. Thus, I have kept my essence and remained pure for thee."

Maria almost giggled when Levi mentioned spilling his seed, but managed to remain quiet.

"My lanterns are of the appropriate and required color. With them I have cast light upon the four Gates of the Earth, and have done so with only the guidance of the moon. I face the Northern Gate. There is no roof or lamp above my head, save for the sky. I have done these things in accordance with the Nomos, which is the Law. And thus, I command thy attention."

Pausing, Levi picked up the broken silver spoon and placed the sharp edge against the ball of his thumb. Maria shuddered, biting her lip to keep from crying out as he pressed the silver into his flesh, slicing his thumb. He didn't flinch or moan, gave no indication that he'd felt it. He held the wound over the copper bowl and squeezed three drops of his blood into the oil. As each drop fell, he repeated the same phrase:

"*Ia unay vobism Huitzilopochtli. Ia dom tergo Hathor.*"

Maria tried to decipher the words. Some of them sounded Aztec or Mayan in origin. Others sounded Egyptian. And the rest seemed like total gibberish. She remembered what Levi had told her about the *Daemonolateria*. She'd commented that it sounded like Latin, and he'd corrected her, saying it was from a language that didn't exist on Earth.

Humming, Levi held his thumb against his pants leg until the bleeding had stopped, and then he continued.

"I sit in the appropriate and required manner, safe inside a circle of protection. You may not molest me. I come here to open a gate. I come with awe and respect. I come seeking passage. I call upon the Gatekeeper, who gave to us the Nomos, which is the Law. I call upon the Doorman, who is the Burning Bush and the Hand That Writes and the Watchman and the Sleepwalker. I call upon he who is called Huitzilopochtli and Ahtu. He who is called Nephrit-ansa and Sopdu. He who is called Hathor and Nyarlathotep. I call upon he who's real name is Amun. And thus, by naming thee and offering my blood thrice, I command an opening."

Levi reached into the basket again and pulled out a worn paperback. The spine was cracked and a sales sticker from the used paperback store was affixed to the creased corner. The book was *When the Rain Comes* by Adam Senft. He held the book over the north-facing candle. It smoldered, then caught fire. He then placed the flaming paperback on top of the copper bowl. Smoke curled out from around its edges. The bowl's contents must have been flammable because the fire quickly flared. The scent of burning oil became almost overpowering. Levi's voice grew louder.

"This is the avatar of the one I seek. By following the Law and naming thee, I command you grant him safe passage to this place. He may not be harmed or molested by those who dwell between the walls or within the halls, or the denizens of Heaven nor Hell, or the realms between them, or the Thirteen, or the things that live in the wastes beyond the levels. Nor may he end up wandering and lost in that realm beyond the Labyrinth, in which there are no exits save death. I command thee, and so shall it be."

Levi breathed a heavy sigh and then sat up straight. His body stiffened, his shoulders tense and rigid. His eyes remained fixed on the burning book. Maria's legs were beginning to cramp. She started to stir, but Levi held up his hand, silencing her. Keeping still, she watched the flickering fire expand as it consumed paper and oil and blood. A plume of smoke curled lazily from the ashes. At its base, the fire remained only as wide as the mouth of the bowl, but the flames reaching into the air grew taller and wider. First a foot, then two. Maria shrank away from it. She felt the heat, smelled the singed hair on her arms. It didn't seem to affect Levi. Beads of sweat ran out from under the brim of his hat and into his eyes, yet he remained motionless, unblinking.

His attention was focused on the fire.

It blazed higher. Impossibly so. Despite the diminutive bowl and the spare amount of fuel therein, the fire towered far over their heads. The flames changed color—first yellow, then orange, then a deep red. The smoke dissipated, leaving only fire. Maria leaned forward slightly and peered into the bowl. The oil and paper were gone, yet still the fire burned, even without any combustible fuel. The flames turned green. Instead of crackling, the fire hissed. Still, Levi did not move. Maria reached out and grabbed his arm, but he brushed her away. Reluctantly, she turned back to the blaze.

There was movement in the center of the emerald flames. As Maria watched, a scene unfolded, as if the fire was a window looking out on somewhere else—the interior of a small room. She saw grayish-white, featureless walls, devoid of paintings or fixtures. The flames expanded, revealing more of the room. There were three more walls, a yellow-tiled floor, and a single, heavily barred window. The details were stark and clear. To her amazement, she could see through the window. Maria realized it was looking out on the hospital's parking lot, directly at the spot where she'd been sitting earlier that morning.

The room was empty of furnishings. A naked lightbulb hung suspended from the ceiling. A lone iron-framed bed sat in the corner against one bleak wall. A man lay on the bed, sleeping. He was covered in a single sheet and gray blanket. As they watched, he sat up, rubbing and blinking his eyes. Then he looked directly at them. His expression was one of astonished disbelief.

He can see us, Maria thought. *Just like we can see him.*

She recognized the man right away. Two years had passed. He looked different than he had in the newspaper clippings and his dust jacket photo. His face was lined and haggard and his once-thick hair had been shaved down to stubble. He'd lost weight. His wrists were twigs and his cheekbones stood out at sharp angles beneath his skin. His goatee, once neatly trimmed and jet-black in the pictures on the inside back cover of his books, was now wiry and washed with white. Not gray, but pure white. But it was his eyes that had changed the most. In photographs, his eyes had always hinted of amusement, or perhaps mischief.

Now, Adam Senft's eyes just seemed haunted.

Maria felt a sudden wave of sadness, but didn't know why.

Adam ran his hand across the top of his head, gaping at them. His mouth moved, but he made no sound.

"Mr. Senft," Levi said, "please don't be alarmed. We're here to help you."

The author's voice drifted out of the flames, faint and far-away. "Y-you . . . this is . . . but I'm awake. They said the medicine would stop this. I'm dreaming."

"You are not dreaming, Adam. I assure you of that. But you must listen to me. We are here to help you. We can get you free. But you have to hurry. The gateway won't stay open for long. Can you move?"

"Y-y-yes . . ."

"Then step through the door," Levi urged. "Quickly!"

"You—you're Amish."

"Not really. It's a long story."

"Do you drive a horse and buggy?"

Levi paused. "Yes. But I don't see what—"

"Why do you drive a buggy if you're not Amish?"

"The price of gas has increased quite a bit since you went into this institution. We're at war. But that's not important right now."

"Why not? It's my dream, right? I get to make up the rules."

"Please," Levi pleaded. "We know what really happened to you. We know about Hylinus and Nelson LeHorn."

Adam cringed, pressing himself against the wall.

"My father was Amos Stoltzfus," Levi said into the flames. "Do you recognize that name?"

Senft's stutter had returned. "H-he was one of LeHorn's p-peers."

"That is correct. And I am his son. I believe your story, Adam. So does my friend here."

"Nobody believes me," Adam sighed, lying back down on the bed. "They don't understand."

"We believe you," Levi insisted. "But it's not over in LeHorn's Hollow, and unless you want what happened to you to happen to others, you'll come with us. We need your help. I can't do this without you. Now hurry!"

Maria heard the rising panic in Levi's voice. Then she noticed that the flames were starting to shrink again.

Adam sat up again, staring at them. Then he shrugged.

"I've read a bit about lucid dreaming. I guess if I don't like where this is going, then I can just change it. Wake myself up again. Right?"

"That's fine," Levi nearly shouted in exasperation. "Just hurry up. Come through the door."

The flames continued to die down, now flickering at a level even with their heads.

Adam put on a pair of slippers and got out of bed. He approached the portal with caution, slowly reaching out his hand. He reached through it tentatively. When he wasn't burned, he stepped inside . . .

. . . and walked out into the circle of protection, nearly knocking Maria and Levi over. Adam toppled, losing his balance. Still sitting cross-legged, Levi reached for him. Adam pulled away, heading for the edge of the circle. His foot hovered over the line of salt.

"No," Levi shouted. "Don't break the—"

Adam stepped out into the thicket. Immediately, the flames changed color again, burning black against the darkness. The scene inside the fire changed, no longer showing Senft's room. Instead, it looked like the surface of another planet. Boulders and red sand covered the desolate landscape. The rocks looked like they were *rotting,* as if they were organic. Something beyond their view roared. The noise wasn't audible. Maria heard it in her mind.

"What the hell is that?" she screamed. "Is that what we're fighting? The thing with no name?"

"No!" Levi shouted. "That's something else. Hold on!"

She stared, transfixed, terrified but unable to look away as the doorway widened. The roar ceased. She felt the air around them rush past her as it was sucked into the rift. Her hair fluttered and her thin gold necklace began to writhe around her neck, slowly defying the law of gravity. The candles wobbled, the flames flickering but not going out, despite the strong wind. The alien landscape grew clearer. A dark mountain range towered over the red desert. Some of the cliff faces looked carved. She studied them closer, and was suddenly dizzy. Like some otherworldly Mount Rushmore, one of the mountainsides had been turned into statues. But instead of four famous presidents, these figures represented something monstrous and obscene. Tearing her gaze away from the creatures, Maria saw a metallic flash on the horizon, just at the foot of the mountains.

"What's that?" she screamed again, pointing at the silver object.

Gritting his teeth, Levi lashed out with his foot and knocked the copper bowl over.

He shouted, "*Ut nemo in sense tentat, descendere nemo! At precedenti spectaur mantica tergo! Ia Amun traust nodrog! Amun, Amun, Amun!*"

The flames vanished, along with everything else. Levi leaned back on his elbows, breathing heavily.

"What the hell was that metallic thing?" Maria asked again.

"That," Levi gasped, "was your tax dollars at work—one of the robotic rovers that NASA abandoned on Mars. Judging from its position and the surrounding landscape, I'd guess it was the Mars Pathfinder."

"Mars? But there were statues! There aren't any statues on Mars."

"Well, that's what it was." Levi nodded toward Adam. "And this is the man that almost got us killed."

Adam shrugged. "Like I said—lucid dreaming."

"Mr. Senft." Levi slowly got to his feet and extinguished the candles. "What you just did—the damage you caused . . . Well, let's just say I'll be paying for that sooner or later. Hopefully later, at the end of my days."

"I don't understand."

"Consider yourself lucky for that small blessing. Let me assure you that this is no dream. We're playing with lives here. Yours, hers and mine. That was a Sumerian spell and—"

"I know," Adam interrupted. "I know. The green fire and the portal—I recognize them from one of LeHorn's books."

"So you did have all of his books, then?" Levi asked.

"Not all of them. Just his copy of *The Long Lost Friend*. And his journal. And parts of another book—just pages, really. Everything else got burned up in the fire."

He hung his head and shuffled toward them.

"I know this isn't a dream," he said, bursting into tears. "And I know I'm not crazy. What I am is fucking scared! I miss my wife and I just want some fucking peace, and I don't want to go through this shit again. Can you help me? Please?"

"Yes," Levi whispered. "We can help you. And more importantly, you can help us."

"How?"

"All in good time."

"Don't play that Phantom Stranger bullshit on me, man."

"First, let's get you away from here. I'm sure they check on patients throughout the night?"

Adam nodded. "Yeah, they do. Fucking Schmidt—he's one of the orderlies—peeks in through the door windows all night long. Shines his flashlight in and wakes us up. He thinks it's funny."

"Is he on duty now?"

"Yeah. He's one of the overnighters. A real jackass. Messes with us all the time."

"Well, let's get you out of here before he notices you're

missing." Levi studied Adam's cotton drawstring pants and short-sleeved, pullover shirt. Both were a bland shade of green. They looked like pajamas, and the institution's name was stenciled across the back in big, black letters. "And I suppose we'll need to find you some clothes."

"Are we taking my car?" Maria asked. It was the first time she'd spoken since the fire had gone out. She'd been unable to find her voice—afraid that if she opened her mouth, she might start screaming, or worse yet, crying. She'd never been more terrified in her life. This was real. No more doubts. No more questions. Levi had ripped a hole in the fucking air. A hole made of fire. And Adam Senft had stepped through it. It was magic, plain and simple. The proof was standing directly in front of her. She felt dizzy and nauseous and her arms and legs tingled as if asleep. She'd just been confronted by something she didn't believe in, and her convictions had been found wanting. She was afraid to breathe, afraid to blink, worried that if she did, something else might happen.

"Yes," Levi said, retrieving the rest of his items and putting them back in the basket. "Can we reach it without attracting attention, or do you think you should go get it while I hide Mr. Senft here?"

"Wait a second." Adam held up his hands. "Look, don't think I'm not grateful. You got me out of there, and I appreciate it. You've got no idea just how much. But I'm not going anywhere with you until I know exactly who you both are. You said you were Amos Stoltzfus's son?"

Levi picked up the wicker basket. "That's right. You may call me Levi."

"And you do powwow, just like your old man and Nelson LeHorn did."

Levi nodded. "Yes, among other disciplines."

"No fucking kidding. I'm pretty sure what you just did wasn't powwow." Adam turned to Maria. "And who are you?"

"Maria Nasr." She held out her hand. "I'm a freelance

writer, currently putting together a book proposal on the hollow and the LeHorn murders."

Adam frowned. "You said murders. Plural. But Nelson LeHorn only killed his wife."

Maria paused. "Well, as I'm sure you know, there are other murders connected to the hollow."

"So you're writing about me, too? Me and Tara?"

"I . . ." Maria turned her eyes to the ground.

"You're just another scavenger," Adam accused. "Trying to make a buck from someone else's pain and suffering."

"No," Maria insisted. "It's not like that."

"Please," Levi said. "We can discuss all of this later, after we've gotten clear of the area. If they find us now, we're all in trouble. We've got more important things to worry about."

He turned to Adam.

"You said you wanted our help. We can give you that. Others can only imagine the pain you're feeling. The things you've been through. But I don't have to imagine them. I move in that world every day. Let me help you."

"You said you needed my help, too."

"I do," Levi agreed. "Hylinus and the tree-spirits weren't the only dangers in LeHorn's Hollow. Something else is there now—an entity more powerful than either of those. It's forcing its way into our world and if we don't stop it by tomorrow night, then the horrors you faced will pale in comparison to what will happen to all life on this planet."

"Jesus . . ." Adam rubbed his shaved head. "What can I do? I don't have any special abilities. I don't know any magic. Not anything useful, at least. All I did was fool around with those books we took from LeHorn's house."

"That's how you can help," Levi said. "The police never obtained LeHorn's copy of *The Long Lost Friend*. It was still in your possession at the time of your arrest, but it was never logged into evidence, nor was it found by the family who moved into your old home since then."

"A-another family lives there now?" Adam's voice cracked.

"I'm sorry," Levi apologized. "You hid the book, didn't you?"

Adam nodded, his mouth working soundlessly.

"And these loose pages you mentioned—do you remember if some of them were inside the book?"

"Yeah," Adam sighed. "About a half dozen of them, actually."

Levi arched his eyebrows, surprised at this revelation, but he stayed quiet.

"They weren't part of the book," Adam continued, "but I kept them anyway. Didn't understand a word of them, but they were sort of interesting to look at. There were some pretty gruesome drawings on them. That's why I recognized that thing you did with the fire."

"Thank you, Lord," Levi whispered. "Your name be praised."

"Excuse me?" Adam blinked.

"Do you remember where you hid the book?"

"Sure."

"I need those pages, Mr. Senft."

"Call me Adam. And that's it? That's all you need—the papers? That's all I need to do to help?"

"Yes, Adam," Levi said. "Just that, and one other thing."

"What's that?"

If Levi heard him, he gave no indication. Instead, he began leading them out of the underbrush and into the field. Maria heard him muttering to himself.

"A necessary evil . . ."

"Levi," she called. "Wait up."

They followed the magus into the field, stepping out into the night.

CHAPTER FIFTEEN

It was almost midnight when the last of the Ghost Walk's volunteers drove away. Ken, Terry, and Tom McNally stood in the center of the field, watching the taillights fade as the departing workers pulled out onto the road. The wide-open area now seemed very empty. The sudden silence was unsettling. In the darkness, it was easier to understand why the forest spooked some people.

"There's still no sign of Cecil," Tom said. "Unless he was here and I didn't see him?"

Terry and Ken looked at each other and then shook their heads.

"I didn't see him," Terry said. "How about you?"

"Me either," Ken agreed. "Although, with the spotlights and everything, it was kind of hard for me to pick people out of the crowd. You're sure he didn't tell you where he was going, Tom?"

"Nope. And his truck is still here. Don't know how else he would have gotten home. Guess he could have caught a ride with someone else. But it seems like he would have at least told me first."

All three of them glanced toward the parking area. Sure enough, Cecil's old pickup truck was still sitting in the same spot, alongside Tom's Dodge Charger, Terry's Jeep, Ken's truck, and Russ and Tina's SUV. The thin moonlight reflected off the vehicles.

"Russ and Tina's Chevy is still here, too," Ken observed. "Anybody seen them?"

Terry frowned. "Now that you mention it, no. What the hell is going on? First Sam and Rhonda. Now this."

Ken shook his head. He had a sinking feeling in his gut. The ground started to spin, so he closed his eyes. He had never been wearier.

"Maybe they're still in the woods," Tom suggested. "We should look. I keep imagining Cecil lying out there after having a heart attack or something. Last time I saw him, he was going off into the woods to piss."

"Yeah," Ken agreed, looking up again. "Terry, go grab some flashlights. We're not leaving here until we find them. Tom, while he's doing that, call their houses. See if they're home, just in case they got a ride with someone else. And call Tina's cell phone, too."

"If she's in the woods, it won't work."

"Call it anyway. It's worth a try."

"Whatever you say, Ken."

"Hold on a minute," Terry said. "Look, Ken. You've been up for how many hours?"

"I don't know."

"I do. You look like death warmed over, man. We've got a big day tomorrow and an even longer night, and you're gonna have to be on top of your game. An operation this size— there's going to be a million little things that need your attention tomorrow night. You need some rest, before shit starts catching up with you."

"Like what?"

"Like that cop, for instance. Did you remember to call him back?"

"I did. Got his voice mail and left him a message."

"And when did you finally remember?"

Ken paused. "After the walk-through tonight."

"That's my point. You're tired, Ken, and you're starting to slip. Now, I know you're worried about Cecil. We all are. And we're concerned about Russ and Tina, too, although I'm willing to bet they're okay. It's this place. These woods, and all the bullshit history that goes with them. It just has us a little spooked. Chances are they're fine. But just in case, Tom and I will go look for them. You go home and get some sleep. You need it worse than we do."

"Screw that," Ken said. "I'm not going anywhere until we know what—"

"Go home and get some fucking sleep," Terry ordered, raising his voice. Then he softened it again. "If we find anything—if something bad really has happened—I'll call you right away. I promise. But as worn out as you are, you'll be helping everybody a lot more if you just get some rest. We need you sharp, man. This is your show. Tom and me can handle this."

"Damn straight," Tom agreed. "In truth, I'm betting old Cecil is just lying up against some tree, drunk as a skunk or passed out. He's always carrying that flask around with him. Drinking that frigging cheap-ass gin. Hell, could be Russ and Tina are out there with him."

Ken rubbed his chin, lost in thought.

"Go home," Terry urged him. "Please? You're exhausted. We've got this."

Ken hesitated. "You promise you'll call me if something's wrong?"

"I promise." Terry nodded. "Have I ever lied to you?"

"Yeah. In the eleventh grade, when you told me you hadn't slept with Alicia Hartlaub on prom night."

Terry groaned. "You're never gonna let me forget that one, are you?"

"Hell, no. She was *my* prom date, man."

"And she was good."

"Fucker."

"Get going." Terry punched Ken's shoulder. "I'll call you if something's happened."

"Okay. Good night. And you guys be careful."

"We will," Terry promised.

"See you tomorrow," Tom said, waving.

Ken walked off to his pickup truck. They watched him go. His head hung low and his shoulders were slumped. He weaved back and forth slightly, as if he were drunk.

"Jesus," Tom whispered. "You were right. He really is beat."

Terry nodded. "His ass is dragging, all right."

Ken's headlights came on and the engine thrummed. They heard the distant strains of Jerry Reed belting out "Eastbound and Down," the theme from *Smokey and the Bandit*. Ken sang along with him. Then Ken tooted his horn and pulled away. They gave him a final wave and then walked toward the storage trailers. As they crossed the field, Tom tried calling Cecil while Terry called Russ and Tina's house.

"Anything?" Terry asked.

"No. If he's there, he ain't answering. How about you?"

"I got their answering machine. I didn't leave a message, though. Don't want to worry their kids just yet. Let's check the trail first."

"Glad I ate something earlier," Tom said. "This might take a while."

"Listen, did you take off work tomorrow?"

"No."

"Well, shit, Tom! Why don't you go on home, too? I can handle this by myself."

"No, you can't. And besides, I don't have to be at my desk until nine. I got time."

"Okay, if you're sure. This might be a wild-goose chase, but I appreciate the help. Ghost Walk or not, those woods are kind of creepy after dark."

"Terry, do you really think they're okay?"

"Do you really think Cecil is laying out there drunk?"

"No. I wish I did, but I don't. This just isn't like him at all. I think something's happened."

"So do I. I'm not sure why. Maybe it's those kids going missing, or maybe I'm just tired, too. Or maybe it's these fucking woods. But I'm starting to get a bad feeling."

"Me, too," Tom said. "You think maybe we should call the cops?"

"Not yet," Terry said. "I mean, maybe we should. But I want to hold off. This time tomorrow night, we'll be open. The last thing we need right now is law enforcement and search parties traipsing through the woods."

"That's pretty harsh."

Terry shrugged. "I don't like it either. Hell, Russ and Tina are friends of mine, and old Cecil seems like a good guy. But I've got other responsibilities to think about, too. Ken's been my best friend since high school. A lot of folks drift apart after they graduate, but that never happened with us. He's like a brother to me. This Ghost Walk means the world to him. It's the first time I've seen him excited about anything since Deena died. If the cops suspect foul play, they could shut us down before we even open. That would kill him. Not to mention the negative publicity."

"You don't reckon the police think we had anything to do with this?"

"No," Terry admitted. "Probably not. But you never know. And if those fucking reporters start sniffing around and asking lots of questions, Ken's not going to be able to deal with it. Not right now, on top of everything else. He's got other shit to worry about."

"Not necessarily. He handled that girl from the newspaper pretty well."

"Yeah, but she was just writing a fluff piece. Look, I don't like it any more than you do. And you're right. My gut tells me we should call the authorities right now. We probably *should* let someone know. It's the right thing to do. But humor me just a little bit longer. Let's have one last look ourselves. If we don't find them, then we'll call somebody. At least this way, Ken will get some sleep before we wake him up."

"I guess you're right."

They retrieved two high-powered flashlights from the storage trailer. Terry grabbed a first-aid kit, as well.

"Think we'll need that?" Tom asked.

"It's just a precaution."

As an afterthought, Terry stuffed two road flares into his jacket pocket.

"Another precaution?" Tom's expression was grim.

"Yeah," Terry said. "If they *are* hurt—and I hope to fucking hell that we're wrong about that—and one of us has to come back up here to call 911, then the other one can light up these flares so the paramedics can find us easily. Especially if we're off the trail."

"That's good thinking."

"Let's just hope we don't need them."

Terry and Tom began the long hike across the field, heading toward the forest. They zipped up their jackets against the late-night chill and slipped on their leather work gloves to keep their hands warm. The high weeds were wet with dew and their pants quickly became soaked below the knees. Neither spoke much. They were too tired, too cold. Too apprehensive. They tried once again to reassure each other that they were probably overreacting, but secretly, both men were becoming more and more convinced with each passing moment that something was seriously wrong. Their fear grew as they neared the forest, as if the darkness magnified it. Unlike the moonlit field, the woods were draped in shadow. They turned on their flashlights. The beams only penetrated a few yards beyond the trees. Somewhere in the branches overhead, a bird cried out. Both men jumped.

"First bird I've heard out here in a while," Terry whispered.

"That was a whip-poor-will," Tom said.

"Oh, yeah? That a good thing?"

"My granddaddy used to say that if you heard a whip-poor-will, it was waiting to carry away someone's soul."

"Now there's a cheerful fucking thought."

"Well, he was drunk most of the time. Used to piss in a coffee can. Nasty old fucker, but I loved him just the same."

"I think," Terry said, "I liked it better when we weren't talking."

Snickering, they stepped into the forest. Their laughter dried up beneath the trees.

"It's dark in here," Tom said. "I can barely see the lime."

"Yeah."

"Want to try calling them one more time?"

"No," Terry said. "Let's get this over with."

Walking side by side, they started down the trail.

Maria drove the speed limit, repeatedly checking the rearview mirror for police. She fully expected to see red and blue lights flashing behind them at any second. After all, she was driving with an escaped mental patient in her car. She knew she was probably being silly. Nobody had seen them. But her nervousness remained.

Levi was in the passenger seat and Adam sprawled out in the back. He'd been nervous at first, still unsure about his new companions. But he'd warmed up considerably by the time they reached Interstate 83. Maria had turned the radio on and Adam reacted with joy. He'd told them that he wasn't allowed to have a radio inside the psychiatric hospital. The only music he'd had access to was whatever the facility's staff played over the loudspeaker—light jazz or easy listening music, depending on who was on duty. Maria tuned in his favorite station.

He stared out the window as they headed south, bobbing his head to the music and watching with interest as the landscape zoomed by.

"I didn't think I'd ever see any of this again," he murmured. "But it's still here. All of it."

"Did you think it would all just go away?" Maria asked. "That it would cease to exist just because you couldn't see it anymore?"

"Maybe. Inside that place, I didn't know what to think. They fucked with my head pretty bad. Put me on a bunch of different medicines and into daily psychotherapy sessions. They said I needed to face what I'd done. Come to terms with it."

Maria glanced over at Levi. He hadn't commented. Instead, he sat with his eyes closed and his hands folded in his lap. His hat was pulled low. She assumed he was meditating.

"They said I had to face my inner demons." Adam's voice cracked. "Face what happened. Why Tara really died."

"Well," Maria said, trying to sound upbeat, "I guess that's a healthy form of therapy, right?"

"Healthy? You don't understand."

"I'm trying to."

"Let me give you an example. There was a woman inside named Karen Moore. I knew her from before. We went to the same high school. She graduated a year ahead of me and was friends with this girl I used to date named Becky Schrum. In 1984, Karen was abducted and raped by a cemetery caretaker. He killed her boyfriend, Pat. Slaughtered him right in front of her. You're young, but maybe you heard about it?"

"No," Maria said. "I moved here from New Jersey just a few years ago."

"Well, Karen and another woman were held in an underground warren. They were both raped repeatedly by this guy. Karen ended up pregnant from it. Nine months later, she went nuts. Had a total breakdown. Karen was convinced that her baby was half human and half monster. A ghoul. That's what she kept insisting—that she was pregnant with a ghoul."

Maria didn't respond.

"I know what you're thinking," Adam said. "Sounds familiar, doesn't it? Just like me and Tara? The crazy writer guy insisted that his wife was pregnant with a satyr? Well, maybe. But think about this. They made Karen confront her inner demons, and you know what happened? Karen had her whole life ahead of her. And instead of living it, she's spent the last twenty-five years in a fucking insane asylum. Her baby went to live in an orphanage. No happy endings for either of them. That's what happens when you confront your monsters. The monsters win. And I'm not going to do that. I know what really happened. I know I'm not crazy."

"Calm down, Adam," Maria said. "I didn't say you were."

"What do you care, anyway? I'm just material for your fucking book."

They drove on in silence. Levi remained quiet and motionless. His breathing was shallow. Maria wondered if he'd fallen asleep.

"Levi?"

He didn't answer.

"Wonderful." She turned up the radio and focused on the highway.

Once they reached the Shrewsbury exit, Levi became alert again, and apologized for his silence. On his suggestion, they stopped at the twenty-four-hour Wal-Mart. Adam told Maria his pants and shoe sizes. Then, while Levi and Adam waited in the car, Maria went inside and purchased him some new clothes—jeans, T-shirt, pullover sweatshirt with a hood, socks and underwear, and a pair of shoes. She also selected a ball cap and a pair of sunglasses. Word of Adam's escape would break soon enough. They might as well try to disguise him. At the register, while she stood waiting behind an overweight woman who was trying to pay for her Hostess cupcakes and carton of cigarettes with food stamps—and arguing with the cashier when told she couldn't—Maria got an iced cappuccino out of the cooler, then added two bottles of water for Levi and Adam.

Surrendering to her growing paranoia, she paid cash for her purchases, just in case somebody had spotted her car leaving the area around the White Rose Mental Health Facility and remembered the tag number. This way, the police would have no record of her movements. No way to track them. Of course, there were the store security cameras to think about, but it was too late now anyway. She wondered if Levi could do something about them, and decided he probably could. Maria was starting to think she'd barely scratched the surface of what he was capable of. She considered mentioning it to him, but decided against it. He'd seemed moody and unresponsive since freeing Adam.

She walked out of the store, nodding thanks to the elderly greeter standing next to the shopping carts, who thanked her for shopping and asked her to come back again. As she crossed the parking lot with her bags, she stuffed the sales receipt in her purse. With any luck, she could claim the purchase on her taxes—if she sold the book.

The book, she thought. *Yeah, like that's ever going to happen now. I'm aiding and abetting a murderer—and the ex-Amish magician who helped him escape by creating some kind of flaming hole in time and fucking space. Maybe I can write the book from prison. What the* hell *was I thinking?*

Then she remembered the voice on her digital recorder. She felt the blood drain from her face.

Maria halted, afraid that she was going to pass out. When the dizziness had passed, she hurried to the car. She climbed behind the wheel and handed the bags to Adam without speaking. Then she gave them each a bottle of water and started the car.

"Thank you," Levi said. "You must have read my mind. I was indeed thirsty."

"Yeah," Adam agreed. "Thanks."

"There you go," she said. "You've got a new suit of clothes. Sunglasses and a hat, too. You're a new man."

"Cool shades." Adam pulled the items out of the bags. "I really appreciate it. I'll pay you back when I can."

"Don't worry about it," Maria said. "You can pay me back by helping us out."

"Should I change now, or wait till later?"

"Wait," Maria said. "Let's get this over with first."

"We're not far," Adam replied. "Just a few more minutes."

"I know the way," Levi said.

"You were really at my house?" Adam asked him as they pulled out of the parking lot.

Levi nodded. "Yes. Right after your arrest and once since then. I was looking for the book."

"The . . . people that live there now. What are they like?"

"They seemed like a very nice family. Husband and wife. Two kids. A dog. Good folk. I didn't speak to them for very long, I'm afraid. Just asked them a few short questions."

"That should have been us," Adam whispered. "Me and Tara and Big Steve. That should have been us. The only thing missing were the . . . kids. We miscarried several times. That's why, when Tara got pregnant after Hylinus, I just . . ."

He stopped talking, unable to finish. Moaning, he buried his face in his hands and wept.

"Adam," Levi said softly, "I know that you are hurting right now. And I know this won't be easy, seeing your old home. But I need you to keep your wits about you until we've retrieved the book. Then we'll talk about this, okay?"

"You don't understand," Adam cried. "The ultrasound . . . the picture . . . the baby had horns! She said it was mine, but it had fucking horns, man! That's why she tried to hide it from me. What was I supposed to do?"

Maria's grip tightened around the steering wheel. She stared straight ahead, slowing as they approached a red light.

"I know," Levi soothed the distraught man. "I know. But we need to focus."

"It should have been mine," Adam wailed. "I was supposed to be the father—not him! Not the satyr."

"Which way?" Maria asked, stopping at the light.

"Left, and then straight through the next light," Levi told her, turning back to Adam. "Mr. Senft, I need you to be with me. Put this behind you for just a little longer. Can you do that for me?"

Sobbing, his face still hidden, Adam nodded.

"Good." Levi turned around again and stared straight ahead.

When the light turned green, Maria made the left. The streets were deserted. Levi opened his bottle of water and drained it without pausing for air.

"Are you okay?" she asked him.

"I'm fine." He screwed the cap back on the empty bottle. "Tonight's occurrence took a lot out of me, and I'm tired. That's all. But I'll be okay. I just need to prepare myself."

Maria sipped her iced cappuccino. "For what?"

"For what's to come. For what I have to do next. I like it even less than flying."

"You don't like to fly?"

"No."

"I love it," Maria said. "I always ask for a window seat."

Levi shuddered.

They passed through another intersection.

"At the next light," Adam said, "there will be a gas station on the left. Go straight through it and then, about twenty feet later, you'll see the firehouse on the right. Turn down that alley."

Maria followed the directions. The gas station was closed for the night. As they drove by it, Adam pressed his palm against the window. His expression was full of grief.

"Did you used to go there for cigarettes or something?" Maria asked.

"A friend of mine worked there. Leslie."

"Did she visit you while you were in the hospital?"

Levi started to speak, but Adam interrupted him.

"The last time I saw Leslie was when she had Merle's dick in her hand. She cut it off with a rock, trying to protect Hylinus."

"Oh . . ."

"She was shot by a police detective named Ramirez," Levi explained, taking over for Adam. "On the night of the fire, Detective Ramirez and Adam, along with several of their friends, confronted Hylinus during a mating ceremony. Mr. Senft's wife, his friend, and several other women were . . . accompanying the satyr."

"Ramirez," Maria said. "I spoke with him on the phone earlier today. Seems like a week ago already."

"He knew the truth," Adam whispered. "And he let them railroad me anyway. Because he didn't want to admit that he'd been wrong. He didn't want to believe, even after being confronted with the proof. He was a coward."

Maria slowed as they approached the alley. She switched her turn signal on, but before she could make a right into the alley, Adam flung the car door open and leapt out into the street.

"Adam!" Levi shouted.

Maria slammed on the brakes. "Oh shit."

Before they could react, Adam had fled into the alley, disappearing from sight.

"What should we do?" Maria yelled.

"Go after him—drive!"

She turned into the narrow alley and her headlights speared the fleeing man. Maria floored it, and the car shot forward. But as they closed the distance between them, Adam stopped running. Holding his sides, he walked a few more feet and then stopped at the rear of a two-story house with gray vinyl siding. The house was sandwiched between the alley and Main Street. There was a detached garage and a driveway at the rear of the property, and a large oak tree in the center of the yard. A red Toyota and a blue minivan were parked in the home's driveway. Adam glanced at them and then collapsed, kneeling in the driveway. He clawed at the stones, his hands curling into fists.

Maria glanced around. To her left was the community Fire Hall's parking lot. Beyond it lay a grassy vacant lot and a

playground with swings and monkey bars. Beyond the playground was a dark line of trees. To her right were a row of
houses, including the one Adam knelt in front of.

"Pull into the parking lot," Levi said. "Turn the car off.
And the headlights, too. We can't attract any attention."

"Tell that to him."

"I'll handle Senft."

He got out of the car and quietly shut the door behind
him. Then he crouched down next to the crying man, put his
hand on Adam's shoulder, and whispered something in his
ear. Maria rolled down her window, trying to hear the conversation.

"They changed the siding," Adam said.

"I know," Levi sighed, patting Adam's shoulder. "But we
have to be quiet. Okay?"

Shaking her head, Maria crossed the alley and parked the
car. She yawned, realizing just how long it had been since
she'd slept.

"Jesus . . ."

She was beginning to wonder if she'd ever have a good
night's sleep again. How could she, with all that she'd seen
today?

Terry and Tom made their way along the winding trail, passing by the papier-mâché Bigfoot cave, the pterodactyl's nest,
the haunted outhouse, the guillotine, and a grove of trees with
fake skulls dangling from their branches. The creek flowed
silently as they crossed over the little footbridge spanning it.
The forest was absolutely silent and their high-powered flashlight beams barely penetrated the darkness. The blackness
was so dense that the lime outlines along the path were almost
invisible.

"We should have changed the batteries in these things before we left," Tom said. "I can't see shit out here."

"It's not the flashlights," Terry replied. "They've got fresh
batteries."

"Well, then why is it so fucking dark? This is like walking through tar."

"I don't know, Tom. Maybe because it's nighttime."

"You don't have to holler at me, Terry. I was just asking."

Terry sighed. "You're right. I'm sorry. I'm just worried, is all. Didn't mean to take it out on you."

They cupped their hands to their mouths and hollered for Cecil, Russ and Tina. The echoes ceased abruptly, swallowed up by the gloom. When their cries went unanswered, they reluctantly continued on their way, reaching the maze house.

"Ain't no way I'm going in there tonight," Tom said. "I get lost in it during the daytime."

"Me, too," Terry admitted. "Let's go around."

They stepped off the trail and skirted the edge of the sprawling, ramshackle building. Twigs snapped and leaves rustled under their feet. Tree branches scraped slowly across the tin roof of the maze house, making them both cringe.

"Man, that's a horrible sound," Terry said. "Like nails on a chalkboard."

Tom tugged on Terry's arm.

"What's up?" Terry asked.

"Just had a thought. What if they're inside the maze? Maybe Cecil had some kind of spell, got disoriented and is stuck in there?"

"Shit. I hadn't considered that." Terry raised his head and called out. "Cecil? Russ? Tina? It's Terry and Tom! You guys in there?"

Again, the darkness seemed to muffle his echoes. Then they heard a new sound.

"Noooooooo . . ."

"Jesus Christ!" Tom dropped his flashlight. It rolled away across the forest floor.

"That sounded like Tina," Terry said. "But where is she? Tina! Tina, are you there? Sound off, hon!"

"Here . . . we're over here . . ."

Tom retrieved his flashlight and made sure the lens wasn't cracked. "Sounds like it's far away."

"It's coming from that direction." Terry shined his light into the woods. "Come on."

Dispensing with caution, they charged deeper into the forest. Branches tugged at their clothing and whipped their faces. In the darkness, the foliage twisted into sinister, menacing shapes. Tree limbs became outstretched, grasping arms. Late-season ferns became claws thrusting up from the dirt. Roots became serpents. Terry's flashlight beam glanced across a blurred, moving shape. White teeth flashed amidst the black.

"The fuck was that?"

"Just an animal," Tom panted. "A coyote or a fox, probably."

"I didn't see any eyes," Terry said. "The light should have reflected off its eyes."

Pausing, he shined the beam around the area, but the creature was gone. The woods grew colder.

"Could be rabid," Tom said.

Terry frowned. "Rabies makes their eyes nonreflective? What kind of bullshit is that, Tom?"

"It could. You don't know. You weren't a veterinarian last time I checked."

"Terryyyyyy . . . Tommmmm . . ."

"We're coming!" Terry shouted.

They started running again, following Tina's frantic cries. The strange sound-dampening effect cleared. Her wails became clearer as they got closer. Several times, they heard branches snapping behind them, but neither man turned around. Instead, they just ran faster.

"It's just a fox," Tom repeated. "Probably as scared of us as we were of it."

"If it is," Terry gasped, "then it's the first one we've had around here. That and the whip-poor-will."

Pressing on, they smelled a faint hint of burned wood. Soon, the terrain sloped downward and the vegetation cleared. The towering, looming trees turned into splintered, broken stumps. In the darkness, they looked like broken stone pillars. The ground beneath their feet grew softer, like they were jogging on baby powder. Terry coughed, tasting ashes in the back of his throat. The darkness deepened, becoming almost palatable.

"Terry?"

"What?"

"You know where we are, don't you?"

"Yeah."

Tina's voice rose out of the darkness, very close by. She sounded weak and tired. "Terry? Tom?"

"We're here," Terry yelled. "Where are you?"

"I'm here. Just a little farther. Please hurry."

"Are you okay? Are Russ and Cecil with you?"

"Yes, we're all here."

"Hurry up," Cecil called. He also sounded like he was in bad shape.

They shined their flashlights ahead of them, sweeping the darkness, but saw nothing. The beams did nothing to dispel the gloom. It was as if the night had become a solid wall, and the beams of light were bouncing off it.

"Terry," Tom whispered, stepping closer, "I don't like this. My butt is puckering."

"I don't like it either. Something's not right here. I can't see shit."

"Then what the hell are we doing? Let's get out of here."

"Where are you?" Tina called.

"Coming," Terry shouted. "Just give us a minute. It's hard to see."

"Yes." This time it was Russ who spoke. "There is no light."

"What do we do?" Tom asked.

"Fuck this."

Terry turned off his useless flashlight and pulled out one of the road flares. He snapped and twisted the end, activating it. The flare burst to phosphorescent life, hissing and spitting sparks. Its tip glowed red. Still, the darkness held. He tossed the flare ahead of them. As it spiraled through the air, they caught glimpses of human figures. There were six of them. As the flare began its downward descent, something long and black whipped through the darkness and seized it. The obsidian tentacle coiled around the hissing flare and the red glow disappeared, snuffed out.

"Holy shit . . ." Terry started to back away.

"No light at all," Russ called.

"What do we do?" Tom whimpered.

Terry spoke quickly and quietly, trying to keep the panic out of his voice.

"Go back to the exit. Call the cops, the paramedics, the goddamned National Guard. I don't care who. Just get them down here, now."

"But what about what you said before? The Ghost Walk—"

"Fuck the Ghost Walk," Terry said. "Just do it. We just saw a black who-knows-what out there. And hurry up. But don't wait for me. I'll be right behind you."

"What?"

"I'm gonna find out what's going on. Now go!"

Tom turned to leave and something stepped out of the darkness behind him. It padded forward, growling, until it was only inches away. Tom shined his flashlight on the creature. It was a coyote—sickly and suffering from what appeared to be an extreme case of mange. Most of its fur was missing, and its hide was covered with raw, red sores. Its eyes were two black holes, but its teeth were white—and looked very sharp.

"T-Terry . . ."

Moving slowly, Terry turned around. His eyes widened when he saw the animal, but he didn't panic. He inched his hand toward his pocket, intending to grab the second flare. Noticing the movement, the coyote growled louder. Terry stopped, lowering his hand to his side. Then they heard something slithering toward them from the rear.

Both men turned in time to see the darkness move. Dozens of black tendrils hurtled toward them. Behind the darkness, their friends stepped forward. They saw Russ and Tina and Cecil, as well as Sam and Rhonda, and another man that neither of them knew. All of them seemed to be suffering from the same illness that plagued the coyote. Beyond them was a stone circle. The darkness seemed to be clustered there, seeping from the circle like water through a sieve. It bulged, as if there were an invisible bubble still holding its bulk at bay.

Terry closed his eyes. "Oh, Ken. I'm sorry, man. I'm so fucking sorry."

The darkness hovered inches from their faces, twisting and writhing. It looked solid and yet incorporeal at the same time, defying natural law. The tentacles waved at them, waiting, stoking their fears higher. Tom began stuttering through the Lord's Prayer. Terry screamed.

Terry?

This voice was different. It took Terry a moment to recognize it.

He'd lied to Ken earlier. Yes, he'd slept with Ken's prom date, Alicia Hartlaub, on the night of their junior prom. What he hadn't told Ken—what he'd kept secret all these years—was that she hadn't been awake when it happened. After the prom, they'd all gone back to Artie Lewis's house. Artie's parents had been gone for the weekend, and the teens held a four-keg party in their absence. Bobby Marsh and Chris Sipe had brought along a bottle of Boones Farm Strawberry wine, and Terry traded them an ounce of weed for it. The party was in full swing. Everybody was hanging out and laughing, having a good time while Foreigner and Foghat and David Cassidy blared from the stereo. Ken wanted to go out into the backyard and get stoned with some other kids, but Alicia had declined. Ken asked Terry to keep an eye on her while he was gone. At first, that was exactly what he had done. But as Alicia drank more wine and chased it down with beer, she'd begun to get sleepy. Terry had escorted her upstairs to an empty bedroom, and stayed with her to make sure she was okay. But he was horny and drunk, and when she passed out, he'd taken advantage of it. It wasn't rape—or at least, it hadn't seemed so at the time. But later, when he'd sobered up, Terry felt guilty for betraying his friend. He lied about it for weeks, before finally confessing what he'd done to Ken.

He'd never given Alicia the same respect.

The guilt had haunted him for years.

The darkness changed, forming a human shape. Alicia stood in front of him, looking exactly as she had all those years ago. She was close enough to kiss. He smelled the wine on her breath and saw the tears in her eyes.

Those eyes were black.

Now it's my turn, Terry.

"I'm sorry . . ." he sobbed. "I was drunk, Alicia. I didn't mean to."

"Terry!" Tom screamed. "Help me. It's my uncle. He's back, just like when we went camping!"

Terry couldn't tear his gaze away from Alicia. She leaned closer, her lips pursed.

Kiss me, Terry. Kiss me like you did that night . . .

"Get away!"

"Terry!" Tom shrieked. "Stop him! He's going to put his thing in me again! Oh, God, help me."

As their fears peaked, their ghosts laughed. Then the darkness lunged forward and consumed them, leaving behind only withered husks.

CHAPTER SIXTEEN

"There." Adam pointed at a garage two houses away from his former home. "Behind Merle's wood shop."

The three of them huddled together in the driveway, hiding behind the blue minivan. Levi had convinced Adam to pull himself together.

Maria frowned. "That doesn't look like a wood shop."

"It's not anymore," Adam whispered. "After Merle died, he left everything he owned to his ex-wife, Peggy. He sold antiques out of the house. She put all of it up for an estate auction—the house, his antiques and personal belongings, the wood shop. Everything. I'd left LeHorn's book in there the night we confronted Hylinus. I got it back that same night. After what happened with Tara, I buried it behind the wood shop."

Levi groaned. "You buried the book unprotected?"

"No. Give me some credit, dude. I sealed it in a plastic freezer bag and put it inside a cigar box. Then I duct taped the box shut. It should still be okay."

Maria stifled a yawn. "Why did you bury it?"

"Because of what it was. What it had caused. I couldn't just get rid of it. I'm a writer. I can't throw a book away, even a book like that. But I didn't want it around, either. So

I buried it, just in case I ever needed it again. I hoped I wouldn't, but I guess now we do, right?"

"You did well," Levi whispered. "You did very well indeed. You were guided by the Lord."

"God?"

Levi nodded.

"Fuck God," Adam exclaimed. "Fuck Him in his all-powerful, all-knowing benevolent ass!"

"Adam." Levi's voice was like ice. He grabbed Adam's arm and squeezed. "That will be enough."

Adam pushed Levi away and laughed. The sound carried down the alley.

"Be quiet," Levi hushed him. "You don't believe in God?"

"Hell, yeah, I believe in Him. And I hate the motherfucker."

"I said that's *enough*! I'm not going to let you blaspheme like this."

"You want to kick my ass? Go ahead. I don't give a shit. What—just because He's always been nice to you, you're required to kiss His holy ass? Well, screw that, Levi. Maybe He's been good to you, but the only thing God's ever done for me is shit all over my life. This whole thing was His fucking fault, man. Do you understand that? I prayed to Him. Begged Him. I fucking begged. And God just laughed. He took everything from me. I'm not Amish like you. I'm not one of the favored ones."

"I'm far from favored," Levi protested. "And I've had plenty of unanswered prayers. You think I don't know about suffering or loss? You think I haven't questioned God? You know nothing about me."

"I know that you still love Him, even if you're not Amish anymore. And I know that I still hate him—more and more every day. All I want to do is spit in His fucking face. You want the truth? I wish the motherfucker was standing here in front of me right now. I'd fucking say it then, too."

"Then I pray that your wish never comes true."

"Look," Maria whispered, quieting them both. "I'm going on well past twenty-four hours with no sleep here, and I'm about to fall over. Can we please get on with this? You two can argue theology and steal lines from *Pitch Black* later."

Levi appeared confused. "Pitch black?"

"It's a movie, and it doesn't fucking matter. I need some sleep before we do whatever it is we're going to do with this book. Let's just sneak over there and dig it up and go home before we get caught. Tired as I am, I really don't feel like sleeping in a holding cell tonight."

"You're right," Levi agreed. He looked at Adam. "I am sorry."

"I'm not. I meant every word of it. I fucking hate Him."

Levi tugged on Adam's arm. "Maria is right. Let's go retrieve the book. We'll discuss the rest later."

"Hey!" Adam yanked away from him. "Let go of me or I'll wake up everybody in this fucking neighborhood."

Levi took a deep breath. "Adam, look over there, beyond the playground. Do you see those trees?"

Adam turned away from him, sulking.

"Do you see them?" Levi insisted, wrenching the man's arm.

"Yes. Now let go. You're hurting me."

"You know where those trees go, don't you, Adam? You remember where that forest leads to. What it's part of."

"Leave me alone."

Levi leaned close, breathing into Adam's ear. "It leads to LeHorn's Hollow. Sure, we're on the far side. There are many miles between us and that place, and the fire destroyed a great portion of the woods between here and there, but it's all still connected. It's all part of the same net. The energies that make that place what it is don't rely on trees or undergrowth or property boundaries. They run through the ground. I can feel them, you know. Pulsing. Turning. Vibrating far beneath our feet. And you can feel them too, I'll bet. Because they've touched you. You've been poisoned by that place."

"Stop it," Adam whispered.

"That's enough, Levi. You're hurting him."

Maria stepped forward and tapped Levi's shoulder. He brushed her away and continued.

"But the energies aren't the only thing brewing there, Adam. Something else is growing in those woods. It's searching for a way into our world, and it's found one. It's seeping through right now, a little bit at a time. Gathering strength. But it's almost to the boiling point now, and tomorrow night, those floodgates won't be able to hold it back any longer. It will swamp the Earth, extinguishing everything that lives, smothering the planet in darkness."

"No . . ."

"Oh, yes. You fought one of its minions before. Fought it and defeated it. Hylinus. But now we have to stop the rest of it. We have to stop the thing that Hylinus served."

"I can't."

"Yes, you can. You have no choice, Adam. You owe it to your friends. To your wife. It's time to finish this once and for all."

"Okay!" Adam shouted. "You win! You're right. Just leave me the fuck alone!"

Maria ducked down behind the minivan again, gasping. She started to speak, but Levi held his hand up, listening. They waited, but heard nothing.

"Shit," Maria breathed. "If that didn't wake anybody up, then nothing will."

"It didn't," Levi said.

"Then this town could sleep through a nuclear bomb attack. Or the Second Coming."

"Perhaps. Or maybe the Lord is with us."

Adam started to speak, but they both silenced him. After making sure his outburst hadn't attracted any late-night attention, they crept out from behind the minivan and snuck across the yard, single-file. The grass was wet with dew and showed traces of their passage. Maria kept glancing at the houses around them, looking for lights, but the homes remained dark and silent.

"Don't any of these people have dogs?" she whispered.

Levi shrugged.

"I did," Adam said. "Big Steve. He was my best friend."

"Where is he now?"

"Hylinus killed him, too."

They crossed over the second yard and then into the third, darting quickly behind the former woodshed. The corrugated steel structure hid them from the view of the other houses. Now all they had to worry about was someone driving down the alley unexpectedly, or the fire siren going off.

Adam moved to the center of the building's wall and stood with his back against it. Then, staring at the ground, he counted off twelve paces, putting his feet together, heel to toe. He stopped and crouched down.

"It should be right here. Which one of you brought the shovel?"

Maria and Levi glanced at each other. Levi closed his eyes and shook his head in frustration.

"Oh, for fuck's sake," Maria whispered. "You didn't prepare for this?"

"Well, I didn't know he'd buried it, now, did I?" Levi protested. "We'll just have to use our hands."

Kneeling next to Adam, Levi began digging at the earth with his hands. After a moment, Adam joined him. Together, they tore up clumps of sod and tossed aside rocks, then pawed through the softer dirt below. Earthworms wriggled in annoyance, disturbed by the intrusion. They'd only dug about eight inches when their fingers grazed the surface of the cigar box.

"See? I knew I didn't bury it too deep."

"I'll be thankful when I get what we need," Levi said.

Adam started to dig again, but Levi gently pushed him back. "Allow me."

"I can help."

"I know you can. But trust me, it's for the better. With all the pain this book has caused you, do you really want to touch it again?"

Adam shook his head, then stood up and wiped his dirty hands on his hospital smock. Levi clawed at the dirt feverishly, throwing it to the side until he could slip his fingers around the edge of the box. Then he hauled it upward and brushed the soil from the lid. He ripped the duct tape away and then opened the box. Inside, just as Adam had told them, was a slim, brown leather book wrapped in a plastic freezer bag. Levi unzipped the bag and held up the book. Maria leaned forward, reading the tiny gold lettering on the front cover:

The Long Lost Friend

A Collection
of
Mysterious & Invaluable
Arts & Remedies
For
Man As Well As Animals
With Many Proofs

Of their virtue and efficacy in healing diseases and defeating spirits, the greater part of which was never published until they appeared in print for the first time in the U.S. in the year of our Lord 1820.

By

John George Hohman
I N R I

"Wow," she whispered. "That looks really old."

Levi flipped it open and glanced at the bottom of the title page.

"It's a 1916 edition. Not the complete translation, but not

as bad as some of the later editions. Certainly better than the abridged versions available on the Internet."

"Is it worth anything?"

"Quite a bit, actually. An antiquarian book collector would pay several hundred for this. A powwow practitioner would pay even more."

Holding the book by the front and back covers, he turned it upside down and fanned the pages. Six folded sheets of paper fell out. Levi closed the book and picked them up. He glanced through them quickly, then settled on the final sheet. His eyes glinted in the darkness as he scanned it. Then he smiled.

Maria tried to read over his shoulder, but the words were in another language. She tried to figure out what it was, but couldn't. The words weren't typeset. They'd been written by hand. There were also several hand-drawn diagrams and figures. When Maria focused on the drawings, her vision blurred. She chalked the occurrence up to her lack of sleep, and rubbed her eyes. When she opened them again, Levi was folding the sheets of paper again. He tucked them carefully in his shirt pocket.

"The book is valuable," he repeated. "These pages from Nelson LeHorn's *Daemonolateria* are priceless."

"Can we go now?" Maria asked, shivering in the damp air. "Do we have everything we came for?"

"Oh, yes. This is exactly what we needed. We've got one more stop to make, but it will be quick." Levi stuck his hand out to Adam. "Thank you, Mr. Senft."

Maria groaned upon hearing of yet another stop.

Adam stared at Levi's hand for a moment, his expression timid. Then he shook it.

"So this really will help you?"

"You've helped me a great deal," Levi said. "I've got one more thing I'd like you to do for me, but we'll talk about that later. For now, this is enough."

"What is it?"

Levi walked out into the alley and headed for the car.

"Something small. Just some closure. But not now. Like Maria, I'm exhausted. We all are. Let's talk about it in the morning, after we've all had some sleep."

"But it *is* morning," Adam said. "It's just not light out yet."

Levi glanced up at the sky. The moon was shrouded in clouds again. The stars seemed dim and cold, and the darkness between them was vast and impenetrable. He turned back to them. His expression was grave, his eyes bloodshot.

"Then let's just hope that when the dawn arrives in a few hours, it's not for the last time."

CHAPTER SEVENTEEN

Levi had Maria drive him back across the river to his home in Marietta. She'd protested. It didn't make sense, driving all the way to Lancaster County at this time of night, especially when they were currently at the far southern end of York County. But Levi said there were items he needed for the confrontation. Reluctantly, she conceded. When they finally arrived, Levi grabbed his wicker basket and got out of the car. He asked her to wait while he went inside. She'd wondered aloud why they couldn't just sleep at his place and then go to the Ghost Walk. He didn't explain his reasons, but Levi was adamant that she and Adam couldn't come inside. He offered to let her wait outside on the porch, but insisted that they not cross the threshold. Fuming, Maria told him to hurry up.

They waited in the car. Maria seethed, fighting to stay awake. Adam snored softly in the backseat, still dressed in his sweat-soaked hospital clothes, now covered with dirt and grass clippings. She was amazed. In the space of a few hours, he'd escaped from a mental hospital, seen a black magic spell almost backfire, tasted freedom, been confronted with his past, and had a near nervous breakdown in his former hometown. Despite this, he'd fallen asleep soon after they'd retrieved the book, and had slept undisturbed ever since. Like a baby—innocent and carefree.

Levi's home was unremarkable—bland and perfunctory, and smaller than she'd imagined. In the backyard, visible from the car, were a small doghouse and a two-car garage. The buggy was parked next to it. One half of the garage had been converted into a stable. She saw Dee peering out the door. Maria rubbed her eyes, struggling with fatigue. She rolled down the window, hoping the chilly, damp air would wake her up.

If I fall asleep now, she thought, *I'm not waking up again. Still need to drive home.*

Levi emerged from the house twenty minutes later, carrying a small canvas bag with the drawstrings pulled tight. Maria noticed that he'd changed clothes. Wet curls stuck out from beneath the brim of his hat. He opened the passenger door and sat the bag on the floor.

"I won't be much longer. Just need to get one more thing, and then check on Dee and Crowley. Give me five minutes."

"Okay," Maria sighed.

He went around the side of the house and disappeared into the garage. Then he emerged again, fed the dog and the horse, and then returned to the garage. When he came back out, he was carrying a bag of something over his shoulder. It was heavy, judging by his posture.

"Can you open the trunk?" Levi asked as he neared the car.

Maria pulled the lever at her feet and heard the trunk latch click. Levi loaded the bag into the back. The car sagged on its shocks and then bounced back up. Levi closed the lid and then got into the car.

"There," he said. "All finished. Now we can go back to your place and get some sleep."

Maria didn't reply. She just stared at him.

"What?" Levi asked her. "Are you okay to drive?"

"I'm fine. Just wondering if you were going to tell me what's in the trunk?"

He shrugged. "Salt. You know, like what you put down on your driveway in the winter. It's just a bag of salt."

"We drove all the way out here for a bag of salt?"

"Yes . . ."

Shaking her head, Maria drove away.

"I hope you know what you're doing, Levi."

"I do," he said. "I only pray that it actually works. The Lord fed hundreds with one loaf of bread. I'm hoping He will do something similar with one bag of salt."

"What? Like a dump truck load?"

He shrugged.

"If it's that important, why don't we get more?"

"Because we're already running out of time. I would if we could, but you and Adam are both exhausted, and you need to sleep. You need your strength for what is to come. Otherwise, the entity can take you easier. And I need to prepare. There are many hours of study, memorization, and meditation ahead before we can confront it. And prayer. Believe me, I'd rather not stop at your home. I'd rather go straight to the hollow. But we have no choice. I only pray the delay doesn't cost us."

Rather than responding, Maria stared straight ahead, watching her headlights beat back the darkness.

CHAPTER EIGHTEEN

Ken awoke at seven, mumbling and incoherent. The hazy vestiges of a dream departed—he tried to remember it, but failed. Something about Deena. She'd been at the Ghost Walk. The last remnants vanished as his alarm clock blared. Ken fumbled for it, knocking an empty bottle of Stella Artois beer off the nightstand. It hit the floor without breaking and rolled under the bed, coming to rest against more empty bottles and some dirty socks. Ken pressed the snooze button and fell back to sleep for another ten minutes. When the alarm went off a second time, he sat up and stretched.

Yawning, he slid out from under the sheets and put his feet on the floor, flexing his toes in the thick, red carpet. Deena had picked it out, just like the rest of the home's furnishings. Some of Ken's friends had suggested that he redecorate now that she was gone—one step toward moving on with his life. But Ken balked at the idea. Things like the carpet were all he had left of her. Everything else had long since waned—her hairs in the shower drain, her scent on the pillow, lipstick-stained cigarette butts in the ashtrays. These things were fleeting. He was left with her sanitary napkins, still sitting beneath the bathroom sink. Her shampoo and

conditioner, sitting lonely and forlorn in the shower caddy.
A half-empty bottle of water, still wedged in the back of the
refrigerator. Even after all this time, he clung to them, refusing to throw any of it out.

To see her, he had to rely on photographs and memory—
and dreams.

Dressed only in a dirty pair of yesterday's boxer shorts,
he padded into the bathroom and pissed. Then, still yawning,
he brewed a pot of coffee and checked his cell phone. Terry
and Tom hadn't called him overnight—or if they had, then
he'd slept through the ringing phone. His cell phone showed
no missed calls and no new voice mail. Ken didn't know if
that was good news or bad news.

While the coffee brewed, he took a quick shower and got
dressed. Breakfast was a banana and a bowl of cereal. Then,
sipping a cup of coffee, he called Terry's cell phone. After
four rings, it switched over to voice mail.

*"This is Terry Klein. I'm not available right now, so leave
your name and number after the beep. See ya!"*

"Hey, man. It's me. Just wondering what happened last
night. I'm assuming everything turned out okay, or else you
would have called. Anyway, I'm heading out to the Ghost
Walk now. Get some sleep. I'll see you later on today."

He hung up and poured some coffee into a plastic travel
mug. For a moment, Ken considered calling Terry's house,
but didn't want to risk waking his wife up. She was apparently already displeased with the amount of time her husband
had been devoting to the Ghost Walk. Instead of calling,
Ken turned the coffeepot off and reached for his jacket. As he
was preparing to leave, his cell phone rang, playing Garth
Brooks's "Friends in Low Places." He answered, hoping it was
Terry. Instead, it was the dispatcher of the rental agency, letting him know that a flatbed truck loaded down with portable
toilets was at the Ghost Walk, waiting for him to sign for delivery.

He apologized for the delay, silently cursing them for

being so early. Who accepted delivery at seven thirty in the goddamned morning? While he was still on the phone with the dispatcher, his call waiting beeped. Then it beeped again. After he'd hung up, he checked his voice mail and found new messages from one of the caterers and a representative from the local NBC affiliate who wanted to film the grand opening.

Sighing, Ken headed out the door. He called the caterer back as he climbed into his truck. The man wanted more space than he'd been allotted. While they spoke, the call waiting continued to beep.

It was going to be a long day.

They pulled up in front of Maria's apartment just after seven. The sun was climbing into the sky. To Maria, the world seemed very normal. Kids waited for school buses. People drove to work. An elderly man raked the leaves in his yard. Halloween decorations adorned many of the neighborhood homes. She tried to reconcile all of this with the fact that hiding in the midst of all this normalcy was a world in which people stepped out of flaming holes in the air and disembodied, sexless voices left messages on digital voice recorders. A world where Amish magicians read minds and viewed the past, and midlist paperback writers buried spell books after killing their wives. It was too much for her. She needed sleep.

They roused Adam. He was groggy and incommunicative as they led him to the front door. Levi carried his extra clothes and supported him while Maria unlocked the door. They walked inside. Levi glanced around while Maria got some clean sheets and pillowcases from the closet and fixed a place on the couch.

"It's only big enough for one person," she said, "so one of you is going to have to sleep on the futon—or the floor."

"Adam can take the couch," Levi offered. "I'll be fine on the floor."

Adam mumbled his thanks and then sagged onto the couch. He curled into the fetal position, closed his eyes, and sighed. A minute later, he was snoring again. Maria half-expected him to start sucking his thumb.

She pulled Levi aside. "Are you sure? The futon is small, but if you curl up—"

"The floor is all I need."

"Well, at least let me get you a blanket."

"No," Levi insisted. "Seriously, I'm fine just like this. I don't intend to sleep very long, anyway. I'm just going to recharge a little bit. Then I'll need to study and prepare. As I said, there is a lot to go over. Passages to be memorized. In truth, I can do that better without distractions, so it will be easier if the two of you are sleeping."

"Are you sure?"

"Yes." Smiling, he took her hand and squeezed it gently. "Please, Maria. Get some sleep. You need it. And you've earned it. I can't thank you enough for your help so far. It means a lot to me."

He let go of her hand. Maria felt a flash of regret when the contact was broken.

"I haven't really done much," she said. "Just drove the car."

"You've done a lot. It helps—not doing this alone. So again, thank you."

She smiled. "You're welcome."

"Now get some sleep."

She glanced over at Adam. "Do you think he'll be okay? What if he wakes up and freaks out? Or what if the hospital staff tell the cops I wanted to speak with him yesterday? Won't they come here, looking for—"

"You're tired. Sleep. Now."

"Okay."

Maria barely made it to her bedroom before collapsing onto the bed. She didn't bother to undress or even close the bedroom door. She was too exhausted. She closed her eyes and sank into the pillow. If only her parents could see her now—hiding an escaped mental patient, fighting the forces of darkness, fooling with magic. And now, two strange men in her apartment, neither of whom she knew very well and both of whom were hiding things. If her parents knew, they'd have simultaneous heart attacks.

Then she fell asleep and thoughts of her parents evaporated like mist.

The sun rose over the burned-out remains of LeHorn's Hollow, but its light didn't penetrate the forest. Wisps of shadows swirled between the trees in place of the morning fog. The remnants of the stone circle were obscured by darkness. It flowed from the seven vacant holes where the sigils had been, forming a pulsating ball ten feet above the forest floor. Tentacles of darkness crept forward from the sphere, searching the hollow for living things. They encountered a few green shoots, buried beneath the thick layer of ashes, and quickly drained them. The fledgling vegetation turned brown and brittle.

Now that all of the sigils had been removed, Nodens no longer required slaves. Thus, they'd been discarded.

Terry's and Tom's remains lay nearby. Their eyes were open, staring at nothing. Their mouths gaped, frozen in eternal horror. Their fingers had curled, clawlike, in death. They'd been emptied. Sucked dry. Their bodies were just desiccated husks, as brittle as the burned tree trunks around them. Cecil, Russ, Tina, and the coyote were in even worse condition. Each occasional breeze that blew through the area stirred more and more of them up into the air, spreading their ashes amongst the rest of the debris. Of Rich, Sam, and Rhonda—there was nothing left, not even dust.

The floating black sphere continued to pulse and swell. Nodens gathered strength. When its feelers reached the limits of their exploration, they returned to the mass. With each passing hour, more of it seeped into the world, spreading farther into the forest, lapping at the vegetation and feasting off their energy.

Come midnight, the walls would shatter and it would surge forward, an unstoppable tide of living darkness, consuming everything in its path until there was nothing left.

Levi waited until he heard Maria's breathing turn shallow and rhythmic. Then he tiptoed across the floor and shut the door to her bedroom. After double-checking to make sure Adam was also sleeping soundly, Levi crept into Maria's office, opened the curtains and let the sunlight stream in through the window. Sighing, he closed his eyes and held out his hands, palms up, bathing in the luxuriant warmth. After a few minutes, he sat down cross-legged on the floor. The sun's rays danced across his face. Levi removed his hat, closed his eyes again, took a deep breath, and exhaled.

It was eight o'clock in the morning. Night would come quickly today.

Before he began his studies in earnest, Levi decided to take an extra precaution. Just reading certain passages of the *Daemonolateria* could invoke things that had no business in this world. It was dangerous—adding Nodens to the recipe was simply playing with fire. Prevention was in order.

He prayed out loud, quiet but fervent, reciting from memory a benediction against enemies, sickness, and misfortune that his father had taught him.

"The blessing which came from heaven, from God the Father, when the true living Son was born, be with me at all times. The holy cross of God, on which He suffered His bitter torments, bless me today and forever. The three holy nails which were driven through the holy hands and feet of Jesus Christ, bless me today and forever. The spear by which His holy side was pierced and opened, protect me now today and forever. May the blood of Christ and the Holy Spirit protect me from my enemies, and from everything which might be injurious to my body and my soul. Bless me, oh you five holy wounds in order that all my enemies may be driven before me and bound and banished. All those that hate you must be silent before me, and they may not inflict the least injury upon me, or my house, or my premises. And likewise, all those who intend attacking and wounding me either spiritually or physically shall be defenseless, weak, and conquered. The cross of Christ be with me. The cross of Christ overcomes all water and every fire. The cross of Christ overcomes all weapons. The cross of Christ is a perfect sign and blessing to my soul. Now I pray that the holy corpse of Christ bless me against all evil things, words, and works."

When he was finished, Levi fell silent again. Outside the window, a bird chirped. He heard a leaf blower hum to life somewhere nearby. Still solemn, he made the sign of the cross four times, to the north, south, east and west. Then he took a deep breath. From this point on, he'd be dealing with methods and benedictions that were decidedly different and far older than the one he'd just recited.

He pulled out the pages from the *Daemonolateria* and unfolded them. He read each one carefully, focusing on one in particular. He began memorizing it, committing the ritual to memory. He needed to be exact. One miscalculation or an incorrectly pronounced word, and he could fail. In truth, he might fail anyway. There were no guarantees with an entity of this magnitude. His only chance was to confront it before it was completely freed. But these pages, and the items currently locked inside Maria's car, should even the odds.

And Adam Senft, as well—the most important ingredient of all.

After several hours of study, Levi folded up the papers again and returned them to his pocket. Then, slipping into a meditative trance, he began to prepare for what needed to be done. The sun was warm on his skin, but inside, he was cold.

In the darkness behind his eyes, shapes moved, twisting and floating. He heard the faint voices of the damned.

Concentrating, Levi ignored the ghosts and prayed.

CHAPTER NINETEEN

"Son of a bitch. You've got to be shitting me!"

"I wish I was, Ken, but I ain't. The generator just won't start. Don't know what the hell is wrong with it. I've tried everything."

Biting his lip in frustration, Ken breathed through his nose, feeling his blood pressure rise. It was just after one in the afternoon, and the Ghost Walk swarmed with people—volunteers, vendors, delivery personnel, community officials, and a handful of people from the media. They bustled about like ants, busy with a hundred different tasks, all of which apparently needed Ken's input or approval. It had started the moment he'd arrived. Before he'd even got out of his truck, he'd been besieged by two delivery drivers and a half dozen early volunteers, each voicing a different concern and needing an immediate answer. Now, several hours later, it showed no signs of abating. If anything, the demands for his time and attention were getting worse.

Dennis can't find his mask. Neil can't find the keys to the storage trailer. The deliveryman can't find a pen so I can sign the bill of lading for these fucking pumpkins. Lisa needs a hammer. Jerry needs a hand setting up. Arlene needs help finding her hiding spot along the trail. Stephanie has to leave early. Greg won't get here until later. Diana's ice-cream

*truck got a flat. The french fry stand doesn't have electricity.
The pterodactyl isn't working. Bayer lost his saw and needs
another. Tessa needs some petty cash to buy a wig. Doug hurt
his thumb and needs to have it looked at.*

"And I need an Advil," Ken muttered. "Or a beer. Or
both."

"What's that, Mr. Ripple?"

Blinking, Ken focused on the man. He couldn't even remember the guy's name.

"Nothing," Ken apologized. "Just a little distracted. Look,
I don't know a lot about generators. But obviously, we're going to need it fixed by tonight. Or else we need a replace-
ment. Either way, we don't have much time. What are you
driving . . . I'm sorry?"

"Craig."

"Craig. Sorry. Got a lot of names to remember. What are
you driving?"

"I got a truck."

"Great! Tell you what. Do you know where Harvey's Rent
All is?"

Craig nodded. "Over near the hospital."

"Right! Can you do me a favor? Take a drive on over
there. Tell them we need another generator and that they
should put it on my account. Have them test it for you before
you bring it back here. Keep track of your mileage and get a
receipt for your gas, and I'll make sure we pay you out of
petty cash tonight. Okay?"

Nodding, Craig dashed off. Ken sighed, turned to take care
of the five things he'd been working on before Craig interrupted him, and then got sidetracked again by David Tate.

"Hey, Ken," the man called, running toward him across
the field. "You got a second?"

"Exactly one second, Dave. What's up?"

"I told Terry yesterday that we needed some more plastic
sheeting. I just checked the storage trailer, but I couldn't
find any."

Ken paused. *Terry.* He'd forgotten all about him. Terry and Tom. Cecil and the others. He'd been so consumed with operations, so caught up in the hectic goings-on and a million other little details and crises, that he'd completely forgotten to check in with them and confirm that everything was okay.

"Listen," Ken said. "Have you seen Terry, today? Or Tom?"

Dave grinned. "Hell, Ken, there must be two hundred people here, and we ain't even open yet. I may have. I can't remember. I know I saw Terry's vehicle earlier."

Ken glanced over at the parking area. It was full of cars and trucks. Row upon row of them—too many for him to spot Terry's with any ease. He tried to remember exactly where Terry had been parked the night before, but couldn't.

"You sure?" he asked.

"Yeah," Dave said. "I parked near it. Definitely his. And I think I saw Tom earlier, too."

"You're absolutely positive?"

"Ken," Dave said, "I'm sure they're just as busy as you right now. Maybe more. Knowing Terry, he's running interference for you. Now what about the plastic sheeting?"

Ken sighed with relief. Dave had verified that Terry was here today, and he was fairly certain he'd seen Tom. And what he was suggesting made an awful lot of sense. Terry probably was busy. Zero hour was approaching rapidly. They'd catch up with one another tonight, at the midnight party. Until then, he had to assume that Cecil and the others had been found safe and sound. Otherwise, Terry would have let him know.

"What about the plastic?" Dave repeated.

Before Ken could answer him, two more people walked toward them, calling Ken's name.

"Check the other trailer," Ken told him. "If it's not there, then they must be using it somewhere on the trail. You'll have to track it down."

Nodding, Dave walked away.

Ken grimaced as the others approached. Both of them were already talking.

"No rest for the wicked," Ken said under his breath. "No rest at all . . ."

Passing its zenith, the sun slowly began its afternoon descent.

Maria opened her eyes and screamed. Levi stood over her bed, peering down at her. She scrambled halfway across the bed, another shriek dying in her throat. Her hands clutched the sheets. Her heart pounded at jackhammer speed.

"Oh my God . . ."

"I'm sorry," Levi apologized. "It's just after two in the afternoon. I've been trying to wake you for the last five minutes. I called your name but you didn't stir."

"You scared the shit out of me—again. Damn it, Levi . . ."

She paused, sniffing the air.

"What do I smell?"

Levi winked, bowing slightly. "Breakfast. Well, technically, it's lunch. Or brunch. But I made breakfast."

She breathed deep through her nose, savoring the aroma of fried bacon and eggs. Her mouth watered.

"You made breakfast? You can cook?"

Levi flinched. "Don't sound so surprised. All Amish men can cook. That's how we keep our women happy."

"But you're not Amish anymore."

He grinned. "Well, I still like to make women happy."

Maria blushed and looked away. Clearing his throat, Levi quickly stepped backward.

"Why don't you go ahead and grab a shower," he suggested. "And change."

"Are you saying I stink?"

"No," he laughed. "Actually, we should hurry. But I'm sure you want to freshen up a bit. We'll wait for you in the kitchen. Although I'm afraid Adam has already started eating."

"How's he doing? Any better?"

Levi made a seesaw motion with his hand. "He's pretty quiet. I think he's most likely depressed. It's probably starting to sink in that he's on the run. And I imagine that without his daily dose of whatever medication they had him on, there will be mood complications. We need him compliant and co-operative. Let's just try to steer the conversation away from his wife and friends. At least until we get to the Ghost Walk."

"And what happens then?"

"God's will."

"Is that all?"

Levi shook his head. "Go shower. I'll fix you a plate and keep it warm."

"Okay." Stretching, she got out of bed. "Don't let Adam eat it all. It really smells good, and I'm starved."

As if to prove her point, Maria's stomach grumbled.

Blushing again, she giggled.

"I'll take that as a compliment," Levi said.

"Told you I was hungry."

After he'd left, Maria shut the bedroom door and then stepped into the bathroom. She closed the bathroom door behind her as well, and turned on the exhaust fan. Then she began stripping off yesterday's clothes and tossing them in the hamper.

"Gross," she muttered as she pulled off her jeans. "These could stand up on their own at this point."

Finished, she turned on the shower and let it run. Then she lit a vanilla-scented candle. While the water heated, she sat down on the toilet. Steam filled the bathroom, coating her body and opening her pores. Maria sighed. She already felt better and she hadn't even cleaned up yet. She got up from the toilet, remembering not to flush because when she did while the shower was running, the water's temperature became scalding. Then she pulled back the shower curtain and slipped beneath the spray. The hot water drummed against her scalp, soaking her hair and running down her back and breasts. It felt luxurious. She stood there for several minutes, just enjoying the sensation. She whistled and hummed. Then she grabbed her loofa and some vanilla bean body wash, and scrubbed, lathering herself in bubbles. Her stomach rumbled again as she rinsed.

Reluctantly, Maria turned off the water and stepped out of the shower. She dried off quickly, wrapped her hair in a towel, and brushed her teeth. Then she got dressed. She chose a sweatshirt and jeans, and pulled her still-damp hair into a ponytail. She put on a ball cap, and then looked at herself in the full-length mirror. Maria liked what she saw. She was a new woman.

Except for the dark circles under her eyes.

"New woman, hell. I look like shit."

She opened the bedroom door and walked out into the kitchenette, catching Adam and Levi in midconversation. Both were seated at her tiny table. Adam was polishing off what she assumed was his second plate of bacon and eggs, along with fried potatoes. A half-empty glass of water and a cup of coffee sat in front of him.

"So, anyway," he said around a mouthful of potatoes, "those were the only three I had published. *Cold As Ice*, *Heart of the Matter* and *When the Rain Comes*. I started a book about the Civil War. It was supposed to be my big literary breakthrough novel. Was going to get me out of the midlist genre ghetto. Make me some real money. But I never got the chance to finish it. I guess I sort of lost my stomach for it, after . . ."

His voice trailed off. A shadow passed over his face.

Sensing his impending mood change, Levi tried to change the subject.

"Did they let you write in the hospital? Surely, they wouldn't let a man of such God-given talents squander his abilities."

Adam's laugh was short and humorless. "Sure. They encouraged it, in fact. But they wanted me to write about what had happened, and I'd had enough of that. Everything an author writes is to some extent autobiographical. Our joys and fears, good times and bad, the people we meet in life—all of that is fodder for the muse. Especially the bad stuff. It's like you cut open a vein and bleed out onto the page. But writing about Tara and Hylinus and the babies and Big Steve and all the rest? That wouldn't have been bleeding for my work. It would have been a fucking hemorrhage."

"So you didn't write?" Levi kept his voice calm and level.

"Oh, I wrote." Adam devoured another slice of bacon. "What little I could, with crayons and paper. But I didn't let them see it. No way. I couldn't. If I had, they would have made it worse on me."

"Why? What did you write about?"

Adam leaned forward, lowering his voice. "I started a new novel. I called it, *Darkest of Dark*. It was all about this thing we're fighting—He Who Shall Not Be Named."

Levi flinched, taken aback. His hands gripped the table. His knuckles were white. When he spoke, his voice was barely a whisper.

"But how—"

"How did I know? Coincidence. I read those books. Read LeHorn's journal. That's all."

"Adam," Levi said, "tell me the truth."

"Okay, you caught me. I wrote about it because Tara came to me in my dreams. She told me a living darkness was coming. It would sweep across the land, consuming everything in its path. A darkness that was darker than dark. Something that could not be named. But we know what the name is, don't we, Levi? Its name is No—"

"Stop! Don't finish that sentence. Don't speak it out loud!"

"I'm not afraid of it!" Adam yelled, instantly changing from conversational to combative. "Not Hylinus. Not God. Not Nod—"

"Hey," Maria interrupted, making her presence known. She sensed the tension in the air, saw which direction the conversation was heading again. Mindful of Levi's warnings to keep Adam happy and calm, she tried to distract him. "I hope you saved some for me, Adam."

His demeanor changed again. Smiling, he nodded, sweeping his hand above the table.

"Oh, yeah," he said. "Check it out. Levi's not too bad of a cook. He even chopped up some onions and fried them in with the potatoes."

"I would have added peppers," Levi said, "but I couldn't find any."

"I'm surprised you found what you did," Maria said, sitting down. "I'll have to check my fridge more often. I didn't know all of this was in there."

"It wasn't."

"Some more of your magic, Levi? Don't tell me you conjured all this up. I'm willing to believe a lot, but that's stretching it."

"No magic," he said, setting her plate down in front of her. "While the two of you were still sleeping, I walked to the store. That was where I couldn't find the peppers."

Maria tried a forkful of eggs. Her eyes closed and she moaned with delight.

"These are delicious."

"I'm glad you like them. Not to rush you, but as soon as the two of you are finished, we should leave."

"So, did you get any sleep at all?"

Levi nodded. "Enough for what needs to be done. I rested. Studied. Prepared."

Adam pushed back from the table. "Man, that coffee tastes good. We had real weak stuff at White Rose. But I'm not used to this strong stuff. Runs right through me. May I use your bathroom before we leave?"

"Sure." Maria pointed him toward it. "Why don't you shower and change while you're at it? I'm sure you want to get rid of that gown and pants."

"Good idea. That okay with you, Levi?"

"Yes. Just please be quick."

"Thanks."

When she heard the bathroom door shut, and was sure he couldn't hear them, Maria leaned close to Levi.

"You know he's bat-shit crazy, don't you?"

"Oh, he's certainly disturbed. Unbalanced."

Maria smirked. "That's putting it mildly. He changes emotions like some women I know change clothes."

"He's mentally ill. But regardless, he's telling the truth about what happened the night of the fire. About the satyr and the rest."

"Doesn't matter if he is—he's still nuts."

"Yes," Levi sighed. "He is. The strain of what he's been through was too much, I suppose. I've heard the expression 'the mind snapped' before, but I never really saw it in action until today."

"So what are we still doing with him? We've got the book and the pages. Why keep him around? Why not just cut him loose before he freaks out on us again? The longer he's with us, the better our chances of getting caught."

"We can't just let him go," Levi explained. "He's like a child in some ways. And those mood swings. He could hurt someone—or himself."

"Then we make an anonymous tip. Drop him back off at the hospital."

"And what happens when he tells them it was us who helped him escape?"

"What? That we burned a hole in time and space and broke him out? They'll increase his medication and think nothing more about it."

"Maria." Levi sighed. "The truth is, we can't let him go yet. We still need him."

"For what?"

"I can't say. The less you know, the better."

"Why? Is it something bad?"

"God forbid you get engulfed by the entity. As soon as it leeches onto you, it not only drains your energy—it also siphons your thoughts. I can't risk it learning of our plans before I have a chance to defeat it."

"So what are our plans?"

"Like I said, I can't tell you all of it. But the first thing we need to do is finish up here. Then we need to contact the owner of the Ghost Walk. This Ken Ripple. We need to ask him to consider not opening."

Maria shook her head. "No way. He'll never go for it."

"We can't let those people go into the woods. Isn't there some way you can convince him?"

"I can try," Maria reluctantly agreed, "but I don't think it will do any good."

She walked into her office, retrieved her cell phone, and scrolled through the recently called numbers. Finding Ken's, she hit redial. On the first ring, it automatically put her into his voice mail.

"He's not picking up," she said. "Probably has a million things going on. They open in like four or five hours."

"Four hours?"

"Well, yeah. When did you think it would open?"

"I assumed an attraction like this would open well after dark—eight or nine at the earliest. That gives us less time than I'd planned for. There must be another way to stop people from going into those woods."

"We could call in a bomb threat," Maria suggested. "Phone the police and tell them there's a bomb somewhere on the trail."

"Do the regional police usually react to such a situation?"

"No," she admitted. "Takes them an hour to arrive on the scene when there's shots fired. I can't imagine they'd take a bomb threat seriously. If Al Qaeda ever wanted to wipe out a place with no resistance or preparation, York County would be a prime target."

Levi's expression was grim. "This is my fault."

"Maybe I could call the evangelical church. Convince the pastor and some of his parishioners to go down there and protest. Slow things down a little. Tell them the Ghost Walk is the devil's work."

"No," Levi said. "Then we just put more people in harm's way. Something like that will attract more attention, not less. We need to get going. Now."

Maria wolfed down the rest of her breakfast while Levi told Adam to hurry up. By the time Adam was showered and dressed, the two were ready to go. Adam pulled his ball cap down low and readjusted his sunglasses.

"Think anybody will recognize me?" he asked.

"No," Maria said, "although they might look twice, wondering who the crazy guy is wearing sunglasses at night."

"Not me," Adam laughed. "I'm not crazy."

Maria bit her tongue as they walked out the door.

Levi said nothing.

They climbed into Maria's car. Levi took the passenger seat again. Adam crawled into the back and flipped open Maria's newspaper, which he'd appropriated from her porch step.

"I've been gone too long," he mused, scanning the local section. "I need to catch up on what's been happening."

Maria glanced at Levi, but he stared straight ahead, still silent.

"Okay, guys," she said, trying to sound brave. "Next stop, the Ghost Walk!"

The sun sank lower as they drove away.

CHAPTER TWENTY

"But we're not even open yet!"

"I don't care," Ken said, trying to refrain from shouting at the older man—Bill Goytre, a volunteer from the Lions Club. "Take a look out there in the road."

"But it ain't even dark. We don't open until dark."

"Tell that to the people who are showing up already, Bill. If we don't have volunteers parking cars, it's gonna be chaos. Now get your crew together and get over there in that field and start directing traffic. Please?"

"Yeah, okay."

Bill ran off to muster his forces. Ken stared at the road in amazement. The number of cars already turning into the field was stunning—a creeping, unbroken line that stretched from the parking area to the road and beyond. Drivers wound their way through the field without direction, parking anywhere they chose.

"Jesus Christ . . ."

Ken hadn't been this nervous since the night he'd proposed to Deena.

Greg Lineberger, one of the farmers who was in charge of the hayrides, approached him, leaning on a faded wooden cane. His cheek bulged with chewing tobacco.

"Looks like we're gonna be swamped, Ken."

"Yeah. Holy shit, they're still coming."

"Want us to open the trail early?"

Ken thought it over. "No, let's stay on schedule. Wait until dusk, at least."

"All right." Greg looked up at the sky. "Reckon that will be soon enough anyway. The sun ain't even set yet, but it's already getting dark. Especially down there in the woods. Hope that doesn't mean there's a storm coming."

"That's all we need," Ken agreed. "But no, I went online with my cell phone this afternoon and checked the weather. It's not supposed to rain tonight."

"Well, I'll head on back to my tractor. You let us know when you're ready."

"Will do. And thanks again for your help."

The old farmer gazed out at the snaking line of automobiles and spat tobacco juice in the grass. "Sure is an awful lot of people."

After the old man left, Ken found that he had a rare moment of solitude. Seeing that the public was beginning to show up, most of the volunteers had gone into action. Ken massaged the back of his neck and sighed. He had a headache. He needed a beer. And there was still a lot to do. He had things to check on and phone calls to return. He'd been playing phone tag all morning with the cop investigating Sam and Rhonda's disappearance. When they'd finally connected, the cop had assured him it was just a few routine questions. Supposedly, the detective was going to show up tonight, take the Ghost Walk, and then quickly interview him.

Ken surveyed the crowd. How the hell was the detective even going to find him with all these people? Ken couldn't find anybody and he was the owner.

Walking back to the midway, Ken grabbed a battery-powered bullhorn and made an announcement.

"Folks, can I have your attention, please? Listen up! Can I have your attention?"

He waited for them to quiet down and focus on him.

"As you can see, we've got some early arrivals."

The crowd cheered. A thunderous wave of applause rolled over him. Grinning, Ken waited for it to die down and then continued.

"We're not opening the Ghost Walk until it's dark enough in the woods. Shouldn't be much longer, judging by the sky. But until then, people can buy their tickets and get in line. They can also walk the midway and check out your stands and booths. So consider this your five-minute warning. Get ready. We'll open for business in five minutes."

Another round of applause greeted this, along with cheers and whistles. Ken switched off the bullhorn and steeled himself.

He hoped that somewhere, somehow, Deena was watching. And if so, he hoped she was proud.

Nodens quivered in anticipation, feeling the walls thin around it.

Soon . . .

The forest shuddered.

"Look at this," Maria exclaimed. "It's unbelievable!"

She'd driven the same route she'd taken the night she interviewed Ken, from the city to the suburbs and then onto the rural back roads. That was where the trouble began. Southbound, there was more traffic than normal, and the closer to the Ghost Walk they got, the more congested the narrow roads became. Maria grumbled, forced to drive the speed limit, then below the speed limit, and then reduced to a crawl. Finally, traffic stopped altogether. A few drivers tried passing the congestion by driving south in the northbound lane, but after a few near misses with oncoming traffic, nobody else dared. One impatient driver honked his horn, but the rest sat patiently—families, couples, and carloads of teens, all on their way to the Ghost Walk, anticipating an evening of getting the shit scared out of them.

"Got to hand it to Ken," Maria said. "He's going to rake in a lot of money for charity tonight. I don't think he had any idea it would be this big."

"They may make a lot of money," Levi agreed, "but they'll never get to spend it if the living darkness is freed."

Maria turned on the radio and switched it to a local news station. They listened to a commercial for a vacuum cleaner service and another for a steakhouse, and then the announcer came back on.

The top news story was Adam's escape.

"Shit," Adam said. "Well, I guess we knew this was coming. Wonder what they'll say about me?"

"Listen," Maria whispered, silencing him.

According to the newscaster, neither the local authorities nor the White Rose Mental Health Facility's staff had been able to determine how Adam had escaped. Nor had they been able to locate him. The authorities did not know if he was still in the area, and were advising residents to be cautious. Adam was considered dangerous.

"I'm not dangerous," he muttered in the backseat.

The announcer made a joke about how this was the perfect news story for Halloween, and then gave the weather and traffic report, including a mention of the traffic jam they were currently sitting in.

"Now he tells us," Maria moaned. "Very helpful."

"I'm not dangerous," Adam repeated. "They act like I'm fucking crazy or something."

Maria glanced in the rearview mirror. Adam's left eyelid was twitching and his lips were pulled into a scowl. She turned the radio off and tried to calm him.

"We know, Adam. It'll be okay."

Levi grabbed the door handle. "Come on."

"You have to piss?" Adam asked him.

Levi didn't answer. Maria activated the power locks a second before Levi opened the door. He turned to her in annoyance.

"Unlock the door," he demanded. "And the trunk, as well, please."

"Where are you going?"

"To the Ghost Walk," he said. "Leave the car right here. We'll hike there."

"Are you crazy? We're still five miles away."

"I've walked farther."

"I haven't."

"Me either," Adam said. "I didn't exactly get a lot of exercise in the hospital."

Levi pawed at the door handle. "Unlock this. We'll leave the car here. That might help slow down this progression of traffic."

"No way," Maria balked. "I'm not abandoning my car in the middle of some country road, especially with all these people around. If you want to make an even bigger traffic jam, then you get out there and conjure up a demon or something."

Before Levi could respond, traffic began to move again, albeit slowly. Maria eased her foot off the brake and the car rolled forward.

"Look," she said. "We're moving again. See? No worries."

"Unlock the door, Maria."

"Levi, we're *moving*!"

"Not fast enough. We don't have a choice, Maria. Look at the sun."

She gazed out the windshield. The yellow orb was just beginning its slow descent beneath the horizon.

"Sunset. I know. But it will be another hour and a half or so before it's dark out, and you said the walls won't thin until midnight."

Levi gritted his teeth. "No, I said that they'll be *at* their thinnest at midnight. They're already thinning. I also said that the entity is already seeping through, and gathering strength. We have to stop it before midnight—before it's completely here. If it breaks through all the way, none of us will be strong enough to stand against it."

"What does that have to do with the sun?"

"The enemy breached our world via the doorway in the hollow. As more and more of it pours through the gate, the surrounding area will grow darker. The more mass that enters our reality, the farther it can spread, continuing to feed in preparation for what's to come. This gathering darkness has nothing to do with the sun. It is a false darkness, a manifestation of the entity. And with all of these people heading to the Ghost Walk, your friend, Mr. Ripple, will welcome an early dusk."

Maria gasped. "He can open early if it's dark enough . . ."

"Exactly."

"Shit."

"Yes."

Maria took a deep breath and fastened her seat belt. Her fingers tightened around the steering wheel. The brake lights on the car in front of her flashed. The procession stopped again.

"Both of you buckle up," Maria said.

"I'm comfortable," Adam said, still sprawled and reading the newspaper.

"Put on your seat belts and hang on!"

"What are you doing?" Levi asked.

Maria swerved left and edged out into the northbound lane. Spotting no oncoming traffic, she stomped the accelerator. The car shot forward. Behind them, annoyed drivers blew their horns and made obscene gestures.

"I'm not crazy," Adam said, reaching for his seat belt. "You are."

The speedometer crept higher.

"After the last twenty-four hours?" Maria said. "Yeah, maybe I am."

Adam turned pale. "We're all going to die."

"Not yet," Levi said. "But perhaps before the night is through . . ."

The darkness began to spread beyond the confines of the hollow, creeping over the burned-out wasteland and reaching for the surrounding forest.

The crowd was getting restless.

They'd descended upon the midway, consuming cotton candy, funnel cakes, barbeque sandwiches, and candied apples. They spent money at the gaming booths, popping balloons with darts and tossing horseshoes and throwing softballs at the elected officials in the dunk tank. They cooed over the baby animals in the petting zoo. They got free pens at the fire department's booth, and free pamphlets from the Methodists' table, and free bumper stickers from a congressional candidate stumping for votes. They stopped by the Baptists' table, where a sign promised that they could find out if they were going to Heaven by answering three easy questions. They promised the representatives at the SPCA booth that they would spay and neuter their animals. They pointed at some of the people in costumes who walked amongst the crowd. But then, after all of these distractions, they purchased their tickets and got in line for the Ghost Walk. As the sky grew darker and the line grew longer, they milled about restlessly.

Ken watched them with growing unease. Some of the teenagers, and even a few adults, were starting to make trouble—roughhousing and annoying those around them. One man had already caused a scene, reacting belligerently when security pulled him out of line for being visibly intoxicated.

The volunteers were also growing impatient. The ladies running the bake sale weren't doing much business because attendees didn't want to carry a shoofly pie through the Ghost Walk with them. Therefore, customers were avoiding the stand, promising to come back on their way out. The folks selling tickets and policing the lines were dealing with a steadily growing mob. Tempers began to flare.

Ken hurried over to the ticket stand and pulled the person in charge, Sammi Horton, aside. She seemed frazzled and tired.

"Have you been in contact with the trail?" Ken asked.

"Yes. They want to know what the holdup is. They say it's dark enough down there now."

Ken checked his watch and the sky. "Really? The sun is still setting."

Sammi shrugged. "That's what they said."

"Well, I wish someone had reported that to me. Where's Terry at?"

"Haven't seen him, Ken."

"Shit."

Ken stomped across the field and told the tractor and wagon teams to get ready. Then he returned to the head of the line, stepped over the stanchion, and advised his security volunteers to go ahead and open. He reminded them to let people go through in groups of twelve, with five-minute breaks between each group. Then he turned on his bullhorn and repeated the information to the people in line.

And then it was time. The sun disappeared below the horizon.

The Ghost Walk—Ken Ripple's pride and joy, the project he'd worked on for over a year, the thing that had consumed his every waking moment, his testimony to his wife—was open for business.

His fears and misgivings vanished, along with his concerns for Terry and everything else—washed away by a tremendous swelling of pride.

The first group boarded the hay wagon. The tractor chugged forward, transporting them to the haunted attraction's entrance. They reached it about the same time the second group boarded their wagon and set forth. The first group entered the woods.

Ken beamed. Blinking away tears, he watched them disappear into the shadows and waited for the screams to start.

CHAPTER TWENTY-ONE

The O'Bannon family—Liam, Connie, and their sons, Connor and Alex—had been looking forward to the Ghost Walk for the last two weeks, ever since they'd heard an ad for it on the radio. At ten and thirteen, respectively, both Connor and Alex were into scary video games and movies. Liam had been the same way as a boy, except that he'd been into horror comic books and movies. He'd never outgrown that infatuation, and he hoped his sons never would either. Connie wasn't a fan of anything scary—be it comics, video games, movies, or books. She preferred the Lifetime Channel and A&E, and books by Nora Roberts and Nicholas Sparks. The closest she came to horror was the occasional Sherrilyn Kenyon novel. But she was a big fan of her family spending time together, and if this was what it took, then that was okay.

Liam had taken the afternoon off work so that they could arrive early. After sitting in the unexpected traffic jam and finally finding a parking spot, they'd made a beeline for the ticket booth, spying a chance to be among the first in line. While everyone else stopped on the midway, Liam purchased four tickets and they took their places, just inches from the stanchion—with nobody waiting ahead of them. While Liam and the boys held the spot, Connie had gone to a nearby stand

and got them slices of pizza and cups of soda. Then they waited patiently for the fun to begin.

The hayride had been fun, if a little too short. So far, it had been Connie's favorite part of the evening. Liam had put his arm around her when they sat down on a bale. She'd snuggled up against him. He was warm and the evening was chilly. She'd closed her eyes and smiled, remembering how it had been before the boys. Connor and Alex had bounced up and down impatiently, anxious to reach the trail.

And when they did, Connie's fun ended and the boys' and Liam's began. They'd laughed at the various scenic locations along the path—the pterodactyl's nest, a guillotine, and a reproduction of a windmill from some horror movie that the three of them recognized and Connie didn't. They'd elbowed each other and shouted in excitement at each stop while Connie recoiled in disgust. Worse was the people in costumes who hid along the trail at random intervals. Some of the costumed monsters jumped out in front of them. Others waited until the O'Bannons had moved past. A man with a chainsaw and a face like a leather sack had chased her twenty yards up the trail while Liam and the boys howled. Somehow, the people hiding along the path seemed to know she was an easy target. Sometimes they acted alone and a few times they had teamed up, trapping the family between them. During one prolonged period of this, Connie had been trapped between Jason Voorhees and Freddy Krueger. She screamed while her husband and children laughed. When it was over, Connie had laughed with them.

It was a good evening.

They just couldn't believe how dark it had gotten already— so early in the evening.

The O'Bannon family, for the most part, loved monsters and ghosts.

But it was their real-life ghosts that threatened to tear them apart.

When Connie was pregnant with Alex, Liam had cheated

on her with a temporary worker from his office. The girl, Tasha, had left two weeks later, assigned to the next job. She'd e-mailed him once since then, to tell him she was pregnant and getting an abortion. He'd responded, but Tasha hadn't answered. He'd never seen her again—but the guilt remained. Both for what he'd done to Connie and what he'd done to Tasha.

During her final year of college, Connie had been unfortunately saddled with a manic-depressive roommate named Celeste. While Connie enjoyed all that her final year had to offer, Celeste usually sat in the room with the lights turned off, listening to Depeche Mode—or, as Connie called them Depressed Mood—and getting high. Once a week, Celeste would threaten to kill herself, but after a half-dozen false alarms, Connie and her friends chalked it up to cries for attention, and ignored her further threats to do the same. Until the night when Celeste did it. Connie had been going to a party. Celeste had begged her to stay and talk. Said she was feeling low. Connie had left anyway, telling Celeste to just get some sleep. Instead, Celeste had sliced her wrists open, straight down, palm to elbow. She'd bled out on the bathroom floor, her blood congealing on the tiles before anyone found her. Connie had never forgiven herself for not staying. For not listening. For not being a friend.

Even at their young age, Connor and Alex had ghosts, as well.

Two years ago, Connor had shot a bird out of a tree with his BB gun. When he walked up to it, he heard frightened chirping above his head. The bird had been a mother, and her four babies trembled in their nest, cold and hungry and scared. Connor felt sick to his stomach. He didn't know what to do. The babies wouldn't stop squawking. So he knocked the nest out of the tree and killed them, too. That night, he hadn't eaten dinner. His stomach hurt too badly.

Although his family didn't know it, Alex was a thief. He stole his brother's toys, change from the jar on top of his father's dresser, and bills from his mother's purse. He stole at school, at church, and even last year at summer camp. At his bravest moment, he'd stolen a video game from a neighbor's yard sale. He liked how it made him feel. Liked the illicit thrill. But late at night, he worried what would happen if he ever got caught.

These were the ghosts they kept from each other—their most private, secret torments. This was what kept them apart, even on nights like this when they thought they were happy and having fun and loved.

Eventually, they entered the maze house. It was pitch-black inside. The boys led the way, stretching out their arms and touching the walls with their fingertips. Connie and Liam followed behind. In the darkness, Liam playfully squeezed her butt. Connie elbowed him in the stomach. They moved slowly, feeling their way along, and hitting many dead ends. Backtracking, they eventually found their way to the center of the building. A flashing strobe light hung from the ceiling. The entire room had been painted in a black and white checkerboard pattern—the floor, all four walls, and the ceiling. As they crossed the room, the O'Bannons marveled at the effect. It appeared as if they were moving in slow motion. It made Connie dizzy. She reached for the wall to steady herself, and noticed that the wall had eyes. And a mouth.

The mouth was grinning.

Shrieking, Connie jumped backward, hiding behind Liam. As they watched, a figure detached from the wall and moved toward them. It was another Ghost Walk volunteer. His clothing had the same checkerboard pattern as the rest of the room. Even his exposed skin—his hands and face—had been painted in the same fashion. Connie smiled in smug satisfaction as the boys and even Liam fled, screaming.

They plunged down another dark hallway, and were back to feeling their way through the impenetrable gloom. Eventually, they reached the maze house's exit and emerged back into the night. This part of the trail had been strung with twinkling orange lights. They reflected off the white lines on each side of the path. After pausing to laugh about their encounter, the family moved along. Behind them, they heard another group screaming as they encountered the checkered man.

"That was awesome," Liam said.

"Yeah," Connor agreed. "Can we do it again?"

"There are people behind us, buddy. We have to keep moving. But maybe after we get to the end, we can go back through if the line isn't too long."

Both boys cheered. Connie groaned. They moved on. Connor and Alex ran ahead. Liam and Connie held hands.

Running footsteps pounded toward them. A man dressed like a werewolf rounded the corner, clutching his rubber mask in his hands. His eyes flashed terror.

"It's my grandma," he shouted, racing past them. "She's down there!"

Liam reached for the fleeing man. "Is she hurt?"

The volunteer werewolf brushed by him, barely stopping.

"No, man. She ain't hurt. She's fucking dead! Has been for twenty years."

He ran past them and disappeared into the woods.

"That guy was weird," Connor said, staring in confusion.

"It's just part of the show," Liam said, trying to reassure his family. "It's all an act."

Connie frowned. "Well, I definitely don't approve of his language."

"Come on," Alex urged. "Let's keep going."

More screams and laughter drifted out of the maze house as they started down the trail again. Curiously, there were now screams ahead of them, as well.

"I thought we were the first ones through," Connor said.

"We are," Liam assured him.

"So who's screaming?"

"It's just the people hiding up ahead. They're trying to psyche us out."

The trail sloped downhill and then began to curve

around, heading in the other direction. Liam guessed they must be at the halfway point. The trail grew darker as they reached the bottom of the hill. The white lines on both sides of the path faded, as if eaten by the dark. It was colder here. Connie and the kids shivered. The string of orange lights flickered. The screams increased in pitch and intensity, and then abruptly ceased.

Liam frowned. "What the—"

As they watched, the lights began to go out, one by one. Then they realized that they weren't going out—they were being blacked out. Something was creeping across them. Something that moved like smoke.

It was the night.

The night was moving.

"Look at that," Alex gasped.

Darkness flowed across the forest floor like water and wound between the trees like a snake. Everything it touched disappeared, encased in an impenetrable, obsidian shroud.

Connor grabbed his mother's hand and squeezed.

"T-this is part of the show, too, right, Daddy?" Alex asked.

Liam couldn't answer him because Liam was speechless. Tasha, the girl he'd had the affair with, stepped out of the darkness, naked and glistening with ebony liquid. The dark matter dripped from her pores. She reached for him, breasts heaving, and Liam gasped, terrified that his worst nightmare—Connie finding out about Tasha—had now come true.

Except that Connie didn't notice because Celeste was gripping her hand. A second ago it had been Connor. But when she glanced down to reassure her son, she saw Celeste's arm instead, sliced from palm to elbow, flayed skin hanging down in flaps, and black blood dripping from the wound.

For Connor, the darkness sounded like a flock of baby birds. Their wings beat against his upturned hands.

For Alex, the sky rained black coins, all stolen from his

father's dresser. They pelted his skin, their impact like bullets.

The O'Bannon family screamed as one and Nodens began to feed.

At the entrance to the Ghost Walk, Ken nodded at each customer as they climbed aboard the waiting hay wagon. Many of them reacted to the sounds drifting out of the woods. Some of them looked frightened. Others looked excited.

Grinning, Ken nudged the security man next to him.

"Listen to that. You hear those screams?"

"I sure do, Mr. Ripple. Sounds like it's a big hit. People are having fun and getting spooked. We should get some great word of mouth tomorrow."

More screams echoed across the field.

"Yeah." Ken smiled. "It really is beautiful, isn't it? That's the sound of success. We're doing good things here tonight."

Nodens continued to feed, sending tendrils and feelers in all directions, consuming every living thing it touched—taking the form of their greatest fears and confronting them with it, waiting until their energy peaked from terror and pain and regret, and then gorging itself, draining them dry and spreading onward.

It pushed more of itself into the world, and felt the walls shake around it. They grew more fragile with each passing minute. Soon, they would shatter altogether and the feast would truly begin.

Until then, Nodens was content with the appetizers. It took pleasure in the horror it caused. It relished the destruction. Reveled in the anguish that it knew the Creator must feel every time it or one of the other Thirteen did this. Every time they snuffed out another of His favored creations.

The darkness continued to expand, engulfing everything in its path.

Another group of people had just emerged from the

maze house when a wave of darkness rolled over them. It
flowed through the building's exit, racing down the winding
hallways—darker than the darkness around it. It crashed
over the roof and wrapped itself around the trees towering
above the maze house. Then it gushed down the other side
of the building and sent ebony tentacles rushing into the entrance, as well, trapping those inside. Their screams faded
quickly.

Tammy Hays had volunteered to be a Ghost Walk runner.
She was delivering hot chocolate to the other volunteers
when the darkness took her. For Tammy, the darkness looked
like snakes.

Benson Nugent was hiding behind a wall of cornstalks,
waiting to jump out at a group of teens. Benson wore glasses
and they kept fogging up beneath his rubber mask. He heard
the screams all around him, but the sound didn't concern him.
There was supposed to be screaming. When the teens faltered,
Benson pulled off his mask and quickly tried to clean his
lenses. He noticed the darkness pooling around his feet. Then
it turned into a pool of water, just like the pond he'd almost
drowned in when he was nine.

Doris Anderson, Philip Nguyen, Steve Midler, and Sara
McCauliff heard Benson's screams. Doris and Sara screamed
along with him, frightened by the outburst. Philip and Steve
laughed, assuming it was part of the show. Then a wave of
darkness swelled out of the forest and crashed down on them.
Doris saw spiders, Philip saw the parents who'd given him up
for adoption, Steve saw his drunken father, and Sara drowned
as the darkness filled her lungs and throat. They were all
swept away in a flood of black.

Jim "Jimbo" Sylva and Brandon Clark had a sweet setup.
They'd located their hiding spaces directly across the trail
from each other. They jokingly called it The Gauntlet.
Passersby had no choice but to walk between them, at which
point Jimbo and Brandon could jump out and give them a
double-whammy of a scare. When they heard footsteps ap-

proaching, they leaped out onto the path—only to be confronted by a nine-foot-tall cancerous tumor and a wall of black fire, respectively.

Some surrendered to the darkness right away. Others, driven mad by its touch, insane by having their fears exposed, pulled away and attacked the others around them.

Christopher Jones had listened to Ken earlier. He'd removed his chain from his chainsaw. But now, after just reliving the car crash that had killed his parents, he'd changed his mind. He dug through his toolbox, hidden behind his wall of cornstalks. The darkness hovered around him, enjoying the emotions pouring from his body. Christopher grabbed a wrench and put the chain back on. Then, repositioning his Leatherface mask, he began to systematically slaughter others along the trail, until the darkness took him completely.

Throughout the forest, the screams grew louder and the darkness grew thicker.

Nodens continued to feed, siphoning off their energies and leaving behind empty husks. With each victim, its mass grew—but its movements were still limited. On the other side, it strained against the walls, felt them weaken. Nodens knew impatience for the first time. It was eager. Ravenous.

Soon.

Ken listened to the screams and stared at the exit. He felt uneasy. Apprehensive. Something was wrong. The shrieks and shouts coming from the Ghost Walk seemed frenzied. There was no laughter, only screaming.

And the exit remained empty.

The tractors had continued taking people to the entrance. Group after group walked into the forest.

But nobody was coming out.

"What the hell is going on? Where is everybody?"

He wondered again where Terry was, and felt the first real pangs of fear.

The screams reached a fevered pitch. Now, many of the

volunteers and attendees were beginning to look unsettled. They kept glancing nervously at the woods.

Ken pulled aside some security personnel and asked them to hold off on sending anyone else in. Then he flagged down the tractors and told the farmers the same thing. Grabbing a flashlight, Ken walked toward the darkened entrance.

CHAPTER TWENTY-TWO

The line of traffic lessened as Maria, Levi, and Adam neared the Ghost Walk. Cars were still backed up, but at least they were moving now. The majority of attendees had already parked. All that was left now were the stragglers. Blowing the horn and flashing the lights, Maria raced past them and zipped toward the entrance. A volunteer in an orange safety vest waved his flashlight at her, making frantic motions and shouting at her to slow down. Ignoring his protests, Maria swerved around the man and barreled through the field. The car bounced on its shocks, jarring them all. Maria's teeth clacked together and Levi held on to his hat. In the backseat, Adam squawked, pleading with her to slow down. Something scraped against the bottom of the vehicle.

"There." Levi pointed at the entrance.

Maria drove toward it, weaving around angered pedestrians. People leapt out of her way, shaking their fists and hollering as she passed.

"Coming through!" she shouted out the window. "Sorry. We have an emergency!"

"All these people," Levi said, staring at the midway. "There must be several hundred, easily. And who knows how many have already entered the woods?"

Two men wearing ball caps with "Ghost Walk Staff"

emblazoned across the front ran toward them. They yelled at Maria to stop, but she gunned the engine, sending mud and grass flying out from beneath her back tires.

"There's Ken," she said, pointing to the entrance.

He stood just a foot from the start of the trail. He turned, blinking, as the car shot toward him.

The screams emanating from the woods were now joined by shouts of alarm from those standing in line. Ken cried out along with them, cringing as the car bore down on him. It slid to a stop about ten feet away from the entrance. Two people got out, but Ken couldn't see who they were. The car's headlights blinded him. Ken shielded his eyes with his hand. Then the shadowy figures stepped in front of the car.

"Maria?"

"Ken, don't go into the woods!"

"What?"

She hurried toward him. With her was an Amish man. A third figure slowly got out of the car and trailed along behind them. Ken grunted in bewilderment. Despite the gloom, the second man wore sunglasses. Far behind them, Ken saw two of his security personnel running across the field. One of them seemed to be shouting into his cell phone. Ken briefly wondered if he was calling the police.

Maria stopped in front of him and bent over, holding her sides and gasping for breath. The Amish man stood next to her, seemingly unruffled. The man with the sunglasses approached them slowly, as if afraid.

"Maria," Ken hollered, "what the hell is going on? You could have killed someone coming in here like that!"

"I'm sorry," she panted. "We had to find you . . . talk to you . . . Jesus, I'm out of shape."

"Well, I hope you had a good reason. My security guys are probably calling the cops right now."

"Excellent," the Amish man said. "They can help keep the crowd back. You mustn't let anyone enter the forest."

Ken flinched. "Excuse me?"

"Anyone who enters your Ghost Walk is damned, Mr. Ripple."

Ken opened his mouth to speak, and found that he couldn't. Behind him, the screams from the woods intensified.

"You were right, Levi," the man with the sunglasses muttered. "I can feel it."

He held his hands up, palms facing the forest, as if warming them over a campfire.

"Look," Ken demanded. "You people better start making some goddamned sense. Maria, I thought you supported what I was doing here?"

"I do . . ."

"Then what the hell is this?"

"It's very simple, Mr. Ripple. You can't let anyone else go into that forest. If you do, their souls rest in your hands."

"I'm sorry. You are who, exactly?"

"You can call him Levi," Maria said.

Ignoring her, Ken glared at Levi. "You're Amish. What is this, some sort of religious protest? You here to picket me or something?"

"No," Levi explained. "This is beyond religious dogma. This is something else."

More screams poured out of the forest.

"Screw this," Ken said. "I want all three of you to get out of here, now."

"Ken," Maria pleaded, "please listen to us. I can explain everything. Something bad is happening."

"Take a listen." Ken nodded toward the forest. "You hear those screams? Those aren't your normal I'm-having-fun-getting-scared screams. Somebody might be hurt. I need to get down there and find out what's going on. What I don't need is this bullshit. Now get out of here."

"Those people are already dead, Mr. Ripple." Levi stepped forward. "And if you go in there, you'll only join them."

Ken leaned toward him, so close their noses almost touched.

"Buddy, I don't know who the hell you are, but after the day I've had, if you don't get the fuck out of here right now, I will knock you flat on your ass. Do you understand me?"

Levi smiled. "You can try."

The flashlight slipped from Ken's grasp. His hands curled into fists. His jaw clenched. He glared at Levi through narrowed eyes.

"It's true," Maria interrupted, pulling Levi back. "It's all true, Ken. Everything they said about LeHorn's Hollow and these woods. The Goat Man. The murders. I know it doesn't make any sense. I know it sounds crazy. We just talked about this the other day. But I've seen things—things you wouldn't believe. And I'm telling you that you need to listen to us. Just five minutes, okay?"

Without giving him a chance to refuse, Maria plunged ahead, giving him an abbreviated account of what she'd learned.

"There's something evil in the forest. It's a force—a living darkness. It drains the energy from living things. If we don't stop it before midnight, then it will expand all over the world. This man, Levi, knows how to stop it."

"And who's that guy?" Ken nodded toward Adam.

Maria sighed. "This is Adam Senft."

"Now I know you're full of shit."

Maria exploded. "Don't you take that tone with me, you son of a bitch. I interviewed you. We had dinner together. Now, I know you don't know me very well, but you damn sure know I'm thorough and skeptical about everything. *Everything*. I know this sounds crazy, but it's fucking true! You said yourself that something was wrong. Listen to those screams."

Adam shuffled forward. "What screams?"

They paused, listening.

The forest was silent.

Ken paled. "What the hell is—"

The sudden silence terrified him more than the screaming had.

"We've got to act now." Levi turned to Maria. "Give me your keys. I need to get my things out of your car. Adam, will you carry that bag of salt, please?"

The two security men finally reached them, breathing hard, their faces red and covered with sweat. Ken couldn't remember either of their names.

"We're sorry, Mr. Ripple," one exclaimed. "She drove right by us."

"We called the police," the other one said. "They're on the way."

"Good." Ken grasped at Levi, spinning him around. "Hold up. You're not going anywhere."

Levi's voice was like stone. "Unhand me now."

"Go fuck yourself."

There was a commotion near the ticket booth. Ken turned to see what was happening and saw Sammi Horton, the woman in charge of tickets, running toward them.

"Ken, Terry's wife just called."

"What now?"

"He never came home last night. She said at first she just assumed he was here, but when he didn't call today, she began to get worried. She's left him several messages but he hasn't called her back. She says she's been calling your cell phone, as well."

Ken's temples began to throb.

"Goddamn it. I should have checked earlier . . ."

"There's something else," Sammi said.

"What?"

"There's a woman over at the booth. She says her

grandchildren went in with the first group and they're still not back yet. She's getting a little worried. What should I tell her?"

"Tell her we are looking into it. And hold off on calling Terry's wife back."

"Are you sure?"

"Yes. And don't sell any more tickets until I tell you to. We're closed."

Maria gave Levi her car keys. Adam and Levi retrieved the salt and Levi's bag from the car. The security guards moved to stop them, but Ken waved them off and retrieved his flashlight.

"Keep an eye on that line," he said. "Don't let anybody else through."

"So you suddenly believe me?" Maria's tone was skeptical.

"No," Ken told her. "What you're saying is ridiculous. But I do think something's happened. Hell, something's *been* happening. I was just too stupid and fucking prideful to notice. And now my best friend is missing, along with a whole bunch of other people. I'm going in there. You and your crazy friends are staying here."

"The hell we are."

"I'm not gonna argue with you, Maria. Stay put until the police get here. If that really is Adam Senft, then you've got a lot of explaining to do."

"Somebody mention my name?"

Adam and Levi had returned from the car. Levi clutched his bag and Adam had the sack of salt thrown over one shoulder. Ken glanced at it and snorted.

"I don't think ice on the trail is a problem right now."

Ignoring him, Levi nodded at Maria and Adam. "Come on. We're running out of time. I can feel it getting stronger."

"What part of 'stay here' don't you people understand?" Ken shouted.

"Ken, please!" Maria shook her head in frustration. "Listen to us."

"Screw this. I don't have time to argue with you. You guys want to follow me, fine. But stay the hell out of my way."

He wheeled around and marched toward the entrance. Levi, Adam, and Maria followed along behind him, walking side by side.

"Are you sure about this?" Adam asked Levi. "I mean, maybe we should get a couple shotguns or something. Maybe some chainsaws. They worked okay when me and my friends did this."

"They'll do us no good this time."

"Okay." Adam shrugged. "It's your funeral."

"No," Levi whispered, "it isn't."

The four of them stepped onto the trail and plunged into the forest. Ken stopped before he'd taken a dozen steps. The others halted behind him.

"Jesus," he wheezed. "Look how dark it is in there. I can't see shit. The flashlight doesn't even penetrate."

"That's because it isn't a normal darkness," Levi said, hunkering down on his haunches and staring at the path.

"It's so quiet," Maria whispered. "What do you think is happening, Levi?"

He didn't respond. Instead, he examined the ground closely, running his hands across it. "What are these white lines?"

Frowning, Ken glanced back at him. "It's lime. We use it to line the trail, so people don't wander off. It's supposed to glow in the dark, but for some reason, it's not doing a very good job tonight."

Levi fell backward, landing on his ass. He began to laugh. The sudden outburst surprised the others.

"Are you okay?" Maria asked, concerned.

"What's so funny?" Ken demanded.

"Lime! Oh, this is perfect. Better than I could have ever

hoped for. This, my friends, is a testimony to the power of prayer."

Ken glanced at Maria. "What's he going on about?"

She shook her head.

Levi gazed upward. "Thank you, Lord! Thank you for this boon."

"LeHorn used lime," Adam said. "I remember, from his journal. He used lime in one of the banishing spells, when he tried to cleanse the hollow."

"That is correct." Levi stood up and brushed the dirt from his pants. "He did indeed. Although lime is not as powerful as salt, it can be used as a substitute. All you have to do is charge it properly."

While Levi examined the lime, Ken turned back to the trail and took another tentative step forward. He thought he sensed movement in the darkness, but he couldn't see anything. He stared harder, trying to peer beyond the black curtain. There it was again—movement, a slight tremor. But from what?

Then his eyes widened.

It was the darkness itself.

As he watched, it crept toward them, slowly, excruciatingly, as if it were a rubber band stretched to its limit.

Noticing his reaction, Maria and Adam followed Ken's gaze. Maria gasped and Adam screamed, dropping the bag of salt. It split open, spilling onto the ground.

"That's it!" Adam shrieked. "He Who Shall Not Be Named! It waits at the heart of the Labyrinth like a big tumor, infecting the universe. And now it's here!"

Maria grabbed Ken's shoulder and tried to pull him backward, but he remained rooted to the spot, staring as the darkness crept closer.

"Ken," she urged, "come on!"

"It's moving slowly," Levi said.

"Not slow enough for me," Maria replied.

Adam ran to the edge of the forest.

"It's sluggish," Levi insisted. "Which means that it's extended to its limits. It won't be able to go much farther until the barriers are down. We still have time. Maria, Mr. Ripple—get behind me. Adam, come here. I need your help."

"No thanks," Adam called. "I'm fine right here. You go ahead. Work your voodoo."

"Adam," Levi insisted, "you promised that you'd help me. You agreed that you owed it to your loved ones. Now I need you to honor that promise—and to honor their memories."

"I can't. I'm . . . *afraid.*"

"We're all afraid, Adam. But this is what we've been called to do. Now please, come here. You have to trust me."

"Trust you?"

"Yes. I've helped you so far, haven't I?"

Adam slowly approached him, while Maria tried to drag Ken away. Ken shrugged free of her and pointed at the darkness.

"Look!"

The night rippled. Ken glanced over his shoulder to verify that Maria had seen it, too—but she was gone. They were all gone. Maria, Levi, and Adam. The woods. The trail. All of it. He floated in a sea of black. There was only him, adrift in an ebony void, completely alone.

His greatest fear. Ever since Deena's death, Ken was afraid of being alone.

The darkness pressed in on all sides, and Ken screamed.

Maria tried to pull him away, but before she could, two figures stepped out of the darkness.

Maria . . .

"M-Mom? Dad?"

Her parents glided toward her. Their skin, hair, eyes, and clothes were black.

You have failed us, Maria. You are an embarrassment to this family. To your culture. Your heritage. Our standing in the community.

"No." Maria closed her eyes. "You're not real. Levi said you take the form of the things that haunt us. The things we fear."

Maria, look at us!

"I'M NOT AFRAID OF YOU!"

Maria opened her eyes again. Her parents reached for her, and her resolve shattered. Maria screamed.

"Adam," Levi shouted, "to me!"

The darkness swirled around Ken and Maria, poised to strike.

Levi scooped up a handful of salt and ran toward them.

"*Ia Ishtari, ios daneri, ut nemo descendre fhatagn Shtar!* God, guide my hand."

He tossed the salt at the entity. The crystals sparked, turning blue as they soared through the air. They pelted the darkness, and it withdrew, shuddering.

"Grab Ripple before he falls," Levi told Adam as he reached for Maria.

Stumbling, they guided Maria and Ken back to the beginning of the trail, out of reach of the darkness. Levi peered into Maria's eyes.

"Are you okay?"

She nodded. "I think so."

"Ripple, how about you?"

"I'll live. The fuck just happened?"

"We've been trying to tell you," Levi said, "but you would not listen. Now I'm afraid I'll have to insist that you stay out of my way."

"Fuck that," Ken said. "I want to help. And for what it's worth, I'm sorry."

Levi knelt, picked up the bag of salt, and handed it to Ken.

"Be careful that you don't spill it."

Ken frowned. "What am I supposed to do with this?"

"If you're being sincere and you really do want to help, then listen to me carefully. I saw an exit not far from the entrance. Am I correct in assuming that this trail loops around?"

"Yeah. So what?"

Levi placed one hand on Ken's shoulder and his other hand on the ruptured bag. Then he repeated the same phrase he'd shouted before throwing the salt. For a second, Ken felt a slight charge go through him, like licking a battery. Then it faded. The air smelled of ozone.

"What did you just do?"

Levi shook his head. "I need you and Maria to take this salt to the exit. Pour a line of it all the way across the exit, connecting to the lime lines on either side. You don't have to use a lot of it. In fact, try to conserve. But the line must completely touch both sides. Think of it as an invisible wall. Okay?"

Ken nodded. "Sure. What will that do?"

"Just what I said. It will create an invisible wall. Once you've done that, I want the two of you to stand on the far side of that line. Make absolutely sure you're not standing on the trail or between the lines. Do you understand?"

"This is like before," Maria said. "With the circle of protection?"

"Exactly. But this time, instead of keeping something out, we're trying to keep something in."

"A trap?"

Levi winked at her.

"Stay clear of the path," he told them, "but be ready for me to call you. When I do, proceed into the woods—making absolutely sure you walk on the outside of the lines, avoiding the path—and sprinkle the salt onto the trail."

Maria coughed. "But won't the salt break the circle?"

"No. I've already prepared it. As long as neither of you cross the barriers, we'll be fine. Be mindful of that as you sprinkle the salt. Don't let your hands or fingers cross the lines. Just the salt. You won't have to go very far. Probably only a few feet. A few yards at the most."

"How will we know when to stop?"

"You'll know."

"You want us to go into the woods?" Ken asked.

"Correct."

"And that thing—that dark stuff—is in the woods?"

"Yes."

"Fuck that."

"Then Maria can do it alone. Three is a better number than four, anyway. In certain Chinese dialects, the word for four is very similar to the word for death. I have no time to reassure you, Mr. Ripple. This is our last chance and we are out of time."

Ken flinched, staring at him. Then he turned to Maria.

"Do you trust this guy?"

She nodded. "If you'd seen what I have, you'd trust him, too."

Ken turned back to Levi. "You're not like any Amish person I've ever met."

"I'm not Amish."

"But you were talking about God. Don't you believe in Him?"

"I do. But I am not Amish and I am not a Christian."

"Well, what are you then?"

"I am something worse. I am a soldier. Now go, please."

Ken and Maria hurried back into the field and over to the exit. Adam studied Levi closely. The man's expression was grim but determined as he opened his bag and began removing items from it.

"Earlier," Adam said, "after we found the book, you said there was one more thing I had to do to help you. I'm guessing this is where that comes in?"

Levi nodded.

"Well, for what it's worth, I just want to say thanks."

"There is no need to thank me. I'm just doing what I'm called upon to do."

The darkness began to gather again, lapping at the forest floor just feet from where they stood. It trembled and quivered, but did not progress farther.

Levi spread the items out on the ground, just at the edge of the forest, on the other side of the entrance. Then he turned to Adam.

"I need you to stand here, just inside the trail."

"But the darkness—"

"Cannot reach this far. Not yet. Look at it. I've weakened it, at least temporarily. It needs to recuperate."

Cautiously, Adam stepped back onto the trail again. He watched the forest carefully, tensed and ready to flee, but the darkness remained where it was. Behind him, Levi picked up another handful of salt and recited the same words over it. Then he took one step backward, just outside of the entrance. Kneeling, he poured the salt out of his hand in a straight line, just as he'd instructed Ken and Maria to do—joining it to the Ghost Walk's outline. For a brief moment, the lime lines seemed to glow blue. Then the light faded.

"Seriously," Adam said, still watching the darkness. "I mean it. I want to thank you. It's been a really long time since I've trusted anybody—or since anybody has trusted me. But you changed that, and I'm grateful."

As Adam talked, Levi sat two candles on either side of the entrance and lit them. Under his breath, so that Adam wouldn't hear him, he prayed.

"Lord forgive me, for I do this in Your name. Please have mercy upon all our souls. Thy will be done, Lord."

"Levi?"

"Thy will be done . . ."

"Hey, man? Are you listening? I'm unburdening my soul here, dude."

"Forgive me, Father."

"Levi, didn't you hear me? I said thank you."

Levi glanced up. "For what?"

Adam smiled. "For believing in me. For letting me help.

I appreciate it. All this time, I've wished there was some way I could redeem myself. Some way to make up for everything that's happened. And you're giving me that. So I'm saying thanks."

"Redemption?" Levi smirked. "There is no redemption for you, Adam Senft. You murdered your wife in cold blood. You slaughtered her—the woman who you swore before God and your family to love and honor and cherish and respect. You made a sacred, holy vow and then you discarded it. You pushed your wife out of the attic window."

"No! I was trying to save her. I just wanted to kill the baby. Hylinus had—"

"You killed Tara. She split open and spilled out all over the ground. By your hand, Adam. By your red right hand. The reasons don't matter, only the results. You fancied yourself one of us—a magician. Yet you were nothing more than a child playing war with a loaded gun. And then, when things turned tragic—when things went wrong—you didn't even accept responsibility for your actions. You blamed it on everyone else. On Hylinus. On Nelson LeHorn. And especially on God."

Still standing on the path, Adam whirled around. "It wasn't my fault."

"Then whose fault was it?"

"It was God's fault!"

"No!" Levi shouted. "It was *your* fault! How dare you blame Him? He gave you everything. Your wife. Your dog. Your friends and family. And how did you repay that kindness? By leading them to their deaths and then blaming Him. You disgust me."

"Shut up, Levi. You just shut the hell up, right now!"

"God didn't do this to you, Adam Senft. You did this to yourself. And now you're damned."

Adam snarled, clenching his fists. "You motherfucking son of a bitch! I'll fucking kill you!"

He charged, running at Levi with his head down and fists

raised. His lips were pulled back, revealing gritted teeth. Levi remained sitting, not moving from his spot on the other side of the entrance. When Adam's foot came in contact with the line of salt, he screamed, flying backward through the air and crashing to the trail with a thud.

"Oh, no," Levi whispered. "Not this time. You already broke one circle. You don't get to break another one."

Groaning, Adam sat up. "Let me out of here. You hear me, motherfucker? I said let me out of here."

Levi shook his head. "I'm sorry, Adam, but I'm afraid that's impossible. It's too late. Look at the darkness."

Stumbling to his feet, Adam turned and stared down the trail. The entity was moving again. It swirled like mist, coalescing into different shapes.

"You're not a man," Levi goaded, trying to stoke Adam's fears higher. "You're nothing. You failed as a writer, as a husband, as a father, and as a friend. You're not a protector. You're a joke. You couldn't save your wife or your children. And now, you can't even save yourself.

"Look at it, Adam! Everyone that you damned. Tara. Big Steve. Merle Laughman. Dale Haubner. Cliff Swanson. Cory Peters. Paul and Shannon Legerski. Shelly Carpenter. Leslie Vandercamp and her boyfriend, Michael Gitleson. Officer Al Uylik. All dead because of your arrogance. Because of your incompetence. Their families grieve while you shirk the blame. Look upon your works, magus. Go on! Look into the darkness and stare upon your ghosts."

Adam's screams echoed across the forest and field. He shrank away, pressing against the invisible barrier behind him. The darkness rushed forward, flowing along the trail.

Levi's voice rose in pitch and drowned out Adam's wails.

"*Eloim shammanta. Barra, Gigum xul. Barra, Maskim xul. Ia idimmu, descente Shtar. Destrato Nud. Destrato Verminus. Destrato Nuada.*"

"Get back!" Adam screamed. "Levi, help me! Let me out!"

"*Destrato Lud. Destrato Shub-Niggurath. Destrato Pahad.*

Destrato Lilitu. Destrato Lamashtu. Destrato Othel. Sator opera verminni. Sator opera fhatagn."

Levi paused, watching. Attracted by the magnitude of Adam's fears and guilt, Nodens was focusing on the distraught man, attracted by his boiling emotional energies. As it narrowed the distance between them, stretching to the very limits of its current boundaries, the entity condensed its mass, shrinking down and thickening. Without taking his eyes off it, Levi reached down and grabbed a candle with each hand. Then he touched the flames to the lime. Immediately, the darkness solidified inside the lines, occupying the Ghost Walk and withdrawing from the surrounding woods. The portion of Nodens that was left in the gateway retreated inside the portal.

"Got you." There was no glee in Levi's voice.

Levi had effectively split the entity in two. The earthbound portion was trapped inside the Ghost Walk. The rest, he knew, was cowering on the other side of the doorway, weakened and—for the first time in eons, he hoped—afraid.

"Levi," Adam begged, "please don't do this. Don't do this to me."

"For what it's worth, Mr. Senft. I am sorry."

The darkness spoke.

Adam . . .

"Tara," Adam whispered. "Baby, I'm so sorry . . ."

"Maria!" Levi yelled. "Ken! Do it now!"

He turned back to Adam and watched him writhe as the darkness slithered over him. Adam's cries died in his throat.

The darkness hovered in front of him, savoring his emotions. Then, overcome with hunger, Nodens began to feed. Levi turned away.

"God forgive me," he wept. "God, please forgive me . . ."

"It sounds like they're fighting," Ken said. "Maybe we should go back over there."

"No." Maria reached out and clasped his arm. "Let's just do what Levi said, and wait for his signal."

Privately, she was concerned as well. Standing where they were, in the field and near the trail's exit, she couldn't make out every word. Their voices were garbled. But Levi's tone had taken on a distinctly ugly sound. It was mean. Spiteful. Full of hatred and disgust—not at all like the man she'd come to know over the last forty-eight hours.

Then Adam started screaming.

Ken started forward again, but Maria pulled him back.

"Wait."

"Why?"

"Because we have to trust him. He's a man of God, right?"

"I don't know what the hell he is."

Ken glanced around the field. The police still hadn't arrived—or if they had, then they were having trouble making it through the surging crowds. Rather than running, the crowds had come closer, drawn like flies at the prospect of some human misfortune—an accident, a heart attack, a murder. Excited by the possibility of seeing someone dragged out of the woods on a stretcher, they waited. The Ghost Walk's staff was holding them at bay, keeping them confined in a rough semicircle near the ticket booth. Beyond the midway, other people were leaving, perhaps anxious to escape the morbid curiosity of their fellow citizens. The upper half of the field was jammed with cars and a long line had formed on the road—another traffic jam, this time leading away from the Ghost Walk. Maybe that explained the cops' tardiness.

Levi's voice rose on the wind, drifting toward them.

"Eloim shammanta. Barra, Gigum xul. Barra, Maskim xul. Ia idimmu, descente Shtar. Destrato Nud. Destrato Verminus. Destrato Nuada."

"Sounds like gibberish to me," Ken grunted. "Maybe he's having some kind of seizure."

"Be quiet," Maria whispered. "I'm trying to listen."

Suddenly, Adam's screams rose in intensity. Then they heard Levi call out to them.

"Maria! Ken! Do it now!"

"Come on," Maria said. "You heard the man."

"I still don't understand any of this."

They began sprinkling the salt as Levi had instructed, careful not to let their hands or toes breach the pathway's boundary lines. Leaves and twigs crunched under their feet, and they had to duck beneath low-hanging branches. They'd gone about ten feet when the white line began to glow.

"Look," Maria gasped.

A blue radiance filled the air. Sparks crackled across the surface of the lime. Then, the entire Ghost Walk began to glow, starting at the exit and racing into the woods.

Ken gazed in amazement. "It's like pouring a line of gasoline on the ground and then lighting a match. Like a long fuse."

As they watched, the blue glow spread deep into the forest, following the trail.

"Maybe we should get out of here," Ken suggested. "Get back up to the field."

"That's not a bad idea," Maria agreed breathlessly. "You're right. It does look like a fuse. And who knows what's gonna happen when it reaches the other end?"

Nodens swept over Adam, gorging itself on the man's overwrought emotions.

Adam shivered in its cold caress. His body felt weak and weightless. He closed his eyes and moaned. When he opened his eyes again, all he saw was darkness. Something whispered in his ear. Then another. And another. His wife. His children. His friends and his dog. Each of them spoke to him, promising in detail the terrors and anguish that waited beyond.

Blinking the tears from his eyes, Levi watched.

Deep in the forest was a blue glow. It grew brighter and

larger as it raced toward them, dispelling the darkness in its path. It reminded Levi of a freight train.

Nodens tried to flee the onrushing light, but was trapped by the lime. It tried to cross the barriers, tried to break free and return to the doorway and rejoin its other half—but it was too late. Already, the cold light had severed its link with the rest of its body, churning in the portal. Now the dazzling brilliance rolled forward. The darkness sizzled at its touch, dissipating like smoke.

Enraged, Nodens poured itself inside the man, Adam Senft. It was furious at this violation—angered that it would have to resort to seeking shelter inside one of the Creator's toys, a bag of flesh and blood and pus. And all because of this little human with the beard. But it had no choice. The light devoured everything in its path, and Nodens grew weaker as it advanced.

Levi mouthed a silent prayer as the light bore down on them. He felt cold fingers dig through his mind, and knew that Nodens was aware of his presence. Sensing its rage and humiliation, Levi smiled.

"I bind and banish you according to the Law. You may not pass through the door. Go now and bother this Earth no more."

Levi tensed.

The light crashed into them.

Nodens screamed with Adam's mouth and then a blue sun burst to life and rose over the forest, before burning out. A few wisps of energy floated into the air, crackling in the silence that followed. Then they faded and the night returned.

The night returned—but the darkness was gone.

So was Adam Senft. Not a trace of either remained.

Still kneeling, Levi leaned forward and pressed his face into the ground. Twigs and stones dug at his flesh, but he didn't care. Then, as tears rolled down his face, Levi slowly climbed to his feet and walked toward the gateway. He could feel its energies in the distance, pulling to him like a magnet.

Sobbing, he begged God and his father and Adam Senft for forgiveness.

And just like always, nobody answered.

CHAPTER TWENTY-THREE

Maria and Ken followed Levi's voice. It echoed across the forest—strange words that had very few consonants. They left the trail and, after a short walk, they found him at a circle of standing stones, putting rocks covered with sigils into holes.

And crying.

Tears streamed down Levi's dirty face. His face and hands were scratched and bloody. His eyes were red. His hat had fallen from his head. The brim was bent. Maria handed it to him while Ken helped him up. Levi thanked her, and put the hat back on his head.

Maria glanced around at the burned-out wasteland.

"This was LeHorn's Hollow, wasn't it?"

Levi nodded. "Part of it."

"Where's Adam?" she asked.

Levi didn't respond. Instead, he placed the bloody palm of his right hand against each standing stone, leaving red handprints on them. Using his index finger, he drew symbols with the blood.

"There," he said. "This gate is sealed and can be opened by none, except for the Gatekeeper. The entity has been bound and banished."

He slowly walked toward the trail. Maria jumped in front of him.

"Hey! Not so fast, Levi. Where is Adam?"

"Gone."

"What do you mean, gone? Did the darkness kill him?"

"No." Levi shook his head. "I did."

Maria stared, stunned. "W-what are you implying, Levi?"

"I'm not implying anything. I'm telling you. To bind and banish an entity as strong as the one we faced, a sacrifice is required. Adam was that sacrifice."

"You . . . *sacrificed* him?"

Levi nodded. Then he brushed past her and continued through the woods, heading toward the trail. After a moment, they followed him. Levi remained silent, refusing to answer their questions.

Eventually, they reached the Ghost Walk. The path seemed normal again. There was no blue glow, no sparks of energy. The lines of lime were just that—lime. But neither were there any dead bodies. Maria and Ken had heard people screaming, heard the slaughter taking place in the woods. But the trail was swept clean. They were gone, just like Adam. Even the bloodstains were missing.

Upon reaching the exit, Levi stepped out into the field, mumbling to himself. His head hung low and his feet dragged wearily. Maria and Ken ran after him.

"Levi . . ."

He didn't turn around.

"Levi!" Maria shouted. "Goddamn it, look at me!"

Sighing, he turned. "Please don't take that name in vain, Maria. I've asked you before."

"You . . ." She shook with rage. "You killed an innocent man."

"Adam Senft was far from innocent. You said so yourself."

"That doesn't matter."

"Doesn't it? Look around us. Is the night closing in on us?

Is the darkness breeding? No, it's not. I've rid us of the threat—sealed the gate and saved this planet and everyone on it, including you. Billions of lives versus the life of one damned soul. Are you telling me the sacrifice wasn't worth it? That one man's life is more valuable than the lives of everyone on Earth?"

Ken cleared his throat. "Sounds like *Wrath of Khan* to me. I didn't know Amish people watched *Star Trek*."

Levi regarded him coldly. Then he turned back to Maria.

"I did what I had to do, Maria. I did what the Lord required of me. I'm a soldier. He asked me to do it, so that none of you would have to. I get to live with that. I get to suffer so that you won't. That's my ghost. I've freed you of yours."

"What kind of a God would ask you to do such a thing?"

"My God—the same as your God. You still believe, don't you?"

Maria didn't answer him.

Levi turned again and strode away. His muscles ached and his bones were sore. He sighed. It was a long walk back to Lancaster and it would be an even longer time before he could rest. First he would need to cleanse himself upon arrival. Then he had to tend to Dee and Crowley.

"Levi," Maria called. "Come back. We're not finished yet."

He paused.

"What, Maria?"

"You asked me what I believe in? I believed in you."

He nodded his head sadly. "Yes, you did. And before you met me, you believed in nothing. But that's the thing with belief, Maria. It's easy to believe in something when it doesn't require anything from you. It's much harder, though, when the object of your belief requires something of you or asks for something you don't want to give. That's when real belief occurs."

She stared at him, speechless. In the distance, police sirens

wailed. Ken glanced from Levi, to Maria, and then back
again.

"What do you believe?" Levi repeated. "Do you believe in
ghosts?"

She hesitated, thinking of her parents and how they'd appeared in the darkness.

"No. I think we make our own ghosts."

Levi asked a third time. "Then what do you believe in?
You don't believe in ghosts. Your belief in me has been shattered. What's left? Do you believe in God—in Allah? His
voice spoke to you, after all. Was that enough to strengthen
your belief?"

"I . . . I don't know what to believe anymore."

He smiled, sadly. "Well, look at the bright side, Maria. In
a few hours, the sun will rise. You can have faith in that. Believe in it. The sun doesn't require much. There are no sacri-
fices to be made in its name. Every morning, the sun rises
and reminds you that it exists, so you can believe in it without hardship."

He turned his back on her and began walking once more.

"Levi?"

He responded without looking back.

"Believe, Maria. The sun will rise and you will never have
reason to fear the dark again."

And then he was gone.

Ken blinked. "Where the hell did he go?"

Fighting back tears, Maria shrugged.

"He disappeared into thin fucking air. I don't believe it."

"I do." Maria wiped her eyes. "That's not the weirdest
thing I've seen him do."

Ken put his arm around her, awkwardly at first, but then
with more confidence. Maria leaned against him. Ken glanced
around, but Levi was still absent.

"Who the hell is he, *really*?"

"I don't know," Maria whispered. "I thought I did, but I
just don't know."

The police sirens drew closer.

"Jesus," Ken muttered. "Jesus fucking Christ . . ."

Levi walked home in the darkness, with only his ghosts to keep him company. They followed along behind him, hovering in the corners of his vision. He knew from experience that if he turned to look, they'd vanish. The only time he saw them clearly was when he went to sleep.

Like always, his ghosts cried out in anguish and anger. They threatened and cajoled, but Levi kept walking. He'd learned over time to ignore them. But now, a new voice had been added to the cacophony. A new ghost.

"Be still, Adam," he whispered. "Be still."

Levi sighed. He still had a long way to go, and it would be a long time before the sunrise. This night seemed endless. Walking the line between the two, he disappeared into the black.

Turn the page for an advance look at Brian Keene's
next terrifying novel . . .

CASTAWAYS

Coming in February 2009

CHAPTER ONE

Becka knew she was going to drown. Gasping, she filled her lungs as another massive wave forced her below the churning turquoise waters. As she plunged downward, all sound ceased, except for her heartbeat, pounding in her ears. The salt water irritated her eyes. The light dimmed. Her muscles ached and her lungs burned as she sank lower. Despite the pain, she kicked and thrashed. Bubbles ringed her body like a halo. Becka's headache, which had tormented her for the last few days, throbbed in steady time with her pulse. She'd spent the last two weeks with very little food or water. Now, exhaustion, dehydration and hunger were taking their toll on her.

She should have never applied for *Castaways*. Watching it on TV every week was very different than actually competing in the show. Watching it didn't require pain or sacrifice or pushing your body to the limits.

What was she doing here, drowning in the waters off an uninhabited South Pacific island? Was being on television or a chance at the million dollar prize worth all this? It was insane. She couldn't do this. She'd applied on a whim, never believing she'd actually make the final cut. She'd filled out the online application, but so had a million and a half other people. There was no way she should have been picked. Yet here she was, one of the twenty who'd been selected—a twenty-two-year-old Penn State graduate who still lived with her parents because she couldn't find a job. A month ago, she'd been at home, attending employment fairs and desperately trying to find herself. Find *anything*. Now, she was here, in the most beautiful place she'd ever seen, and Becka was so tired and demoralized that she couldn't even enjoy it.

She was tempted to just close her eyes, exhale, and slowly drift to the bottom of the sea. The other people on the island craved fame or notoriety or wealth. Let them have it. She didn't want those anymore. Maybe she had, at one point, even if it was just a whim. Otherwise she wouldn't be here. Now, all Becka wanted was oblivion—the blessed bliss of unconsciousness. The smothering kiss of death. A very long sleep.

The water felt like a blanket.

Becka closed her eyes and let the blanket engulf her.

. . . sleep.

No, fuck that.

Her depressed futility gave way to a sense of frustration and competitiveness. Screw it. She hadn't come all this way just to give up now. She was in this to win. No matter how much she hurt, there was no retreat, no surrender. Not yet. Her family and some of her friends would understand if she quit, but they weren't the only people Becka had to worry about. There were others—the countless, faceless millions on the Internet, eager to log on and share their opinions and critiques on countless trivial pop culture icons, including her. A month ago, she'd been nobody, with a grand total of eight subscribers to her blog. Now, after this aired, her face and name would be recognized by everyone in America that owned a television or read the newspapers. She was a reality television star—or would be, once this aired.

In just a short time, Becka had learned what other public figures before her had known, as well—fame or infamy (because the two were often synonymous) sucked in equal measure. You craved them until you got them, and then you didn't want them anymore.

And she didn't even have them yet.

But there was no going back.

Spurred on by anger, Becka gritted her teeth and kicked hard for the surface. A vibrant rainbow of tropical fish darted around her, chased by a grayish-white sea snake with prominent dark bands encircling its body. Becka paused. Eyeing the serpent's paddle-shaped tail, she tried to remember if this particular type of sea snake was venomous or not. Before her arrival, she'd studied the Pacific Islands as best she could, memorizing the flora and fauna. Despite all her preparation, she couldn't remember if this one was poisonous. Becka gave the sea snake a wide berth, just to be safe. Ignoring her, the serpent continued pursuing the fish. A stingray glided by, oblivious to both Becka and the other marine life, or perhaps indifferent. She stared at it, carefully avoiding the barbed tail.

The aching in her oxygen-starved lungs grew stronger. Above her, Becka saw the wiggling legs of the other castaways. She swam toward them. Her head broke the surface. Coughing, she spat salt water and gasped for air. Her throat was sore. The sun was blinding. Waves buffeted her about. Another big one almost sank her, but she fought to stay afloat. Blinking the water from her eyes, she glanced around.

A television camera stared back at her.

Ignore it, she thought. *It doesn't exist. Remember that. I'm supposed to pretend it isn't there.*

Becka treaded water next to a small boat. Aboard were four men—a camera operator, a sound engineer, a field producer, and a pilot—all network employees. As Becka coughed, they merely glanced at her, impassive. They didn't speak or even nod in acknowledgement. Becka drifted away from the craft, debating whether she should break the rules and ask for assistance. Contestants weren't supposed to talk to or interact with the crew unless it was a dire emergency—or unless the crew initiated the contact first.

"Think they'll give us a ride?"

Jerry treaded water beside her, droplets rolling off his shaved head and chest. Like Becka, he was in his early twenties and in impressive physical shape. He was cute, and she'd noticed him checking her out several times since they'd arrived on the island two weeks ago. She didn't know much about him—just that he owned a video store in Santa Monica, California. Under different circumstances, Becka might have considered getting to know him better, but there was no time for that out here. It was every man or woman for themselves. Confiding in the wrong person, or trusting someone just a little too much, led to disaster. After twelve seasons of *Castaways*, even a novice knew that.

"Give us a ride?" She struggled to catch her breath. "You know the rules. Initiating contact with the crew means immediate disqualification from the—"

Jerry held his hands up. "I know, I know. Jesus, Becka, I was just kidding."

Another wave crashed over them. Becka fought to keep from swallowing more water. This wave was smaller than the last, and she managed to stay afloat. The two of them bobbed up on its crest and then back down again as it rolled past.

Three times a week, Becka and the other castaways had to compete against each other in a series of contests and challenges. Sometimes, they were physical. Other times, the puzzles focused on intelligence and wits, or trivia knowledge based on the region where the current game was being played. The winner of the challenge gained temporary access to the circle of protection, and was safe until the next challenge. The other castaways would then select someone to exile—meaning the chosen person was ejected from the game. Any contestant was fair game for exile, with the exception of whoever had won the circle of protection.

For today's challenge, they'd been brought offshore by boat, and then told that they had to race to shore. Now that Becka had surfaced, the other castaways were swimming away again, leaving just her, Jerry, and the camera crew on the small boat.

Becka frowned. "Shouldn't you be trying to finish the race?"

"It doesn't matter now." Jerry shrugged. "Simon already won this round."

"Shit."

"Yeah. Pompous Brit bastard. Jeff and Richard were right on his ass the whole way. All three of them made it to shore at the same time, but Simon crossed the finish line first. He's got his place in the circle of protection, now, so somebody else will have to go home tonight."

"Who?"

"I don't know. Any ideas who you'd like to see gone?"

Becka's response was cut off by another bout of coughing. "You okay?"

Jerry sounded genuinely concerned. Becka eyed him carefully.

"I don't like the water."

She immediately regretted revealing her weakness to him. Now, if he wanted to, Jerry could exploit it to advance his own standing in the game.

"This?" He grinned, dog-paddling. "This is nothing. Just some minor swells."

"I thought there was a storm coming. That's what one of the crew—Mark, the guy with the mullet—said earlier."

"Maybe." Jerry glanced up at the sky. "But the sun is out and there ain't a cloud in the sky. These aren't storm waves. The sea is choppy, sure, but it's nothing to worry about. I surf waves bigger than this all the time back in Santa Monica. Hang on to me and I'll get us both to shore."

"I'll be okay. It's just . . . I had a bad experience in a swimming pool when I was little. My brother pushed me in the deep end when I was like four years old. The water scares me a little bit, but I'll make it."

The boat's engine throttled up, and the small craft raced ahead. The camera crew's lenses were now trained on Paula and Roberta. Coughing, Becka watched the two women swimming toward shore and felt a twinge of jealousy. Even Roberta, a middle-aged librarian, was doing better than she was.

"Come on," Jerry insisted. "Let me give you a lift."

Becka hesitated, still not trusting him.

Jerry's grin vanished. "Look, that million dollars isn't going to do you much good if you drown before reaching the island. You're coughing and hacking and obviously worn out. Use your head. The challenge is over, anyway. Simon already won."

"Yeah," she said. "I guess."

He held out his arm. Becka paused, and then took it. His muscles were hard as stone beneath his slippery skin. She shivered, and felt a warmness in her belly. If Jerry noticed, he didn't comment on it. Instead, he propelled them forward with strong, confident strokes. They rose and fell on the crests of the waves. Seabirds circled overhead, riding the breeze and squawking incessantly.

The boat slowed, engine idling softly, as it reached Roberta and Paula. The two women were quite a pair. Roberta, fifty-four, was a librarian at the Ulster County Community College in Poughkeepsie, New York. Paula, forty-one, was a dancer, model and former NFL cheerleader from Tampa, Florida. Roberta was kind, soft-spoken, and sedate. Paula was gregarious, manic, and possibly crazy—or, at least, that was what her fellow castaways believed. Still, despite their differences, the two had formed an alliance within their first day on the island. They swam next to Troy, a skinny, tattooed, foul-mouthed auto mechanic from Seattle, Washington.

Jerry didn't speak as he guided them toward the beach.

"Are you okay?" Becka asked. "Am I too heavy?"

"No, you're fine. Light as a feather."

She blushed. "That's because we've had nothing to eat at base camp except rice and fish for the last five days."

"Yeah," Jerry agreed. "Lucky for us that Randy and Ryan have been so good at catching fish."

"Lucky for them, too. Keeps them from getting exiled."

"Even so, I'd kill for a pizza right about now."

Becka started to pull away from him. "I think I'm okay now. I've got my breath back and I don't feel like I'm going to pass out anymore."

"Well, maybe you'd better hold on to me a little longer, just to be safe. You can let go when we reach the boat. That way, they don't capture this on camera. Wouldn't want your boyfriend back home to see this when it airs and get jealous."

"I don't have a boyfriend."

"Really?"

"You sound surprised."

"I am," he admitted. "I figured you'd be fighting guys off with a stick."

Becka blushed again. Before she could respond, they neared the camera boat. One of the crew members had noticed their approach and was beginning to swing the camera back around on them. Becka felt a twinge of regret as she let go of Jerry's arm and began to swim on her own. They drew alongside Roberta, Paula and Troy. The rest of the castaways were already on the beach.

"Hey." Roberta waved her hand in greeting. "Looks like Simon won again."

"We saw," Jerry said. "Which sort of screws up our whole plan. Anyone have any ideas on who to exile from the island instead?"

"We were talking about Jeff," Roberta said. "Thoughts?"

Jerry nodded. "Good choice. He's physically fit, and kicking ass in the challenges. He's definitely a threat."

"But he's so nice," Paula said, treading water. "Can't we pick someone else? I hate voting to exile the nice guys."

The cameraman leaned over the side of the boat, focusing on their conversation.

"Nice?" Troy smirked. "You mean you think he's hot. Ain't that right?"

Paula shrugged. "Sure. What's wrong with that."

"Nothing," Troy said, "except that Jeff's got you and every other chick on this fucking island not voting to exile him because he's a goddamned pretty boy."

"Don't forget Ryan," Becka teased. "He thinks Jeff's pretty cute, too."

Troy poked his cheek out with his tongue and mimed fellatio.

Jerry rolled his eyes. "With your sparkling personality, Troy, I bet you never get exiled."

"Fuck you, baldy."

"Great retort, tough guy."

Scowling, Troy swam ahead of them, muttering a string of curses that grew louder when a strong wave knocked his battered Seahawks cap off his head. Arms flailing, he surged after it. The hat drifted back to Paula, who plucked it from the water and waved it over her head. Her breasts bounced up and down as she did, and the camera zoomed in on them.

Becka frowned, noticing the leering expression on the crew's faces. No doubt this footage would make it through the editing process and end up on the air.

Paula held the hat out to Troy.

"Thanks." He reached for it.

Laughing, she jerked the hat back and swam away.

"Hey," Troy shouted. "You're playing with you're fucking life, sweetheart!"

He chased after Paula, and the camera crew followed them, forgetting about the others and instead, remaining focused on Paula's attributes. Somehow, her ass stayed above the surface as she swam, and her thong bikini, threadbare from all this time spent outdoors, left little to the imagination. It certainly kept the interest of the four men on the boat. Becka was certain that Paula was aware of it. So far, her strategy for winning had been to use her sexuality—flirting with the men and playing the helpless damsel in distress, or worse, sucking up to the other women when the men weren't around.

"She's certainly got no problem staying afloat," Becka said. "Wonder how much she paid for those things?"

Jerry laughed. "Remember, all of America might hear you say that."

"No they won't. The camera crew went chasing after her."

But even if they didn't hear me, Becka thought, *Roberta did. She and Paula are pretty tight. If she tells Paula what I said, and Paula gets offended, it could be me who gets exiled tonight. Shit! What was I thinking?*

Roberta swam ahead. Frowning, Jerry watched her go. Becka noticed the worried lines on his face.

"What's wrong?"

"We may have just screwed up really bad."

"Why?"

"Paula and Roberta are part of Simon's clique. So is Jeff. And we just told them we thought Jeff was a threat and that maybe we should vote to exile him tonight."

"Yes, but they were the ones that brought him up in the first place."

"True. But why? Why would they do that, unless maybe they were testing us? Find out our plans and then report them back to the rest of their alliance."

"Shit."

"Yeah."

A helicopter roared overhead, filming aerial footage of the race. Becka watched it swoop toward land. Over the last two weeks, she'd come to hate the island, but despite the treacherous living conditions, she was still impressed and awed by its beauty. It loomed before them, a foreboding but yet picturesque mass of hills and jungle. Towering, volcanic mountains descended into blue green bays, and white sandy beaches. Far above the peaks were a few thick clouds, but otherwise the sky was clear. If there was a storm on the way, as Becka had been told, then it was a long way off.

They swam for shore, and caught up with Roberta. Becka continued staring at the island. Jerry and Roberta followed her gaze.

"Pretty, isn't it?" Roberta asked.

Becka nodded, watching the sunlight glint off the highest peaks.

"We don't have anything like it back in Poughkeepsie," Roberta said. "Even if I don't win, it doesn't matter to me anymore. Just seeing this place—just being here—has been worth it. Never in a million years would I have ever thought I'd get to do something like this."

"It looks like something out of *Jurassic Park*," Becka said, eyeing the lush, green tropical foliage.

"Yeah." Jerry flicked water from his eyes. "But on this island, it's not the raptors you have to watch out for. It's our fellow castaways. They're the predators. Everybody's out to get paid. That's why we should form an alliance. What do you say? I'll watch your backs and you guys watch mine. Deal?"

Roberta shrugged. "I've already got an alliance with Paula, so you'd have to bring her in."

"Do you trust her?"

"Sure," Roberta said. "I mean, she's sort of flighty, but I don't think she's deceitful."

"What about Simon and Jeff and Randy? Aren't you loyal to them?"

"It's a game, right?"

"Okay," Jerry said. "I'd be up for that. How about you, Becka?"

Becka tried to catch her breath. Exhaustion was creeping back into her muscles.

"Let's focus on getting to shore first."

They reached shallow water and found their footing. Then they waded toward the beach and joined the rest of the contestants, who were killing time while the crew put makeup on the show's host, Roland Thompson. Becka sprawled in the white sand, next to Shonette, a twenty-five-year-old single mother of two from Detroit, Michigan, and Ryan, a strikingly handsome, twenty-one-year-old beautician from Los Angeles. Jerry joined them after a moment, sitting cross-legged next to Becka. She wondered if he was being friendly, or just waiting for her decision on forming an alliance.

Further up the beach, Roberta joined Paula in a game of keep-away with Troy's hat. The feisty mechanic was frothing, now, letting loose with one string of curse words after another. A few feet away, Sal, a thirty-three-year-old stockbroker from Paramus, New Jersey, and Richard, a thirty-five-year-old drummer from a small town in Kansas that none of the other contestants had heard of, were involved in conversation. Becka wondered if they were scheming about tonight's choice for exile. Beyond them were Simon, Jeff and Randy. Simon was Welsh, but had moved to the United States several years ago and now worked as a music producer in Nashville. Jeff was an adventure tour guide from Estes Park, Colorado. Along with Jerry, the two were the most physically fit contestants, and therefore, among the most formidable in most of the challenges. Randy, who hailed from Philadelphia, was overweight and worked in a machine shop. And finally, standing apart from the rest of the group was Matthew, a lanky, dirty twenty-eight-year-old from the small town of Red Lion, Pennsylvania. The laconic loner didn't interact much with the other castaways, and his rat-faced features seemed frozen in a perpetual scowl. In Becka's opinion, the only reason he hadn't been exiled yet was because he was so uninvolved with the other players that he was often forgotten when it came time to vote. Currently, he was drawing stick figures in the sand with a six foot length of bamboo. He'd used the implement as a walking stick since their second day on the island, sharpening one end against the rocks to form a makeshift spear. He took it with him everywhere, and even slept with it. Becka had to give him credit, though. Matthew's spear had come in handy a few times. He'd used it to catch fish in some of the island's shallower pools.

All of the contestants did their best to ignore the cameras flitting between them, filming their every word and action. More crew members worked on Roland Thompson's hair and clothing, making sure the host looked his best before going back on camera again. He sat removed from the contestants, occupying a small pavilion above the high tide line. As a longtime *Castaways* viewer, Becka was secretly disappointed with Roland. On television, he was charming and witty and handsome. Here, in reality, he was haggard, cranky and usually sipping a gin and tonic. He stank of cologne, cigar smoke, and sweat. When he was actually on the island, he spent much of his off-camera time hitting on Paula.

The beach was noisy. Snatches of conversation blended with the shrieks of seabirds as they circled overhead or darted across the sand, looking for crabs. The waves crashed against the shore. Further inland, the treetops rustled in the breeze.

As Becka watched, Troy succeeded in reclaiming his hat, and gave a victorious, profanity-laden cheer. Paula began stretching, bending over to touch her toes and then reaching for the sky. She brushed grains of sand from her coffee-colored skin. Becka frowned. Her own skin was blotchy and peeling from overexposure to the elements, while Paula's stayed smooth and unblemished. As Paula's acrobatics continued, Randy, Sal and Richard openly leered at her, while Jeff and Simon cast furtive glances in her direction. Troy seemed oblivious. Ryan was checking out Jeff, rather than Paula. And Matthew . . .

Matthew was also staring at Paula, but his expression was one of contempt.

Despite the warm sun on her skin, Becka shivered. She glanced at Jerry to see if he was also captivated by Paula's aerobics, and then wondered why she cared. Even so, she felt relieved when he turned his attention to her and smiled.

"When this airs," he said, "I'll be amazed if Troy gets any screen time."

"Why?"

"Because they'll have to bleep everything he says. Dude swears more than a sailor."

Becka, Ryan and Shonette laughed. Noticing them, Troy walked over and joined the group. He plopped down on the sand and scowled. Becka studied the tattoos covering his forearms, back, and chest. Most of them were basic black, and the ink had faded in spots.

"What's wrong?" Shonette asked him. "You got your hat back."

"I need a fucking cigarette," Troy said. "Thirty days of this shit without a fucking smoke? What the hell was I thinking, man?"

Jerry brushed white sand from his forearms. "Why didn't you just bring some cigarettes as your luxury item? Each of us were allowed to bring one thing to the island with us."

"Because the fuckers at the network made me pick between my hat and my smokes."

"But a hat is clothing," Becka said.

"They didn't see it that way, and I don't go anywhere without my fucking hat."

"Why not?" Jerry asked.

"Because it's my lucky fucking hat!" Troy's tone was incredulous, as if Jerry should have already known that. "I've traveled all over the fucking place, and this hat is the only thing that's been with me each and every time."

"You're from Seattle, right?" Becka asked.

"Yeah. But I moved around a lot. I was born in New York. Brackard's Point, armpit of the fucking world. Me and my older brother, Sherm, ran away from home when I was fourteen. Our parents didn't give a fuck. We went from New York to Florida, and stayed there for a while. Then we lived in Texas. Then Wisconsin, which was even worse than New York. Eventually, we ended up in Seattle. Been there ever since. My hat stayed with me the whole fucking time."

"It's funny," Jerry said. "Seeing as how you've lived in

Seattle for so long, I would think you'd be craving a Starbucks Caramel Macchiato rather than cigarettes."

Troy scowled. "And you'd be wrong. I hate that fucking shit. Starbucks tastes like hot cat piss. Whatever happened to just plain old coffee? Black, no flavors or fancy names that sound like French and Italian run through a fucking meat grinder. This country is going down the fucking tubes. Not every person from Seattle is a Starbucks-loving asshole. I hate Starbucks. Give me fucking Folgers any day of the week. If I want vanilla, I'll eat some fucking ice cream. You know what I'm saying?"

"I guess so." Jerry shrugged. "I kind of like their iced cappuccinos."

"So," Becka said, trying to change the subject. "I bet your brother will be pretty excited to see you on TV, then?"

Troy lowered his head and stared at the sand. "Not really. Dumb-ass got in trouble a few years back and had to bail. Moved his ass to Pennsylvania, and got shot during a fucking bank robbery."

"I'm sorry."

"Don't be. It was his fault. Stupid son of a bitch. He was always doing shit like that."

Seeing that Troy's mood had soured even more than normal, Becka tried to distract him again by returning to the original subject.

"You should have hidden some cigarettes underneath your hat."

"Na," Troy said. "Wouldn't have worked. They checked us all pretty good. What'd you bring as your luxury item?"

Becka blushed. "My diary."

"No shit? That's cool."

"I've been keeping them since I was a little girl."

Troy turned to Jerry, Ryan and Shonette. "What'd you guys bring?"

Before they could answer, Stuart, one of the field

producers, grabbed a battery-powered megaphone and shouted directions.

"Okay, everyone, if you could please gather together here, we're ready."

The contestants made their way to a large, makeshift stage that the construction crew had built before filming had commenced. The stage was lined with bamboo torches and authentic native masks and carvings. Above it, out of sight of the cameras, were rows of lights, microphones, and other equipment. The group gathered on the stage after each contest, and when they voted on who to exile from the game. In the center of the stage was a white circle, painted directly onto the planks—the Circle of Protection. When it was time to vote, whoever had won the previous contest stood in the center of the circle, granting them immunity from exile. The contestant who was exiled had to leave the island immediately, and join the game's other losers on the network's ship, floating off shore—a large freighter that housed the camera and sound people, helicopter pilots, medical personnel, the director, Roland, and all of the show's other crew members.

When they were all onstage, arranged in a semicircle, Stuart flashed a cue, and Roland Thompson strolled across the sand toward them. A camera filmed his approach. He was dressed in a safari outfit, and when he smiled, his capped teeth gleamed in the sunlight. There were dark sweat stains beneath his armpits, but Becka knew now that the producers would edit those out before the show aired.

"Prissy fucker," Troy muttered. "I'd like to see *him* spend a night in this fucking place."

Becka and Jerry stifled their laughter.

"Hello, everyone." Roland's deep baritone boomed across the stage. "And congratulations to Simon, who won today's challenge."

"Thank you." Simon smiled, flashing his own perfectly capped teeth. "I never had any doubt."

"As you know," Roland continued, "the last castaway to

leave this island will go home with one million dollars. You are now one step closer to that prize, Simon. Tonight, you will stand in the Circle of Protection, and one of your fellow castaways will go home. The rest of you have until sundown to figure out who that will be. Head on back to base camp, and we'll see you tonight."

Roland began to turn around, but Richard raised his hand. The host called on him, visibly annoyed.

He probably can't wait to get back to the ship, Becka thought. *Sit in the air-conditioning with his feet up and have a drink. Or take a shower. God, what I wouldn't give for a hot shower.*

"Any word on the storm?" Richard asked. "There was a rumor going around that a cyclone might be coming?"

Roland glanced at Stuart, motioning for him to join them. The assistant producer stepped forward and cleared his throat. The cameraman and sound engineer turned off their equipment.

"There is indeed a tropical storm warning," Stuart confirmed. "But as far as we know, it's not going to amount to much, at least not here. It's currently tracking further north. We've got a staff meteorologist back aboard the ship who's keeping an eye on things, and he'll let all of us know if things change. They've named the storm Ivan, if that matters to any of you."

"So what if it does hit?" Shonette asked. "That mean you're gonna pull us off the island until it passes?"

Stuart smiled. "As I said, we're keeping a watch on things, and if the situation changes, we'll let you know. Now head on back to base camp. We'll have more information for you tonight, after exile."

They filed off the stage and began walking along the beach, heading toward their camp. Becka noticed that everyone had split off into subgroups. Sal and Richard walked together, laughing at some shared private joke. Simon, Jeff, Randy, Paula and Roberta celebrated Simon's victory as a group. So much for Roberta and Paula switching alliances. Jerry had been right to worry. Becka glanced from side to side. Ryan, Jerry, Shonette and Troy walked next to her.

Our own little cabal, she thought.

Jerry must have been thinking the same thing.

"That's trouble." He nodded at the group in front of them. "Simon and the rest of the big dogs. Unless we come together, they can start picking us off one by one. There's five of them, and five of us. If we make an alliance, and get Sal and Richard to vote with us, we can come out on top."

"Count me in," Ryan agreed. "I say we exile Jeff."

"I thought you had the hots for him," Becka said.

Ryan shrugged. "Sure, he's cute and all, but this is a million dollars we're talking about."

The others laughed.

"I'm in, too," Shonette whispered. "And I bet you can convince Roberta to switch sides."

"Yeah," Jerry said, "we talked to her earlier. She wouldn't commit to anything though. In fact, I'm a little worried that she might rat us out to Simon and the others."

"She wouldn't do that," Shonette said. "Paula might, but not Roberta."

"We'll see." Jerry turned to Troy. "How about you?"

Troy shrugged. "Fuck it."

"Is that a yes?"

Troy shrugged again. "It ain't a fucking no, dude. Yes, I'm in."

The cameras filmed it all.

"Aren't you forgetting someone?" Ryan asked.

Jerry frowned. "Who?"

Ryan glanced back over their shoulders. Matthew trailed after the group, slinking along behind the camera crew.

"Yeah," Jerry said. "I guess I did forget about him, after all. Kind of easy to do. He never says anything."

"He's flying under the radar," Shonette said. "Hoping that if he doesn't get noticed, he won't get exiled from the game."

Troy snorted. "He's a fucking weirdo. Always watching people. Like a snake. Dude never fucking blinks."

Becka turned, and sure enough, Matthew was staring at them. His expression was sullen.

She moved a little closer to Jerry, feeling Matthew's eyes crawl over her exposed skin.

They continued along the beach, unaware that other eyes were watching them from beneath the jungle's greenery, as well.

CHAPTER TWO

The males of the tribe crouched, hidden within the foliage, watching the intruders as they walked along the beach. The tribe's females and few young were hidden in the caves, where they'd been since the strangers had first arrived. Both had to be guarded. With each passing year, the females bore less young, and many of the newborns were severely deformed and unfit to live.

The tribe did not like the newcomers. They were noisy and destructive, and had chased away much of the island's wildlife. Their unfamiliar scent wafted through the jungle, souring everything it came in contact with.

The tribe had watched them from the shadows since their arrival, studying and learning, unsure if the intruders were predators or prey. At first, the tribe was afraid. Like them, the newcomers walked on two legs, but they were clearly not the same. There were far more differences than similarities. The intruders' bodies were mostly hairless, except for a few of the males, who had a sparse covering of hair on their chests and backs—but nothing like the thick, curly hair covering the males of the tribe. The hairless ones' heads were bigger, but their brows weren't quite as sloped as the island's inhabitants. Their feet weren't as broad, nor were their lower jaws. While the tribe members could crack a coconut with their teeth, the strangers had to use rocks to penetrate the hull. They were much taller, and their language was different. Most bizarrely, they covered their bodies in a colorful, unknown material—not animal skins, or at least, not the hide of anything that lived on the island. They used strange and frightening tools, the purpose of which the creatures couldn't discern.

Perhaps the new arrivals were distant cousins—a missing tribe from far-off shores. The tribe members knew that other islands existed somewhere beyond the vast waters that surrounded them. Occasionally, debris washed up on the beach—items that were not native to the island. And their legends told of a race of hairless visitors who had arrived on the island many generations ago, crossing the water on long, hollowed-out trees. The strangers had spoken in a strange language. They carried shiny sticks that were harder and sharper than stone, and had spears that belched smoke and flame. Eventually, the tribe's ancestors determined they were a threat and had slain them all. From that point on, whenever a stranger arrived on the island, they were met in the same manner, until, eventually, the others stopped coming.

Now, a similar decision faced this new generation of tribe members.

After a week of observation, their fears and misgivings had now given way to cautious urgency. The tribe was overcome with conflicting desires. Clearly, the strangers were a threat to the island's ecosystem. Their continued presence was throwing everything off balance. If the tribe did not act, and soon, their entire existence could be in jeopardy.

The time for watching was over. It was time to act.

Leaving a few sentries behind to keep track of the intruders' actions, the tribe withdrew to the island's center. There, in a deep, hidden valley that they used for important gatherings, .

the males hooted and grunted among themselves in their gut-tural language. Finally, the elder stood up and hissed for atten-tion. The others fell silent, eyeing him with respect. His body was covered in thick, silver hair and long, ragged scars of old battles crisscrossed his massive arms and chest. Despite his age, he was still strong and had almost all of his teeth. He was a formidable opponent, and the few younger males who had dared to challenge him for leadership had been torn apart at his hands.

Growling, the elder pronounced judgment.

Meat was scarce. For generations, the tribe had supple-mented their diet of fruit, bark and plants with birds, turtles, snakes, insects, spiders, crabs, and whatever sea creatures happened to wash up on shore. There had once been wild pigs on the island, or so they'd been told, but none of those living had ever seen one, or knew what they tasted like. For refer-ence, they only had the pictures, drawn on the cave walls by their ancestors.

The males among the hairless newcomers would be caught, killed and eaten. Perhaps they would taste like pig. Perhaps not. In either case, they would fill bellies. The tribe had long kept the practice of eating their own dead, when sickness, in-jury or old age took them. This would not be so different. In fact, the new arrivals might taste better. They appeared well fed, for the most part. Many of them had succulent layers of fat around their abdomens.

The females would be taken to the caves as breeders. If they could not bear children, or if the fruit of their wombs was defective, then they would be eaten, too, along with the deformed infants.

The wind blew in from the sea, and the treetops rustled and swayed.

The elder raised his tiny head and sniffed the air. The breeze ruffled his hair.

A storm was coming—more proof that the intruders had upset the natural balance.

They would act tonight, under cover of the darkness and the weather. They would be swift and merciless. And then they would feast.

On the island, even the night had teeth.

CHAPTER THREE

The contestants made their way back to the base camp, followed by camera operators and sound technicians. They reached a point along the beach where a narrow trail cut into the jungle, and turned toward it. The path was only wide enough for three people to walk side by side at a time, and Becka noticed that everyone continued to stick to their various cliques. One crew member took the lead, walking backward and filming the procession. Becka was surprised he didn't trip.

Sal and Richard walked slightly ahead of the others. Becka couldn't hear their conversation, but both men were snickering. Simon, Jeff, Randy, Paula and Roberta strolled along behind them, but Roberta was just a few steps behind the others. Becka wondered if maybe Jerry and Shonette were right. Maybe Roberta could be swayed over to their side after all. A few more crew members—Mark, Jesse and Stuart—followed Simon's group, recording their conversation. Ryan and Shonette were in front of Jerry and Becka. Troy stumbled behind them, slapping at mosquitoes. Becka glanced over her shoulder. Matthew trudged along silently with his spear, keeping several yards' distance between himself and the rest of the group. He stared straight ahead, as if trying to bore a hole between Troy's shoulder blades with his eyes. His face was expressionless. Another cameraman brought up the rear.

The network's construction crew had built the path. It was outlined with lime, so that the contestants could see it at night. (For safety reasons, midnight strolls through the jungle were discouraged, unless, of course, they were something that would bring in ratings.) Bamboo handrails were positioned at swampy or hilly spots. But despite the conveniences, the dense tropical undergrowth crowded the path on both sides. As they walked, Becka noticed how still the jungle was. Normally, the terrain was alive with insects and birds. The trees and sky were usually filled with parrots, albatrosses, honeyeaters, frigates, gulls, and boobies. At times, their noise was almost deafening. Now, there was only silence.

Jerry paused, staring into the jungle. Becka and Troy stopped with him.

"What is it?" Becka asked. "Is something wrong?"

"I don't know. Hear that? It's quiet. No birds, nothing."

"I was just thinking the same thing. Maybe the helicopter scared them all away?"

"Maybe," Jerry agreed.

Troy slapped another mosquito. "Or maybe these fucking bugs got them all. Swear to Christ, I'm down a fucking pint of blood."

Grinning, Becka and Jerry started forward again.

"So, do you have a girlfriend?" Becka immediately regretted asking.

"No," Jerry replied. "But I'm always on the lookout. I figure that once I win the million dollars, finding a girlfriend will be a little easier."

"That's why you wanted an alliance," she teased. "So you could win."

Jerry feigned mock surprise. "Well, why else would we form an alliance?"

"I don't know. It would be nice to have someone to trust."

"Yes, it would," Jerry agreed. "But an alliance doesn't mean you'd be able to trust me. What if we play the game all the way to the end, and avoid getting exiled, and then it comes down to you or me? What then?"

Becka grinned. "Then I'd have to kick your butt and win the million. But don't worry, I'd give you a loan."

"Thanks."

Ahead of them, Shonette let out a frightened squeal. All of the contestants stopped walking. Ryan and Shonette stared at the ground. Shonette stumbled backward, pointing.

"What the hell is that?"

Mark and Jesse jostled past the others. Mark trained his camera on the disturbance and Jesse leaned closer with his microphone.

The group gathered around them. Only Matthew remained in the background, leaning on his spear and looking disinterested. Troy pressed up behind Becka, craning his neck to see, and accidentally shoving her forward. She recoiled in disgust.

In the center of the path was a small, wormlike creature, as narrow as pencil lead and about eight inches long. It was so small that Becka was amazed Shonette had noticed it at all. The thing was slate gray in color, with pink patches along its length. The thing's head was not offset from its body, and Becka couldn't tell which end was which. She peered closer and saw two tiny black dots on one end—the creature's eyes. The worm wiggled back and forth. Becka thought back to the research she'd done on the region before leaving home but didn't recognize the wriggling creature.

"What is it?" Shonette asked again.

"Disgusting," Ryan said. "That's what it is."

"It's a fucking worm," Troy said. "What's the big deal? Step on it. Or better yet, eat the fucker."

"Oh, man," Randy moaned. "You'd eat a worm, dog?"

Paula scowled, hands on hips. "That's gross."

Troy shrugged. "Hey, we're all sick of eating rice, right?"

"I think I'll stick with rice," Roberta said. "It doesn't move when you eat it."

"I'd eat a worm," Richard said, in his slow Kansas drawl. "I used to eat possums and squirrels and groundhogs. A worm ain't much different. I bet it tastes just like chicken."

Sal nudged him. "You'd eat shit if somebody paid you five bucks to do it."

"Yeah," Richard agreed. "You got five bucks on you?"

"It's not a worm," Simon said. "Unlike some of you, I prepared for this contest by familiarizing myself with our locale. I did my homework."

Troy yawned. "Well, aren't you just fucking special?"

"I'll certainly outlast you, you foul-mouthed little troglodyte."

Troy turned to Jerry. "What'd he just call me?"

Jerry shrugged. "I'm not sure. Nothing good."

Becka considered telling Simon that she'd done her homework as well, but decided to keep quiet. There was no sense in drawing attention to herself. Otherwise, she might be the next one to be exiled.

"Anyway," Simon said, "this isn't a worm. It's called a 'blind snake.'"

"A snake?" Roberta knelt for a closer look. "But it's so small."

"Well, this one is rather large, all things considered. They rarely exceed twelve inches in length, if I remember correctly."

"Is it poisonous?" Jeff asked.

"Not at all. They're timid creatures. Harmless, unless you're an ant or a termite, like our friend Troy here."

"Fuck you, motherfucker."

"No, thank you. You're a bit too greasy for my tastes."

"You think you're better than me, Simon? Is that it?"

Simon rolled his eyes. "Heaven's no. I'm sure you make valuable contributions to society."

"I bend wrenches for a living. Maybe I'll take one upside your head when we get home."

"You'll get there before me. I *will* be the last person left on this island."

"Not if we cook you and eat you first, you yuppie fuck."

Ignoring him, Simon turned his attention back to the blind snake. "Interestingly enough, they're an all-female species."

Ryan peered at the snake. "What does that mean?"

"It means that they lay eggs without the benefit of a male snake to fertilize them."

"Where's the fun in that?" Paula asked.

The men laughed obligingly at Paula's joke, and Becka gritted her teeth to keep from responding. A dozen different sarcastic replies came to mind. She glanced at Shonette, who rolled her eyes.

The group began to split up again. Simon, Jeff, Randy, Paula and Roberta walked on, along with half the crew. Jerry pulled Sal and Richard aside, and watched until the others had disappeared around a turn in the path. Then he gathered Sal, Richard, Troy, Shonette and Ryan together. Mark and Jesse remained behind as well, filming their discussion.

Becka tugged on Jerry's shoulder. He leaned close.

"What about Matthew?" she whispered.

Jerry glanced over at the loner. Matthew stood apart from the group, staring off into the jungle. Jerry sighed.

"Matthew, you want to join us for a second?"

Shrugging, he stepped forward.

"Here's the thing," Jerry said. "Simon, Jeff, Randy, Paula and Roberta have a pretty strong alliance. We think we may be able to pull Roberta, but the others are sticking together. Simon and Jeff need to go. They present a physical threat in the challenges."

Troy interrupted. "Not to mention Simon is an asshole."

"Yes," Jerry agreed. "There's that, too. And after what just happened, I think it's a good bet that he's gunning for you tonight. Let's make sure he doesn't get the opportunity."

"How?" Richard asked.

"Me, Becka, Shonette, Ryan and Troy were talking. There's five people in their alliance. We were thinking maybe you guys would want to join us. You, too, Matthew, if you like. We don't know for sure who they're going to vote for tonight, of course. It'll probably be whoever Simon says. Like I said, I'm guessing Troy."

"I heard them talking earlier," Sal said. "It is Troy."

"That motherfucker!" Troy yanked his hat from his head and threw it on the ground. "So he was planning this shit even before he talked smack just now?"

Sal nodded. "Looks that way."

"Simon's untouchable," Jerry said. "He's got the Circle of Protection—for now, at least. But if you guys join up with us, we could exile Jeff tonight. That would leave Simon's alliance weaker. Then we could start picking them off one by one. We could take out Simon next week."

"Unless he wins another challenge," Richard said.

"If he does," Shonette replied, "then we exile Paula or Randy."

"Exactly," Jerry said. "If we can't get to Simon, we can at least take out his supporters. Leave him vulnerable. That's gonna fuck with his head, and then he'll start slipping up."

Sal frowned. "Okay, but what happens once we've exiled all of them? You realize we'll have to turn on each other, right?"

"Well," Jerry said. "It *is* a game, right? No hard feelings at that point. Agreed?"

Sal and Richard glanced at each other, and then back to Jerry.

"Fuck it," Sal said. "I'm in."

Richard nodded. "Yeah, let's do it."

Jerry turned to the others. "You guys still up for this?"

Troy picked up his hat, brushed the dirt off it, and plopped it back on his head.

"Fuck that fucking fuck. Let's exile his ass, and all his little cronies, too."

Ryan laughed. "I'm with Troy."

"Let's do it," Shonette said.

They all turned to Becka.

"Okay," she said. "Sounds like a plan, I guess."

"Matthew?" Jerry smiled. "Will you help us?"

"Sure." His voice was a sullen monotone. "For now. But this doesn't make us friends. Like you said, it's a game. Simon and Jeff are the most immediate threats. Taking them out will level the playing field."

"The enemy of my enemy is my friend?"

Matthew's smile was tight-lipped. "Something like that."

"Gotta admit," Jerry said, "you didn't strike me as the type of guy who reads Sun Tzu's *The Art of War*."

Matthew's smile vanished. "That's because you don't know anything about me. None of you do."

He raised his bamboo spear, pushed past the group, and trudged away. They watched him go, shaking their heads.

"Nice guy," Ryan whispered.

Troy began slapping mosquitoes again. "Dude's an asshole, if you ask me. Not as much as Simon, maybe, but still . . ."

"Well," Jerry said, "as long as he keeps his word with us, and helps take down the alliance, I don't care what he does. We can exile him out after we finish with the others."

Tired, hungry, thirsty, and pestered by mosquitoes, they plodded along the trail, making their way back to the base camp.

As she walked, Becka got that weird feeling of being watched again. She tried to ignore it. Although she'd never admit it to the other contestants, the island was pretty spooky at night, and even during the day, if she happened to be off by herself. As a result, she tried to stay close to the others—or at least near the base camp. Maybe it was just her imagination, or perhaps it was the island's local lore. Upon their arrival, Roland had filled them in on all of its history. Tradition held that the island was haunted. The region had been inhabited for over seven thousand years, but in all that time, the island had remained uninhabited because the natives avoided it at all costs. Legends were passed on from each generation to the next that many of the caves scattered across the island were actually mouths leading into the underworld. A tribe of small, inhuman creatures were said to emerge from these caves to rape or devour anything in their path. Unlike the Indonesian folktales of the little people of Flores—cave-dwelling South Seas leprechauns who accepted gourds full of food that the Floresians set out for them as offerings—the diminutive creatures on this island were said to be savage and demonic.

Over the years, various traders, explorers and adventurers from as far away as Europe and America had vanished in the region. There was also the legend of the *Martinique*, a merchant vessel that had anchored on the island in the early 1900s. The crew had supposedly stayed one night on the beach and then fled, swearing never to return. And a Japanese squadron had disappeared in the vicinity during World War II. According to several television documentaries, they crashed on or near the island, and were never heard from again. Supposedly, their spirits still haunted the jungle.

Becka knew that Roland had told them this as part of the show—a bit of local color to enthrall the viewers—but that didn't make her feel any better late at night when she was lying in the darkness, listening to the jungle.

And it didn't make her feel better now.

Jerry tapped her shoulder. "Earth to Becka. Penny for your thoughts?"

"Sorry. I was just thinking about our first day here—all the stuff that Roland told us."

"I liked that part," Jerry said. "The celebration they threw for us aboard the freighter? That was cool."

Becka nodded, remembering. Before they'd been transported to the island, the network had treated them to a welcoming party aboard the ship. Natives from the surrounding islands were brought in to share their culture and traditions.

There was a great feast and live music, and the contestants were treated to displays of dancing, tattooing, wood carving, and other regional pastimes. She'd especially been enamored of the women's colorful tribal garb.

"Yeah," she said, not telling him that hadn't been what she was thinking about, "it was pretty cool, wasn't it?"

"It was," Jerry agreed. "Even if I don't win, I'll never forget that. I mean, how often do you get to experience something like that? We're very lucky to have been picked. Good thing we fit the stereotypes."

"What do you mean?"

"Oh, come on. Think about it. You've seen past seasons, haven't you? Each of us are here because we fit a certain profile that the producers were looking for. We've got a black guy, a black girl, an older woman, a hick, a handsome stud, the bad boy, a yuppie, a gay guy, a hot chick, and you—the pretty, nice girl next door."

Becka blushed. "And you're the handsome stud?"

"Me?" Now it was Jerry's turn to blush. "No, I'm just the regular dude."

"Goddamn," Troy muttered behind them. "I really need a fucking smoke. You two are so fucking sweet, you're gonna send me into a diabetic coma."

They turned to glare at him, but then realized that Troy was laughing. He winked conspiratorially and, after a moment, they laughed, too. The noise disturbed a roosting parrot, who voiced its displeasure.

They walked on.

Once more, Becka felt eyes on her, but when she glanced around, it was just the camera, filming everything that they did.

☐ **YES!**

Sign me up for the Leisure Horror Book Club and send my FREE BOOKS! If I choose to stay in the club, I will pay only $8.50* each month, a savings of $7.48!

NAME: _____

ADDRESS: _____

TELEPHONE: _____

EMAIL: _____

☐ I want to pay by credit card.

☐ **VISA**　　☐ **MasterCard.**　　☐ **DISCOVER**

ACCOUNT #: _____

EXPIRATION DATE: _____

SIGNATURE: _____

Mail this page along with $2.00 shipping and handling to:
Leisure Horror Book Club
PO Box 6640
Wayne, PA 19087
Or fax (must include credit card information) to:
610-995-9274

You can also sign up online at **www.dorchesterpub.com**.
*Plus $2.00 for shipping. Offer open to residents of the U.S. and Canada only. Canadian residents please call 1-800-481-9191 for pricing information.
If under 18, a parent or guardian must sign. Terms, prices and conditions subject to change. Subscription subject to acceptance. Dorchester Publishing reserves the right to reject any order or cancel any subscription.

GET FREE BOOKS!

You can have the best fiction delivered to your door for less than what you'd pay in a bookstore or online. Sign up for one of our book clubs today, and we'll send you *FREE* BOOKS* just for trying it out...**with no obligation to buy, ever!**

As a member of the Leisure Horror Book Club, you'll receive books by authors such as **RICHARD LAYMON, JACK KETCHUM, JOHN SKIPP, BRIAN KEENE** and many more.

As a book club member you also receive the following special benefits:
- **30% off all orders!**
- **Exclusive access to special discounts!**
- **Convenient home delivery and 10 days to return any books you don't want to keep.**

Visit **www.dorchesterpub.com**
or call **1-800-481-9191**

There is no minimum number of books to buy, and
you may cancel membership at any time.
*Please include $2.00 for shipping and handling.